"Once Bitten, Twice Die"

Antony J. Stanton

Book one from 'The Blood of the Infected' series

Published by Antony J. Stanton

"Once Bitten, Twice Die"

Published by Antony J. Stanton
Cover: Adnan Saleem of DestinationCreation.com

Copyright © by Antony J. Stanton 2015

ISBN: 978-0-9934285-0-0

"Once Bitten, Twice Die"

Book one from 'The Blood of the Infected' series.

The end of the world was just the beginning…

Coming soon…

"Once Bitten, Twice Live"

Book two from 'The Blood of the Infected' series.

When death is the best option, survival is no longer enough…

"Twice Bitten, Twice Die"

Book three from 'The Blood of the Infected' series.

When there's no one left to hear you scream…

Dedicated to friends and family… and a bet amongst mates.

The end of the world was just the beginning…

The Players

Group Captain Tristan Denny. RAF. Station Commander
Royal Air Force Headley Court
Captain Thomas Lewis. Army. Royal Artillery. 2nd in
Command RAF Headley Court
Sqn Ldr Anna Singleton. RAF. Station Medical Officer

Security
Sergeant Garrick Straddling. RAF Regiment
Sergeant Matteo Abbott. RAF Regiment
Sergeant Sinna. Army. Gurkha Regiment
Corporal Bannister. Army
Lance Corporal Dean Millington. Army
Private Giuseppe Campos. RAF Regiment
Private Sharp. Army
Private Rohith. Army. Gurkha Regiment

Supply / Logistics
Flight Lieutenant Andrew Walkden. RAF. Officer in
Charge of Admin / Logistics / Engineering
Corporal Bamburac. RAF
Senior Aircraftman Richard Masters. RAF. Wife = Vida
Private Bruce Matthews. Army

Admin
Cpl Gillen. RAF
Leading Aircraftman Mayoh RAF
Leading Aircraftman Allen. RAF

Military Transport (MT)
Sergeant Harper Hutchison. Army
Lance Corporal Ward. Army
Private Darby. Army

Medical
Dr Handley. Civilian
Corporal Newman. Army
Corporal May Williams. RAF
Senior Aircraftman Freddie Samuels. RAF
Senior Aircraftman Dan Hobbs. RAF
Private Howes. Army
Private Hanson. Army

Catering
Sergeant Vallage. RAF
Corporal Bell. Army
Leading Aircraftman Neale. RAF
Leading Aircraftman Patrick Scovell. RAF

Patients
Sergeant Liam Wood. Army. 1 Para
Corporal Charlotte Collins. Army
Corporal Reggie Pethard. RAF. Wife = Emma
Corporal Kevin Berthon. Army
Corporal Elliot Gray. Army. Coldstream Guards
Corporal Pellegrini. Army. Coldstream Guards

Aero-Medical Students
Flight Lieutenant Jonny Parsons. RAF
Flying Officer Oliver Frost. RAF

Once Bitten, Twice Die

CHAPTER 1

This is the end.

The thought was only fleeting. In reality the end had been and gone a long time before. Sinna had warned him not to do anything stupid, but here he was fighting for his life. What he really should have done was to just give up and let Death claim its prize. If he had known what the future held in store for him he may well have accepted the inevitable. He may have sought a more agreeable means of dying; something a little less brutal that did not jeopardise the lives of others. Perhaps something that did not involve kitchen implements. Had he been aware that he himself was soon to become a vicious murderer he might not have battled quite so hard. But Abbott was not gifted with foresight. At that moment all that consumed him was trying to stay alive just a little longer. Besides, what kind of death can any one person choose for their first experience of it?

His aggressor advanced with surprising vigour. Abbott was forced back onto the table. He was fit, well-trained and considerably larger than the other. Nevertheless, he found himself unable to contain the onslaught, the triumph of wrathful incognisance over strength and experience. Only certain kinds of demise permit the luxury of reviewing your existence as it flashes in front of your eyes in glorious Technicolor. Some keep you fully engaged and struggling for salvation until the very end. In such cases even a brief perusal of your life in black and white is asking too much. Abbott's situation fell firmly into the latter category.

He frantically grasped the lunatic's forearms. His assailant however possessed unnatural surges of power dredged up from his inner demons. A trail of phlegm and a guttural snarl escaped his lips. Hands clawed and teeth

1

snapped. He lunged repeatedly at Abbott's face. He was virtually within reach now. Abbott dodged his head to the side with a grunt. He tried to get a knee under his attacker's body but the man was writhing too much. It was just not possible. Yet without doing so he knew he would not be able to hold him off much longer. His strength, along with his hope, was fading fast.

Abbott was flecked with spittle. The stench of warm, rancid breath was overpowering as their heads slowly came together. Some of the man's teeth had rotted and fallen out leaving open sores in blackened gums. His face was mottled with an unhealthy, purple tinge. It was covered with scabs and flaking skin. Red lines like those of a habitual drinker covered his cheeks. His eyes were bulging and blood-shot, and darted about as though without focus. Yet the most chilling factor was the absolute lack of perception. The pupils were dilated and blank like those of a shark. It was as though he was just lashing out blindly. If the eyes are a window to the soul, then these particular portals looked out onto a vista of pure hell. And then there was the rage; unprovoked yet wanton and plentiful. There was just an overpowering urge to kill.

Abbott's arms burned. His attacker still showed no sign of tiring. If anything he grew even more frenzied and ironically that may have provided an invaluable reprieve. Death took a reluctant step back and waited, denied its reward for now. As the man thrashed about there was a loud crack. The back legs of the table splintered. The pair were sent tumbling. Abbott hit the floor hard. Pain shot through his shoulder and he was winded. Nevertheless he managed to slip a leg between the two of them. Deftly he launched the man over his head, slamming him against the wall. This was his moment to save himself. This was his one chance to live. If the other reacted more quickly then he would surely be dead. He rolled and scrambled to his feet grabbing at whatever he could reach - a heavy, pewter candlestick discarded nearby. He swung as his opponent started to rise. It struck with a thud across the temple. The force jarred right up through Abbott's arm. Nevertheless his adversary somehow did not go down. As he leapt, Abbott backed up and swung, again and again.

Each blow solidly found its mark leaving deep, red gashes. The man sagged to his knees, a trail of blood at his nostril. He flailed forwards with an enraged gargling as the liquid dripped from his chin. Abbott struggled to maintain balance. He desperately hit out once more and cracked the skull right on the top. This time it made a different sound, more hollow and decisive.

This time the candlestick embedded itself.

This time the man went down.

Abbott sank to the ground. The body lay at his feet with one leg twitching, disturbingly. A small pool of viscous blood gradually took shape around the head forming a macabre halo. Abbott gulped down air as his hands started trembling. He was in an upstairs room with bookshelves lining three of the walls. The house was identical to all the others in the street and presumably in most this would have been a bedroom. However the owners of this one, almost certainly dead - or worse - had turned it into a reading room. The shelves were made of cheap, knotted pine and books were lying on the veneer flooring, torn and discarded. He noticed that only one tome remained standing - the Bible.

As he sat trying to regain composure, the violence of the confrontation made it hard to focus. He found himself fixing on irrelevant details, a mist enshrouding his mental faculties. He looked around vaguely for a matching candleholder, as these would probably have come as a pair. The random notion surfaced that it was just like a

3

scenario from Cluedo; Colonel Mustard, or in this case
Sergeant Matteo Abbott, in the library, with the
candlestick. He wondered again where Sinna was as he
should have arrived a long time before. It was most unlike
him to screw up. Only now did he start to appreciate that
something had gone badly wrong.

Sergeant Abbott had left the relative safety of RAF
Headley Court earlier that afternoon but later than was
prudent. Headley Court was a small military station to the
north of London, near the town of Bishop's Stortford. It
was a medical establishment specialising in rehabilitation,
as well as research and training. Abbott had been driven
by Private Giuseppe Campos in convoy with another
Land Rover carrying Sergeant Sinna and Private Rohith,
both soldiers from the Ghurkha regiment. They had gone
to a supermarket and had carefully and quietly loaded
shopping trolleys with bottled water, tinned food,
cleaning products and other essential supplies. Sinna kept
an anxious vigil over the three of them throughout.
    Campos had become agitated as the afternoon
progressed. "Sarge, you know my parents live around
here, don't you?" He looked at Abbott through veiled
eyes.
    "Hmmm," Abbott replied cautiously, not looking
forward to the next few words.
    Sinna had heard the comment too. He stood in the aisle
a few metres away, gripping his SA80 assault rifle as he
scanned all around them, listening for sounds of anyone
approaching in the gloom. Their afternoon had been
uneventful so far although the threat of attack always
lingered ominously. To let one's guard down meant
courting death. They all knew it, the RAF station had
experienced it and they did not want to add to the
obituaries. Sinna flashed Abbott a look with a hint of a

warning but there was also empathy in his expression. Abbott respected Sinna. He was a fastidious and dedicated soldier but had a big, compassionate streak running through him. He was charismatic and the troops took to him well.

"Sarge, what d'ya think?" Campos took a step nearer to Abbott, his hands fidgeting. "Is there any chance that we could swing by my house? Just for a moment? I mean, they're almost certainly dead but I'd really like to make sure, just in case, you know?"

Abbott rubbed his chin and avoided looking at Campos who's pleading eyes drilled into him.

"Sarge?"

Abbott glanced at Sinna who just shrugged and looked away.

"All right, all right. We'll drive over to their house when we're done here but we're not getting out of the Landy. We can beep the horn a few times, maybe shout out of the window but we're not getting out. Is that clear?" he answered sternly but Campos was no longer listening, his face had lit up and he was chattering away to himself. He was a nice lad, always cheerful and keen to help as best he could. Abbott knew how much Campos thought of his parents and how much he idolised his father. For a moment Abbott felt a flush of bonhomie. Even in this terrible world that they all barely existed in now, he had been able to brighten someone's day, albeit briefly.

Sergeant Sinna turned to Abbott with a grin, sharing in the moment. "I think we're just about done here. Why don't you two poke off and we'll catch up with you at the house?"

Abbott's smile vanished as he was jerked back to reality. He was aware that every second spent off base exposed them to significant risk and whilst he wanted to

5

help Campos find his parents if at all possible, he did not want to put himself or his colleagues in any greater jeopardy than was absolutely necessary.

"Are you sure?" he asked with a frown. "Wouldn't it be better if we waited and went together?"

"This is the last lot of stuff to chuck in the Landy. It'll only take a mo and we'll be right behind you losers. I'd rather we get back to the station as fast as possible and certainly before sunset."

Sunset was at six thirteen; it was now five forty-two. That did not leave them much time. Abbott was about to argue until he saw the look on Campos's face. He shrugged. "Sure, okay we'll get cracking then. And thanks – this means a lot to the boy."

"Yeah I kinda gathered that," Sinna laughed. "Go on, just stay in radio contact and don't do anything stupid, okay?"

'Anything stupid' - did that include allowing Campos to persuade him it was safe to leave the vehicle after there was no reply to their shouting? Did that include going into the house even though Abbott knew it was lunacy to be confined in such close quarters? If only Sinna knew how stupid he had been since last they spoke.

Abbott now shuddered and the makeshift weapon slipped from his grip as he passed a hand across his face. Only then did he notice the throbbing in his arm. It was a small bite mark. The skin was barely broken, hardly worth mentioning really, with just a slight prick of blood. He could tell where the man's teeth had fallen out with the marks on his arm representing those that remained. He rubbed his flesh ruefully and pulled the sleeve down. As he sat hugging his knees to his chest the temptation was to remain there, hidden and safe from the horrors of the outside world, horrors that were never far from one's conscious thoughts, horrors that temporarily submerged when one was preoccupied but then resurfaced like a bloated corpse.

However he knew he could not stay there. It was hard to find motivation but he had to leave the house, and fast. He rebuked himself for his inactivity; come on, get moving soldier. This is no time to rest. Wearily he rose and crossed quietly to the door. With every step the floorboards creaked. He stopped and held his breath, listening for sounds. The house was still; evidently the scuffles had not attracted any further, unwanted attention. Yet!

He drew his gun and flicked the safety catch off, taking no chances this time, then raised his radio and operated the 'press-to-talk' button. "Sinna, this is Abbott, do you read?"

Nothing.

"Sinna, this is Abbott. Come in."

Deathly silence.

Odd, he thought. The only explanation he could think of was that they had got confused and gone straight back to base. Ordinarily Abbott might have been angered by this. Ordinarily alarm bells might have started to ring. But now he just clipped the radio back onto his belt, rubbed his arm and continued, survival mode dictating his actions.

He paused on the landing and listened again, then slipped quickly down the stairs. Campos's body lay at the bottom, his head twisted unnaturally to the side where his neck had snapped. His eyes and mouth were open in the grimace he bore as he was savaged and fell. Abbott felt for a pulse but he already knew there would be none. Above him on the wall was a photo, a portrait in a wooden frame. It side-tracked Abbott and he stared at it for a moment. It was a typical family pose of much-loved

7

mother and idolised father with their arms around each other's shoulders. A boy, Private Giuseppe Campos of perhaps only seventeen years old, was sandwiched between them, kneeling down as though in the stance of a football team. Campos was not much older now and had hardly changed since that photo was taken. He reflected on the photo a moment, the familiar ease with which the three of them embraced each other and thought with sadness for a moment of his own parents.

Now however was not the time for reminiscing; there would be time for that later, he thought, although in this he was wrong. He was conscious that it was not level and dimly aware that normally his fastidious nature would have prompted him to straighten it. But not today. Not now.

Abbott had served in three war zones and accumulated several medals for his efforts. He had witnessed death, both amongst his own troops and the enemy and was on first name terms with it. Recent dealings however were all very new and strange. Perhaps in times before he might have been more traumatized by this most recent attack but now he steeled himself, shook off the mental fog and moved with the intent of someone focussed on staying alive. The prospect that Death has not yet left the building but is somewhere nearby sharpening his scythe and having a quick breather before returning to the scene of the crime does wonders to one's motivation.

He looked down at Campos's lifeless body. "Sorry pal. Heaven knows you're better off where you are now."

He crossed himself although since very recently he no longer believed in God. He reached down and took Campos's holstered pistol and dog tag. It did not escape his attention that like himself, Campos had not even had time to draw his weapon.

Suddenly there was a creak from upstairs which made

him freeze. He hoped it was merely the noise of the house groaning in the wind rather than his attacker walking to the top of the stairs. Silence returned. In fact there was an eerie stillness in general. There were no noises of traffic or any kind of life from outside, none of the background chatter that one normally expects from living in an urban area. Creepy. At that moment a car alarm sounded, screaming out into the quiet with its shrill tones and the noise was even more alien in this world devoid of the usual detritus of life. The house was in disarray. Furniture lay overturned and broken, there was smashed crockery on the carpet and a bloody stain smeared down one wall. A stale smell pervaded throughout. With a nervous glance at the stairs Abbott moved to the front door. He looked at the sky although in truth the weather did not matter. The weather would never be of consequence again, just as the date no longer meant anything. He was more interested in the time of nightfall. The sun was scuttling quickly westwards, unwilling to loiter and neither was Abbott. He really did not want to be off station and alone when it got dark. The road, although gloomy and unlit, was quiet. There was no movement until a dog ran past, its tongue lolling out. It seemed unconcerned and happy as though everything was normal and for that he envied it. The dog stopped briefly to scratch and sniffed at a wall before continuing. Abbott slipped out and moved guardedly towards his Land Rover. Glass crunched beneath his feet and he tried to walk as quietly as possible checking all around him as he went. It was predominantly a residential street and there were signs everywhere of hysteria. The gate to Campos's house was off its hinges, rubbish was strewn all around and the windows in many adjoining buildings were smashed. Old newspapers danced in the breeze like modern age tumbleweeds, and there was a distinct smell of burning. On the garden path he noticed the head from a plastic Barbie doll. In the garden next door was a child's plimsoll lying in a patch of dried blood. The shoe was small and pink and Abbott had to force himself to look away and not think too deeply. There was still no sign of Sergeant Sinna and Private Rohith. At the gate he looked all around and felt confident that he was not being watched. Not for the first time that day, he was wrong. Not for the first time that day Lady Luck was smiling upon him more than he would ever know.

He got into the vehicle and with shaking hands he started the engine. He was well aware that there would be questions on his arrival back at base. He could imagine the anger as to why they had been out alone with no backup. He had no answers, no good reason for their actions, other than the emphatic plea of a young man desperate to find his parents, a plea that he himself could well understand.

On the short drive back he could not help but notice various corpses arranged in their final resting places. He had to swerve around a body lying in the middle of the road. Another, an elderly gentleman in a pinstripe suit, was slumped against the front door of a house as though asleep. Abbott saw them all but felt nothing. It was as if the attack upon himself, or perhaps the proximity of his own demise, had left him emotionless and unable to empathise. By the time he arrived back at the base the shock and exertion of the violence and the effect of Campos's death were starting to affect him. He felt exhausted; sweat had dried on him giving him a chill and his arms and back ached as though he had flu.

Corporal Bannister from the army security regiment at Headley Court was smoking in the guard room. He had been sat on duty with his feet up on a table for the last half hour, his green, military shirt crumpled and open at the neck more than uniform standards would normally permit. His rifle rested on the desk in front of him, pointing into the distance down the empty road leading to the station. He allowed the smoke to escape from his lips, slowly bleeding away until recapturing it in his nostrils, a trick he had admired in an old movie featuring Humphrey Bogart and an attractive lady whose name he could not remember. With his spare hand he casually played with his cigarette lighter. It was in the style of a metallic Zippo but had the caricature of a naked woman on the side, a tacky souvenir from a recent beach holiday with mates. Colleagues had teased him for possessing such a crass object but he liked the fact that the lighter was a vague source of controversy and rarely cared for other people's opinions anyway.

From the main road any car that turned to enter the base had approximately forty metres to drive up to the guardroom. When he saw Abbott's Land Rover swing into the approach lane he took his feet off the table but did not extinguish the cigarette and remained leaning back in the chair. As the sergeant brought the car to a halt he flicked a length of ash on the floor. Slowly he got to his feet and wandered out to unlock the gates.

"How was your day at work honey?" he began as Abbott wound down his window, then stepped back in surprise and cursed. "You look dreadful," he spat out.

Abbott shot him a glance but said nothing. He took in the decline in uniform standards and the informal, almost disrespectful way in which Bannister addressed him, the fact that he was smoking whilst on guard and had been slow to open the gates. However he could not muster the enthusiasm to say anything, something that Bannister would later recall as having struck him as out of character.

"Where are Sinna and Rohith?"

"Dunno. They haven't got back yet?" Abbott asked listlessly.

"Nope. Hey, where's Campos?" Bannister asked with real concern in his voice now.

"Dead."

"What?" Bannister covered his mouth with a hand as he digested the news. "How?"

From beyond the guard room they heard a bellowing. "Bannister, are Abbott and Sinna back yet?" Station Commander Group Captain Tristan Denny approached the gates but stopped short as soon as he saw Abbott. "Good lord, what on earth happened? Where's Campos? Are you okay?"

Not sure which question to answer first, Abbott just repeated himself in a monotone voice. "Dead."

Denny stood for a moment staring as he too processed the information and then deflated a little in the shoulders and back, as though certain sections of his body had been punctured. His reaction was similar to Bannister's; he brought his hands together in front of his face like a monk deep in prayer and closed his eyes. Then they flicked open and fixed nervously on Abbott. "You don't look so good yourself. How are you?"

"I'm okay sir, a little tired but otherwise all right."

Only then did Denny realise that the other Land Rover was not there. He looked confused. Bannister noticed the vein on his temple stand out as he started to go a little red in the face.

"Where are the others? I thought two cars went off base?"

Abbott found it hard to meet his scowl. "Err, we got separated sir. I thought they should be back already."

"Separated?" Denny was incredulous. "How on earth did that happen?"

"It was Campos sir. His parents live close to where we

were looking for supplies, so we just popped by to check if anybody was there. We only took a moment and Sinna was supposed to come and join us but he never showed up…" Abbott trailed off as the Station Commander threw his hands in the air.

Overreacting again, Bannister thought. Finally Denny took a deep breath, heaving his shoulders up and forcing himself to calm down. He turned away from the two soldiers and rubbed his head frantically for a moment.

"Look, this is really unacceptable," he said, trying to keep his voice calm. "I thought we had introduced procedures to avoid this kind of event. Totally unacceptable. But that can all wait. The important thing now is the whereabouts of Sinna and Rohith. I need you to show me exactly where you left them and where you arranged to rendezvous. Then drop the Land Rover at MT, but I want you in my office later for a debrief."

Bannister stood fidgeting awkwardly. His gelled, brown hair made his naturally impish features seem decidedly more boyish and mischievous than his twenty-eight years would imply. His dark eyes, ever alert and restless, darted about anxiously. As Abbott drove away Denny did not even acknowledge him at first but stood swaying slightly with his head bowed. A light moan escaped him. He had never looked as tired and defeated as at that moment. His ginger hair was greying and slightly unkempt and smudges under his eyes indicated how badly he was sleeping, yet his uniform was still immaculately pressed and his army boots were gleaming.

"How long has he been back?" Denny finally asked.

"He just arrived that minute sir."

"He looked terrible."

"Yes sir." So do you, Bannister thought. In truth they all looked haggard nowadays and the stresses were beginning to tell on Denny more than most.

"Radio Captain Lewis and tell him to meet me in my office in five minutes."

Denny turned and stalked away from the guardroom. Bannister was left feeling vulnerable and alone as he searched up and down the road for any sign of Sergeant Sinna, before going to recheck the padlock. He sank back into his chair, lit another cigarette and nervously picked up his weapon. He looked out at the setting sun, half veiled by clouds. He often thought that the most beautiful sunsets he had ever seen were in England, the frequently overcast sky lending itself to dramatics. The red shafts of light poked through and illuminated the cloud from beneath, as though the roof of the heavens was aflame, although tonight it felt to Bannister more like hell itself was boiling over, spewing forth its contents unto the earth. He was morbidly becoming a little more resigned to the prospect of his own fatality with the passing of each day and every death. He sat staring at the outside world beyond the safety of the fence as the shadows lengthened and gathered around him.

"Bugger!" Captain Thomas Lewis cursed as he left Group Captain Denny's office. The news was bad - really bad. Another soldier killed and the whereabouts of two more unknown. As well as that, the thought of going out now as twilight shrouded the station was not one that he relished, and the nonchalant way Denny had mentioned it made his mood even worse. Still, he would have it no other way; as second in command on the base, if two of his men were missing then he would damn well go and find them. He was certainly not going to go out alone though; he wanted three of his best soldiers with him. They would most likely go unmolested but you never knew...

In less than five minutes they were driving away from

14

the station with Corporal Bamburac from the supply and logistics section hastily locking the gates behind them. Captain Lewis turned to look back, as he always did, as the protection of RAF Headley Court receded out of reach. He was from the Royal Artillery and had been at Headley Court for only six months. However he had served in the army for ten years and like many of his colleagues a lot of that time had been spent in Northern Ireland, Iraq and Afghanistan and thus he had a fair amount of frontline experience.

"Stay alert lads; let's not get our names on the list of deceased for today. We don't want what happened to Parsons to happen to us, do we?"

With the news of Private Campos's death and the other two still missing the atmosphere in the car was sombre. Sat in the back even Bannister's normally incorrigible manner had been quietened. Beside him sat the dark, hulking mass of Lance Corporal Dean Millington, a black man-mountain from the army security regiment and a reassuringly solid soldier to keep handy. Driving them away from safety was his most senior sergeant, a Scot named Garrick Straddling. He had served for more than twenty years in the army and was one of the most experienced men on the station. He was fairly short and stout with a large chest and belly and thick arms. His gruff, cynical attitude to life in general reflected perfectly his physical appearance and he seemed to have an idiom of doom for every occasion. He had an enormous auburn moustache and was balding on top with a wispy comb-over at the front. Although Lewis found him stubborn and uncooperative at times, he was definitely someone to take along on just such an excursion.

"Where to boss?" Sergeant Straddling asked.

Captain Lewis had a map with the locations marked on it by Abbott. As Sinna had not arrived at the house of

Campos's parents by the time Abbott had left, it seemed reasonable to start at the supermarket.

The onset of nightfall shielded their eyes from the worst of the scenes of pandemonium that now littered the roads; scenes that these four soldiers were all-too familiar with and were grateful not to be reminded of yet again. Occasional creatures scurried out of their way as Sergeant Straddling whisked them wordlessly through the streets to their destination, hands gripping the wheel tightly as he scanned their path.

They arrived at the store and Straddling warily brought the Land Rover to a halt. No one spoke. Lewis peered out trying to see any movement or sign of their comrades.

"Odd," Straddling said.

"Huh?" Lewis turned to see what had caught his attention.

Straddling pointed. Near the entrance to the store was the Land Rover. "They never left."

"So they're here somewhere," Bannister said as he leaned forwards from the rear. "Let's go get 'em I say, and then get the hell outta Dodge. Being away from home gives me the willies."

"Okay, okay. Just go easy," Lewis frowned. "There's something not right about this. Why is their car still here? Why haven't they left yet? They should have been back at Headley Court a long time ago." He spoke into his radio. "Sergeant Sinna? Private Rohith?" but there was no answer. He turned to his sergeant, "Before we get ourselves into any trouble, do the honours please."

Straddling honked the Land Rover's horn a few times, destroying the evening hush and making them all uneasy. Attracting such attention when away from the security of the station was never a wise idea but in this case Lewis considered it inevitable. Only silence answered them back.

"I guess there's nothing for it then," Lewis said.

Tentatively they all got out of the vehicle, brandishing their SA80 rifles before them.

"Straddling, bring up the rear and keep checking your six," Lewis whispered. "Let's keep it as quiet as possible,"

"But he's only just been blasting out the Landy's micking horn," Bannister muttered to Millington, earning him a scowl from Straddling.

They examined the other Land Rover but it gave no clues. The rear had been half-loaded with supplies and all seemed completely normal. Lewis motioned towards the entrance of the supermarket and the four shuffled forwards with Straddling casting nervous glances over his shoulder.

By now night engulfed them, and with no lighting the store was in total darkness. They crept along, torches probing back and forth. There was a putrid smell of decaying food mingling with the stale funk from the dirt of animals. The aisles were littered with goods that had been knocked off shelves. Some had split spilling their guts, making every step crunch painfully. At the end of the first aisle Lewis raised a hand to bring them to a halt. They clustered together, breathing rapidly but as quietly as possible.

Cautiously he called out into the threatening blackness. "Sinna? Rohith?"

Nothing.

They proceeded down a second aisle. It was when they got to the third that they encountered something strange. The produce displays had been absolutely decimated. The shelves had been toppled and packets and cans strewn all around. Something serious had happened here. This was not the action of marauding animals. The shelf units were substantial. To knock one over would have required

17

considerable force, to break one even more so.

Lewis looked back to ensure the others were aware of the potential significance. Still there was no sign of either missing soldier as they stood amidst the mess. He scanned around but it was Straddling who noticed it and gave a hiss.

"What is it?" Lewis asked.

Straddling just pointed. Down - at their feet.

Blood!

They were standing in a pool of it; lots of it. It must have stretched for several metres, along the floor and was splattered on the shelving.

"Bugger me!" Bannister exclaimed with a low whistle.

Frantically now they widened their search but there was no sign of the soldiers anywhere, just the ominous streak of blood that looked like something or somebody had been dragged through it, smearing a gory trail along the aisle until it suddenly stopped. There were no bodies or indications as to the source of it. As they stood bewildered back at the scene of so much carnage Lewis was no closer to an explanation. He could not determine from where the blood had come or why the smudged trail ended so abruptly.

"What the hell happened?" Lewis asked. "If they've been killed where are the bodies? And if they haven't been killed, then where are they?"

It was all too surreal, too inexplicable. He could not shake the feeling that at any moment they would be attacked themselves. His torch picked up something reflective in the dark and he stooped to pick it up - dog tags. They were printed with the name 'Sinna' and his staff number.

"Oh god no," he mumbled as his last hope disappeared. Then he shouted - an unnatural sound in the silence. "Sinna? Rohith?" No one answered. His voice died in the darkness.

There was a trace of blood on the dog tags and the chain had been severed. There was nothing else. No other sign that either soldier had ever been there, no weapons, no bodies, nothing.

They checked outside and all around the store but there was still no indication as to their whereabouts. The soldiers appeared to have vanished, spirited away for some dark purpose. Finally Lewis turned to his men with a baffled look and repeated his question.

"What the hell happened?" but there were no answers. They bunched closely and looked about them, feeling ever more vulnerable.

"Boss, they're not here," Straddling murmured, not sounding his usual confident self. "We would've found them, we've searched everywhere. They wouldn't have just abandoned the Land Rover. Whatever has occurred, they're long gone."

"They're dead!" was all Bannister could manage as he peered into the darkness, voicing what they all believed. Millington just stood impassively as always, watching and waiting.

"I don't know what's happened but we can do nothing for them," Lewis said, speaking quickly and quietly. "I hate to go without finding any answers but I think you're right. They're dead and I suggest we get out of here fast before the same thing happens to us."

Bannister nodded a little too enthusiastically. "Abso-bloody-lutely."

Swiftly they manoeuvred their tight huddle, rifles swinging wildly at every noise as they scurried back to the vehicles. The keys were still in the ignition of the other Land Rover so Bannister and Millington took it. With a remorseful glance towards the supermarket Lewis got in as Straddling started the engine and floored the

19

accelerator, whisking them back to the protection of the base.

Safe.

For the time being at least.

CHAPTER 2

As Captain Lewis and his soldiers sped through the deserted streets towards their safe haven all the devastation was a clear reminder of what had led to their current circumstances. The gruesome proof was all around. Lewis had a rough idea of what had triggered the chain of events - that was inevitable. The name of 'GVF Laboratories' was very familiar to them all, as was the 'Dem-buster' drug. However, he did not know exactly how things had gone so terribly wrong, nor the name of the man chiefly responsible for their precipitous situation now, Dr Boxall.

Several months before and a little distance from RAF Headley Court towards the north west of London, Dr Jason Boxall had finished work and returned home. His daughter Isabelle greeted him at the front door with a kiss. With her freckles and shoulder-length brown hair she was a little carbon-copy of her mother Julia.

As Jason joined his wife in the kitchen he called out, "Mum, dinner," but there was no answer. "How's she been today Jules?"

"Same, same," she replied. "She's been upstairs most of the day. I got her out of bed around nine and brought her down but she went back just after lunch. She just seemed to want to watch TV in her room." Julia could see the pain in her husband's eyes as she spoke and put an arm around his shoulders. "She's fine, really. She's happy."

"Yeah I guess," he lapsed into silence. Several years before, his mother had been diagnosed with Pick's disease, a form of dementia similar to Alzheimer's. Her mental functioning had declined considerably in recent months and she was now becoming a hazard to herself so

Julia and Jason had decided to look after her in their own home.

Jason was happy that they were able to do this but it did not assuage his feeling of guilt. He knew his mother would have loved to have visited more often over the previous years but somehow they had not made enough time for her until it was too late. Jason realised now to his cost that those were precious years that he would never get back. Dementia is an insidious fiend that steals into your home when you are not looking, sits down next to you on the sofa and before you realise it, has made itself an unavoidable part of your life, stealing away the person that was once there and leaving nothing more than a husk bearing scant resemblance to whom the person once was. For him the guilt would always be there but at least they could now take care of her.

When he went up to her room she was sat in a faded red armchair in the corner, watching the television. She turned and stared vacantly at him for a long moment before offering a limp smile but he was not sure if that was a sign of recognition or just a reflex action.

"It's dinner time mum. Are you hungry?" he asked.

"Yes dear," she replied and made a muted kind of laughing sound like a swan's hiss.

He looked into her eyes and she returned his glance without any obvious emotion at first but then, as though she could read his mind, she patted his arm.

"It's okay dear, it'll be all right," she smiled. He wasn't quite sure to what she was referring but her positive reaction gave him a fleeting warm glimmer. He wondered exactly when she had stopped being the woman she once was, when her personality and humanity had died.

When they had all finished dinner Isabelle went to slip off her chair but Jason tapped his water glass with his fork. "Attention, attention, Boxall family meeting in progress."

"Oh Daddy but I want to go and play."

"Well, you know the rules - meeting first. There may be something that you want to add. There may even be talk of your birthday if you stick around long enough."

"I want add something," Rory piped up.

"Of course you do my love," Julia grabbed his head and kissed the top of it. "You always want to add something, usually a ruddy great mess."

"Okay," Jason continued, "it's been a pleasure for us to have Nanny Boxall staying with us for the last couple of weeks hasn't it? How would you like it if she stayed with us for a little longer?"

Rory cheered but Isabelle paused in consideration for a moment before speaking, her six-year-old brain already learning the subtleties of feminine guile. "That's really great. So she will be here for my birthday?"

"Yes poppet."

"Does that mean I will get an extra present from her?"

Julia laughed. "Yes, of course you will." In fact they had already bought her present on behalf of Nanny Boxall, a furry rucksack in the shape of a dog's face with floppy ears and a big, brown nose.

"Great. I do have one other thing to add," Isabelle said with a sly look.

"Yes?" Julia arched her eyebrows enquiringly, trying to contain the smirk.

"Now can we talk about my birthday party please?"

After the children had gone to bed, Jason and Julia sat in the living room with a bottle of wine.

Jason took a slow swig and turned to his wife. "That was not the only thing we had to discuss tonight." Not for the first time that evening she arched her eyebrows but said nothing, waiting for him to proceed.

He cleared his throat. "It seems I am being promoted at work, kind of."

"Really? That's fantastic. Kind of? What does that mean?"

"There is a new project that I am going to be involved with, it's being pushed through as top priority and getting unlimited funding, kind of." He could not contain his grin and she could tell he was bursting to blurt it all out but was teasing her with the slow drip-feed of information.

"Yes?" Again the eyebrow, this time accompanied with a gentle pinch of his leg. "Well go on then, tell me."

"As you know I have been involved with neurological synaptic networks, their functionality and connectivity, and…"

"Whoah! Hold your horses there Einstein. Layman's terms please else you get to do the washing-up for a week."

She was a smart lady but he was a neurological scientist, and when he started talking about mitochondrial synaptic junctions it left her, like most people, feeling a little lost. She had fond memories of when they first met at a friend's dinner party. They had been placed together although her friend subsequently swore that there was no intended element of match-making. In fact her friend had hoped to set her up with the man sat on her other side, a TV producer called Gavin, but he had been chatting to the lady on his right all night so Julia and Jason had spent most of the night talking.

When she had found out that he was a brain scientist she had mocked him by yawning and pretending to fall asleep in her dish, poking herself in the face with her spoon in the process and splattering soup on the tablecloth which set them both off giggling. She challenged him to tell her the most interesting fact he could think of about brains.

"Well, did you know that there are more potential pathways to connect the cells in the average human brain than there are molecules in the known universe?"

"Wow!" She had been genuinely amazed, although she did not really know what synaptic pathways were or what function they served, but she was impressed by this statistic nonetheless. "So what do these pathways do then? And why is it so important that there are so many of them?"

As he had started to explain she became a little lost but nevertheless found herself desperate to understand and appear intelligent. She remembered thinking how intense and piercingly blue his eyes seemed and she felt herself being drawn in. She had liked this man right from the start although she had no idea why and she found herself laughing a little too readily at his jokes.

Several years and two children later, and she had given up work at least until Rory, their youngest, was old enough to join his sister at primary school in just under a year. Jason was now employed by a small yet esteemed company in the neurological research industry. He himself was also highly regarded in his field and never short of well-paid offers from rivals. He was extremely good at his job. What he was not so good at was describing what he did, in layman's terms. He tried to explain.

"I have been investigating how electrical charges flow between cells in the brain, how the patterns of these flows relate to a person's thought processes, storage of memory etcetera, etcetera." He paused to ensure she was following him.

"Hmmm," she gave a faint nod.

"Well, we have always been notoriously under-funded. Compared with companies in the US we work on peanuts. Now however it seems that some wealthy hot-shot called

Gautam van Firstenburg has taken an interest and we are going to get an unexpected cash-injection. He's been bank-rolling a company that researches certain brain diseases including types of dementia. This is what our studies have been dabbling in for a while, only he has been looking at these issues from a genetic point of view. It seems he's really keen to try to come up with a cure for dementia as soon as possible."

"Really?" Julia said. "I thought that dementia meant the brain was slowly dying and since dead brain cells can't be repaired or replaced there's no cure for it?"

"Not exactly. Yes, dementia does mean that brain cells are, in effect, dying. However, considering the brain is really only three pounds of gelatinous mulch it is the most incredible organ. In the last twenty years our understanding of it has improved drastically but we still have a heck of a lot to learn. We used to think that once the cells of the brain died, through trauma, illness, even alcohol..." he raised his glass and clinked hers, "...then that was it, there was no getting them back. But that is not necessarily the accepted truth any more. Certainly the brain *can* learn to adapt and other areas can relearn the functions that are lost when one part of the brain is damaged. There is a possibility also that the damaged cells can even be repaired. We are working on both angles but we are encouraging it to do this really quickly, sort of speeding up the metabolism of the brain so the chemical processes operate a lot faster."

"And how exactly does all this affect you?"

"This Gautam van Firstenburg chap is in the process of buying our company and amalgamating it with his own. He was quoted in the press as saying something about dementia being a war against individual humanity and he intends to develop a 'neurological nuke' that will end the war once and for all. He wants to combine our research with his. Once we have introduced the elements of change the brain will continue to adjust itself, evolving even as the damage repairs itself. I mean we're talking about radical alteration in the DNA of how one's brain works. With the amount of funding we're going to have, we'll be able to do so much more than ever previously." His eyes were really lighting up now and he was talking a lot faster.

"That's amazing, really. So who is Gautam van Firstenburg, and what's his background?"

"He's a billionaire of Indian-German descent living in London, and his company is called 'GVF Laboratories'. He isn't married and has no kids, but wants to do something philanthropic with his money, to leave his legacy for society. I understand that his parents have both recently been diagnosed with different forms of dementia and so he decided to try and help them, hence the need for speed. I guess he wants to go down in history as the man responsible for curing dementia, sort of like a modern day Marie Curie. A cash injection this large, and all in one go, means that we should be able to make huge progress in a really short space of time."

They both paused, contemplating how this could affect people's lives, and especially their own and that of Jason's mother. At that stage they could not possibly have envisaged exactly how everybody's lives would indeed be altered forever.

There was the sound of light footsteps on the stairs followed by the living room door creaking open and a sleepy, young girl wandered in rubbing her eyes.

Julia rose first. "Are you okay darling?"

"I had a nightmare about Nanny."

In the ensuing weeks and months Jason's job at GVF Laboratories was more intense than ever before.

27

Typically when he arrived home at the end of the day he would check on his mother. Slowly her mental state declined.

One evening over another glass of wine the conversation returned to his project.

"How's work?" Julia asked. "Any developments?"

"Huh? Oh yes, actually we have been making considerable progress. We've been hampered a little by some internal politics though."

"What's the problem?"

"Van Firstenburg has stated he is not keen on animal testing so we are having to find alternative methods which are making matters more difficult."

"Wouldn't that be a good thing though? Not harming innocent animals?"

"This is true," Jason sighed. This was an issue that he had struggled with, like most people involved with such research. "No one actually *likes* testing any medical procedures on animals but unfortunately in this business there really is very little substitute. I mean it *is* possible in some cases to use alternatives such as growing human tissue cultures or computer modelling, and we do both, but unfortunately these methods are just not accurate enough. Doing experiments on animals is almost as realistic as experimenting on humans; almost. So we will be doing some animal testing, just not nearly as much as we would do normally.

"We've had a few breakthroughs though. At the moment we're making some really aggressive DNA modifications that speed up the cell functioning like crazy. I told you before that Gautam van Firstenburg is keen to push this ahead as fast as possible, possibly even too fast. It's caused a few problems trying to slow things up and performing enough of the correct trials. But anyway, the point is that all the results look promising and he wants to go ahead with human clinical trials."

"But surely *he* is not the expert, you are. Do *you* think it's too soon for that?"

"No you're quite right, he's not the expert but he *is* the money. Without his backing we would certainly not have made the advances that we have made to date, not in my lifetime anyway. It's sooner than we would have liked but it *is* safe."

"Well that's incredible. And?"

"Hmmm, well, they're looking for volunteers, human guinea pigs with advanced dementia of various types. You'd be surprised exactly how few people actually have advanced Pick's in the UK."

"Ahh. And you were considering volunteering your mother." It was not a question, just an uncomfortable realization.

"Yes. With virtually all new drugs or medical procedures there will come a time where you need to test the results on humans. This has just come slightly sooner than we would have liked. Now the life expectancy of a sufferer of Pick's can be as little as three years from diagnosis to as long as ten years in some. My mother was diagnosed with this, what, six years ago? So we really are living on borrowed time. It's her best chance, her last chance and I really think it will work."

"What exactly does it involve?" Julia's natural sense of caution meant that she did not particularly like the sound of this plan, but then what other options did they have? As with Van Firstenburg's parents, time was running out.

"There is a long course of drugs to take that may have some unpleasant side-effects for some, such as nausea or headaches. There will be some therapy called trans-cranial, magnetic stimulation, which involves using electro-magnets to excite deep areas of brain tissue, and a little radiography will help with this stimulation. The drugs will be administered over the period of about a week then a couple of weeks off and repeated several times."

"And are you sure that you are not rushing into this, because of your mother?"

"Absolutely not. Not all research programmes progress at the same rate. This is just one of the faster ones."

Julia took a deep breath. This really was a big decision to take but, if he was sure… "Well then, I guess it's the right thing to do for her."

They both laughed a little nervously.

"Think I need another drink. You?"

Until recently the drug had unofficially been named the Dem-buster, a reference to the Dam Busters squadron of the Second World War, implying its triumph over dementia and alluding to Van Firstenburg's mention of developing a 'brain bomb'. Now however it had been given an official brand name, 'Mnemoloss', taken from Mnemosyne, the Titaness of Greek mythology, daughter of Gaia and Uranus and the personification of memory.

Jason's mother was taken for a rigorous screening procedure. The medical research facility of GVF Laboratories was to the north east of London, just outside the city of Cambridge. It had a small unit that provided accommodation for patients. Standing blankly by the front door waiting for Jason to bring her suitcase down she looked lost and afraid. Julia had to go into the kitchen to avoid the children seeing her with tears in her eyes. However the programme went smoothly for her. After just over a week she was released and Jason took her home until the second stage of drugs were to be administered.

Julia and the children were all waiting for her when she arrived back. On seeing her walk unsteadily through the front door Julia burst into tears and flung her arms around her. Jason's mother stood for a second not reacting then slowly returned a frail hug. Over the next week she seemed to recover quickly but she did experience some side-effects in the form of nausea and terrible headaches. She had always been fairly steady on her feet but now a couple of times she stumbled and fell. Otherwise so far everything seemed well.

Extensive clinical trials were required before a licence could be obtained to produce the drug commercially. In order to speed up the process GVF took an innovative approach and involved large pharmaceutical concerns from overseas. Human volunteers were found initially in twelve other European countries with more non-European nations added as the tests proceeded. This was an unusual arrangement and although nobody could have predicted, it contributed significantly to the events due to unfold. In days and weeks to come Jason would have time to rue some of the decisions made and how they foolishly thought they were infallible. Although like some of his colleagues he was uncomfortable with the speed with which the human tests were pushed through, he was not vocal enough in his protestations to make a difference. They were all swept along with the euphoria of the huge financial boost from Van Firstenburg and his unshakable desire to succeed, and Jason in particular with his own agenda to cure Nanny Boxall. They were so concerned with developing this neurological nuke that they forgot to treat Mother Nature with the respect that she deserves. Instead they showed her an arrogant level of disdain and sometimes Mother Nature bites back.

More sessions of drugs followed. Always though at the back of Jason's mind were the doubts. Were they going too fast? Were the normal safety procedures being ignored? His fears were mainly that the drugs would not

31

work as they hoped and they would ruin this unique opportunity to achieve excellence and cure dementia. Nanny Boxall gradually became more responsive. She would often look up with a smile as Jason checked on her, or would speak of her own volition. To Jason these were priceless moments that helped to assuage his concerns. However, his worries were trivial in comparison with the horror that even now was building.

Finally the drug was released onto the open market with huge acclaim and a celebratory party for 'significant' employees, of which Jason was one of the most important. He received a special mention at the party which he found highly embarrassing, and promise of a pay rise which he found highly agreeable. As Mnemoloss had been created in such unusually international circumstances the promotion of it was immediately opened up to medical practitioners all across the globe. The world press had incredible coverage of this new 'wonder drug' and the nickname 'Dem-buster' became better known than the actual brand name. After a couple of days the media, always notoriously fickle and with the attention span somewhat akin to the dementia sufferers that GVF was seeking to cure, turned its gaze elsewhere.

Although Mnemoloss was now being prescribed freely they continued to examine its long-term effects in the laboratory. It was having excellent results with neurological recovery. What was not so good however was that in a small yet growing number of cases there were unpleasant examples of personality change. People with dementia are often fairly amiable and pliable having lost aggressive instincts along with most other basic drives, but increasingly those taking Mnemoloss were starting to become irascible. In a smaller number of instances that irascibility was becoming something decidedly more unwelcome…

A short while after its release date Jason returned home
from work to find Julia looking disturbed. When the
children were out of ear-shot he asked what was
bothering her.

"It's nothing really, I'm sure I'm being silly. It's just
that earlier when I was in your mother's room I was
chatting away to her and she told me to shut up."

"What?" Jason was stunned. It was very unlike his
mother to be bad tempered, but also he wondered whether
the drugs were reversing her decline to such an extent that
some of her emotions and instincts were returning? He
was not sure whether to be disturbed or delighted by this
news.

Julia looked distraught. "I mean for starters I didn't
know she was capable of having or even expressing
feelings anymore. But also it was the aggression with
which she said it."

"It may just be that as the drugs take effect emotions
start to come back in a random order. The brain is trying
to juggle with an awful lot of change and things get a bit
confused in there. Or maybe she did not really know what
she was saying. Let's face it she has been talking garbage
for quite a while now."

"Oh she knew what she was saying all right. She even
turned and glared at me when she spoke. She's said daft
things to me before but this was different. This time it
was as though there was real hatred."

There had been vague mention of such incidences with
other volunteers from the Mnemoloss programme.
However these were people he did not personally know
so it was easier to write them off as over-reactions. To
hear this report about his own mother was very
disturbing. He went upstairs to check on her but she was

asleep, breathing in a soft, rasping rhythm. She looked more at peace now than she ever did while awake and he could almost believe that she was her normal self again. He sat on the chair in the corner, watching her for a while and feeling decidedly troubled.

A couple of days later and her headaches returned. She would lie in bed moaning and sweating at night and although she was indeed becoming more vocal and communicative, she was still not quite coherent enough to formulate complex sentences. It was like trying to deduce from an eighteen-month-old child what is bothering it. Jason wondered whether that frustration brought on by pain was the reason for the irritable behaviour.

Despite the drug having attracted a huge amount of press coverage, the first attack ironically went by virtually unnoticed by the media. An elderly man called Howie who lived with his wife in Stuttgart, Germany, had been diagnosed with Alzheimer's six years previously. He had been put forward by his family doctor, Doktor Rourke, for the initial trials, and although there had been some doubt over his suitability, Doktor Rourke was most insistent and they had pressed ahead anyway. Herr Howie had completed the first two courses of Mnemoloss but the side-effects had been so severe that he had been withdrawn.

One Sunday afternoon after he had been removed from the trials Frau Howie was in her garden. She looked up to see her husband advancing towards her. He looked distracted and seemed irritated by something. She had risen to her feet and as he neared he had suddenly struck her, knocking her to the floor. The neighbours, a quintessentially English couple called the Clarksons, were in their garden at the time. They heard a commotion and peered over the fence, only to see Herr Howie crouching

34

over his stricken wife and biting her. They rushed round and restrained him, Mr Clarkson receiving an injury on his wrist in the process. The four of them were taken to hospital. Herr Howie had calmed down already but was sedated. Mrs Clarkson was treated for shock and the other two were treated for bite wounds. Doktor Rourke visited them in hospital but there was nothing to initially lead him to believe it was linked to Mnemoloss. The incident made page seven of the local newspaper, the 'Stuttgarter Zeitung', but otherwise it went unnoticed.

It was only a few days later when Doktor Rourke was in his surgery he came across some information pertaining to the drug trials. Out of professional courtesy he rang his local connection associated with GVF to mention the incident. His report eventually found its way to GVF Laboratories in Cambridge and finished its journey in the office of a man who worked near Dr Boxall, where such post-trial information was being collated.

The second attack happened a week after the Howie occurrence in the town of Penn just outside Manchester. A teenager walking to school saw an old man he knew, called Mr Abra, tottering out of his front door wearing only his pyjama trousers. The boy stopped and laughed at Abra who seemed to take offence, turned and chased him. When he was later questioned the youth said that the old man had been shouting something at him but that it did not seem to make any sense, as though he was talking in tongues. After a short distance the teenager realized he had outpaced his attacker and turned to see him instead attacking another elderly gentleman. The gentleman, who was eighty-four years old, later had a heart attack and died. When the media got hold of this story it made larger headlines in the UK and the fact that Abra had been using Mnemoloss *was* mentioned this time. Now alarm bells started to ring at GVF, although at this stage they were still reasonably muted.

Dr Boxall was summoned for a meeting the next day and asked to relay his research to some of the more senior managers. First he returned to the animal section to check on progress and to speak to the head clinician, a small, twitchy man called Bennett who had an impressively bushy moustache that he waxed to a point. When he looked at the moustache Boxall could not help but think of the whiskers of the rats in the cages, especially since Bennett spent so much time amongst them. If any man was ever suited to their job it was he.

Bennett led him down the lines of cages that housed the rats, row upon row of them stacked on work benches that ran the length of the room. The room was austere with white floors and scrubbed surfaces. The smell from the many rodents mingling with the scent of mass-produced cleaning products was quite nauseating at first until one got used to it. Boxall had worked there with Bennett for several long months, interspersing his theoretical computer modelling with live tests in the early stages of drug development, but he spent much less time there now and Bennett had more current information on the progress of the animals.

Bennett briefed him as they strolled down the ranks of cages. "Of course a few of the specimens have died through natural causes. As you know we don't include them as 'Death From Drug'. Here are the statistics." He handed some charts to Boxall. "They basically say that ninety-five percent of the test cases took to the drugs okay, the other five either DFD'd within the first couple of days or through other complications within the first week. Otherwise, as clinical trials go, it was remarkably smooth and straightforward, one of the better ones that I have ever seen."

Boxall felt a brief flush of satisfaction with this news as they both knew how important he had been in the design of Mnemoloss. He was about to thank the man and leave to study the charts further when Bennett added an afterthought that made Boxall stop short.

"At least, the earlier rats we used all seemed to go through the tests without problem. It was only the latest batch that for some reason has started to skew the stats somewhat."

"How do you mean?" Boxall had a sudden feeling of alarm, those old, nagging doubts coming back to the surface chanting 'I told you so.'

"It's not that there have been many more DFD's. It's just the latest group of rats have exhibited behavioural changes. At first we put it down to a coincidence. As you know that kind of thing happens sometimes, but there were so many of them that we thought there must be more to it than that. I assume the drugs have been tweaked in the latter stages of development and for some reason it has just not agreed with them."

"Behavioural changes? What kind of changes?"

"Well recently the rats have been becoming quite aggressive. Often it is a struggle to get them out of their cage without claws and teeth flying everywhere. Three of my techies were bitten only last week. Most odd, I have never seen anything like it."

The hair on Boxall's neck literally stood on end. For a second the world receded and he felt faint. He had heard about the attack in Manchester and whilst an isolated case is nothing to go by, the fact that the animal trials were reflecting the human reactions was worrying; very worrying. He thanked Bennett without enthusiasm and left the laboratory as quickly as he could without wanting to seem in a rush. A small prickle of sweat already ran down his throat like a talon gently tracing a path over his skin.

At nine thirty-five he arrived back in his office. Immediately he checked the data from Bennett and then re-checked. The results were not conclusive, merely suggestive, but he was worried nonetheless. During the development phase of the programme Boxall had commanded a team of up to eight technicians working directly for him and he could still contact them and use them if he needed to. The next twenty-five minutes he spent doing just that.

By half past ten they were all assembled in his office and he quietly closed the door. It would be very easy to panic them but at this stage there was not much to go on, nothing more than a disturbing hunch and the slightest spectre of a problem. He decided to keep it low key and for the moment just to gather more information, just to be sure.

It was five past eleven when they left the conference room. Whilst apologizing for the short notice, he gave them all until three o'clock that afternoon to report back to him on their various assignments. "No lunch breaks today I'm afraid, no cigarette breaks, you've barely even got time to breathe. This takes precedence over everything else you were doing and over anything that anyone asks you to do. If someone has a problem with that then tell them to come and talk to me about it. Is that understood?"

The last one out of the room closed the door leaving Boxall alone with his thoughts and the ticking of the clock. His doubts were speaking to him again in the silence and the one word he heard loudest was one of the most feared words in drug development – 'mutation!'

He sat there pondering. Drugs do cause mutation over time and viruses and diseases will evolve and adapt eventually. Such a fast alteration however was practically unheard of. Mnemoloss had been manufactured to target certain neurological functions and change the way the brain codes information. As such, it was in reality actually created to teach the brain to mutate, after a fashion. Not only that but it was designed to act quickly. Could it be that they had somehow got it wrong and it was indeed aggressively causing mutation, only not as they had planned?

Until twelve o'clock he looked through some of his notes that he had stored on his laptop. Then he donned his white lab coat and went back to see Bennett. Regardless of what his team of technicians found out he decided to check over all of his work and retest the drugs. It was a little late to be doing this now, after Mnemoloss was already commercially available, but it would put his mind at rest. After all, had he not felt that the whole development programme had been forced through too quickly with insufficient animal trials? When he presented his findings to the medical board later that day he would insist on a lot more testing in the laboratory.

He returned to his office at two fifteen. By three o'clock he had received most of the data from his team. He sat watching the clock and fiddling nervously with a sheaf of papers. By half past three they had all got back to him and he went to see his managers who were having coffee and biscuits in an office at the other end of the building.

He entered the room, politely refusing the drinks he was offered. Boxall had regular dealings with the two men and knew them well. The woman he had met only a couple of times and knew mostly by reputation. His direct boss, Dr Michael Rhind, was wearing a light grey suit and yellow tie. He was a tall, slim man in his late fifties with thinning light brown hair in a side parting and always seemed to have a five o'clock shadow and a cup of black coffee. He was a neuroscientist like Boxall, and had been ultimately responsible for overseeing the neurological aspects of the drug and liaising with other departments. After Boxall, more than anybody else he understood the drug and its application, and the two of them had worked closely throughout its development. Next to him sat Dr Robert Cannon who had been responsible for integrating and coordinating the various aspects of medical science. He was a slim man who looked fit, was always extremely energetic and enthusiastic, and had very blond hair and eyebrows which in certain lights made him appear nearly albino. Dr Rhind reported directly to him and he, in turn, to Gautam van Firstenburg. He wore a standard, grey suit with light pin-stripes that seemed to lack imagination and was going threadbare at the elbows. Lastly, sat on the far right, was Ms Zoe Jenkins who had recently been promoted to the position of general manager responsible for sales of Mnemoloss. She was relatively young for such a senior position, being only in her early thirties. She had a fine head of glossy, red hair that clashed particularly badly with the red blouse that she wore. All three of them had clipboards resting purposefully on the table.

"Gentlemen, Ms Jenkins, I am sorry for being slightly late..."

Rhind waved his hand dismissing the need for apologies. "You know presumably why we asked for this 'chat'; there has been a media report of a patient from the trials acting aggressively and clearly we need to cover ourselves. We would like a few facts so that we can exercise a little damage limitation with the press. We just need to know what caused the attack, if there have been any other incidents and whether you think there is a significant likelihood of this happening again."

Boxall placed his notes on the table in front of him and

cleared his throat. "I have got my technicians to gather whatever data they could since this morning. I looked into three main areas; animal tests, results from the human trials and contacting as many of the volunteers' families as possible, or failing that - their doctors."

He paused and looked up but none of them spoke, they were all scribbling furiously, so he continued. "Firstly, the animal tests." He placed some graphs on the table in front of them. "Ninety-five percent of our test cases took to the final drug without problem. Of the five percent that died, one percent were from unrelated causes, two percent died within the first week of administering the drugs, likely due allergic reaction, and two percent lasted as long as two weeks before DFD'ing."

Jenkins looked up in confusion. "What was that, 'DFD'ing'?"

"Sorry, Dead From Drug. In the tests we found no signs of drug distortion and no side-effects at all with the final drug compound. The only comment I would add is that today the Chief Lab Techie reported some possible behavioural change in the rats." The three of them paused and looked up intensely, waiting and not interrupting. Boxall continued uneasily. "The rats have been exhibiting increased episodes of violent behaviour although at this stage that could be for one of many reasons."

"Such as?" Jenkins interrupted sharply. Boxall could see quite clearly how she had been promoted so quickly.

"Well, we were initially limited to the number of animals or rats we were permitted to use, which meant that the trials that we did have were of a greater duration than normal. So it could just be a function of that, literally they have gone a bit stir-crazy. There have been previous studies into just that condition which suggested that this kind of behavioural change does sometimes occur. We're examining their diet to see if something might have affected them. Lastly, the strain of rat we have been using is not the typical kind used here in the UK. We imported them from Germany. So we're considering that possibility and contacting our counterparts there to find more info."

"Yes, please do," said Rhind, "and get back to us as soon as you have anything more on that."

"Absolutely. Next were the results from the human trials. The trials officially ended a little over three months ago and the drugs have been commercially available for the last month and a half. As we were short of time we concentrated on those in the UK. We were able to get hold of the doctor involved in the case in Manchester. I'll come to that in a moment. Basically all of the families and doctors we spoke to said that Mnemoloss had enhanced the patient's quality of life through improved memory, linguistic functioning and social skills. We estimate the improvement at the moment to be equivalent to roughly two years of steady dementia degeneration and that should increase."

Jenkins stopped writing for a moment and looked up. "Were there any other side-effects reported by the volunteers? Character changes, increases in hostility or such like?" she asked.

"There have been character changes, but to some extent at least, we predicted that would happen. Dementia by its very nature involves changes in personality. As parts of the brain degenerate people lose social norms, forget whom they are and how to act. Our patients are regaining functions that they lost possibly years ago and with that they are re-experiencing some of the feelings of confusion that they will initially have had.

"But, no one else has experienced an increased level of hostility like that in the Penn incident. There have been isolated episodes of minor aggression but not the same as in that case. We spoke to the doctor in Manchester. It seems that the patient, a man called Abra, was fairly hot-tempered in general so it's possible that the incident had nothing to do with Mnemoloss but just that he was reverting to type, perhaps exasperated by his condition. However I am still not one hundred percent on that and I need to look into it a lot more."

Boxall's last few words had been largely lost on the three of them, due to the collective sigh of relief. In drug development 'mutation' may well be one of the most feared words; in the manufacturing industry in general another is 'recall'. There are various reasons why a product may be recalled and most of them are health-related. Invariably whatever the reason, the cost will be high and if people have been harmed by faulty products then the following law suits can be disastrous. Clearly they did not want to hear that their drug was causing episodic violence. As they sat back and each started to express relief, Boxall's mind returned to his wife's words: 'This was different. This time it was as though there was real hatred.'

Dr Cannon put down his clipboard, clasped his hands on his knees and smiled for the first time. "That's great news Jason, just what we wanted to hear. You will obviously examine all this further, yes?"

Boxall nodded vigourously. Cannon's smile lessened but he seemed genuinely keen to be of assistance. "Is there anything we can do to help you?"

"All I would like is to have my original team of eight lab-techs back working exclusively for me for the foreseeable future. Also given that the animal tests were cut down to the bare minimum originally, I would like to go back and extend those trials and complete them thoroughly. As I said, my findings are not yet conclusive and we really must look into it all a lot more." He stared

43

at Cannon expecting the worst.

The other two also looked at Cannon who sat thinking for a second, then nodded. "Of course. Yes to all your requests. Put it in a brief memo to me and I will action it immediately. I know that Van Firstenburg did ideally want to limit animal tests but I think this has been enough of a scare for us all and will do our PR some good. I am sure I can sanction at least a limited number of further tests."

Leaving the meeting Boxall felt an enormous sense of relief, although he was bothered by the word 'limited' that Cannon had slipped in at the end of his sentence. As the data had been collected for him throughout the day it had gone some way to allaying his fears, but only now could he relax a little. After a brief phone conversation with Bennett he packed his laptop into his suitcase and left for home. The material he had presented to them had been correct, at least at that moment in time.

Next morning Jason sat in his kitchen having a leisurely cup of tea whilst contemplating his plan of action. Unbeknownst to him, this was to be one of the last happy moments he would have together with his family.

Arianna Beugg had started using the Dem-buster several weeks previously. She had been diagnosed with Alzheimer's three years before and whilst she *could* still recognize her husband Viktor and their children, she was rapidly becoming more forgetful and confused. On the final night of Viktor's life they had gone to sleep as normal. Despite her worsening condition they still shared the same bed, as they had done for the last forty-two years since immigrating to Brooklyn, New York from Holland. She had been experiencing more frequent and severe headaches over the past couple of weeks but they were not serious enough to link them to any changes in medication, and the fact that she had suffered from migraines throughout most of her life unfortunately masked their significance.

Viktor would never again see daylight. That night Arianna found herself in excruciating pain with the impression of blinding light thumping through the front of her head. Confused already, she tried to scream but no words would form, just a wild, rasping noise that made her husband stir in his sleep but not enough to rouse him to full consciousness and save his life. The pain continued but as the radiance subsided, so did any last remnants of cognitive awareness. The agony gave rise to a ferocious rage that needed assuaging. Like an injured animal she turned in the darkness and blindly attacked the person nearest to her, biting part of him that was exposed above the duvet, Viktor's neck.

Neighbours were alerted to a problem by a banging at around three in the morning. The police were phoned and Sergeant Gerrard of the NYPD arrived at the Beugg house at approximately four o'clock. He could hear noises coming from within and was sufficiently worried to force open the door, only to find Arianna lying in the hall on her stomach. Her face was covered in blood and her legs skewed at an odd angle as though she had broken them in a fall down the stairs. She was moaning something although he could not make out any recognizable words as she tried to crawl towards him. As he knelt by her side she grasped him by the wrist with surprising strength and pulled him down towards her. Because he thought she was going to whisper something to him he did not struggle until he felt her teeth clamp on his ear.

When reinforcements arrived a search of the house was made and the body of Mr Beugg was discovered in bed with his throat ripped apart. The blood on Mrs Beugg's face was found to be his, not, as Gerrard had suspected, her own. Gerrard was taken to hospital and his half-severed ear was reattached. Two days later he went into the police station to fill out a report and have a debrief with his commanding officer, although by the time the meeting was over he already had the first of the migraines so he excused himself and returned home to bed.

Gerrard did not return to active police duty and the headaches continued to get worse. He started to become irritable, withdrawn and acting quite out of character. Although during this period he was bed-ridden a lot of the time, when he was able to go out of the house he started to frequent a local lap-dancing club called Valentines. He regularly withdrew large sums of money from his bank account but by the end of the day had no recollection of what he had done with it. All the while he was plagued by nausea, headaches and a distinct feeling of paranoia.

A clerk at his police station phoned after three days to check on him but got no reply. He rang several more times without success, so his police lieutenant became concerned and a squad car was sent to his house. There was no answer but the two officers, Shirvell and Sparrowhawk, could see through the half drawn curtains that the place was in disarray. Later that evening they returned but there was still nobody home so they decided to wait, which did not displease them as there was a café opposite that served excellent coffee and pastries.

Shirvell had not even had time to take the first bite of his chocolate praline doughnut before his radio crackled into life.

"Disturbance reported in Valentines Bar on Union and Third. Officers needed to respond."

"Shirvell and Sparrowhawk currently on Fifth and Garfield," Shirvell answered. "We're going to Valentines now."

46

By the time they arrived a small crowd had gathered. A few of the women who worked in the bar were standing in a huddle on the street corner sobbing. One, who they recognised by name - an exotic dancer by the name of Charity - wearing nothing more than a leopard print thong and a feather boa, was hysterical. Officer Sparrowhawk noted she had blood on her hands and neck from an open wound. There were also a few of the bar's clientele nearby. Two were sat on the ground looking stunned with temporary bandages applied to various body parts. It transpired that a man had gone berserk inside and attacked one of the other customers before turning on the staff. The officers calmed the scene and called for backup before striding purposefully towards the bar's entrance. As they walked they released their side-arms from their holsters; both carried the Glock, one of three types of semi-automatic 9mm pistols issued to NYPD officers.

Shirvell pulled open the large, outer door and they entered a small hallway. The door swung slowly closed behind them and they stood by a cash register in a foyer where they let their eyes adjust to the dim lighting. Both of them had been here before whilst off duty and knew the layout inside as much as they recognised its stale, musty odour. The smell had never previously bothered either of them but today it seemed unusually unpleasant.

Music was playing from within. The current song was 'Boys, Boys, Boys,' a track from the 1980's by a sultry Italian popstar called Sabrina.

"Seems like they're playing your song, hey?" Shirvell whispered to his partner with a smirk.

They moved further into the club, through a ribbon curtain and into the main dance area, their shoes sticking slightly to the floor. There was a stage to their left with benches around low, plastic tables. To the right was the bar area, illuminated with tacky neon lights and bar stools with red, heart-shaped seats. Some of the stools had been overturned and it was to this area that their attention was drawn. Lying face down by the bar was an enormous black man. His legs were twitching and underneath his torso there was a small pool of blood that looked unnatural in the artificial light. He was wearing a string vest and his arms were thick and muscled; he was clearly the doorman. Just beyond him lying on the floor was another man who could easily have passed for a homeless person. He was dressed in ill-fitting jeans, grey plimsolls that had worn through at the sole and a dirty white t-shirt with the name of a rock band, "Battleborne," emblazoned on it. Another dark puddle was slowly growing around his upper body

The bar was curved and from where they stood they could just see the legs of a third person slumped at the far side. Cautiously they manoeuvred around the tables whilst checking for anyone else. The man looked up and stared at them.

"Strewth!" Shirvell exclaimed. "Gerrard, what on earth have you done?"

Sergeant Gerrard did not move; he just glared balefully at them with bloodshot eyes and moaned. He had clearly not shaved for a couple of days, his hair was dishevelled and his clothes were a mess. The bandages that the hospital had applied were hanging loosely by the side of his head and his ear was covered in blood. He wore stained jeans that were torn at the knee and a scruffy jacket.

"What have you done?" Shirvell repeated as he edged forwards carefully, his gun trained on his sergeant but his other hand held out in a placating gesture.

Gerrard did not react or speak; he just stared down at his fingers that Shirvell now noticed were dripping with blood. There was more blood around his mouth and down the front of his jacket. As Shirvell moved slowly towards him from the front, Sparrowhawk slipped closer from the side along the edge of the bar. In one hand he too held his weapon but with the other he had unhooked handcuffs from his belt. He would not get a chance to use them however. Suddenly Gerrard's head jerked up. The wild unfocused stare had been replaced with a brief glimmer of recognition. His expression became apologetic for a moment and then his features rippled. He snarled and anger flooded his face, as though a mask had been dropped seamlessly into place. His hand moved under his jacket to a bulge that neither had previously noticed.

"Keep your hands where I can seem them," shouted Sparrowhawk as Gerrard pulled a gun from his trouser belt. He held it at an unusual angle as though it was unfamiliar to him but swung it menacingly in their direction. Without hesitation two shots blew Gerrard's head apart, one fired by each policeman.

The ensuing investigation exonerated both officers of any guilt. Forced into a situation which left them no other option they had fired upon their colleague only as a last resort. The erratic actions of Gerrard, both in Valentines and over the previous days, were put down to the acrimonious divorce he had been enduring. Other colleagues had found he had become somewhat bad-tempered and withdrawn, and had clearly been bottling up his emotions. The divorce distracted attention from the attack he had suffered at the Beugg house which was subsequently overlooked and no association was ever made.

Gradually across the planet a pattern of uncharacteristic aggression was emerging and spreading faster than anybody could ever have envisaged. Still the appropriate connections between Mnemoloss and the attacks were not being drawn. Time was running out and unfortunately the opportunity for effective intervention was dwindling and all but gone.

CHAPTER 3

Dr Boxall decided to dedicate himself to retesting laboratory animals and rats. He was still assessing information and trying to satisfy himself of what he badly wanted to believe, but all the while his doubts chattered away to him, hinting of a mounting problem. He kept a radio on in the background, tuned to a news channel. A small but growing number of violent outbursts involving people who had been using Mnemoloss had come to light. After much deliberation he decided to go back to his boss, present his findings and make some strong recommendations. They were sure to be unpopular but he could just not ignore them anymore.

The catalyst for this decision was made for him by an abrupt rise in media attention. From several countries around the world there had been reports of an increasing number of vicious and unprovoked attacks perpetrated by elderly people, either on loved ones or on random strangers. In each case the aggressor had fairly recently started using Mnemoloss. It was just too much of a coincidence. At this time, unfortunately, nobody had yet recognized the preponderance of secondary attacks.

Boxall rang Dr Rhind's office and found it engaged. He tried five more times over the next thirty minutes but as it was still unavailable he went to see him in person. Before he left he rang through to Bennett, who answered on the first ring.

"Bennett here."

"Ah Stephen, it's Jason."

"Thank goodness, I was just about to call you. I'm worried."

"Really? Maybe we're thinking the same thing. The tests we've been re-running on the rats, I'm not sure we did enough of them before the drugs went to human trials and I'm not sure we now have enough time left to continue them. I've been listening to the radio. There have been reports of a few more incidents worldwide, which probably means there have actually been *many* more incidents. A trend seems to be developing. I think we need to stop looking at the animals; it's too late for that. We need to move onto humans now. I'm going to recommend to Rhind that we recall Mnemoloss immediately and I think we have got to start considering the possibility of mutation."

Most people would like to think that at critical moments in their life their brains will be racing and they will be leaping to all kinds of brilliant solutions. In truth, as adrenaline kicks in, it is extremely difficult to focus on even simple tasks. Bennett found himself twiddling his moustache, completely numb, almost unable to hear his colleague as those two disastrous words hijacked his thoughts and demanded his total attention; 'recall' and 'mutation'. He found himself staring uselessly at the hairs that had risen all along his arms.

"Yes, right, I see."

"I also think we are now at the stage where we have got to try to find a cure. We have to try to reverse the effects of Mnemoloss and we have to do it as fast as possible, in case this is as bad as I think it might possibly be. But God help us I'm wrong." There was no answer from the other end of the phone, so Boxall raised his voice. " Bennett? Bennett!"

"Yes, yes sorry. My word, I was thinking along the same lines, I guess just not as far along as you. Okay, yes. Can you pop into my lab and we can talk this through a little further? I will assemble all my technicians for say, about half an hour?"

"Fine. I'm going to Rhind's office now. I'll come straight to you after." He hung up and sat for a short while, feeling hollow and sick. All the work of the previous months and years, his reputation, his job, everything was about to come tumbling down but at the moment all he could think about was his mother. His mother, who had taken the Dem-buster. His mother, who had recently started to exhibit worrying outbursts of aggression. His mother, who was sat in the same house as his unsuspecting wife and children at that very moment! He made one more vitally important phone call, more important to him than anything else, and then he quickly went to find Dr Rhind.

When he arrived there were several other men that he did not recognize standing around Rhind, all talking loudly and excitedly at each other. When Rhind saw Boxall he immediately slipped through the bodies, took Boxall by the elbow and led him away to a nearby drinks machine. Whilst stabbing coins into it with trembling hands he spoke rapidly.

"Jason, good lord, it's all going crazy. I assume you've heard?"

"Heard what?"

"The media. It's on the TV and will be in the papers by tomorrow. The press are linking Mnemoloss to these unprovoked attacks. Surely that can't be right, can it?"

"Actually that's what I came to see you about. I'm afraid it seems as though there might be a connection and I don't think we have a choice any more. We have to issue a recall."

Rhind slumped down into a chair holding his chin in his hands, not noticing the steaming black coffee spilling out from the paper cup. "Really? You think?"

Boxall nodded slowly.

Rhind went pale and looked as though he was about to retch. A soft, moan escaped his lips as he hung his head. "Yes, yes, you may be right."

"Immediately. This very afternoon. We can't have Mnemoloss administered to even one more person. Apparently an investigative journalist in North America called Elizabeth Carpenter broke the story. It's been picked up by various radio stations and now it seems to be echoed all around the civilized world."

"Good lord! This is really bad. This is going to cost millions, hundreds of millions, I dread to think. Are you absolutely certain?"

"I'm afraid so but that's not all," Boxall continued. "We have got to contact all the people who have taken Mnemoloss, every single one of them, and test all of them, world-wide. I believe the media reports may be correct; there may be a link after all between Mnemoloss and these behavioural changes. I'm afraid until I've done more tests I just can't rule it out." He felt an incredulous sense of unreality, as though his mouth knew things that his brain had not yet accepted, but what else could he do? With the possibility that their drug, his drug, was turning people into violent maniacs, they had no other choice.

Rhind buried his head in his hands. "Yes of course," he mumbled. "That's absolutely right. I just can't believe this is happening."

Boxall left Rhind to come to terms with reality, feeling not a little angry. From the start his hands had been tied as to how he ran his own experiments. He had tried to mention this to his superiors but had been ignored and now they were facing the consequences. He wondered though whether he had been vocal enough in his protestations. He had been wracked with guilt over his mother's condition. Because of that he had been as desperate as Van Firstenburg to see the drug succeed, tempted by the possibility that it might make a difference. Had that clouded his judgement? He did not think so, but how could he be sure? And did it even matter now?

54

In pharmaceutics as in any other industry requiring research and development, advances tend to be made at a steady pace, balanced with progress in other fields, insightful leaps forward then periods of stagnation, reconciliation and review. With Mnemoloss however, so much money had been made available which had meant their progress had been positively meteoric. After each seemingly successful result they had forged ahead in a self-congratulatory environment without stopping to consider any possible flaws. Ironically it seemed that this massive amount of funding was ultimately leading to their downfall. As the Four horsemen of the Apocalypse slowly drew into view on the horizon they were not the traditionally accepted faces of War, Famine, Pestilence and Death. Instead they each wore a different guise; that of Progress, Charity, Pride and Arrogance.

It was Tuesday when Boxall went to see Rhind. At that moment, as he was making his way back to Bennett's laboratory, there was a knock at the front door of his home. For some reason Julia felt a sense of unease as she went to answer it and checked on Isabelle and Rory first. She went to open the front door but paused and took a breath, steadying her nerves. Jason's brother, George, was standing there, looking at his feet and shifting back and forth.

"Oh George, it's you. Hello." She was surprised to see him, in fact slightly taken aback. Although he lived reasonably close and often went to a martial arts club at the end of their street, he did not normally come to the house unannounced, and especially not when he would surely know that Jason was at work.

"Yeah, hi," was all he could think to say and just stood there awkwardly. She noticed he was carrying a small sports bag. "Errr," he paused, "can I... come in?"

"Yes of course, sorry." She led him into the kitchen. Checking that the children were still playing in the lounge she quietly closed the kitchen door behind them.

"Why are you here George? Is Jason okay?"

"Yes, he's fine. I guess he didn't have a chance to call you then?"

"No. Why?" She started to feel a flush of panic but tried to calm herself. After all, there was nothing to worry about, was there…?

"He phoned me a few minutes ago and asked me to pop by. Well in fact he asked me to stop by - for the night."

"What's going on?" Julia's voice was rising with her sense of apprehension.

"It's nothing, please don't worry. Or at least I hope it's nothing. You must have seen some of the reports on TV of elderly people going nuts and attacking strangers, or… even loved ones? Well it seems they have all been taking the Dem-buster drug."

"Yes, but…" and it slowly started to dawn on her. "You can't possibly mean your mother?" She was aghast.

"I'm sure she is okay but Jason said to say that he might not make it home tonight and just wanted me here. Just in case."

"Oh my god!" She crumpled into a chair, clasping her hands together. The children must have heard her as they ran in at that moment, Isabelle looking worried.

"Hi Uncle George. What's wrong Mummy?"

"Nothing sweetheart," she replied somewhat lifelessly, trying to sound cheery. "Everything's fine," but as the children turned to go she spoke a little more sharply, "…but come and play in here, both of you. Now!"

"How is she?" George gestured upstairs to his mother. "Mind if I go and check on her?" He ran upstairs without waiting for an answer.

She was sat in her armchair watching television. When

he entered she turned with a scowl that transformed into a vague smile. "Hello dear."

"Hi Mum, how are you?"

"Yes, dear." He was not sure if that was a positive reply to his enquiry or if she was just saying anything, but he decided to leave it at that. She appeared completely normal. He frowned and went back downstairs closing her bedroom door behind him. He noticed that there was no lock to it.

When Jason had phoned earlier George had initially thought his brother was being ridiculous and over-reacting but something in Jason's voice had quieted his protestations. Now he too was starting to feel alarmed although he could not say why. The children were still in the kitchen and complaining that the toys they wanted were in the lounge and why couldn't they just play in there? Julia however wanted them in her sight and wanted to keep herself between them and her mother-in-law; just in case.

Jason did not get home that night, but he spoke to Julia on the phone, telling her there were problems with the drug. It was possible that it was linked to hostile attacks around the world and that he had to stay and work round-the-clock on the issue. He asked after his mother and was told that she was okay, the same as always. His parting words to her were to be careful and not take any risks. That did nothing to put Julia's mind at rest.

George slept on an inflatable bed on the landing outside his mother's bedroom. In his younger years he had served in the army and so was quite used to roughing it. He had checked on her several times throughout the evening and she seemed fine. Julia had put her to bed as normal and he then went in to say goodnight. As he turned out the light he thought she glared at him and muttered something dark under her breath, but when he turned the light back on her eyes were already closed and there was a peaceful expression on her face. Perhaps it had just been his imagination.

On Wednesday morning the story of Mnemoloss was on the front page of every newspaper and dominating every television news report. There were many more acts of aggression reported. This could have meant that other unconnected acts of aggression were mistakenly being attributed to the drug, or that there was indeed a rapid rise in their occurrence and the press was more alert to them.

Like his brother, Jason had spent the night on an inflatable bed although in truth he had only managed to sleep for two hours. He had now turned his efforts to frantically searching for a way to reverse the effects of Mnemoloss. Theoretically that should not be too hard - he hoped. They understood what Mnemoloss was designed to do and hence knew, or thought they knew, how it reacted in patients' bodies. Reversing it should therefore be more straightforward than developing it had been in the first place. The key factor now was time and they did not have enough of it. Jason did not make it home that day and neither did George who remained in his brother's house with a growing sense of alarm.

One of Boxall's staff called Montgomery was extremely busy phoning their contacts overseas who had been involved with the foreign trials. Invariably though the call was not needed as the contacts had seen the horror-show on television and knew the alleged link between the Dem-buster and the violence. It was with growing revulsion that Montgomery made each subsequent call as many of them had terrible stories of their own, most of which had happened in the past few days, as though someone had just thrown a switch and all around the planet the drug had morphed into its evil alter-ego. Montgomery was a petite lady with blonde locks scraped back in a severe bun. As the phone calls progressed she played with the strands of her hair in agitation and the bun increasingly came apart in her hands, leaving her looking more and more dishevelled and fraught.

The journalist Carpenter seemed to be making a name for herself on the back of GVF's misfortune. Because she had been responsible for breaking the story she unwittingly became a lightning rod for further reports and found herself swamped with calls from strangers who all had tales of violence. After her first mention of a potential link between Mnemoloss and the outbreaks, she then went further and suggested the hostility might not be confined to people who had been administered the drug. She had received an undisclosed number of accounts suggesting that those who came into contact with Mnemoloss users were also becoming hysterical and acting strangely. She briefly hinted at secondary effects although did not mention the word 'mutation' and did not yet know the exact method by which the condition was being passed on. Speculation in the media was rife.

In Hong Kong two men working for an electrical goods company were delivering a refrigerator to an old woman on the third floor of a block of flats. The front door was open when they arrived but there was no answer when they called out. Fearing the lady might have taken a fall they tentatively ventured further into the flat.

They found her sitting in her living room wearing a nightdress and mumbling to herself. She ignored them and it was only when one of the men called Tai shook her gently by her shoulder that she seemed to react. She stood with surprising vigour, grabbed at his wrists and started biting him whilst making a strange gargling noise. His friend Patel came to his aid and forced her back onto the couch where they were barely able to restrain her. In the process he was bitten as well. At first it was hard to contain her, even though there were two of them and she was just an old lady, but after a few moments she suddenly seemed to calm down and just went limp. Tai took the opportunity to phone the police and she was still sedate when they arrived.

Both men went to have their wounds checked in hospital but the bites were not serious. Tai went back to work the next day, feeling a little queasy and with a passing headache. Patel did not appear and had not phoned in sick. Over the next two days there was still no sign of him so Tai went to his apartment. He arrived at the flat to find a commotion outside. The police were questioning the doorman who said that he had been advised of a disorder by some of the upper floor residents and was about to go and investigate when a 'wild man' had rushed past him, pushing him to the floor. The man turned out to be Patel. He had run into the street attacking passers-by at random. People fled from his path and Patel, who was frothing at the mouth like a lunatic and yelling in some foreign language, disappeared into the subway station opposite.

He had made it down to the platform from where he normally caught the subway to work and had been attacking and savaging everyone within reach. Many people were taken to hospital and treated for shock or bite wounds. Patel himself did not need any medical care as he fell onto the train tracks whilst struggling with two men who were trying to subdue him, and went under the wheels of a train. The events of the day made Tai feel peculiar. He still had the headache which now grew in intensity and a raging thirst that he was unable to slake. He returned home and by the time he got there was feeling worse. He rang his work the next morning to say

60

that he was ill and that would be the last rational conversation he would ever have.

By Wednesday evening Boxall was absolutely exhausted and had been working feverishly throughout the day. He had been granted all available resources by his superiors and was urgently repeating previous experiments, tests and computer models but this time in reverse. It felt as though up until this week matters had slowly been gathering like distant, wispy clouds on the horizon. Now they were converging, building into the mother of all Biblical storms. The situation was speeding up and he was struggling to keep pace with it. Things were no longer under his control and he felt as though he might just flounder and sink beneath the surface at any moment.

He spent a large part of his time working in the laboratory directly with Bennett whose moustache had never received so much twirling and tweaking. Boxall periodically returned to his own office to keep track of what his team of technicians were doing and giving them new directions. In the background he had a television tuned constantly to a news channel but there was never any good information. Reports were tumbling over each other, struggling to the fore like an angry crowd of shoppers at a Thanksgiving sale, all outdoing the previous one for grief, shock and savagery.

That night none of the team of scientists left the building. Food was brought to them and basic sleeping arrangements were provided. Otherwise they all worked continuously. On Thursday morning Boxall found himself sat in his office feeling numb and staring blankly at the television. It took him some time to register that everything had gone quiet. He turned to Montgomery who was hovering outside his office.

"Hey, the news channel has gone dead. That's the first

break in the reports in the last forty-eight hours."

"Oh yeah, so it has. I wonder what that means."

Montgomery put down a clipboard and picked up some half-moon glasses from the desk. The channel was just showing the view from a roof top, looking out over the city where previously a reporter had been standing and reading the latest bulletin. As they stared they saw the clouds moving in the background, a couple of birds fly past but otherwise nothing else happened, no reporter holding a microphone, no news subtitles being pasted to the bottom of the screen, nothing. Just still, eerie silence.

"I'm not sure I like this," Boxall stood then rang his wife.

Julia, George, Isabelle and Rory were all sat quietly in the kitchen. They were not really waiting for anything, just marking time with a sense of dread constantly lurking in the background. They had not been outside for the last two days and had mostly spent their time watching the news channels. Nanny Boxall was upstairs in her room as usual. They took her meals but otherwise preferred to leave her alone. The children seemed to perceive the unfolding horror and had become sullen and miserable. George had tried to remain upbeat and keep them all preoccupied but even his normally boundless reserve of energy had been exhausted.

When the phone rang Julia jumped and snatched it up. "Yes?" she answered quickly.

"It's me, how are you all?"

She could feel herself on the verge of tears and panic. "We're okay. We're in the kitchen, apart from your mum. She's in her room. How are you?"

"Ah, we're all fine here, just really tired," Jason replied. "I think we *are* making progress though. Just thought I would make sure you're okay. We've got a TV news channel on here but it all seems to have gone quiet.

I mean, the picture is still playing but there is nothing happening; nothing at all. There's no one even in the frame, it's really spooky. Have you heard anything lately?"

"No. We'll go and check the TV and let you know if we hear anything."

Boxall stood staring for a moment, lost in exhausted distraction and then dragged himself back to his work.

A short while later a harassed-looking presenter returned to the screen and announced in a shaky voice, "The Indian Government has declared a state of emergency and is mobilizing the army in order to control the mounting violence and lawlessness." He informed anyone watching that this was an action that had not happened since 1977 and effectively introduced martial law. There had been a sudden rise in violence across the UK as well, which had taken the form of looting, rioting and unprovoked aggression, but as yet no such measures had been taken. Boxall did not hear any more details. He was already thinking about his family and what he should do.

Within a few minutes he was driving home. The streets had an eerie quality to them. There were not many vehicles. What cars there were on the road seemed to be driving fast and not stopping at traffic lights. Relatively few pedestrians were out but there did seem to be a lot of police, either on foot or flashing past in police cars and vans. Those on foot were never by themselves and always wearing full riot gear. Every time he saw someone else walking or loitering he could not help but consider them with suspicion. What were they doing? Were they looting? Or even more dreadful to contemplate, were they crazed people who had taken his Mnemoloss?

Occasionally he saw a smashed shop window and twice cars that were actually ablaze but with no sign of

fire engines in attendance. It reminded him of the prelude
to the Brixton riots of 1981. This was the calm before the
storm. The quiet intake of breath before the screaming
begins. The recoil of the hand before the fist strikes.
People were largely hiding in their homes, waiting and
watching. Frightened, but not quite sure of what they
were afraid.

Yet…

As his keys rattled in the front door his family all
assembled in the entrance hall. Julia immediately threw
herself into his arms in tears. The children were crying
and George stood back, watching the stairs suspiciously.

"What's going on Jas?" George asked. "The TV says
there's been a state of emergency declared."

"Yeah, I saw. I guess that means India is now under
martial law."

"No," Julia was confused. "Here. A state of emergency
has just been declared here."

"What? Oh my god!" He sagged against the wall and
suddenly felt almost as though he was watching the scene
from above. He tried to focus and concentrate. "Are you
all okay?"

"Yes, yes." They were fine.

"And how has Mum been?"

Julia did not answer and George avoided his look.

"Tell me." Jason felt panic rising up inside. "How is
she?"

"She's fine bro," George said quietly. "She's just been
acting a little… odd. I thought she'd snapped at me a
couple of times but couldn't be sure. She's not been
chatting much and although recently she had seemed to
be getting more lively and talkative, the last couple of
days she has hardly come out of her room, hardly said
anything. Then last night Isy just popped her head into
her room and your mother yelled at her. She told her to

64

get out in no uncertain terms. There was real venom there. We heard it all over the house."

Jason was shaken but also thankful. It could easily have been so much worse, judging by the news reports from around the globe. "But you are all okay though?" He stroked Isabelle's head; the stress of being away from his family at this time had been enormous. "Look, I'm probably being a little drastic, I'm sure this will blow over in a few days but I think you should all come with me. Now."

"What?" Julia was alarmed and panicking again. "Where?"

"Back to the labs. It's totally secure, there's a guard on the gate and it's a lot safer than anywhere else. There are crude but acceptable sleeping arrangements that we have all been using for the last few days and it means I don't have to worry about you anymore. A lot of the staff have been staying there and some have gone to get their families already. I have got to go back; more than ever I have to be there now. And it will help me a lot if I know that you are all there and safe."

Julia nodded. Rory was whining and George was still looking upstairs. Jason checked his watch impatiently.

"We have got to go immediately though, in case a curfew is imposed here and the roads are all blocked. Is that okay with you all? You too George."

"Just one thing," George said looking doubtful, "what about Mum?"

It was Jason's turn to avoid his younger brother's eyes.

"We can't leave her," George frowned. "She isn't capable of looking after herself."

"We can't take her with us, it's too risky. The fact that she's been getting more aggressive, I just think we can't take that chance. We don't know what she's going to do…"

He trailed off, not sure exactly what he thought or what to say. This was not something that he had planned. When he drove home he had not had any firm ideas, he only wanted to get back to his family. But now that the UK was in a state of emergency and things were deteriorating at such an alarming rate, this was definitely the right action to take, to protect his family. And his mother? He could not even bring himself to think of it. George was right, she was not capable of looking after herself but worse than that, if she was becoming aggressive like so many others now, then she really was a danger to everybody.

He put a stop to his train of thought as it was heading somewhere terrible and unacceptable. He focused on his family instead. "Okay kids, we are going to go away for a few days. We have got to go right now though so I need you to be good, get a couple of games to bring with you but that's it. Please go to your play room and choose what you want to bring."

They scampered off chatting to each other, sounding quite excited and Jason turned to Julia. "Right, just bare essentials. Pack a quick bag with a couple of changes of clothes, toiletries, only what you really need, and then let's go. Whatever happens we must *not* get stuck here."

Julia disappeared immediately upstairs but George lingered a moment, holding his brother's stare; the futility reflecting in his eyes what Jason felt in his heart.

"Jas, I can't just leave her. You go, I'll stay."

Jason started to protest but George raised a hand, silencing him. "Look we're wasting time and as you said, we haven't got much of it. I can't go with you bro and you know you'd do exactly the same in my position. I'll stay and look after her. When you're able, then come and get us. It'll be all right."

Jason was close to tears. He looked George in the eyes

and it actually seemed that his younger brother believed what he was saying, that everything would work out and they would be reunited sometime soon. Jason tried to believe him but his doubts told him otherwise. Finally he shrugged and nodded.

"Okay but listen - be really careful with her. Find a way of barricading her in the room and every time you go in check first that she is not aggressive. And carry some kind of weapon with you at all times. All of that military training might come in handy after all."

George snorted incredulously but Jason took hold of his shoulder sternly. "I'm not joking, I mean it. She may become violent and dangerous, even towards her own son. Be careful and we'll come for you as soon as we can."

George took a step back but the sceptical look had gone and been replaced with one of acceptance; or was it fear?

The children were assembled first and waiting by the front door. Rory was wearing his Spider Man outfit and Isabelle had on a pair of jeans and a red and white striped jumper, her training shoes that flashed every time she took a step and her doggy back-pack which she had called Muffy. Julia solemnly walked downstairs holding some blankets and an overnight bag that was bulging. She was wearing the pink duffle coat that he had bought her for her last birthday and her white gym shoes. Poking out of the top of the bag Jason could see her hair-dryer; he smiled thinly as this was hardly an essential survival item, but he did not have the heart to say anything. George came last. His expression was grim and resigned and this time neither brother could look each other in the eye.

"Okay, everyone outside, I forgot to say goodbye to Mum so I'll just nip upstairs, won't be a sec. Please get everybody in the car George and start it up for me."

He could feel the lie stumble as it tripped off his tongue and his cheeks burning with guilt as the rest trudged outside, leaving him alone in the house with his mother and his shame.

She lay quietly asleep under her bed-covers. Her breathing was slow and rasping as though she had a terrible chest infection. He watched her for a moment and tried to convince himself that she was all right but the pallor of her skin, the red blemishes and small lesions that had formed even since he had last seen her were evidence that she was most definitely anything but okay.

"I'm so sorry Mum, this is all my fault. I'm so very sorry."

He felt a terrible surge of guilt and tears welled up in his eyes, but an excited screech from Isabelle reminded him of his responsibility now and he forced the tears away, wiping his eyes on the back of his hand. He picked up the red cushion from the chair in the corner and grasped it in his hands for a moment whilst regarding her with an unreal, discorporate feeling. He walked slowly towards her, stopped by her bedside and hesitated. Could he really do it? Her condition was certainly deteriorating and it was only a matter of time until she became violent. He was almost certain of that. Was it better to leave George alone with her to be attacked and injured? Or could he really do this thing to his mother? Just then her breathing became a little irregular. She frowned and let out a small gasp as though in pain. He looked at her again and shook his head, straightened and tossed the cushion back onto the chair. No. No, he had done her enough injustice as it was, merely by creating this monstrous drug. He could not wrong her further. He bent down to kiss her gently on the forehead.

"I love you Mum. God bless you. Goodbye."

At that her eyes flickered open. The whites were

bloodshot and smouldering. The pupils were nothing more than vacant holes of wrath and insanity. Her mouth contorted into a snarling sneer with a hiss. Her hand grabbed him firmly by the wrist, pulling him down towards her stained and snapping teeth.

CHAPTER 4

The gates of RAF Headley Court were locked just before the state of emergency had been declared in the UK. Those in the guardroom could see down the driveway which was shrouded by trees to the main road. In the final hours before the curfew and martial law were introduced, cars sped by the entrance to the base, probably driven by people trying to get to family or seeking a safer location in which to hide from the ensuing insanity. The roads then fell silent for some time with only the occasional police riot-van or army vehicle screeching past. Finally even those reminders of humanity ceased. Not all personnel had actually been on the base at the time. The normal operating staff numbered between sixty and seventy which included those involved with security, catering, administration, supply and logistics, the medical branch and those responsible for military transport otherwise known as MT. Most of these were either from the army or RAF, the remainder being civilian contractors. Together with families there were anything up to roughly one hundred and fifty people associated with the station at any one time and at full capacity there could be as many as thirty patients being cared for and going through rehabilitation. In addition there was a capability to handle approximately twenty-five students in aeromedicine lectures. After the gates were locked only forty-two people were on the base, an alarmingly small pool of resources.

Basic amenities had continued to work for a while after the state of emergency and there had been irregular news updates on the TV and radio for a couple of days. The military had taken to patrolling in large numbers and a strict curfew was introduced. Unfortunately the situation seemed to bring out the lowest common denominator

70

onto the streets. As the emergency services became more and more stretched, accepted behavioural norms started to erode, buildings were burned and some inner-city areas became inaccessible for the police. There was widespread looting as people sought to take advantage of the situation which centred on luxury goods at first. After a few days as the situation deteriorated, people began to realise just how serious it was. Hysteria spread like the sickness itself. Even normally law-abiding individuals became determined to protect and provide for themselves and their families, and many people started looting for food and water. This led to the military being far busier. Not only did they have to prevent this societal breakdown but also they had to try and identify and contain any people who had contracted this strange illness. Not knowing who was sick or healthy made matters extremely difficult and many more people were exposed to the condition than would have been if the curfew had been more strictly observed.

Mobile telephone reception had ceased and normal landline telephones sometime thereafter, so anybody who had become separated from loved ones during that period no longer knew if they were alive, dead, or worse still – infected. The TV broadcasts soon stopped but the radio announcements came hourly. They included information on the curfew, how large a military presence was in each area, the state of amenities including water and electricity, basic survival advice and information on the diseased. The last broadcast was repeated a few times over a period of several hours without being changed, as if those responsible for gathering and disseminating the information were no longer in a position to provide that service, the last words of a dying society. Then suddenly, without warning or explanation, even those updates ceased. The voices were replaced by static leaving all at

Headley Court feeling isolated, alone and very, very scared.

They saw no one, either on foot or in a vehicle for a week before they next had any outside contact. Corporal Bannister of the army security regiment had been smoking in the guardroom at dusk with Corporal Gillen from the admin section when they noticed a man shuffling along the main road.

"Hey there's someone there, look," Corporal Gillen was on his feet immediately and pointed excitedly.

Bannister peered through the gloom at the figure but something instinctively just seemed wrong. It might have been his unsteady gait as he made his way slowly forwards or perhaps merely the fact that they had not seen anyone else until now, but Bannister was about to advise caution. However he was not quick enough as Gillen rushed outside and called out to the man. He was dressed in jeans and a striped shirt but it was not until he approached that they noticed he had only one shoe on and the shirt was ragged and half undone. When Gillen had shouted he seemed not to have heard at first and Bannister felt a surge of relief, but then the man stopped, turned, raised a hand almost in a salute and made a haunting, moaning sound like an injured stag. He started gradually lurching towards them. Both soldiers slowly took their SA80 rifles off their shoulders. They switched the safety catches off whilst walking cautiously backwards away from the fence.

"Now look what you've done, fool." Corporal Bannister angrily rounded on his colleague.

"Sorry, I didn't realise," Corporal Gillen replied but it was too late.

The man was running now with both arms held out in front of him as if he were blind or feeling in front of himself in the dark, and he was still howling at them in all-consuming rage. He hit the fence without even attempting to stop, as though he had not seen it and despite the fact that the gate was locked both soldiers recoiled, unsure of what to do and feeling entirely unnerved. This was the first time either had seen any of the infected and it was a truly frightening experience. The man crouched at the fence clawing and banging it in fury as he snarled at them. Phlegm and froth sprayed out of his open, twisted mouth which had dried blood stains around the edges. His enraged, red eyes flickered between the two of them as though he held them responsible for some heinous slight against him. His skin was pale and flaky with a purple tinge to it and thin red veins spread out from his nose and eyes, across his cheeks.

"What's wrong with him?" Gillen asked, looking frightened and puzzled but Bannister just shrugged and kept gaping.

They stood back indecisively from the fence with their guns trained on him for a few moments. Finally Bannister told Gillen to go back to the main building and get help. When he was gone Bannister cautiously approached the fence, horrified but fascinated in a truly morbid way, by the man whose nonsensical tirade had not let up once. In fact the man seemed to be getting louder and started trying to climb the fence which really unnerved Bannister who followed his progress closely with his rifle. He did not get far before he slipped off. Just then Gillen arrived back with Group Captain Denny and Private Bruce Matthews, an athletic and loquacious black soldier from the supply and logistics section who was fresh out of training and had been at the station for only a week. For a while they all stood staring and flinching periodically at the outbursts.

"Well we can't just leave him there," Denny finally snapped.

Bannister raised his weapon and pointed it at the man but Denny admonished him. "No idiot, we can't shoot him. He may be sick but he *is* still human you know. Hang on a sec, I have an idea."

Corporal Bannister and Private Matthews approached close to the man which made him even more animated. They then slowly walked around the perimeter of the fence a short way, with him following and pawing at the barrier between them in irate frustration. Gillen then opened the gates so that could Denny drive a Land Rover out. Bannister and Matthews disengaged from the man and with the gates locked behind him, Denny attracted his attention with shouts and blasts of the horn. The man turned, threw his head back and howled like a wild animal before doubling over practically on all fours and tearing after the vehicle. Denny led him at a fast running pace sufficiently far from the base, several road junctions away before turning the vehicle around. The streets were eerily deserted. He started to feel vulnerable and brought the car to a sudden halt. With a knot in his stomach he attempted a three point turn but the road was not quite wide enough. For a frantic moment he had to reverse and turn once more. The extra time spent fumbling gave the man opportunity to reach his quarry. With a scream he thumped into the driver's window of the Land Rover. The glass cracked as he splattered it with spittle. Denny flinched and gave a yelp. With shaking hands he slammed the gear lever forwards and stamped on the accelerator, knocking the man to the floor as he fled back to the station.

It was the first time any of them had ventured out since the state of emergency had been declared. He passed just one other vehicle, a car that had crashed and caught fire. There were the remains of a charred body in the front of it and the sight truly disturbed him. To have gone off station alone had been a mistake and the experience had really traumatised him. He hated being outside and could not wait to be back in the shelter of Headley Court. By the time the gates were safely locked behind him again he was trembling and felt nauseous.

Like many military establishments the station had its own backup electricity supply provided by generators, but there was only a limited amount of diesel kept on base for that purpose. The generators would not provide enough power to run everything that required electricity and the supply of diesel quickly dwindled. Candles were predominantly used at night and only the most essential services were run during the day. It was quite possible to get more fuel, both petrol and diesel, from local petrol stations, but it was thought best to avoid too many journeys out, if at all possible.

It caused greater problems when the mains water supply failed. Drinking water could be sourced from local shops and supermarkets for the immediate future, large containers were filled up from the nearest reservoir and simple purification methods were used in order to make it safe for consumption. Washing obviously required larger supplies and so the Logistics and Engineering branch, under Flight Lieutenant Andrew Walkden, had rigged up some vessels to catch rain which was supplemented from the indoor swimming pool on the station. They were all allowed two buckets to shower with per day. Some of the first bucket was used to wet the body, soap was then applied and the remainder used to rinse clean. It was not a very comfortable way of washing but it proved effective. Walkden proudly told whoever would listen that he had used a similar system in ordinary life as he was extremely environmentally friendly. Bannister kindly offered to help Corporal Charlotte Collins pour the buckets over herself if she had any difficulties as he was just extremely friendly.

Lavatories were now also inoperative so until a store or warehouse that had chemical porta-loos could be located, two deep holes were dug near a side entrance to the mess, by the kitchens. Simple wooden huts had been constructed over each hole, and basic long-drop toilets created. Any waste organic matter was disposed of here and although they were reasonably hygienic, there was a fairly unpleasant odour from them. The duty of disposing of the organic matter was not a favourite task and was usually awarded to the most junior kitchen hand, Leading Aircraftman Neale.

"It's character building; you'll thank me one day," his boss was fond of reminding Neale. "Besides laddie, effluence rolls downhill."

Leading Aircraftman Neale disagreed. To him, using the word 'rolls' implied some form of movement and suggested that the 'effluence' had started its journey elsewhere than right at the bottom. As far as Neale was concerned the effluence had *started* its life with him at the bottom and remained there throughout its existence. 'Shit just lives downhill,' would have seemed a more accurate expression to him. He always accepted the job of waste disposal without complaint until he was out of ear shot of his boss, Sergeant Vallage, a large, cumbersome and stereotypically dour Scot with grey hair and a bushy moustache. When a safe distance away Neale would then curse him vociferously. Sergeant Vallage was not the kind of man one insulted to his face.

Although the station's primary roles in normal times had been medical rehabilitation, aeronautical education and research, as it was a military base it did hold an amount of firearms. When communication with the outside world had ceased, maintenance of their own

76

security became the number one priority for everyone. As provisions dwindled it quickly became apparent that if life did not return to normal very soon they would run out of supplies, so they had started to consider sending out scavenging patrols in the Land Rovers. Most urgent was food and water but there was also a long list of other requirements including weapons and ammunition, medical supplies, cleaning products, batteries, candles, torches and fuel.

At first there had been daily briefings from Group Captain Denny for everybody on the base which included any relevant new information, recent occurrences, anything of interest from the patrols and tasks for that day. Denny and Lewis both considered it very important to keep everyone busy and give them a purpose in order to prevent morale from sinking too low, although that was inevitable in such circumstances. They had involved all personnel on the station, it brought them all together and helped build a feeling of solidarity and reliance, but as time wore on it seemed as though Denny himself was not impervious to the stress. His briefings had become more disjointed and erratic until finally they ceased altogether. The station's medical centre had an open clinic which now provided more counselling than actual physical treatment. They did try to continue the bodily rehabilitation of the patients as well, both to keep spirits up but also to prepare them all as best they could in case any kind of drastic physical action was required.

The Engineering branch of RAF Headley Court had been incredibly busy adapting processes and appliances for the new circumstances. Previously the standby electricity generators had rarely been used and then only during weekly tests. They therefore needed a fair amount of attention to keep them working. Walkden's section was also responsible for maintaining the radios which were considered absolutely vital to safety and any future salvation. A transmission containing information on the whereabouts of the base, its survivors and the date was played on a constant loop on the international emergency frequencies. Senior Aircraftman Ric Masters of the Logistics section was given the task of monitoring the radios, although having listened to static for several hours he was usually completely exhausted and demoralized. Either his Spanish wife Vida or his direct superior, Corporal Bamburac, would take over when Masters could face no more.

Vida was one of only two spouses who had been on the base when the gates were closed; she had heard nothing from any of her family in Madrid and found listening to the white noise of the radio to be therapeutic. From conversations with her husband she was aware that the static came from a number of sources such as the atmosphere, other electrical equipment and even, incredibly, an amount from the noise of radiation emitted in the origin of the universe's Big Bang. To her however, it was the sounds of the souls of countless millions of people who had perished in this international disaster, brushing past her in the ether on their way to the afterlife. To her it was soporific. It made her feel closer to her Spanish family and she almost went into a meditative trance when she took over from her husband. After the general information and emergency broadcasts from all commercial radio stations had ceased there had been no further human contact with the outside world. At Headley Court the radio station was situated beside the medical department so Senior Aircraftman Masters and his wife were given the quarters that were closest.

The MT department, also under the auspices of Flight Lieutenant Andrew Walkden, had been busy as well. It was imperative that all vehicles were in absolutely prime condition because if one of them broke down when off base it could prove fatal. They had fortified the Land Rovers as best they could, enlarged and improved the front and rear crash bars and created several convenient places where weapons could be placed around each vehicle and easily retrieved in a hurry. Sergeant Harper Hutchison effectively ran this section and he joked with Private Darby that it felt like an episode of 'The A-Team'.

Two days after the incident with the man at the gates, everyone at Headley Court had been getting skittish, not knowing what had happened to loved ones or even if society *had* completely broken down. The appearance of the man aroused their curiosity and it was felt that they had to know what was occurring outside.

A preliminary reconnaissance group was sent out in two Land Rovers with four soldiers in each. Other than Denny's brief foray this was the first time anyone had left the station since the state of emergency. They were lightly armed with standard issue military Browning 9mm pistols. These were considered sufficient for the purpose as they were traveling in the safety of the two cars and did not expect to have any truly hostile encounters. They had assumed that outside the gates there would probably be a discreet military presence mostly confined to vehicles, the majority of the population under strict curfew and perhaps the occasional sick person roaming freely until being contained. It just seemed totally unbelievable that the situation could possibly be anything different.

Captain Lewis was in the front of the lead vehicle driven by Sergeant Garrick Straddling, with the comfortingly large figure of Lance Corporal Dean Millington and Senior Aircraftman Dan Hobbs from the medical branch in the rear. The second vehicle was driven by Sergeant Matteo Abbott and carried Lance Corporal Ward and Private Sharp, who both worked in the MT section, and Flight Lieutenant Jonny Parsons, a RAF helicopter pilot who had been undergoing aeronautical studies at the base. They had left Headley Court just after sunrise and drove slowly through the deserted streets in strained silence. Every so often each vehicle would radio the other, as much to break the unnatural hush as to check the equipment. At first the roads seemed relatively normal with not much out of the ordinary but as they neared the town things started to take on a more sinister air. They frequently passed cars that had been abandoned by the roadside for reasons that were unclear, their doors wide open alluding to dark secrets. Under the chassis of one car they could not help but notice the broken body of a man, his spine warped like dried driftwood. A small murder of crows hopped around the body, examining and pecking at it. On seeing the corpse Senior Aircraftman Hobbs let out a choked gasping and pointed. Millington raised an eyebrow but looked otherwise unmoved and remained silent.

Hobbs was obviously shaken. "Did you see him?"

"I'm afraid so my man," Millington nodded grimly. "Steel yourself, I think there will be many more of those yet."

"Do you think he was contaminated?"

Millington said nothing. Lewis looked at Straddling, who shrugged.

"Impossible to say," said Lewis, "but his clothes were really dishevelled and he wasn't wearing any shoes? Which makes me think he probably wasn't of sound mind. If that's true then I guess whoever was driving the car saw him and didn't want to stop."

"Can't say I blame them," Straddling grunted. "I'm ney

80

bloody stopping for anyone."

They drove into Bishop's Stortford and headed towards the police station which seemed to be a natural place to start looking for any surviving humans. Lewis had a megaphone and sporadically called out to anybody who might be able to hear, such as survivors hiding in fear in their homes. He announced whom they were and to come forth in safety. Straddling accompanied him with hoots on the vehicle's horn.

It was a pretty town, Lewis thought, displaying an abundance of attractive, red-brick houses with bay windows and manicured gardens. He could not imagine anything overly dramatic ever occurring there; it had a general feel of sleepiness and inactivity, the kind of place to raise one's children in safety. Now though litter was festooned in the streets. Black bin liners had been torn, spilling their guts out onto the pavement, and shopping trolleys seemed to have been deposited randomly. In many of the houses the ground floor windows and doors had been hastily boarded up, although some had subsequently been forced open and smashed. Broken furniture was strewn across front lawns and there were occasional blood stains smeared down walls. Every once in a while these stains were accompanied by soiled items of clothing, a shoe here, a torn shirt there, but nowhere did they see any living humans. They saw several more corpses however; not all complete cadavers, which mostly bore the indications of having been ravaged or dismembered. The soldiers all sat in grim silence, captivated yet distraught by the disturbing scenes of chaos. None of them could help but wonder what had occurred in each house, what had led to all that destruction; the doors off their hinges, the discarded accrual of everyday life, or the bloody hand print on a wall. The situation seemed far grimmer than any of them had previously feared. There were absolutely no signs of human life, no survivors waiting to greet them and no military presence. Lewis was aware that the shocking scenes would have an effect on them all and was determined not to allow his attention to wander. His soldiers needed him sharp and in command, now more than ever.

They stopped in front of the police station and sat peering out at the building, unwilling to leave the safety of their vehicles. Only now the seriousness of the situation was starting to hit home with Lewis, as with them all. In RAF Headley Court they had been totally sheltered from whatever horrific scenes of death and pandemonium had occurred. Like hell on earth, it must have truly been horrendous. The doors and windows of the police station were all closed and intact. It looked relatively normal and felt as though there might just be people sheltering inside.

"Where is everybody?" Hobbs asked, aghast and pale, craning his neck back and forth.

"It's not what I had imagined it would be like," Straddling muttered.

"No, you and me both," Lewis replied. "I hadn't expected there to be such bloodshed. There's absolutely no sign of anybody alive so far."

"No, and I'm starting to doubt there will be either," said Straddling.

Lewis called on the megaphone again but there was no movement or noise from within. Reluctantly he decided to get out and investigate. Straddling stayed in the car with the engine running but Millington and Hobbs nervously accompanied him, all with their Brownings clutched tightly. In Millington's large fist the weapon looked nothing more than a toy. After checking that the street was devoid of life they shuffled towards the building and Lewis gingerly pushed the front door. It slowly swung open until it knocked into the door-stop making them jump. Get a grip, he told himself. He looked back at the Land Rovers with trepidation in his eyes. As he peered into the building the first thing he noticed was the stench, fetid and decaying but with background hints of smoke. He called out but there was no answer. Followed by the two soldiers, he entered and disappeared from view.

He had his radio on and gave a somewhat disjointed commentary. "I'm just going in, moving through the front reception now," followed by a crackle of static. "Blood on the wall, there's nobody here so far." More static. "It's a real mess, looks like there's been some sort of fight," then a hiss. "We're checking the first holding cell, it looks empty. Hang on, Millington what on earth is that over there? We're just checking something out. Oh my god!" Then the radio went dead.

The alarm in his voice left Straddling fidgeting nervously. He sat holding his radio and trying to see any movement in the police station windows but there was nothing. He turned and looked back at the other Land Rover. Flight Lieutenant Parsons returned his worried expression with a perplexed shrug. Moments passed and there was no more sound from the radio. Straddling shifted again in his seat, scanning all around.

"I don't bloody like this," he said to himself and cursed.

After another ten seconds Straddling spoke sharply into his radio. "Captain Lewis?"

Silence.

"Captain Lewis, what's going on?"

Lewis heard his sergeant on the radio but was distracted by a dismembered corpse he had found in a holding cell. "Wait," he answered, stepping back and away from the stench and the flies, then the fizz of interference again.

The next thing Straddling heard was a bang as though Lewis had dropped his radio. Just then a dark shadow clipped his periphery of vision and he jumped. His own radio nearly slipped from his grasp. Parsons with Ward and Sharp moved past his vehicle. Parsons indicated to him that they were going in after Lewis.

"Flight Lieutenant Parsons," Straddling called out, winding down his window a fraction. "I'm not sure that's a good idea? Captain Lewis said to remain here."

"They may need help. We're only a few metres away. If you need us then call on the radio."

"Okay. Captain Lewis, are you there? Parsons, Ward and Sharp are coming in."

There was more static, then Lewis's voice again. He stepped gingerly around some blooded debris that littered the bottom of the flight of steps, before answering.

"Sorry, I missed that, we were just looking into something. There's nobody alive downstairs. We're moving upstairs now." He signalled to his two soldiers to follow him and slowly they ascended the staircase.

Straddling puffed a sigh of relief. Parsons was just about to enter as a crash sounded from the building beside the police station. It was a Thai restaurant with a large, ornately carved elephant over the dark, wooden door which was wide open like a gaping mouth. A broken, ground-floor window had red, velvet curtains flapping in the breeze like a tongue lapping up spilt milk. Above the upstairs windows some ivy had taken root and clung to the wall looking like scowling eyebrows and the whole effect was of a leering face that left Straddling feeling troubled. Parsons, Ward and Sharp were about five paces from the front door. They heard the noise which made them jump. Sharp looked nervously around at Straddling.

His handsome young face and shock of blond hair now looked less the boy-band member he normally resembled and more a scared youth. Parsons quickly looked back at Straddling and pointed at the restaurant indicating his change of intention. He said something to the two soldiers and the three of them slowly approached the front door.

Straddling spoke softly into his radio. "Captain Lewis, there's a noise from the restaurant next door. Parsons is going to investigate."

"No!" Lewis replied immediately, urgently. He sounded scared. He had a room of utter carnage in front of him. Bodies and limbs were scattered in front of him, decorating the upstairs rear office of the building. Blood had sprayed over the walls and even ceiling. There had clearly been a horrendous struggle. The thing that struck him most though was the smell; a sickly, overpowering stench of dead, decaying flesh, like nothing he had smelled before, that had him gagging as flies swarmed about him.

"Everyone's dead here, it's a bloody massacre. Tell them not to go in. Parsons, wait, that's an order." With that Lewis and his two soldiers started running back through the building towards the entrance.

Parsons had heard the instruction as well. The three of them had paused on either side of the front door, peering in warily. Straddling did not realise that he was actually holding his breath. As he leaned forwards his attention was caught by movement. The curtains flapped rhythmically, the beating pulse of the restaurant. The tongue flicked out lazily marking time, like a snake testing the air for the scent of food. Straddling was about to speak again into his radio to say that something was odd about it when the pulse skipped a beat. The velvet was thrust out of the way by a bloody hand and a man launched himself with a shriek in a full-length dive through the window. He caught Parsons around the shoulders from behind and the two of them hit the floor hard. Parsons's weapon was sent flying from his grasp. A second man and then a third followed him. They bounded through the window, stumbling over the bodies on the ground and added to the melee. With an instinctive reaction Private Sharp whipped his gun around. There was a loud bang as he squeezed off a round into the stomach of the third attacker before an arm seemed to dart out of the gaping mouth of the restaurant like a chameleon ensnaring a fly. He was pulled back into the darkened doorway, out of sight.

Flight Lieutenant Parsons was pinned face down on the pavement screaming with the three attackers all biting and scratching him. Lance Corporal Ward leapt forward to try to aid him but with the writhing bodies it was difficult to get a clear shot. In a panic he repeatedly smashed the handle of the gun down on the head of the nearest assailant who was astride Parsons, clawing at his back.

"Shoot him, shoot him," screamed Straddling.

On the third strike the blood started welling up at the man's temple. He finally seemed to realize that he was being hit and turned with a toothy snarl to face Ward. The wound from Sharp's bullet did not seem to have slowed him down at all. He started to rise and lunged forwards. Ward took his opportunity and fired down at him from point blank range. The shot skimmed the man's cheek, entering his body just by the collarbone. It sent him tumbling onto his back but only for an instant. With a blood-stain spreading across his chest and merging with that on his stomach, he came at Ward again. Ward stepped backwards, away from him and closer to the doorway of the restaurant in order to get a clearer shot. Just as the man leapt he fired again. This time he blew the crown of the man's head clean off like the top of a hard-boiled egg. He sprawled and crashed into Ward's legs. Ward was sent stumbling further back and into the beckoning doorway. Straddling watched helplessly as the drama unfolded in a blur before him. The speed with which the situation had deteriorated had shocked him into inactivity. Seeing the developing menace he yelled out a warning but it was too late. More hands grasped Ward from within, pulling him off his feet. His scream was choked out of him as the hands and teeth fastened on his throat. He staggered back through the doorway into the same darkness that had swallowed Sharp.

All of this happened in the briefest of moments. Straddling had barely had time to draw his pistol and get out of the vehicle. He heard from behind him the horn of the other Land Rover blaring out. The engine gunned as Sergeant Abbott rammed it into gear and the vehicle jolted forwards. It clipped one of the attackers wearing a torn black jacket hard enough to send him reeling head-first into the wall by the entrance to the police station. He got back to his feet without respite and was about to jump on Parsons once more. There was blood gushing from Parsons's shoulder and neck and still his initial attacker straddled him and bit down hungrily at his exposed flesh. Then suddenly there was a swift movement from the edge of the fracas. Black Jacket lurched at Parsons but was plucked in mid-air and abruptly changed direction as the bulk of Lance Corporal Millington burst onto the scene with a bellow. He snatched hold of Black Jacket, arrested his flight and yanked him back. In a tremendous display of brute force and adrenalin-fuelled strength he twirled the man around. He hurled him through the air and over the bonnet of Abbott's Land Rover, where he fell between the two vehicles. Straddling leapt out of the way then turned and fired twice at his head. Black Jacket flinched but did not move again. Another attacker rushed forwards from within the darkened doorway of the restaurant. Millington whirled around and leapt, meeting the assailant head-on. He kicked out in mid-air, knocking the man decisively straight back where he had come from. Blood exploded over his ruptured face. Another man appeared at the window right beside Millington. Like a ballerina he pivoted in a flash and smashed an over-sized fist into the man's face sending him flying backwards into the bowels of the restaurant.

Lewis had been a step behind Millington. He tore out of the police station and without a second to consider his actions, grabbed the first assailant who was still on Parsons's back and shoved him aside. As he flailed on the floor and started to rise, Lewis shot him three times, twice in the stomach and as that seemed to have no effect, again in the face.

Lewis gesticulated quickly to Straddling and pointed at Parsons. Then he turned back to the open front door. The two sergeants hastily turned the vehicles around, ready for a swift escape. Straddling's head was still ringing from the shooting and his pulse was racing in his chest, but he was thinking quickly and clearly.

"Quick," he barked at Abbott, "help me get Parsons in."

As they bundled the lifeless, bloody corpse into the back of Abbott's vehicle they could hear terrible sounds coming from within the restaurant. There was crashing, snarling and screaming, although it was not clear if they were the screams of the diseased or the soldiers. Lewis, Millington and Hobbs shuffled into the gloomy doorway with weapons held out in front of themselves like protective amulets.

The light was dim inside and there were overturned chairs and tables blocking their path. Lewis unclipped his torch which picked out a messy trail of blood leading into the restaurant. He strained to see further into the interior. There were thumps and growling sounds from somewhere indeterminately close. Then the entrance hall opened up into a larger dining area. Thin, cotton drapes were hanging from the ceiling, partially obscuring the main section of the room. Nevertheless Lewis was able to see through the gaps in the cloth. There was a shambles of broken crockery and furniture and a group of the infected all gathered around something in the half-light. They were on their hands and knees, fighting each other now to get access to their meal as they feasted like wolves around a kill. As Lewis played his torch beam over them, through the mess of writhing limbs he could make out the lifeless, desecrated body of at least one of his soldiers being literally torn to pieces. Someone shrieked, although Lewis did not know if it had been one of his troops or one of the infected, and the three soldiers started firing indiscriminately into the jumble of crazed lunatics.

Straddling and Abbott had just finished manhandling the body of Parsons into the rear of Abbott's Land Rover when they heard the shooting. They froze in situ, unsure whether to go in aid of their comrades or remain where they were in preparation for a swift departure. A second later and their question was answered for them. The three soldiers emerged from the restaurant's depths at a desperate run.

"Go, go, go!" Lewis screamed.

Millington was a half-step behind and both leapt into the rear doors of Straddling's vehicle. Neither saw Hobbs trip in the gloom and fall. Immediately the pack was upon him in a frenzy of shrieking, snapping teeth and claws. Hobbs cried out as mouths clamped upon his neck and hands tore his hair and ripped at his clothes and face.

Another of the infected came stumbling into view up

the road, then another, perhaps due to the commotion caused by the shooting. Lewis had not realized that Hobbs had fallen but Straddling had seen. He wound down his window and started firing at the throng. Abbott, from his vehicle, did likewise and their shots found their mark. Straddling's first clipped the shoulder of a woman in a blue dress, spinning her round. His second ripped half her face off and left her slumped across Hobbs's body as he struggled and screamed. The woman was replaced by a young man with a deep wound down one side of his face. Straddling fired again, missing this time but the man screeched in rage and then charged at the Land Rover. Straddling steadied his aim and fired again and again, just as the man was about to lunge at him, blowing his head apart. There was another right behind him. Straddling's pistol clicked uselessly as he aimed at the second attacker.

Lewis also aimed and fired but nothing happened. "I'm out."

"Me too," said Millington.

Just then one of the infected jumped on the bonnet of Abbott's car. He jerked. His foot slipped off the clutch and it lunged forwards sending the man tumbling. The vehicle stalled. For a tense moment he fumbled with the ignition. Just as the attacker regained his feet and ran at him, Abbott urged it into life, cursing. He shoved it into gear and floored the accelerator. The man roared in rage and leapt as the car shot forward but he was struck by the front crash bars and went under the wheels with a satisfying but sickening crunch.

Lewis shoved his door open, forcefully smashing it into another attacker just as the man tried to break through the window and claw at his face. The man howled as he was knocked back but was on his feet again immediately. This gave Straddling the moment he needed however and he too hit the gas. As the man swiped again the wheels span for an agonising moment before they bit down and the car raced after Abbott.

"We can't go, we can't go. Hobbs is there," Millington pleaded, looking helplessly back at his fallen comrade.

For a second Straddling paused and his foot came up off the pedal, but Lewis shouted decisively.

"He's gone, we can't help him. We're out of ammo. We'll die too if we don't get the hell out of here. Go!"

Another man came running at them, tearing out of a darkened house, intent on death and destruction and screaming mindlessly. He leapt on the bonnet and Straddling flinched but ignored him as he bounced harmlessly off. They continued racing after Abbott with Lewis still staring helplessly out of the rear window at his fallen comrade. It was a heart-breaking decision for him to have to make but he had no choice. If they had stayed they would all surely have died. The stench of rotting flesh remained in his nostrils, polluting the back of his throat like a disease, long after the police station had disappeared from view.

CHAPTER 5

After that disastrous initial foray and the deaths of the
four soldiers, everyone had been extremely shaken up and
nobody had been off station for several days. As supplies
dwindled however it became clear that they would have
to venture forth again and several successful missions
were carried out without further loss of life - until Abbott,
Campos, Sinna and Rohith had ventured forth on the
latest sortie. At roughly the same time that they had been
loading supplies in the supermarket, a gathering had been
taking place in an upstairs room of a nearby presbytery.

A gnarled figure slumped in an ornate, wooden seat that
resembled a throne. The chair had come from China, from
a minor royal court in the late Ming Dynasty. Its arms
were covered in blood-red leather and its back was carved
intricately into the pattern of a dragon entwined around
itself as it appeared to bite its own tail. Its wings were
small and its legs were spindly, and the carving lacked
realism. This had not been an oversight in the eyes of the
carpenter who created it however; the beast was not
supposed to be swallowing itself, but instead spewing
forth its own body from its mouth, signifying its
metamorphosis into what it was to become - a serpent
evolving into a dragon. The chair's current occupant,
Darius, was even older than it was.

"We hunger, Darius." The voice was dry like the
withered bones of the dead, shadowy and ancient, without
warmth or conscience. Darius said nothing but shifted
slightly in the Chinese throne so the comment was
repeated. "I said we hunger."

"I heard." Darius now stirred and turned to glare at
Farzin who was not cowed but continued speaking.

"It has been such a long time that we go hungry, such a

long time since proper sustenance. And now, when nourishment is at hand…" He trailed off leaving the sentence unfinished. Flavia stirred restlessly at his side and took a small step closer and Alec stood impassively as always right behind. Farzin returned Darius's hard stare and his voice grew louder. "It is time we end our fast. It is time for us to feast. It is time to take our rightful place, seize the moment that has presented itself and create for ourselves a new life, a new existence. We must emerge now as the new ruling class."

He stood 6' 6," not overly tall by vampyric standards and reasonably slender, but wiry and lithe. If he were a human he would have been considered gangly but as a vampire he looked sleek and efficient, like a machine. His eyes were taciturn and watery blue, unnerving and unflinching in their gaze, and totally devoid of emotion or empathy. They did not allow the slightest glimpse into his being, just reflected coldly back at the observer. He always gave the impression that he was not focussing on the eyes of whoever he was speaking to, but a thousand yards beyond as he burrowed into their soul. He wore dark trousers tucked into black, knee-high, leather boots and a sash was tied at his waist as a belt below a dark brown jerkin. He applied a faint cologne that lingered briefly after he departed from a room, a clinical, crisp reminder of his presence that carried overtones of winter. Farzin's sinewy arms ended in misleadingly delicate fingers with long, malicious nails and a deep red ring on his left index finger. His face was drawn and framed by his black, wispy hair, his lips were thin and pale as with most malnourished vampires and the whole effect was of one whose body is half empty of life – or perhaps half full of death.

Darius leaned forwards; his broad shoulders puffed up and his powerful hands clawed at the arms of his chair, causing the tendons and muscles on his large forearms to flex. He was not used to being spoken to in such a confrontational manner and he struggled to keep his voice level.

"These are indeed unusual days, unprecedented even. We are entering a time when our place in the world must change, which is why we must tread carefully. These events in human society are still unfolding and I will not risk playing our hand too soon."

He paused a moment as his brow furrowed in consternation. This clash had long been coming. He knew it was overdue and that he must handle Farzin carefully. For all of his apparent fragility, Farzin was a ruthless and effective killer whose wary economy of movement belied his speed. His two constant companions were entirely devoted and loyal, and doubtless would stand by him faithfully. Now was not the time to be causing a rift in the clan.

"If I were I to solicit your opinion, what would you have me do?" Darius asked.

Farzin did not hesitate but replied fervidly. "Civilization has crumbled and collapsed. Many humans have died or become sick. Those that remain are spread out, disorganized and often undefended. Slowly their numbers dwindle as yet more are killed or diseased. They can barely defend themselves against the tainted and they most certainly cannot stand against us. We are unopposed by humans. We are the dominant species. The only ones who can possibly offer any opposition to us now are others of our own kind."

"Yes, all this I know already. But what would you actually have me *do?* What course of action do you advocate?"

"The humans are our future. Too long have we dined upon vermin, afraid to reveal ourselves to these inferior creatures. They cannot survive without our help and we need to keep them alive. We must forge a beautiful relationship of interdependence, of symbiosis. Just as they have done to other inferior species, we must corral the survivors as much for their own safety as for our benefit." He hesitated, seemingly uncertain of how much of his plans to reveal, searching for the best way to persuade the older vampire.

"You mean we should 'farm' the humans? Treat them as cattle, imprison them and feed off them at our leisure?" Darius's voice was rising in tone and incredulity. He was half-out of the seat now, his bespoke, pitch black suit and black shirt pulled tight by his solid frame as he tensed his shoulders in agitation. His silvery hair fell over his craggy face and put his grey eyes in shadow. After such a long life he was not handsome but he was certainly charismatic, although when angry he was a truly terrifying apparition. The last few days and weeks seemed to have aged him more than the past few decades had, with the weight of leadership of the clan falling solely upon his shoulders like the Sword of Damocles. His lips drew back in a sneer revealing his long teeth, still pointed and sharp after so many years of hunting and killing.

Farzin nodded passionately. "It is for their benefit as much as ours. They will not survive without our intervention. It may seem cruel at first and it is just the initial fear of the unknown against which they will struggle. But once it has the welcome feel of familiarity they will realize there is no alternative.

"We should establish ourselves in some location, some haven which we can defend from the impure and protect our new charges. Then we venture forth and gather survivors unto ourselves and quickly we spread our dominion. We can provide them with safety, a structure and even a future. Without us they have none of that, just constant fear and a doomed struggle to survive. Now is the time to re-write civilisation according to *our* needs."

"And how do you propose we restrain them? Do we keep them isolated, chained, under lock and key, bound and blindfolded? Or do we put them in a field with bales of hay and a milking machine?"

"You mock me Darius, yet you would do well to listen. Things will change whether you like it or not and we should be the instigators of that change, not just follow in its wake and accept events as they unfold. It is in our interest to keep them safe from harm and in time we may even decide to 'turn' some, a specially selected and fortunate few, into vampire brethren, as our supremacy widens. It is now time to step out from the shadows as we deserve." His eyes were shining with a clear zeal and he was becoming more animated as the resentment of the aeons bubbled up within him.

Darius was enraged and shouting. "No! We must not be governed by a desire for revenge for our centuries of concealment. Now is the time to seek a measured reaction, not a settling of scores. They do indeed need us as protectors but when has a subjugated people ever accepted that their conquerors act in their best interests? Sooner or later they will rise up against us and we will forever be watching over our shoulders lest the time for revolt is nigh. Better to attain this position in a more civilized manner after approaching them with open discourse and agreement. Better to have their ultimate consent in this matter."

"Civilized? Consent? What are these words to them? They are not a civilized species. They are not interested in open discourse and they will not see the benefits that we will bring. We have waited an eternity for a chance like this. It is time to act *now*." He thumped a fist angrily into his open palm as he spat the words out.

Standing behind Darius in the shadows by the wall was Luca, Darius's protégé, and potentially the future Clan Leader. He shifted uneasily as the atmosphere became heavy with hostility. He glanced briefly at the vampire standing beside him, seeking some kind of reassurance. Max was Darius's closest confidant. He was not as tall as Darius but unusually for a vampire his chest was broad and his somewhat hairy arms were stout and knotted like an ancient tree. He was at least as old as Darius but he had never sought to become Clan Leader, happy instead to remain subservient. He had the same aquiline features common to many old vampires whose bodies have altered subtly over time and through repeatedly feeding on human blood. His dark eyes were deeply set beneath bushy eyebrows, his teeth were slightly stained and there were deep scars across his pale face. He wore a dark blue jumper with the sleeves rolled up as though ready for manual labour - or action. His grey trousers and black boots were all unfussy and more for practical rather than sartorial reasons. He stared expressionlessly at Farzin and his cohorts, assessing their disposition and preparing himself lest the argument should turn violent. Lately Farzin had become more insolent, like a young buck testing the leader, and Max could foresee confrontation looming. He looked at Darius, his sharp nails digging deeply into the leather on the arms of the chair and slowly shredding it as he rose from the seat.

"No. Once we emerge unto the sunlight there is no return to the shadows of myth and fable. When we stake our claim for our place at the head of this emerging world we must be absolutely certain that the time is right."

"You spend too long hidden away here procrastinating," Farzin replied. "You have no idea what has been going on out there in recent days. The time is now. We can determine the way forward and then negotiate from a position of power."

Darius slammed his hand down on the chair's arm causing it to crack. "*No!* I have decided. We wait."

On Farzin's right Flavia stirred and placed a calming hand tentatively upon his shoulder. As a female vampiress she was shorter than the males, but she still stood 6'4" in her black, heeled boots that reached just over the knee. She wore black, leather trousers that were so smooth and tight they were mirror-like in their reflectivity, beneath a corset-style top with lace trim like something that might have been sported in the aisles of the Moulin Rouge. The corset was close-fitting and tied at the front by thick, black string, and merely served to accentuate her curves. Despite the inevitable slimming and shedding of excess weight through the vampyric passage of time, she maintained a very feminine figure which her outfit only exaggerated, hinting at the voluptuousness she must have displayed whilst still human, many years previously. This had been an attribute she had used to her advantage while working in bawdy, French, backstreet hostelries before she was 'turned', and it was a feature still appreciated in her life now. Her hair was jet-black like the unfocussed eyes of the insane and cut short at the back with the sides layered to the same level as her sharp chin. Her cheeks were pronounced in an attractive manner that many a human female would envy, and her blue, feline eyes seemed at odds with the darkness of her mane. Unlike the male vampires, her lips were still fairly full and she applied deep red lipstick and dark eye shadow. The effect was very attractive and unashamedly vampish.

She regarded Farzin out of the corner of her eye. He had been unpredictable of late and he was now becoming incensed. This argument was going nowhere, she thought, and best delayed till another time. She spoke to him in soothing tones with the sing-song accent of the French.

"Come, my love, we have done all we can for now. Let us not push this further tonight."

Darius caught the last words in both sentences and their significance was not wasted on him. He wondered whether Farzin would be less confrontational if he were not trying to please the female stood beside him. We are so different from the humans we once were in so many ways, he thought to himself, yet still so alike. He had ill forebodings about the influence Flavia had over Farzin. She may not deliberately have tried to manipulate him but the fact that she was the only female amongst six males, and clearly bestowed with a flirtatious nature, inevitably led to tensions. Did Farzin perhaps act differently in order to keep her allegiance? The vampire to their left, Alec, was less of a threat. Slighter than Farzin and more placid and predictable, he was dressed simply in pale grey trousers, a white shirt and brown pumps. His emotionless eyes shifted uneasily and he sneered unconsciously as he shifted from foot to foot. Darius thought he would perhaps be reluctant to become involved in an actual physical struggle. Perhaps...

"This conversation is not yet over Darius. This is too important to me, to us all, to get it wrong," and with that Farzin span and fluidly strode from the room, arms held out at his sides with open hands as though stirring the air in his wake.

Flavia paused a moment, pouting as she glared at Darius, her chest heaving with intent. She quickly measured the demeanour of all three vampires standing poised in front of her, an instantaneous and instinctive action, before she too turned and stalked like a cat, following the other two from the room. As she reached the door she glanced towards the corner where another figure sat quietly on his haunches, hugging his knees and calmly observing the proceedings. She looked into Sebastian's eyes and held his gaze a moment. Her lips parted in a slight sneer, or perhaps smirk - it was not clear, but her expression did not hold the venom that she had shown towards Darius. If it came to it, she wondered, whose side would Sebastian take? He had always been an enigma to her. Normally she could predict men and their transparent thoughts so easily. Although this one should, in reality, be easier than any of them, she could not decipher him at all. Maybe that was why he held such fascination for her. A soft, rasping sigh like a purr escaped her, then she was gone leaving a breathless vacuum in the room. Sebastian had calmly watched the entire exchange, just as now he watched her with intrigue as she departed, his thoughts shadowing her closely from the room.

Darius had noticed the brief look between them and wondered at its significance. For a second or two he sat holding his grey head in his hands and no one moved. The hush was uncomfortable and made them all feel on edge. Sebastian frowned slightly as he noticed Max's reluctance to say anything before his leader. His complete subservience puzzled and frustrated Sebastian. In his opinion loyalty was an admirable quality, but rare is the ruler who does not benefit from a second perspective. So they waited until finally the Clan Leader slowly stood and drew himself up to his full imposing height, taller than any of them and decidedly striking. He was possessed of innate gravitas; the others naturally deferred to him and revered him. His council was accepted usually without question, his word taken as binding, and hence to query him thus seemed highly unusual to Sebastian. This made Farzin's outburst all the harder to accept. Darius stretched as though he had just woken from a deep sleep and everyone in the room shifted and stirred.

"I have grave misgivings about the future," he said turning first to Max. "Our path is no longer clear to me and that is the not the last we have heard on the subject."

"Hmmm," Max looked disturbed. "These recent changes have come upon us with little warning and, as amongst the humans, we deal with them in our individual ways. Whilst our greater life span does permit us to be somewhat more patient, nevertheless we still retain many basic human traits."

"Indeed," rumbled Darius, "and when threatened, like all species of the animal kingdom, we strike out impetuously."

Sebastian noticed a frown crease Luca's brow as he opened his mouth to say something but quickly changed his mind. As though sensing the internal dilemma Darius turned to meet his look with an enquiring arch of his thick eyebrow but Luca merely lowered his head and shrugged.

"And what do you think…" Darius turned and stared out into the room, "…Sebastian?"

Sebastian had remained impassive on his haunches, regarding the scene from the shadows in the corner but now he stood. The clothes he wore were more conventional than the others, reflecting his younger years, the comparative recency of his turning and the fact that he had not yet relinquished some of the mores and values from his life as a human. The shirt was fitted, pale linen but the ends hung loosely outside his dark jeans. He wore a black, mid-length, leather jacket with sunglasses protruding from a chest pocket, and black, slip-on ankle boots.

In modern day London Sebastian would not have stood out as much as the others in the clan. As he was relatively newly vampyric his features had only just started to alter. He was tall and under close inspection one might have noticed the slight angulations of his face, but these changes were as yet still subtle and merely looked like good bone structure as often seen in Slavic people. He was paler than he had been before, but since he was of Mediterranean stock and somewhat olive-skinned, he now looked a fairly normal shade amongst the fairer skinned British. His eyes had become strikingly piercing but this would only be viewed as strange, rather than supernatural. On passing him in a shady back street at night a more perceptive person might have unconsciously noticed something unusual and turned, only to find he had vanished into the gloom, leaving the observer walking a little faster and checking repeatedly over their shoulder, unsure as to what had triggered the spectre to pass over their mind, their pulse to quicken or their hackles to raise.

At Darius's question he cleared his throat as he stepped forwards. "I think that we have waited this long to come out of the shadows, I am not so impetuous that I cannot wait until the time is exactly right."

"Diplomatically put," Darius replied with a curious smile. "You are the most recent member of our clan. You were a human long after I had been turned. What approach do you think best?"

Sebastian was indeed the newest member and as such he was surprised to be consulted before Luca. He paused, still looking at the floor, then raised his eyes and held the hard stare of Darius. He could see truth in what Darius said, but perhaps Farzin also had a point. Time was indeed running out and Darius had barely set foot outside the church where they had sheltered over the previous couple of weeks. They did have to proceed with caution but if they delayed too long they may well find that the human population would be wiped out beyond recovery and of little use to them. He did wonder however if both might be wrong. Perhaps a third option might prove to be better. Perhaps they should remain in the shadows entirely. He was not convinced yet that humanity and vampires could coexist.

"I think that if we *are* to emerge and reveal ourselves then the time is all but upon us, yes," he said, choosing his words carefully. "Ultimately with all that has recently befallen them, they might be more ready to accept our existence than ever before. Some may indeed see a symbiotic relationship as a positive thing, humans and vampires for the first time working for mutual benefit. Many however will not. If we *are* to approach them, then their reaction should guide us."

Darius was silent a moment in contemplation. Then he slowly turned back to Max. "And what say you my friend?"

Max stood uncomfortably for a moment, unhappy about saying anything contradictory. As Darius waited he slowly started to speak. His voice rumbled, sonorous and dry like a tomb stone sliding across a crypt. "I agree that caution is needed but by now any humans may be open to our aid. Perhaps it is now time that we leave our self-imposed hiding and re-enter the world of humans."

"Hmmm, I have not ventured forth as much as I possibly should. I have not seen the new world that has befallen humankind of late. Perhaps that will prove to be my mistake."

He remained silent a moment, then lastly turned to Luca who still stood at the wall and called him forward, not to ask his guidance but to address the three of them together.

"We have spoken before about this group of humans, these soldiers, who seem to be based somewhere in this area. They may well represent our best prospect of paving our emergence into their world. We need to know more about them. Venture forth. Find out all you can about them and report back to me as soon as possible. Go swiftly my friends; let us forge a new future for our kind."

The gathering dispersed. Sebastian was the last in the room. He remained, listening to their imperceptibly soft foot-falls as they departed, with doubts tormenting his mind. The course of the clan's destiny no longer seemed as smooth as before. He wondered where Farzin and his cronies were now, probably searching for a victim and venting their anger on whatever innocent stray dog or unfortunate person they chanced upon. If so it was unlikely that any mercy would be shown. The poor wretch would be ripped to shreds be it hound or human, not that Farzin would differentiate between the two. He shuddered to remember what it was like to encounter a vampire for the first time, thinking back to his own experience so many years before. How many first-bloods had he taken in the intervening years? How many lives had he altered irrevocably or ended completely?

Sebastian could see that Farzin no longer reconciled his state of being with the human he once was so long before, and he now despised mankind with a seemingly irrational vehemence. To Farzin it really was simply a case of survival of the fittest, and now here they all were being challenged as to that very fact. They all believed it to be true, that they were indeed the fittest; stronger, faster and better able to survive than their human counterparts. In reality would that prove to be the case though? As if survival was their God-given right; not that 'God-given' really came into it in the case of a vampire. And what would he, Sebastian, personally do to survive? How far would he go? Would he make a pact with the Devil and treat humans like cattle? And was that even wrong? Humans did treat other animals and even other humans disgracefully, subjugating, killing and using all other species for their own, arrogant designs. Sebastian wondered what was to stop vampires from adopting the same attitude. After all, he thought, he who lives by the sword dies by the sword, although he was fully aware of the irony of a vampire quoting the Bible. He looked down at his hands, long and slender and ending in small but capable talons, all lethal, deadly little swords of his own. Then he balled them up into fists as though hiding the evidence. He walked slowly to the window and stared out as the sun started its journey towards the horizon, staining the sky scarlet, grateful to be leaving behind once more all the horrific scenes of carnage and chaos.

From his position by the window he did not see Farzin storm alone from the building, fury engulfing him as he marched out in search of a victim for his frustrations. His quest did not take him long.

Farzin left the presbytery shaking with incandescent rage. Flavia had watched him depart and was tempted to follow but something stayed her. Whatever her reason, Farzin stormed into the evening alone.

Although he walked without pretence of covertness, nevertheless his movements were swift and stealthy and within minutes he had encountered a cat. It did not hear his approach, did not detect his pounce until his fingers fastened upon its fur. With the subtle flick of his wrist its neck was snapped. He discarded it without even tasting its blood, casting it forcefully aside in disgust, taking its life purely through anger and spite.

Moments later and he entered an area that was more urbanised. There were a few houses, a supermarket and an apartment block. He slowed down now. Some innate sense replaced his anger with cunning and savagery. For the first time since leaving the presbytery he crouched and trod warily. Automatically he merged with the approaching dusk, becoming barely more than a shadow.

He neared the buildings. His focus narrowed. His attention and all his senses now concentrated almost entirely in front of him, the perfect hunter. He was sure he would not be going hungry tonight.

"Go on, just stay in radio contact and don't do anything stupid, okay?" Sergeant Sinna had called out to Abbott's retreating figure as he hurried from the supermarket. The scavenging mission was virtually complete. It was five forty-two. Sergeant Sinna was keen to finish the job and join Abbott and Campos as soon as possible at Campos's house, before heading back to the security of RAF Headley Court. They had already been off base longer than he liked. Every minute that passed left him feeling more on edge.

"Let's get this last load in the Landy double-quick and then go." He indicated the shopping trolley laden with water bottles.

"Yes Sarge," Private Rohith grabbed its handles and started to push it towards the exit.

Sinna had turned away for a moment, just the briefest of moments, as his private rounded the corner out of sight. One swift last sweep of the aisle behind him and he was about to follow. Then something caught his attention and made him stop. Possibly the lightest of sudden breezes or a slight shadow stirred in his peripheral vision. The hairs on his neck abruptly stood on end. There was the clatter of something being dropped - a bottle or tin can nearby. He turned and stared into the darkness where his colleague had just disappeared.

"Rohith?" he called. There was no answer. He took a step towards the exit. His pulse quickened although he did not know why. For some unknown reason his instincts were screaming at him, 'Run!' He stopped and listened. Now silence. He raised his gun nervously and took another step. There was the crack of glass beneath his boot. "Private?"

Still nothing. He must be hearing things. He was going crazy. There was nobody else about, just Rohith. But again, from the corner of his eye there was movement. He whirled around to face emptiness. His heart was beating hard and he tried to control his breathing. He was backing up now towards the exit. He turned once more. There, directly in front of him, a demonic apparition loomed, tall and menacing. He had not heard its arrival. There had been no warning sound or crunch of litter under foot. It had just materialised right beside him. He gasped and staggered back in shock. He raised his rifle and managed to squeeze off a short volley. The blast of the weapon drowned out the hellish roar of the figure. He caught a glimpse of its mouth wide open and looming closer. It was filled with impossibly long, sharp teeth as it leapt at him. Somehow he seemed to miss his target, despite having shot from so close. By all rights the bullets should have torn the creature in half. They should have ripped a hole in its chest and flung it back across the aisle. They should have saved Sinna's life. But they didn't. They missed their mark completely, even from such a short distance. The creature moved with unbelievable speed and managed to get to him before he could react again. Before he could fire another shot. Before he could even scream.

It lashed out with a single, deadly hand, smiting him across the neck and sending him flying to the side. He crashed into shelving, toppling and breaking the display. There were no more shots. No second opportunity to fight or fly. Just as Private Rohith had not even stood the slightest glimmer of a chance of escape, Sergeant Sinna was dead before his body slumped to the ground, now spraying blood out of the fresh wound that the creature's talons had opened across his throat. Talons that had sliced the chain to his dog tags, leaving them behind with the pool of blood as the only evidence he had ever been there.

CHAPTER 6

Having arrived back at RAF Headley Court and been
confronted by Denny, Sergeant Matteo Abbott then
deposited the Land Rover at the MT section and went
back to his room. He closed the door and rested against
the door frame. His head was literally buzzing with
random thoughts that felt like alien voices being spoken
from all around him and he had developed a thumping
headache. He fought back waves of sickness and reached
into his wash bag for some pain-killers but before he
could find them he had forgotten what he was looking for
and collapsed down onto his bed. He lay there panting
and holding his head, waiting for the nausea to pass.

A while later, Lewis and his three soldiers arrived back
at the base with no explanation for the disappearance of
Sinna and Rohith. Lewis felt extremely relieved to be
behind locked gates once more. He radioed through to
Denny who instructed him to come immediately to his
office, along with the Station Medical Officer, Squadron
Leader Anna Singleton.

Denny fidgeted in his chair and stared at the map on
the wall behind him as he waited for the others to join
him. He was in his fifties and hence one of the eldest on
base but kept himself in reasonable shape with a strict
exercise regime. As he sat, he too pondered the events of
the preceding weeks that had seen them all thrown
together into what some had called the beginning of
Armageddon. Denny however did not believe in the
religious connotations associated with the horror they had
all witnessed. He believed in science and fact, in the
ammunition that he loaded each day into the gun that
never left his side, and in the discipline of his military
background and training.

RAF Headley Court was primarily a military hospital.

There was also an aeromedical branch that researched, taught and applied learning from that particular field. Amongst other things this involved teaching pilots all about the atmosphere, the pressures and distribution of different gases, the potentially disastrous effects of hypoxia on the brain and how the body copes with the various stresses of aviation in general.

Headley Court had once been a stately home owned by Lord and Lady Lloyd-Mostyn who had bequeathed the estate to the Ministry of Defence. It was built in the late eighteen hundreds with a sweeping gravel drive, impressive, red brick-work and marble pillars. The main building was a beautiful, old house with white columns and grotesque, mocking gargoyles staring out relentlessly over the front of the edifice. There were eighty-five acres of land providing ample space for physical activity, various open, grassy areas and small wooded copses with ancient oak trees, and the grounds were surrounded by a reassuringly imposing twelve-foot brick wall. The station had been used during the Second World War for the treatment of RAF pilots, and had now expanded that role to include men and women from the army and navy. In recent years additional buildings had been added to provide medical facilities and accommodation for staff although most of the more modern buildings were hidden away towards the rear of the estate, sheltered by trees. Denny's office was on the ground floor in the main part of the building.

There was a knock on the door. Captain Lewis and Squadron Leader Singleton entered and stood briefly to attention.

"Hi Thomas, Anna, have a seat."

Captain Lewis was in his early thirties, a handsome and reasonably tall man with a quick wit and full head of dark hair. He had a relaxed, friendly demeanour and always seemed to be dating more than one lady at a time. Perhaps it was because of his laid-back, louche attitude and his slightly irreverent sense of humour, but Squadron Leader Singleton and he had never exactly seen eye-to-eye. There was always an underlying, bickering tension. She had served in the RAF for fourteen years and although Lewis was second in command she officially outranked him. However the fact that he did not seem to defer to her experience or years in service was not well received. This was something Lewis instinctively knew but he could not help but push her buttons, never with malice but usually resulting in animosity from the ever-officious Singleton.

Lewis quickly filled them in on his excursion to search for Sinna and Rohith. They sat quietly in the flickering candle light as he outlined his findings. There was a stunned silence. Lewis had had some time to digest the events and it took Denny and Singleton a while before either was able to speak.

"Are you quite sure their bodies were not there?" Singleton asked but it was a stupid question and she immediately regretted it.

Lewis gave her a dismissive glare. "Yes of course I am. We searched everywhere. Very carefully. You can't just hide two bloody corpses without any giveaway signs. They were not there. And besides, why would any of the septics try to hide the bodies? It doesn't make any sense."

"What do you think might have happened?" Denny asked. "Do you have any ideas at all?"

Denny pronounced each syllable of every word, making sure he enunciated clearly and correctly. Lewis always felt that it made him sound a little too stiff and formal and thought he should loosen up a bit.

"Only that they're dead, that's all," Lewis replied. "But how, and by whom, I have no idea; none whatsoever."

They were still talking when there was a second knock

on the door.

"Come in," barked Denny. Abbott entered and stood stiffly to attention.

"You look tired Sergeant Abbott," Denny said. "How are you?"

"I'm okay sir. Yeah, a little tired I guess."

"Captain Lewis has just been filling us in on his trip to try and find Sinna and Rohith. I'm afraid to say that it seems they've been killed."

Abbott bowed his head, closed his eyes and looked as though he was about to fall over.

"Please, take a seat." Denny half stood up and waved Abbott to the remaining chair.

"Also, we're all really sorry to hear about Private Campos. I know this must be hard for you but we may as well get down to business. Can you tell us what happened?"

Abbott looked down at his hands in his lap. They were damp with sweat and clenched tightly. "Well as you know we were out on a scavenging mission. We've done that a couple of times over the last week and never had much of a problem, I mean occasionally we've had to take evasive action and get outta there pretty fast but that's about it. We haven't had to draw our weapons for a few days now.

"I don't know if you are aware but Giuseppe - sorry, Private Campos, was a local lad. His parents live... lived, not far away. The supermarket was near his house so we just thought we should stop by, you know, just in case there was any chance of anyone surviving and still being alive in there. He was desperate to check. We'd nearly finished the scavenging and Sergeant Sinna suggested that we go ahead to the house whilst they finished up. That way we would be done quicker. They were due to come right behind us but they never showed up."

The three officers said nothing, already feeling absolutely terrible that more soldiers were dead and dreading to hear the horrific details. Denny held his head in his hands as he listened, emotion and responsibility weighing heavily upon him.

Fresh from his own visit to the supermarket, Lewis was brimming with questions but deliberately spoke calmly and evenly, trying not to distress Abbott further.

"Sergeant, I couldn't find any trace of their bodies, just a large pool of blood and Sinna's dog tags. I've got to ask you, when you left the supermarket was there anything suspicious? Is there anything you can tell me to shed any light on their death and disappearance?"

Abbott thought for a moment then looked up. "No sir, nothing that I can think of. It was all quiet when we left them, otherwise we wouldn't have gone. They were almost finished. They should have been done in less than a minute, so I really can't understand what happened."

"But presumably they had their weapons on them at all times?"

"Yes sir. Sinna was guarding us all while we loaded the trolleys so he was holding his SA80, locked and loaded."

"And they were still in the store when you left?" Lewis was desperately searching for any information that might give a clue to the mystery but he was no closer to the truth.

"Yes sir. We were all near the entrance but they were still inside when we left." His voice wavered and faltered and Lewis took pity on him.

"Okay, well if you think of anything else, anything at all that seemed odd or out of place then let me know. And please, carry on with your account."

Abbott nodded, took a deep breath and looked as though he was about to vomit but swallowed hard and continued. In the dim light Lewis did not notice the perspiration forming on his brow or the hollow expression in his eyes.

"It all seemed quiet and there was no one around so we popped into Campos's house, just to have a quick look. I didn't really want to go in as I thought it might be unwise to get out of the Landy but he was desperate to check whether one of his parents might still be alive and hiding in the house."

Lewis exchanged a glance with Denny. Everyone had lost loved ones in the recent events and although it was not a safe thing to do, Lewis could understand that desire. He knew that now was not the time to reproach Abbott for his actions, although they would most certainly have to reiterate standard operating procedures for all activity off base.

"We went in. It was a right state, all in a mess. Furniture was broken, plates and bowls were smashed and blood smeared down the walls. We had our weapons drawn at first but the house was so quiet and still that we were sure no one was there, so we put our weapons away. We looked in all the rooms anyway and when we went upstairs he attacked us."

Now Denny, Singleton and Lewis were all looking down, unable to meet his gaze. There had been plenty of unimaginable events in the last few days and this was opening fresh wounds for all of them.

Abbott looked worse as he relayed the story but forced himself to finish. "He was a crazy man and went for Giuseppe first only because he was closest. It was his father. He was killed by his own father. I tried to help but Giuseppe had only made it as far as the top stair and the attack forced him back. He fell and broke his neck as he went down. Then his father came at me. I didn't have time to draw my weapon before he was upon me. He must have been fifty-five or sixty years old, maybe more, and he was smaller than me but he was so strong. I could hardly hold him off."

Abbott described to them in detail how the fight had ended with the candlestick. He stared vacantly into space as he finished his account as though he had been mechanically relaying a shopping list. None of them spoke at first as they digested the news.

"That's absolutely terrible," Lewis broke the silence. "I'm so sorry. And you're sure it was his father?"

Abbott nodded.

"Were you hurt at all?"

He hesitantly shook his head.

Singleton leaned forward, interested in the development of the sick man, her professional curiosity kicking in. "How did Campos's father look? I mean the colour of his skin, the look of his eyes, whether he was saying anything coherent, that kind of thing; do you remember any of that?"

Abbott wearily rubbed his forehead between his eyes; his headache was making it hard to concentrate. "Err, yes ma'am; I got pretty close to him. I mean, I was not really bothered about what he looked like at the time but I guess I did kinda notice."

He again rubbed his head and Denny took it as tiredness and interrupted. "I've no doubt Sergeant Abbott could do with some rest now? I am sure these questions can wait until morning, if that's okay with you Anna?"

She frowned but let the matter drop. "Yes, yes of course but please come and see me first thing. Not only do I have some questions for you but I would also like to check you over to make sure you're okay after your ordeal. Is that all right? Be in my surgery first thing in the morning."

"Yes ma'am." Abbott stood and left the office. None of them noticed in the candle light how much his hands were trembling as he saluted. When he was gone Lewis checked outside the door and closed it softly.

"That's dreadful, killed by his own father. I can hardly think of a worse way to go."

"Also it's quite incredible that his dad was still in the house after so many days," Singleton added. "That must imply some kind of resorting to previous behaviour patterns."

"Either that, or he had indeed been in hiding and only recently contaminated," Lewis replied.

"Unlikely but possible I suppose," Singleton said acidly. "I can't imagine he'd have survived this long in a house that was not all barricaded up."

"Well yes," Lewis answered with a note of irritation himself, falling all too easily into their habitual bickering, "only that we don't know whether the house was previously secure. Maybe he was only recently infected and started smashing furniture and tore open the front door. So if they had only got there earlier…" he finished, turning to Denny.

"What are you getting at?" Denny retorted sharply.

"You know what I think Tristan. I don't think we can afford to shelter behind our walls any longer. I believe that we should get out there and try to find some survivors. There are bound to be more people like us who have managed to hide from the infected."

"Actually they are not, as you say, 'infected'," Singleton interrupted brusquely. "That is to say, as far as we know it is not really an infection. Originally the sick people had some form of dementia which is a disease. Then their brains reacted badly to the Mnemoloss and it transformed into something else."

"And then those who were bitten? Surely they've subsequently been infected?" Lewis replied wearily. They were getting nowhere. Stress and tiredness was affecting

116

them all.

"Well again we can't be certain yet of the exact method of transmission, but fluid transfer through biting does seem to be the most likely cause, yes. And as to exactly whether it's an infection, a contagious disease, a virus or something else, without proper study it's impossible to say."

"Okay well you say tomato; I say to-maah-to. The fact is they're dangerous and to be avoided if at all possible. If they're not actually infected per se, then they are certainly carrying something unpleasant and I for one don't want to get it. But even so I do think that we should be out there looking for other survivors. We can't just stay here and wait for all this to pass and then to re-emerge and see what's left. What kind of people would that make us?"

For once Singleton nodded enthusiastically in agreement with Lewis, taking him aback.

Denny held his hands up covering his ears, and closed his eyes with an angry expression like a child. He spoke loudly over the top of them and sounded as though he was reciting some well-rehearsed script. "We also have a responsibility to protect those who are here, not to endanger their lives but to keep as many safe as possible. The only reason any of us are still alive is because we have remained secure on the base."

Even before the state of emergency was declared Denny had ordered the gates to be kept closed and locked. This had helped to keep the station free of the illness and the only losses they had sustained were when they had started going out into the surrounding areas. For that reason he was unhappy about venturing forth any more than was absolutely necessary, preferring to remain on the station and closed off to the outside world.

He removed his hands from his ears and continued, although still in the same droning voice. "If we find no other survivors and we lose half of our remaining people whilst looking for them, then that puts those who remain in a very vulnerable position indeed, and we have already lost too many over the past few days."

Lewis sighed, realising he was going to get nowhere with this head-on approach. He raised his hands. "Okay, okay, look - there are bound to be other survivors hidden away. Or perhaps other military units and such like, where they already had a secure entry system. But I do agree with you, we need to take more care out there. We cannot afford any more losses. However this should be no different to patrolling the streets of Kabul or Belfast. In fact as this 'enemy' is not organized or intelligent, it should be a lot easier to survive."

"Well we don't actually know that they're unintelligent and disorganized, do we?" Singleton interrupted again. "I mean after all, if Private Campos's dad was showing retained behaviour patterns, then as I was saying earlier, maybe they do have some residual intelligence. Obviously I have not been out on patrol yet, but I understand they show signs of cohesive, organised behaviour. They still group together and act collectively for whatever reason and they recognize who are, as you say, 'infected' and who are not."

Lewis was trying hard not to become antagonistic in his reply and was confused because for a moment he had actually thought that Singleton was on his side for once. "Even a Giant Schnauzer can recognize that a Chihuahua is another type of dog, but that does not exactly make them 'Brain of Britain' does it," he replied cuttingly.

"No, but it *does* imply at least some basic level of intelligence which is a lot more than everybody seems to be attributing to the 'infected' so far," she snapped. "All I'm saying is that if we're going to start venturing out more then it would help us if we could learn about what we're up against. And the best way of doing that would be by capturing one of them and studying it. We could see exactly how intelligent they are, what they eat, how long they live without food. We can find out whether they can be distracted by flashing a torch in their eyes for example, or loud noises, or fire. Do they feel pain, can they learn to perform simple tasks, that kind of thing."

Denny raised his eyebrows incredulously. "We have been trying so hard to keep those creatures out of here and now you are suggesting that we actually bring one of them in ourselves?"

"I know it would be risky," she said, "but at the moment I'm afraid we're living in tough times. Whenever anybody steps outside the base it's unsafe and everything that might help us to survive has got to be considered. Apart from anything else, we may actually be able to work out how to cure them. Surely that is the ultimate goal? I mean, they aren't monsters, they *are* human beings. They may be acting more like zombies from some horror film but they *are* still people."

Both Lewis and Singleton were silent but turned together to stare at Denny who held his head in his hands again.

"Okay these are all valid points. Just… let me think about it a while please…" He was almost whining at them in despair and Lewis and Singleton exchanged a glance. Denny did not see the look but continued. "To let one of them in just feels so very wrong. And yes, there may be other survivors out there, but they have survived without our help so far, so to go out and put more of our men in jeopardy goes against the grain. Look, please, let me think about it all for tonight and we will talk more, first thing tomorrow."

The conversation ended and they left him alone. Singleton strode away quickly, leaving Lewis to dawdle behind. He knew that they were all under a lot of stress. Nevertheless that just made it even more important to work together. He was worried about his commanding officer and he needed to figure out how to bring Singleton around and onto his side. If Denny could not handle the pressure then he would need her assistance like never before.

Denny sat quietly contemplating their ideas. Certainly there was merit in the thought of getting outside more to try to find other survivors. Much as he hated to admit it there was also some sense in Singleton's plan. He was very aware however, that whilst they had these great notions of what they should all be doing, the ultimate responsibility for everyone's welfare lay with him, and he was having to consider not just what might be the positive side to their ideas but also what might be the worst case should these plans go wrong. He sat in his chair staring out into the dark night a while longer, all kinds of confused thoughts plaguing him.

After the debrief Abbott had got back to his room, staggered through the door and sank onto his bed for the second time that evening. The voices in his mind were practically intelligible now, focused towards the front of his head, reverberating like a dentist's drill. He had experienced many hangovers in his life and aspects of this pain were similar to the worst; the pounding, spinning, compressing feeling that his brain was being kneaded and squashed and wanted to burst out, accompanied by the waves of nausea. This time he was able to find his painkillers and washed down an irresponsibly large handful with a swig of whiskey from a small bottle on a shelf, before drinking deeply from some water beside his bed to try and quench his growing thirst.

He had been close to Campos. They had worked

together for a couple of years, but the pain of his death had been tempered by the very real need to survive himself. When he had related the experience to Lewis and the other two he had felt detached and cold, and although he could see that they were stunned and deeply affected by his words, he no longer felt any emotion about it. Similarly hearing that Sinna and Rohith were also probably dead had not moved him as much as it should. He was not sure if that had been due to shock setting in or the terrible thumping in his head, but he was angry with Sinna for not having made it to the house as arranged. He was finding it increasingly difficult to concentrate on anything or continue any chain of rational thought, but the image of the child's pink shoe in the garden next to Campos's house continually tormented him. He pushed the door to and started to undress. He got as far as taking his top off before he collapsed and passed out. The door had just clicked shut, so unfortunately nobody would see his deterioration and come to his aid before it was too late.

CHAPTER 7

Corporal Charlotte Collins walked her dog, Cujo, towards the dining area. Her left knee was stiff and often ached first thing in the morning until she had stretched a little. She was a dog handler in the army and had been on patrol in Northern Ireland when she had tumbled out of a first floor window during an altercation. After she had fallen Cujo had gone berserk and attacked her assailant, putting the fear of God into his soul and several teeth marks into his arm. Although Collins had injured her hip in the fall it was the damage to her leg that was taking longer to heal. Her recovery had progressed well however. She had done a lot of exercise whilst at Headley Court and was in excellent physical shape, perhaps better than she had been for many years. She was on the verge of being sent back to her unit when the state of emergency was declared. It is never particularly wise to separate a military dog from its handler for an extended period of time as the special bond that has been created between the two needs constant reinforcement. Special provisions had therefore been made for Cujo to be kept at the base with her.

As she walked along the corridor she heard strange grunts and muffled groans coming from somewhere ahead, as though someone was in pain. She slowed up, trying to work out what was causing the weird noises. Everyone was a little twitchy these days and the slightest thing out of the ordinary made one suspicious. She started to feel uneasy. Her pace slowed and Cujo checked himself and fell into step beside her. She was getting closer to the source of the sounds and looked nervously behind her, hoping someone else might be nearby. It was only as she approached the entrance to the gym that the cause became apparent. She peered through the wide, double doors in relief. Inside Corporal Bannister was wearing black gym shorts and a tight, pale blue t-shirt that now had dark sweat rings around the neck and arms. He was holding two boxing pads and it was he who was making the moaning sounds as his friend, Lance Corporal Dean Millington, laid into the pads with precision and ruthless aggression in the form of punches, knees and the occasional flying kick. Bannister was not a small man and neither was he slight, but Millington stood a good head and shoulders taller and looked like a cage fighter. His limbs were thick and powerful and he appeared to have virtually no neck as the muscles on his shoulders rose to meet his ears. He was, without doubt, the fittest person Collins had ever seen. That kind of supremely muscular physique always reminded Corporal Collins of pictures she had seen when she was at school, of the bodies of flies under extreme magnification; their limbs seemed overly developed as though they were pumped up on minute quantities of steroids with all segments of their anatomy looking very distinctly separate. He was black, his head was shaved and his nose bent out of shape either from rugby or fighting injuries. There was a collection of small scars on his hands and around his cheeks and eyebrows that each alluded to an interesting story. He was not classically handsome, but despite his build he was very laid-back. Collins found the combination of strength with kind-hearted gentleness very attractive and he had the biggest grin that was never far from the surface. He was topless and sported an array of tattoos on his arms. The one that always caught Collins's attention was the extremely colourful British Bulldog smoking a cigar on his shoulder, a canine representation of Winston Churchill, she supposed.

With each blow to the pads Bannister was sent staggering a few feet back. They were the most unlikely of friends. Bannister was from the Wirral, just outside

Liverpool. He had been a young offender, committing petty theft and stealing cars, and was well on his way to a life of crime when a sudden change of direction motivated by the death of his older brother saw him join the army. Millington was a youth champion kick-boxer from Hackney with a mild Jamaican twang. As well as their geographical differences though, there was the dissimilarity between their characters which was just as extreme. The two of them would never have developed a friendship had it not been for the military bringing them together and giving them something in common. Now as often as not they were inseparable. Collins stood quietly observing them for a while. When they saw her watching they stopped, both flush and panting.

"I worry about you boys you know," she quipped, "spending so much time half-naked and sweaty in the gym together. I mean this man-love is a beautiful thing but please, keep it under wraps."

"Ah you know I only have eyes for you," countered Bannister without faltering. "Whenever you're ready."

"In your dreams and besides, what would your boyfriend think of that?" She nodded towards Millington.

"He does what I tell him to." Bannister punched him hard on the arm but Millington did not even flinch. "More to the point, what would *your* boyfriend think of it?" He looked at Cujo.

Collins laughed and then quietly muttered a word to Cujo who was still standing attentively by her side and they walked on. Charlotte Collins had lived all her life with banter of a sexual nature from men. That had only increased when she joined the army and she was used to ignoring it, especially from Bannister who seemed to be more ready than most with a flirtatious comment.

As she left, Bannister watched admiringly as her toned figure disappeared from view and then turned to his large friend. "Now there's a sight that'll awaken the bacon. Clearly her arse has never heard of Newton."

"Huh?" Millington looked puzzled.

"Sir Isaac Newton? Gravity? Ah, nothing numb-nuts, I'm just saying she's mighty fine. She so wants me. Did ya see the way she couldn't take her eyes off me?" His Liverpudlian accent was strong but Millington had grown used to it and hardly noticed it now.

"Yeah, like she said - in your dreams," he drawled sonorously with a grin. "She's only got eyes for one male and he has two more legs and a lot more bite than you do."

"Pah! It's just a matter of time. And with a rapidly diminishing gene pool to choose from, it's gonna be me and her before she knows it."

She heard the coarse laughter as she walked away and although she did not know what was actually said, she felt sure she could guess the subject matter.

In the dining hall there were half a dozen people sat having breakfast already and a vague smell of cooking coming from the kitchens. Meals were not what they once were, as supplies dwindled and patrols had to go and scavenge for food from outside the base. Recently though four chickens had been found in the rear garden of a nearby house and they were now kept by the kitchens. Sergeant Vallage was in charge of catering on the station and had assumed the responsibility for looking after the birds himself, although he readily admitted that he knew next to nothing about their care. Three of the chickens produced eggs and were clearly female, so he called them Cath, Harriet and Caz after his own daughters. The fourth, a mangy looking bird, did not lay any eggs. Vallage was fond of remarking that all it produced was 'jack shit', so he named it Jack and constantly swore at the creature, promising that it would be first to be cooked as soon as it had some meat on it. He fed Jack and the three hens on scraps and leftovers. Occasionally the standard breakfast of porridge, cereal or tinned fruit was spruced up with the addition of a small omelette. Meals quickly got boring but these were desperate times so nobody complained to the chef. If they had it would have fallen on deaf ears anyway; Sergeant Vallage was not exactly renowned for trying to create meals that actually *pleased* his diners. He had been serving food to the Royal Air Force for over thirty years and his menus seldom varied in times of plenty, let alone times of thrift.

As Collins entered the dining area there was the sound of banging and shouting from within the kitchens. Leading Aircraftman Neale came scarpering out, casting a troubled look over his shoulder and almost collided with her.

"Valllage is in even more of a foul mood than usual," he confided in her. "Make sure you don't criticise the porridge."

Although Collins was hungry the thought of breakfast did not fill her with joy. She collected a tray with food on it, having made suitably complimentary noises, and something simple for Cujo. She glanced around the room before choosing a table with Corporal Reggie Pethard, his wife Emma and Sergeant Liam Wood who was a patient at Headley Court and always seemed to Collins to keep himself very much to himself. Other than Vida Masters, Emma was the only other spouse on base. As Collins reached the table Sergeant Wood half rose and slid her chair out for her, which made her smile and Reggie Pethard laughed mockingly. Collins liked Wood. They did not know each other well but he seemed to possess much of the self-assured strength that she admired in Millington, albeit perhaps without the warmth or compassion.

Emma dug Corporal Pethard in the ribs. "Why don't I get treated like that?"

"See what you've done now mate," Pethard pointed a fork accusingly at Sergeant Wood. "You give the rest of us a bad name."

"Sorry pal, I got it from watching your Bond movies and if it's good enough for him…" They all laughed. Even when there was such extreme tragedy and adversity on a daily basis, Collins still appreciated the all too brief moments of mirth. She knew it was just a way of coping; without it they could all easily have broken under the pressures they now faced. She spent a moment settling Cujo who seemed unusually ill at ease and restless. I know how you feel, she thought, then turned back to the people at the table.

"Careful with that offensive weapon babe, you'll have someone's eye out." Emma put a hand on Corporal Pethard's and lowered the fork.

"Okay, I have a question," continued Reggie Pethard, "best Bond actor ever?"

"No doubt about it," Collins answered. "The last one, whatever his name was. That body and tight blue shorts, say no more. And about time there was a blond Bond."

"His name is Daniel Craig and no, he isn't the best," replied Emma. "Pierce Brosnan does it for me."

It was not usual for wives, let alone dogs, to eat on the base at Headley Court. Patients did not bring their spouses with them but were given a single room in the mess. Those who were permanent staff serving at the station had the option of having one of the married quarters, within the boundary wall but behind and out of sight of the main building, or living off base in the local neighbourhood. Either way the partner would only come to eat in the main mess building on special occasions. In the light of recent events normal protocol had been forgotten and now everyone possible had rooms in the main building. Emma Pethard had been visiting her husband, who was there for injuries to his shoulder and head, when the gates had been locked. As there were so few women, they had all bonded and Collins was close to her.

"Nah, I think old Brosnan was too affected. Too much quivering and pouting, too much emotion," Wood said quietly, having the final word on the matter. "You can't really beat Connery I'm afraid, the quintessential Bond - suave, detached and ruthlessly cold."

Collins wondered, not for the first time, whether such a description might be applied to Wood as well.

"Well maybe you're right but I'm afraid I just don't have time to debate such deeply philosophical issues," Emma stood up to take her leave, picking up a glass to carry to her room. "I have things to do."

"Oh yes?" asked Collins. "What's on the agenda for today?"

"Well I have a hair appointment at nine, followed by my tennis lesson and lunch with the girls. Then I'll do a spot of shopping in London followed by a show and cocktails. Coming?"

"Thanks, I'd love to, after I've walked the dog."

Cujo was still unsettled and had started whining. Collins frowned. Odd, she thought. She stroked his head to try to comfort him. He looked up at her, licked his lips and then returned his unflinching stare to the door.

"Yeah, I think he probably needs a walk right now from the sounds of him," Emma said. She kissed Corporal Pethard tenderly for a moment which made Collins smile and Wood turn away, before she flounced off, leaving the dining room.

"I'll catch up with you in a mo, babe," he called after her retreating back as he finished his breakfast.

The corridor led from the dining hall down a small stair case and around a corner. There were military pictures on the walls, including a selection of World War Two airplanes and some old photos of pilots, many of whom had slicked back hair, arrogant expressions and, surprisingly enough, walking sticks, a reminder of the perils of their art back in those days.

The Pethards were in a room just along from Abbott. As Emma rounded the corner and neared her room she could see a figure hunched over and shaking on the floor. He was moaning with his head down as though he was vomiting. He wore light green khaki trousers but no top and he was covered in sweat. Emma took five more steps towards him before she paused. She called out to the figure. When Abbott looked up at her, his eyes were bloodshot and blazing in ungrounded fury and she felt her strength sapped away. She faltered, putting a hand on the wall to steady herself. He was hardly recognizable. He had a crazed look in his eyes and a long line of saliva hanging from his lips which drew back from his teeth like a dog. His face was contorted into a hideous grimace. The expression was bestial and held no hint of humanity.

She reached out a hand in a placatory gesture and spoke to him again in a shaky voice. "Are you okay? Can I get a doctor?"

This was clearly futile but she was trying to remain calm and act as though nothing was wrong. He started to rise to his feet and snarled a feral, wild sound that had no place coming from a human mouth. She tried to scream but the sound caught in her throat. The glass slipped from her fingers and smashed upon the floor as she turned. She fled in the only direction she could go, back the way she had come. She rounded the corner and the safety of the dining area beckoned, so close now, so tantalisingly close. He slipped in the turn giving her opportunity to get

129

further ahead. She could hear the sound of conversation. Cujo was barking, dishes clattered, and there was the faint scent of food and normality. She neared the door, reaching her hand out. Only a few strides to go. He was too far to catch her. She was safe. She had almost made it and stretched for the handle just as her shirt was tugged back, just as Abbott caught up with her, just as he pulled her back and away from the door.

Although he was not the nearest to the exit, Pethard was the first to get to it. He was about to stand up anyway and leave the two at the table when he saw his wife through the glass upper-half of the door. She seemed to fling herself at it with a look of terror on her face and then someone jumped on her from behind and dragged her down, out of sight.

Had Emma not taken those last five, critical steps towards Abbott she probably would have made it into the dining hall, but he just caught her as she grasped for the door with a scream. He grabbed her shirt, then threw one arm around her neck and clawed at her back as he sank his teeth into her and they both fell. The average human jaw exerts approximately one hundred and eighty pounds of pressure per square inch. The tender flesh on her lower neck provided absolutely no obstacle to his ripping incisors.

Cujo was on his feet, snarling and barking as he tugged at his lead. Pethard vaulted the table and got to the door a moment before Wood. Through an old design fault that had never been rectified it opened outwards. As he slammed into it, it knocked into his wife and Abbott who both lay right in front of it. Through the glass he caught a glimpse of Abbott biting into Emma as she frantically tried to defend herself. He heaved himself at the door again and this time sent Abbott sprawling and the door flew open. Emma was feebly trying to stand with blood

spouting. The maniac launched himself at her again when
Pethard jumped on him. He grabbed him around the
throat. Like a champion wrestler Abbott's slippery body
writhed out of Pethard's grasp in an instant and he turned
his fury on his new attacker. He lunged forwards at
Pethard, all teeth and growls, and pinned him effortlessly
to the floor. He bit down but Wood landed a boot with
full force on the side of his head. He knocked Abbott off
his new victim and saved Pethard's life. Wood rounded
on him again but received a swipe that knocked him hard
across the corridor.

Bannister and Millington had heard the commotion and
ran towards the noise. They turned the corner in time to
see Pethard hurl himself again at the madman. He
plunged the fork that he still grasped, deep into the soft
part of Abbott's oesophagus, screaming like a lunatic
himself. Frothy blood gushed forward and Abbott paused
for a moment coughing and choking. Then without even
bothering to remove the fork, he struck out sending
Pethard crashing into the wall. He turned his attention
back to Emma who had only managed to crawl a few feet
away. Wood recovered first and jumped on him just as he
reached the flailing woman. He pinned Abbott face down
on the floor. Pethard was still screaming and returned to
the fray. He clamped his hands around Abbott's neck in a
strangle hold, trying to choke the life out of him as Wood
battled to stop him from rearing up and kicking them both
off. Despite the blood flowing freely from Abbott's
wound he still had some strength in him. He was bucking
and snarling like an enraged animal when Sergeant
Vallage put an end to the fight with the aid of a heavy,
wooden rolling pin. Despite his large, ungainly size he
nimbly avoided the thrashing limbs and bodies with
surprising agility. He dodged around to Abbott's head and
brought the kitchen implement down hard on his skull

with a loud crack, just as Abbott himself had the day before with the candlestick. The first strike went unnoticed and hardly had an effect but after a couple more solid blows Abbott stopped struggling and pitched forwards as blood now seeped from wounds on his head. His shaved skull had dented and the skin now furrowed with creases resembling a partly deflated football.

Charlotte Collins was screaming at the dining room door when Lewis arrived a moment later, followed by Denny. The scene that greeted Lewis was of absolute carnage and devastation. Blood was all over the walls, floor and ceiling. Corporal Pethard sat cradling Emma in his arms, sobbing and whispering to her while he rocked gently back and forward. His hand pressed her neck tightly but blood seeped out in spurts between his fingers. Her eyes were still open and stared up into his face although they did not appear to be focussing properly. Her hands flapped weakly by her sides while her mouth opened and closed uselessly. Bannister stood over Abbott guardedly in case it turned out that he was not dead after all and Millington crouched beside his friend, still topless and shining with sweat. Sergeant Vallage stood holding the bloody instrument of death and he looked grim and pale. The corridor seemed frozen in time. Anyone who has been in such situations of extreme stress will know the feeling of being outside of, and detached from, one's body, watching the action as though it were a film. Stress affects people in different ways. Some become hyperactive and irrational, some remain calm and efficiently revert to training or gut instinct and some would rather curl up in a ball and wait for the situation to pass. Sergeant Wood had seen slaughter and bloodshed in the front line many times and knew how to deal with the trauma. By the time Lewis had taken stock, Wood had already quietly and competently started handling the situation.

When Emma was rushed to the medical centre she was still moving feebly, but by the time she had arrived she lay still. Abbott was also taken there but in his case it was clear that he was dead already. The stain of their mingled blood was now a gruesome welcome mat for anybody entering the dining hall. Pethard was utterly inconsolable. Wood helped him to the medical centre and gently cleaned the worst of the blood and gore from them both whilst Pethard sat numbly by Emma's corpse.

Collins watched the various soldiers mostly moving with slow, methodical actions, like ants following a prescribed route. Conversation was kept to a muted minimum and eye-contact was avoided. It seemed to her that Denny was rushing around faster than anyone but achieving very little, whilst Wood and then Lewis dealt with the situation and organised everybody. Vallage exchanged the rolling pin for a mop and set about trying to clean up the mess with the aid of his kitchen hand Corporal Bell. Collins was still very shaken and emotional but she had calmed down a little and stood drinking a cup of sweet tea that Vallage had thrust into her hands without saying a word. As Wood led Pethard away, Bannister sidled over to her and gently placed a comforting arm around her shoulders. He seemed genuinely concerned.

"Are you okay?"

At first she did not seem to notice his arm, or the question, but then she jolted back to reality. "Yes, yes I'm okay I guess, thanks," but she started to sob again. "Poor Emma and Reggie, that's so terrible." Her conversation was coming out in choked gasps.

"I know, it is dreadful. It's a dreadful time we're all going through. Those poor people."

She carried on weeping. She had held it all in for so

long but could now feel the emotions determinedly seeking an exit. "I mean we have all lost loved ones, we've all lost just about everything, our lives, our friends and family. Everyone has dealt with death and all the killings over the last couple of weeks but to lose someone you love like that, it's just so awful."

"I know, I know, it doesn't bear thinking about, it's so terrible. Now we've got to be there for each other."

"When is this all going to stop? It's so hard," she sobbed.

He hugged her close, allowing her to weep for a while before speaking softly. "Yeah, it is, 'cos that's all we've got now. We're family now, there's nothing else. We've all got to watch each other's backs and be there for each other."

She nodded. Suddenly she was aware of his proximity and the physical contact. Her sobs subsided a little as she composed herself.

Spurred on by this apparent sign he continued. "Look if you need to talk, if you need a shoulder to cry on, or a drink even, I've got some vodka in my room. I could pop by later and check on you, make sure you're okay?"

She smiled weakly. She had stopped crying although her eyes were red and she straightened, blowing her nose and wiping her face as she did so. She just wanted to be alone now. "Hey that's really kind, thanks, I appreciate it."

"No probs, any time. Like I said, we've got to be there for each other. So if you need to talk again, just let me know."

"Thanks, I mean it," and she turned and slowly walked away leading Cujo.

"Nice work bro." Millington had been standing nearby with his arms folded and an impassive look on his face.

"What do you mean?"

"Hitting on a girl when she's just witnessed a brutal, bloody massacre. Get them when they're vulnerable huh? You're really something man."

"Nah, I was just trying to be nice, that's all. Can't a fella help a lady without the sweaty finger of accusation pointing at him?"

Millington did not answer but dispassionately, coldly, stared at the bloody mess.

"So who d'ya reckon's gonna be next?" Bannister asked as he too surveyed the carnage. Millington just shrugged and shook his head.

"Well, if they try to get you pal, they'll have to do it over my dead body," Bannister said. "Till death do us part, bro," and he punched Millington on the arm.

Five people dead in two days – that was an unsustainable rate of depletion. It was not the first time Bannister had wondered who would be next. These days it was a common question in everyone's thoughts. Till death do they part, indeed…

Neither Pethard nor Wood had been bitten, but as it was still not known if that was the only means by which the disease was passed on it was decided to quarantine them. Singleton and her senior doctor, Dr Handley, were worried that the condition might be transmitted through the mere exposure to blood. Both soldiers were locked in separate bedrooms upstairs in the main building for a nominal period of twenty-four hours. Bannister was placed on guard outside. As soon as she was able, Singleton went to check on Pethard. He was absolutely inconsolable, crying hysterically and not making any sense at all, so she sedated him and left him to sleep for a few hours.

"Sit outside their rooms please," she told Bannister. "If they need anything then please get it; something to eat or drink but nothing alcoholic. Don't let them out and don't let anybody in, in case they have contracted this, 'condition'. I'll send someone to relieve you in a few hours and when Pethard wakes up please come and find me."

"Yes ma'am," he stood briefly to attention and then sagged down onto the chair. He had also been affected by the killing although he would never show it. They were all stretched a little thinly at the moment like rubber bands about to snap, on the verge of exhaustion, hysteria and full mental breakdown. Like many of the military personnel there he had seen war directly and its bloody consequences. He knew better than most how it is not just the body that gets broken in a conflict zone. He had witnessed friends reduced to emotional wrecks, hallucinating through tiredness and pressure and becoming totally irrational and dangerously unpredictable. RAF Headley Court was there to fix their bodies and it was very good at that, but it was not quite so easy to mend the spirits or the minds of those who had seen such brutality, and this really was the most brutal of all conflicts.

Denny, Singleton, Lewis, Sergeant Straddling, Dr Handley and Flight Lieutenant Walkden all met a little later in one of the rooms set aside for meetings, functions and small medical conferences, in order to discuss their next actions. The room was carpeted in light RAF blue and had a wooden, oval table in the centre with a dozen chairs around it. In the corner there was a white board with pens and an overhead projector on a side table. Windows looked out onto the front lawn and trees beyond which swayed lazily in a breeze, indifferent to all the death and savagery. It was a pleasant day with a warm sun breaking through scattered clouds, quite at odds with the mayhem that had occurred. In normal circumstances they might all have been expecting tea and biscuits to be brought into them while they chatted about pleasantries before getting down to business. Today there were no refreshments and no amenable small-talk. They had all witnessed death but this had been the first killing actually *on* the base, their sanctuary from all the atrocities, their Shangri-La. It seemed that Paradise had been well and truly lost. All of them were stressed and completely fatigued, and the events of the day had left them stunned. The mood was understandably muted.

They sat in sombre silence for a long while. Each was lost in thought before Denny got up and cleared his throat. Unusually for him his hair was dishevelled and he could hardly bring himself to raise his eyes off the table to look at them all.

"Look, I don't really know what to say any more, this was a tragic loss. After our initial disastrous foray off base just over a week ago we have been a lot more careful with good results, until now. We need to discuss how we have let this happen. The fact that Sinna, Rohith and Campos were killed was terrible - really terrible. But to then exasperate the situation with the deaths of both Abbott and Mrs Pethard on base and then the possible contamination of two more men, this is just unacceptable. Clearly we let complacency in and have paid the price. What could we, no, what *should* we have done better? How did we fail them?"

No one said anything for a few seconds; they sat ruminating and staring sullenly at the table or out of the window, avoiding eye contact. Lewis surreptitiously scrutinized them all, trying to assess their states of mind and in particular that of Denny.

Finally he shifted in his seat and replied. "I guess when he returned to base there was no sign of blood and so there was no reason to suspect anything. Campos had been killed but there was no obvious indication of Abbott having been bitten as well."

"That is assuming that he got the infection through a bite. Do we know if there's a bite mark on his body?" Denny's question was directed at Singleton.

"Yes, I think so. I examined his corpse and there are obviously a few wounds from his fight here. I did find one bite mark on him though. It's on his arm and I assume that he was bitten when he and Private Campos were attacked by Campos's father. It's not a large bite and could have been hidden beneath his shirt sleeve but it did break the surface of the skin so that may well have been how he became ill."

Handley nodded in agreement but Lewis was puzzled. "I wonder why he wouldn't have said anything to anyone about being bitten. Everybody knows now that biting is a probable method of disease transmission. Why would he jeopardise the rest of us and not say anything, given what's at stake?"

"Why indeed and we'll never know," said Denny. "Maybe he was in denial and didn't want to face the fact that he was most likely sick or maybe he was just so exhausted and shocked after Campos's death that he was not thinking clearly."

"Or perhaps he was already beginning to suffer the effects of the contamination and was not thinking straight for that reason," Dr Handley chipped in.

Lewis stared at him but said nothing. It was a terrifying thought to contemplate, that the illness could cause such a rapid change.

Handley looked around at everyone slowly before continuing. "Look, I know we were all following the news flashes during the initial few days when the state of emergency was declared. The best medical information then was saying that the first people to use the drug took possibly months before they started displaying any adverse symptoms. By the time they realized what it was doing to people and withdrew Mnemoloss, the last people to be taking it might have been displaying aggressive traits within as little as a few weeks. Then there was a sudden rash of outbreaks of violence, as though someone had opened the flood gates.

"The final few broadcasts that I saw before the TV channels went off air said that people who had been bitten by Mnemoloss patients were themselves displaying antisocial behaviour within a week and some considerably less than that, possibly even within a day or two. The evidence seemed to be inconclusive, often contradictory, and clearly no one had had a chance to run any proper studies, but it does indicate that secondary effects of the drug are not precisely the same as the primary effects. As I said, this was only journalistic speculation based on stories gathered from around the world. We don't know how accurate these reports were and there are certainly other factors that would have had an influence, but that is the best information that we have got to go on - at the moment."

"So although we don't know for sure, we have to assume that it could take as little as one day from being bitten to becoming infected?" Lewis was aghast.

"Absolutely. As I understand it the drug was manufactured to aggressively target the damaged parts of the brain. I studied many areas of medicine including pathogens during my initial years as a trainee doctor, as all trainees do. I am a little rusty on that general field, but from what I heard on the news and read in various medical journals, Mnemoloss was designed so that it would go after the damaged parts of the brain as rapidly as possible, altering various basic qualities of that area. It was designed to be fast-acting and it would seem that it is doing exactly that."

Singleton stepped in at this point. On medical matters she was the commanding officer and carried herself with obvious authority. She was a tall, slim woman with short, blonde hair cut to her chin in a somewhat severe style. She hardly ever wore makeup and Lewis found her demeanour to be somewhat standoffish. However she would not have been unattractive if she would only relax a little and Lewis was often frustrated by her seemingly unnecessarily hostility towards him.

"After finishing medical school I actually worked with neurological disorders for a while before joining the RAF. That was how I got into my current field. My training in such disorders and neurological functioning led to me studying the effects of aviation on the brain, hypoxia, spatial disorientation, and other things that affect pilots, which is partly what I have been doing at Headley Court for the last few years, along with the medical rehab. So this business with Mnemoloss probably meant more to me than anyone here as I had been involved with that kind of research.

"What Dr Handley says is quite correct but also what the news reports didn't properly cover, largely because no one really knows, is what the condition itself is doing."

"What do you mean? You mean what is actually happening inside people's heads?" Denny, like the rest of them, had a lay-man's knowledge of medicine and so was on uncertain ground now, and this lack of knowledge meant he was starting to sound irritable.

"Exactly. People who took the drugs reacted very differently to those who have contracted the condition in other ways such as by being bitten, which would imply that it has changed significantly even in recent months. Viruses, diseases and bugs can all mutate and possibly the fast-acting nature of the drug *has* been adopted by the condition and it has undergone aggressive mutation. We are possibly seeing the evidence of that change in the fact that Abbott became sick less than twenty-four hours after having been infected. Of course there are certainly individual factors at play as well. We won't all respond the same to a drug just as we won't all react in the same way to a disease, so perhaps Abbott was just more susceptible to it and hence became sick much faster than someone else might."

Lewis was even more troubled now. "So isn't it also possible that if we all might react differently to this condition, whatever it is, that actually Abbott reacted to it rather slowly and someone else may feel the effects a lot faster? As in, considerably *less* than twenty-four hours even?"

Everybody around the table stared hard at Singleton who looked pale when she answered. "Yes, that too is correct, although I truly hope to God that is not the case."

There was silence as this thought was digested by them all until Denny gruffly spoke up. "Okay, so back to my earlier question then. What should we have done better?" He slapped the table as he spoke and this time his tone was a little too sharp, verging on petulant.

Lewis tried to calm the mood. "It seems to me we can't really trust anybody to own up to the fact that they have been bitten when they return to base. So we have to assume that *everyone* has been bitten, until we can make sure they are clean. Whoever goes off base should be quarantined in a holding area on their return until they have been checked for bites."

"Guilty until proven innocent?" Singleton asked scathingly.

"Absolutely. And why not?" he retorted. "If we all accept that it's a necessary safeguard then no one should

141

mind. If it prevents another situation like today then I think that's a small price to pay. Don't you?"

Denny held up his hand, his turn to try and ease the tension. "Yes I think you're right, unless anyone has any better ideas?" He looked around the table but no one, not even Singleton, had an alternative. "But we'll have to arrange procedures so that whoever goes off base gets checked the moment they return, I can't have people cooped up in a cell for hours unnecessarily."

Singleton was not satisfied. "What if it's a woman returning to base and the guard is a man?"

"Well obviously I can see that in normal times that might be a sensitive issue but these are not normal times," Denny answered brusquely. "We are talking about survival here. We're all adults; I suggest that we just get on with it, until someone can come up with another solution."

"Let me know when you're going off base and I'll take guard duty ready for your return," Lewis smirked at Singleton, receiving a scowl from her and a rebuff from Denny.

"That's enough. We're all pretty strung out, try and remember that we're on the same team here. Let's move on. That covers measures on the station. What about off base?"

Straddling now spoke for the first time. He was reasonably gruff and blunt, and was never afraid to say his piece.

"I think we can agree that something went drastically wrong with their basic procedures in order for them to become separated and then get caught out by an unarmed man. Starting with their separation, why did that happen? What the hell were they playing at?"

Lewis turned to his sergeant with a sad, resigned expression. "The supermarket was very near Campos's house."

"So?" Straddling was not impressed by this argument. "That's not good enough. We had decided upon procedures to be adopted when off station and separating from your team was not one of them. They should have stayed with Sinna and Rohith, and you shouldn't be defending their actions."

"Yes I know," Lewis sighed, feeling weary at having to fight his corner on all sides, "and I agree with you. But I think we can all understand why they did it. That doesn't make it right and they paid a heavy price for it but it's been done so there's no point in arguing about it further. Let's just ensure that it doesn't happen again. Okay?"

"What happened to Sergeant Sinna and Private Rohith?" Dr Handley asked. The room fell silent and all eyes fixed on Lewis.

He felt even more troubled now and brushed the hair out of his eyes. This had been bothering him since his return, and only the death of Abbott and Emma Pethard had distracted him from wondering about it. Slowly he recounted the experience. The hush remained for several seconds after he finished talking.

"I still don't get it," Straddling said finally. "As far as I'm aware the festering masses just wouldn't remove the corpses from where they fell. And what about their clothes or their weapons? It doesn't make sense to me."

"You're sure you searched everywhere?" Handley asked.

"Yes, I'm afraid so," Lewis replied. "There's no doubt in my mind. I have lain awake half the night thinking about this but I just can't see it any other way. Something killed them both and then removed the corpses, leaving hardly a scrap of evidence."

"Maybe it was some other survivors?" Straddling pondered. "They could have been watching and waited until one Land Rover left and then ambushed the two of them."

"It's possible," Lewis agreed. "To be honest that's my best guess too. In the absence of any other information I can't see any other likely answer."

"Okay, we're wasting time, move on," Denny interrupted. "I want to discuss procedures off base. We've agreed that the four of them should never have split up. What else did they do wrong? What can we improve?"

"Well for starters," Straddling answered, "we should reiterate the principles we agreed upon before, some of which were obviously not followed here. No one goes off base alone. No one leaves base on foot. We use a minimum of two vehicles if at all possible, with at least two people in each; more if going into enclosed situations. The vehicles do not separate. We all have a radio which is tested before leaving the station. Everybody has a Browning *and* a rifle where possible. Make sure that the guardroom knows your exact route and don't deviate unless you absolutely have to. Check in with the guardroom every hour and let them know if you're leaving your vehicle and when you return to it.

"Also, when you're out of your vehicle your weapon is out of its holster and ready for use at all times, locked and loaded. We need to re-emphasise proper search techniques in buildings; arcs of fire, covering your buddy, doorways, corners of rooms, scanning techniques, stairways, the whole works. And if we do encounter any crazies then I would suggest going for a headshot. After all, a fork in the throat didn't seem to make much of an impact on Abbott did it?

"Make no mistake people, we are at war!" He looked around the table at each of them with a deadly serious expression, daring anybody to contradict any of what he had said. "This is not like any enemy that any of us have ever faced before, but it is an enemy nonetheless, and the sooner we start treating them as such the better our prospects of survival. They are no longer human; they are nothing better than animals now and all they want to do is kill us. Here on this base we have a wealth of experience and tactics from many conflict zones around the world. We just need to adapt that to this new theatre of war. And fast."

Lewis was quiet, watching Straddling and aware of the sense that he spoke. He did not have the easiest of relationships with his senior sergeant. Sometimes, with his confrontational manner, it felt as though the older man resented the fact that Lewis was younger and yet still his commanding officer. Notwithstanding that, he was a valuable asset and Lewis was grateful of his experience. He just wished that he did not continually have to justify himself to Straddling. It was draining and unproductive. They should be acting as a cohesive unit, not pulling in different directions, especially at a time when solidarity was imperative for survival.

Denny turned to Lewis. "That all sounds sensible. Can you ensure everyone is made aware of exactly what is expected of them from now on? We have got to maintain our patrols in order to acquire essential supplies so let's make them as safe as possible.

"On that note, we spoke last night about having more patrols. I agree with you Thomas, perhaps it is time we extended our interests and tried to find more survivors. I don't mean that we should all go and look to see if any of our friends or family are still alive. After all, everybody has lost loved ones, but that may prove to be too much of a risk and right now there is more at stake than personal grieving. Our number one priority is to preserve the security of the base and not have anyone else die. But if we *can* find other survivors whilst out looking for

145

supplies then that is a good thing. I think that our patrols could be extended to incorporate not only finding provisions but people as well. Any thoughts from any of you on where we might find survivors?"

"I guess," Singleton said, "like this base, if anybody has managed to stay alive then they may well be in places that are easy to seal up and defend, which could mean hospitals. Especially on the upper floors, it would be quite easy to block off all entrances and control access."

Lewis, as always, was quick to contradict her. "But that may well be balanced by the fact that anyone who became sick could quite possibly have been taken to hospital. They then go berserk and attack and contaminate others. Hospitals could easily have become breeding grounds for these zombies."

They all winced at his choice of words but no one challenged his assertion.

Denny interceded. "Okay, what other options are there?"

"For people to have survived they would not only need to be in a location where they could stop any sick people from getting in but also where they were self-sufficient and didn't need to venture out," Flight Lieutenant Walkden mumbled. "I mean, we're armed and trained in warfare and yet we have sustained causalities when we're out there, so your average Joe Public would not stand much chance at all. I am thinking places like supermarkets. They could be made reasonably impregnable and you'd have enough supplies so that you wouldn't need to go out for weeks, even months."

"Yes, a reasonable option," Denny concluded. "Okay, let's come up with more ideas on where to search and try to incorporate some possible locations in our patrols. Thomas, can you get some local maps and work on that? Dr Singleton has also expressed a desire to capture one of

146

these diseased people and bring it back on base to study and potentially gain useful information on what we are up against." He turned then to face Singleton. "I am not sure we're quite ready for that yet but we'll think about it further and try to formulate a strategy. If it becomes possible without exposing ourselves too much then we will do it, so let's try to be ready with a plan, just in case."

"But…" she started to remonstrate as he raised his hand to silence her and the look on his face cut her short.

"That's the best I can do at the moment. It's just too chancy and there have been too many deaths of late. Please, leave it there."

As they all trooped out of the room Denny remained in his seat staring blankly into space. He turned just as Lewis was about to leave the room. "Shut the door behind you Thomas." He looked exhausted and for the first time Lewis noticed the dark circles underneath his eyes.

"Certainly sir," Lewis stared at him thoughtfully for a moment and then closed the door quietly behind him.

Denny sank forwards in his chair, elbows resting on the table and his head held in his hands. He remained like that for a while before slowly, gradually at first, his shoulders started to shake as the sobs finally broke free.

CHAPTER 8

From upstairs in the presbytery Sebastian had a perfect vantage point as he stared over the town's skyline. He opened the window, perched on the sill and looked out into the dusk. The Roman Catholic church had seemed to be an ideal place for the clan to seek refuge; the presbytery attached to the main building of the church was warm and comfortable. It was slightly displaced from the road so they could see anyone approaching, and it was easy to barricade and defend. They had bolted the presbytery doors on the ground floor, preferring instead to enter and exit through an upper floor window in order to keep the newly infected out, and so far it had worked well.

When Sebastian thought of the 'infected' he was aware that the term could easily be applied to themselves. Their blood was no longer as it had once been, untainted by outside influence. In many ways they had more in common with the newly infected than they did with the humans. Now all was peaceful in the streets as he contemplated the occurrences of the previous few weeks. He and the other clan members had watched with growing unease as the disaster affecting society had unfolded, and whilst none of them had suffered any actual harm, their lives were inexorably bound to the humans with whom they had long and secretly shared the planet. They felt uncertainty as to what the future held and appreciated that their existence, just as that of humanity, would never be the same again and now swung in the balance. Their actions over the next few days and weeks were pivotal and clearly there was serious disagreement within the clan as to the correct way to proceed, disagreements that threatened the unity that had bound them together for longer than he cared to contemplate;

perhaps too long.

Ever since becoming vampyric many years before his existence had been one of concealment and adventure which he had not always welcomed, and he missed many facets of his life as a human. As a general rule they avoided excessive contact with people and tended to live relatively isolated from society, generally in remote and heavily superstitious areas. They remained on the fringes, mixing occasionally with the undercurrent of humankind where one tended to be mindful of one's own business and ask no questions of others. They only rarely frequented shady, drug-fuelled haunts, and in such settings, mixing with people whose grasp on reality was often fairly tenuous, they could generally pass themselves off as nothing more than unusual looking; exotically gothic at best and freakish at worst.

As society slowly began to dissolve they had lurked in the shadows and witnessed the horror develop. The state of emergency turned into civil unrest with people rioting and looting, initially through greed and later through necessity. Panic and violence spread as fast as the mania induced by Mnemoloss and acts of aggression were perpetrated not only by those who were diseased but also by those defending themselves against would-be attackers. The clan had watched with growing revulsion, or fascination, as the secondary effects of the drug turned more and more people into mindless, wrathful lunatics who respected neither fear nor pain, and fed their insatiable hunger upon the flesh of dogs, rats, humans, or whatever else they could scavenge and kill, the fresher the better.

As he sat motionless and invisible, the street was devoid of all but the occasional dog which now roamed with impunity, apparently enjoying the new-found freedom with no one but infected humans to spoil their fun; infected humans and the occasional hungry vampire, of course. Looking out at the skyline, tendrils of smoke rose slowly like talons tearing at the sky, fires blazing with no one to extinguish them. Litter blew in the wind and cars had been abandoned on the pavement, in people's gardens, or in the middle of the street. The drivers having found they could proceed no further either due to people or objects barring their path, had left them where they were, sometimes managing to continue their journey on foot, sometimes being dragged out by screaming crowds of rioters - or otherwise.

Sebastian watched as a woman shuffled along the road wearing a pair of torn jeans, a red sweat-shirt and a single shoe. Her trousers were muddy and stained with vomit and her hair was dishevelled. She made a moaning sound as she staggered and she pawed the air seemingly at imaginary flies circling her head. A dog that was sat in a doorway looked up as she neared and got warily to its feet. Its tongue lolled out, it held its head low and wagged its tail in hope, a gesture of supplication. It was quite clear to Sebastian that dogs, although entirely capable of surviving without humanity, most definitely benefitted from their proximity. Not unlike his own kind. As the woman saw it she bellowed and lurched towards it with sudden rage. The dog turned and fled for its life.

Sebastian eased himself off the window sill and dropped to the roof of the shed below. Without pause he leapt through the air and hit the ground soundlessly. He moved quickly through the graveyard to the street slipping from one shaded area to the next. He too needed sustenance, although that would not come from humans tonight. He did sometimes feast on human blood, and while all vampires found it preferable over blood from other animals in terms of taste and nutrition, he personally felt a moral twinge every time. On the occasions when he set aside his ethics, he justified it with the argument that it did not have to mean actually killing the person or their becoming a vampire; not in every case at least.

Towards the end of the street a fox scurried by. It was unaware that it was being watched or of its imminent demise. That will do, makes a change from rat or dog, Sebastian thought. The fox disappeared into a side alley and he stealthily followed it. At the entrance to the alley was the corpse of an adult male lying on its front. There was blood splattered all over the torso, it was only half clothed and its body had started to decay, but for some reason animals had avoided it and there were no signs that the body had been eaten at all. It gave off a foul stench and Sebastian moved past it quickly, trying not to breathe in the funk.

The alley ran between two-storey buildings and narrowed at a dead-end where some large rubbish bins were overturned, spilling their noxious contents. Sebastian assumed the fox must be hiding amongst them. As he neared he suddenly became aware of someone else just by the garbage. He froze to the wall as a man with blood smeared around his mouth looked up holding the fox's limp corpse. Hunger was making efficient and cunning killers of them, Sebastian thought. At that moment there was the sound of a foot scraping on tarmac and he half-turned to see a second man enter the alley just behind him. The man holding the fox now noticed the vampire for the first time and snarled, shielding the fox's body defensively. He raised the animal to his mouth and ripped at the flesh one last time, coming away with a chunk of meat and fur which hung from his jagged teeth. Then still clutching the creature to his chest, he hurled himself at Sebastian. There was a screech as the second man also charged forwards, realising that food was within his grasp.

Ordinarily Sebastian should have smelled either of them before getting so close, a vampire's senses being a lot more attuned than those of a human, much more akin to the senses of the now dead fox. Their odours must have been shielded by the stench of the corpse at the alleyway's entrance. That did not however explain why he had not heard the man killing the fox, nor the hapless creature's death-cries. He chided himself for getting sloppy and careless as he lashed out with a well-placed boot at the first assailant's midriff, sending him crashing back into the rubbish bins. He span round just in time as the second bore down upon him with hands reaching. He grabbed hold of the man's forearms and continued the momentum, twirling and launching him onwards, sending him flying through the air and straight into the first man in a pile on the ground.

Either fall would have knocked the wind out of a normal human and that should have ended the altercation, but these diseased crazies were more resilient. Driven by rage and hunger they were both on their feet again in a moment, screaming in indignant anger. However Sebastian was no longer there. He imagined that Farzin would have taken great pleasure in tearing them limb from limb, possibly toying with them for a while first, but personally he could not get over the fact that the infected were once human and a lot more recently than *he* had been. He preferred avoidance to violence. In the time it took the men to scramble to their feet he had leapt high at the wall, and using a couple of indentations in the surface, managed to kick himself off it and upwards to the roof above in a move that would have made the most accomplished urban free-runner gawp in astonishment.

Farzin again ventured out, striding contemptuously along

the centre of the road, no cowering or fear for him; he felt an enormous sense of release which temporarily masked his constant, gnawing resentment. He took no precautions, did not attempt to walk quietly or skulk in the ever-darkening shadows of twilight. Eventually he stopped and holding his hands up to the heavens, threw his head back and inhaled deeply into his lungs.

"I do not know why you are being so cautious," he smirked. "There are none who can oppose us. We no longer need to prowl out of sight, afraid of discovery."

On this occasion Flavia had kept pace with him silently and was almost invisible to all but the most observant and perceptive. She now stepped forth and approached him. He smiled and held out a slender, delicate hand to her.

"Tonight my love, we feast. It has been too long since we have tasted the blood of man but tonight I feel as though we may be lucky." There was a look of greedy malice in his sneering eyes and something else she could not quite identify. Normally she could read him plainly but unless she was very much mistaken, his eyes were veiled and there was something she thought he may be withholding.

Even at night the red brick buildings of Bishop's Stortford reminded him of blood. Blood of the many victims he had taken, blood of the people whose lives he had violently ended, blood of the animals and rodents he had been forced to feed off for far too long. But no more; his was now a life of freedom, of self-gratification, of revenge.

Flavia regarded him closely, reading his mood and his impulses, calculating his next words and his next move. She saw his eyes widen subtly, the pupils flare, the increase in his pulse as he turned to her with a lustful smile. There was something he was not telling her, she was certain of that.

153

"I think I detect our dinner," he said.

She watched as he started to walk towards a group of buildings. Only now did she sense a delicate hint of something on the wind, a promise of sustenance and reward, a trace that they could so easily have missed had they not stopped still. She wondered how he had detected it so much more easily than she had. Normally she was the more perceptive of the two.

As he neared he became more rapid, direct and unwavering. He looked at a block of flats and again turned to look at her, before pointing upwards. On the third floor in one of the apartments the slightest of shadows passed by the window accompanied by a faint noise and Farzin let out a moan as he felt the excitement of the pre-kill build. He was truly looking forward to this. He smiled with one thin corner of his mouth. More of a sneer, the expression held no warmth.

"Come, my love," and with that he quickly started to climb.

She again watched for a moment, marvelling at how he had detected the scent, before following him up and arrived a moment after him, just as he was about to enter. The window was slightly ajar and he deftly slipped his fingers through the small gap and prised it open, then vaulted quickly and soundlessly through. The apartment was small and in relative disarray with the stale smell of sweat and fear. Children's toys were scattered over the floor and a selection of kitchen knives were on a small dining table, some of which had been bound to wooden chair legs with masking tape. Bottles of mineral water and tins of food were stacked against a wall beside a mound of medicinal items but he hardly paused to consider any of that as the aroma of fresh human blood filled him with uncontrollable urgency. He knew instinctively where the target was and crossed the space in a single stride, just as a figure holding a candle emerged from an inner room. The man did not have time to gasp as the cold, lifeless hand fixed around his neck like a mechanical vice and hoisted him off the floor. The candle slipped from his grasp as his eyes rolled back in terror, confronted as he was by this sudden, terrifying apparition. The fingers around his throat squeezed tightly, preventing any cry from escaping his lips and he struggled with his feet flailing and scratched at the hand that held him as effortlessly as a hound would hold a rabbit.

Farzin regarded him keenly, trembling now himself in expectation. Nevertheless he prolonged the kill and savoured it, licking his lips like a snake. For him the anticipation was key, almost as important as the actual experience itself. Flavia could see the resentment in his eyes, could almost smell the feelings of revenge that pounded through him. As Farzin slowly brought the man closer, taking in the heady scent and enjoying the terror he saw in the man's face, Flavia turned away. This was Farzin's enjoyment but not one that she shared any more. The Farzin that she had known for so long was changing rapidly. As was she.

Farzin paused with the man dangling in front of him. He knew what fear looked like in a victim. He was well acquainted with its scent and relished its taste. He brought their faces so close they were nearly touching before he started to whisper in a voice rich in gloating, sanctimonious evil.

"Your kind has always arrogantly believed in your own innate superiority, always believed you can unlock the ultimate mysteries of the universe, attempted to answer the great unknowns and divine the truth. But you are not superior and you do not have all the answers. I do though. Do you know, for example, what the meaning of life is?"

The man's eyes desperately tried to avoid looking into Farzin's baleful stare as he continued, enjoying the moment and the, quite literally, captive audience that hung before him.

"The meaning of life is what happens now, *right* now, in the last few seconds before you die. How you are in the final, tedious glimmer of your pathetic existence before death claims your unworthy essence. It is so very easy to be magnificent when everything is proceeding according to your grand designs. But how you behave when all hope has gone and the end draws near, that defines the meaning of your pitiful life. Invariably your kind dies pathetically; blubbering in fear and saying anything to try and save themselves. I have seen so many of you die in such a demeaning manner, and believe me, many more *will* die if they refuse my dominion, when I break away from the yoke of obeisance and realise my destiny. Not long now."

As he spoke the man's thrashing gradually started to subside. It seemed to Farzin as if he realised that there was no escape and was resigned to his fate, as though he wanted his demise to come as fast as possible and end this torment. The man slowly focussed and tried to return Farzin's stare although he could not hold it. His hands still grasped at the talons around his neck but his thrashing eased. Farzin recognised this and it gave him pause. Normally at such a time his victim would be beside himself with uncontrollable terror but there was something else that he noticed in this victim's countenance, something that made him hesitate whilst he tried to identify what was lurking behind the fear.

He stared intently into the man's bulging eyes unable to detect the hidden emotion, but his vague uncertainty had taken the edge off his pleasure and slightly dulled the shine of the pre-kill. With a sudden hiss of venom he plunged his teeth into his victim's neck. The warmth of the liquid that filled his mouth quickly washed away his anger as he felt the life force flowing through his weary veins, causing him to spasm as he drank deeply. His own shudders mirrored those of the dying man whose choked gargling was already starting to weaken and fade. The pleasantly acrid, metallic flavour always brought back to him memories of previous feeds. So many images of surprised and terrified victims, each of which had died in a wondrously different manner, each of which had delighted his taste buds and held a special place in his cold, cold heart. A heart that had become twisted after the first that he had ever turned and loved - as much as he was capable of - had been plucked from his side by the misguided action of fearful humans, leaving a void where resentment and hatred could thrive.

Eventually with a gasp he pulled away from the open vein, and as he staggered backwards he nonchalantly handed the lifeless corpse behind him to Flavia waiting patiently in the darkness. For a moment he turned inwards, looking into the depths of his being as the heat from the man's blood warmed his core, filling him with energy and making every molecule of his body tingle and vibrate in ecstasy.

Flavia too drank but hers was less the action of a lion feeding with complete disregard at a corpse, more a gazelle at a watering hole, always watchful and aware, never letting her guard down. Even whilst her lips were at the man's throat she could tell that Farzin was still dissatisfied and searching for something else.

As the feeling of euphoria subsided and he reluctantly surfaced back to the present he was reminded of that final fleeting look in the man's eyes. A look that had suggested it was not his own life that he was afraid for. That he was resigned to his own death and meekly accepted it as one might wake to watch the sunrise with a feeling of inevitability. There was a delicate groan of floorboards from somewhere within the apartment. The door to a bedroom creaked slowly open and a small figure stood peering out uncertainly. A smile cracked across Farzin's face like an insult and instantly his confusion was assuaged. Flavia watched as his shoulders dropped slightly and his head tilted. She knew what he was thinking and what he would do next. The man had been fearful of his own demise, yes, undoubtedly. But more than that, she realised now, he had been afraid for this child. He had wanted, indeed craved his own swift death in the hope that this little one might live, might be overlooked. Farzin could not help but feel a certain amount of grudging admiration for his latest victim; there had not been the usual, final, plaintive appeal for clemency, just an ultimate desire for the benefit of another. Highly commendable, he thought, and highly misplaced, as he turned with a malicious grin on his face and extended his hand. Once again Flavia looked away.

A few hours after Emma Pethard had died, when the chaos had subsided a little and following the meeting in the conference room, Singleton went to pay Corporal Pethard a visit. Bannister was slouched in his chair outside the two rooms fiddling idly with his lighter when she silently walked up to him, her footfalls cushioned by the carpet. He practically leapt out of his chair when she tapped him on the shoulder.

Despite all his bravado he's pretty strung out, she thought. Just like everyone else. "How are our boys?" she inclined her head towards the two rooms.

"Yes, all good ma'am. Woody's fine. He's been a bit thirsty so I had to fetch him some water. Quite a lot of water in fact," Bannister said in a vaguely conspiratorial manner.

Singleton wondered if perhaps he was trying to intimate that Sergeant Wood was ill and starting to show symptoms but she ignored his insinuation. "And Pethard?"

"Yeah, he's only just woken up. He hasn't asked for any water yet though."

"Okay thanks Corporal." Then she turned to the bedroom doors and called out first to Wood who answered quite coherently and politely. Reassured, she unlocked and entered the room and sat chatting to him for a few minutes. Satisfied that so far he was still healthy, both physically and mentally, she left him and repeated the procedure with Pethard. When she said his name there was a pause and silence for several seconds before he replied. He sounded groggy and distant but coherent enough for her to believe he was uninfected, as yet anyway. She cautiously went in.

Pethard sat on a chair beside the bed, leaning forwards with his head cradled in his hands. He did not stand up as she entered or even acknowledge her presence. Singleton perched on the bed beside him.

"How are you Reggie?" She put her hand gently on his arm and slowly he looked up at her. His eyes were bloodshot and seemed to stare right through her with a vacant, emotionless expression. He opened his mouth to speak but only a soft rasping sound came out. She suddenly wondered if perhaps she had misjudged and he *was* sick after all, and she edged imperceptibly away from him. Then he closed his mouth and tried to swallow and speak again. Reassured, she passed him a glass of water from the bedside table.

"The sedation often leaves you feeling thirsty," she reassured him with a sigh of relief. It was all too easy to jump to conclusions these days. Clearly she too was feeling edgy.

He nodded, rubbing his head. "I'm okay I guess, thank you ma'am."

"Well you look terrible," she said it as a joke but it did nothing to lighten the mood. "I'm so sorry for your loss, really I am." Again she put her hand on his arm and saw the tears well up in his eyes.

"I just can't get that image out of my head, of her at the door and him pulling her down, on top of her biting her neck and blood, blood everywhere..."

"That's so terrible for you, I really am so very sorry. No one should have to witness something like that. I can't even begin to imagine..."

"...I mean I know we have all gone through a lot but just, to go like that. We've only been married a year, we've just had our first anniversary last month, we were about to try for children, it's just so unfair." He started sobbing, violent gasps that wracked his entire body. She leant forwards and put her arms around his shoulders and held him tightly for a long time without saying anything else, feeling his body convulse with the anguish. She said nothing. What could she possibly say that would help assuage his grief? His heartache cut right though her and as she held him, her own pain came gushing to the surface and she silently wept too with her eyes screwed tightly closed, trying to block out her own memories and heartache for lost loved ones, dashed opportunities, wasted dreams.

After a time his body stopped shaking and she released her grip on him. They sat facing each other with their heads just touching, their eyes red and his hands clasped in hers. They didn't speak; words were quite useless now, redundant in such a situation. Just her proximity and the knowledge that another human being empathised and shared the anguish was all she could offer.

Finally he spoke in a voice that was little more than a

croak. "I'm sorry. I know we have all been through a lot. It's not just me; I guess I should man-up a bit." He tried to suppress a sob which then came out as a snort through his nose and started them both laughing for an all-too brief moment.

He wiped his face and continued. "It all seems so unreal, these past days and weeks. I keep on thinking I'm going to wake up in a moment and it'll all have been the most horrible nightmare and Emma will be there lying beside me." He wept quietly again as he talked, the tears flowing freely down his cheeks. "I just can't believe what's happened to me, to Emma, to us all."

"I know exactly how you feel." Something in her words or the slight tremble of her voice must have triggered a reaction in Pethard, as for a moment he looked at her differently, seeing beyond his own grief.

"I guess you have lost loved ones too ma'am?"

She breathed deeply willing the tears away, fighting the urge to break down again but she was unable to stop. It all came tumbling out, boiling and bubbling afresh between the two of them, a torrent of anguish and uncertainty and suffering, about her child who lived with her ex-husband and his partner that she had not heard from since the day after the state of emergency was declared, how virtually every minute of every waking hour was filled with profound despair and how she had to force herself to carry on, not because she thought there was much chance that they were still alive but because she knew that there was so much more at stake now, that every one of them had their part to play to ensure the safety and survival of them all, that she could easily just curl up in a ball and give in right now but where did that leave any of them? For a moment she forgot her rank and her position of responsibility and just grieved as a woman and an utterly distraught mother.

Corporal Charlotte Collins arrived beside Bannister and gave him another fright as he had not heard her quiet tread either.

"Strewth, you scared the beejezus out of me." He smiled at her and mockingly stood to attention for a moment with a comedic salute.

"At ease soldier. How are you doing?"

He grinned and flushed a little. "Fine here thanks," then looked down and noticed the two plates of food she carried. "You're too kind. Are we having a romantic meal together?"

"For our captives I'm afraid. You'll get yours when you're relieved from guard duty and before we get briefed for our patrol in the morning."

"Ahh, so I have the pleasure of your company this time do I? A lovely drive for two in the countryside?"

"Make that for four," she said, ignoring his clumsy attempts at flirtation. "I'm bringing Cujo and we've also got Freddie Samuels along for the ride." It was hoped her dog Cujo could be of use in detecting the infected and in adding extra protection for the soldiers. Senior Aircraftman Freddie Samuels worked in the medical branch but had frontline experience. As the medical centre needed fresh supplies Lewis had considered it would be a good idea to send him along.

"How are they?" She inclined her head in the direction of the locked rooms.

"They're fine. Singleton's in with Pethard now. If you leave me the food I'll make sure they get it."

"Hey no probs, I thought I'd pay Sergeant Wood a quick visit anyway whilst I'm here, I mean I guess he's probably pretty bored by now."

Collins noticed Bannister's grin faded a little and a small furrow formed above his eyebrows. "Well actually I was told no one was allowed in, in case they've turned nuts, so I'll get the food to them. Don't worry I won't eat it."

She spoke then in a louder voice. "Sergeant Wood, are you okay in there? Have you gone nuts yet?"

"Hi Charlotte," he answered immediately. "Hmmm, I don't think so, though I am going a little stir-crazy with boredom."

"He sounds okay to me, don't you think?" she said to Bannister, flashing a smile at him, hoping to win him over. "Come on, just let me pop my head in and say hi, I'll only be a minute, then we can both go and get briefed before exploring the big, bad world together tomorrow. If he gives me any trouble I'll call you for help."

He thought for a moment and then nodded curtly. "Well okay, but make it quick."

She heard the door lock behind her, then crossed the room to where Wood sat and handed him the plate. He stood up for her and pulled her chair out again as he had at breakfast and she tried to suppress a smile. His politeness was endearing but was also tinged with a little stiff formality, a subtle aloofness that seemed in keeping with his distancing himself. She wondered if that distance would keep *everyone* at arm's length.

"Thank you very much, I'm starving."

"Well you'll have to be, in order to enjoy that," she pointed with disgust at the amorphous brown rice dish that slopped over his plate and he smiled thinly as he regarded it with apprehension.

"Strewth, this is gonna take some forcing down." They both grinned.

They sat on chairs by the bed chatting whilst he ate. She already knew that he had been in the Parachute Regiment. After distinguishing himself over a number of years he had been selected for a tour of duty in '1 PARA', the Special Forces unit, where he had excelled. He had

163

arrived at Headley Court with a whole range of scars and injuries that looked like he must have been in a bomb blast, although he seemed reluctant to discuss it. Each of them had been there for over a month but their rehabilitation regimes had not coincided and she did not know all that much about him. There was an instant spark of friendship or attraction, or something. Their previous conversations had been relatively light and mostly passing banter and gentle, good-natured flirting although he had always appeared more reserved than men were usually in her presence.

Remembering the earlier occurrence he lowered his fork and looked at her with genuine concern, placing a hand on hers. "How are you? I mean, after this morning…"

She tried to smile but it was not very convincing. "I'm okay, thanks for asking. And you?"

"Yeah I'm fine. I know I'm in here in case I have been contaminated by Abbott's blood but I'm not ill, I'm absolutely normal. Poor Pethard though, and Abbott and all of them."

"I know. Words can't do it justice. That really is horrific."

They were quiet for a moment, both staring at the floor, plunged into their own personal abyss of grief until Collins took a deep breath and shook herself, as though to purify the unpleasant thoughts. The mood on base was depressed enough as it was. Nobody liked to dwell on the horror and killings. Everything was all so very unpleasant at the moment anyway and like most of the others she tried to continue life without thinking about depressing matters where possible, to concentrate on easier, less disturbing things than the terrors of the outside world. She looked up at his face again and wondered, not for the first time, how he had got a scar that ran from just below his right cheekbone as far as his mouth. He had a handsome face, she thought, very symmetrical with deep, brown eyes that were alert and engaging but ever vigilant and rarely smiling. His cheek bones were pronounced, his hair was cut very short and his body seemed taught and disciplined beneath his uniform through years of training. She always had the impression that he sat on the side-lines watching; watching her, watching everybody around him, always watching and quietly thoughtful.

"How about you," she asked. "Have you lost a 'significant other' in all this mess?"

"Me? Nah," he shook his head ruefully. "I was engaged a while back to a girl called Mina, but I think she liked the idea of the army and the uniform more than the reality. My job meant I was away a lot and I guess I was a little detached when I was at home. I didn't pay her enough attention and I think I probably neglected her a bit. So she saw the light and got out while she could. Can't say I blame her."

"Ah well, her loss, I'm sure," Collins smiled warmly and Wood felt a slight flutter in his stomach, a welcome yet unusual feeling, besieged on all sides as it was by all the misery and hopelessness. He banished the thought immediately, feeling guilty for harbouring a pleasant sensation in such difficult times.

"And you? Do you have anybody significant out there?"

"But of course, the love of my life." She grinned again and he tried to return her smile but felt a small pang of disappointment. He attempted not to look crestfallen and did not know if he had succeeded or if his face had momentarily betrayed him.

She let her smile linger a moment before continuing, teasing him. Ordinarily she would not have been so flirtatious, but these days when nobody knew how long they had to live, it gave them all a very different attitude to life. "Cujo, of course. Who could want for anyone better?"

Wood laughed, perhaps a little too hard and stopped himself short. The disappointment was instantly swamped by a surge of relief. "But of course, faithful and fearless. What more does a girl need?"

"Well that's a good start but I also want someone who is aesthetically pleasing, and let's face it, he is." And he was. A beautiful Alsatian with gleaming, groomed fur and a proud, alert demeanour. "Not only that but he does what I say, hangs on my every word and comes at the sound of my voice. Perfect." She giggled and he laughed again, although he was not sure whether she had intended the innuendo or not. She was enjoying playing with him, for a brief moment transported away from the morning's brutality.

"How could a man possibly compete with that? I may as well just give up now," he joked.

"Well that would be a shame," she held his glance for a second and again he did not know if she was flirting or just talking in general terms. Before he had a chance to find out she stood up smoothing her trousers down, beamed at him and turned to leave.

"Think I'd better go before old Bannister starts shouting at me. I've got to go for a briefing now as I'm out on patrol tomorrow morning," she gulped in mock terror, although she did feel fearful about going, a very justified emotion.

"Well you take care; it's bloody dangerous out there. Don't take any unnecessary risks, don't do anything stupid and don't talk to any strange men, okay?"

"You bet. Don't worry about me; I'll have Cujo to defend me. And you get well soon and don't go crazy on me."

166

He really was struggling to decipher her meaning throughout the conversation and was unsure again whether she was saying not to become infected and lose his mind, or not to fall head over heels for her. He assumed the former although he hoped the latter. It was safer and easier that way and less presumptuous.

"That's a deal."

He stood as she turned to leave and not for the first time admired her physique. Just as the door opened she looked back briefly and flashed him a beautiful smile once more. She had full lips and white, even teeth and it really was a dazzling smile. She was a pretty girl, just naturally very eye-catching without having to make too much effort, with stylishly short, glossy black hair, attractively angular features and endearing blue eyes. Her character was particularly bubbly and engaging and the entire package was very desirable indeed. He could see Bannister scowling at him from without; there was clearly no love lost there, then the door closed and he was left alone in the silence, in a spin, with new inner tumult of a pleasant nature for once, to distract him.

CHAPTER 9

The Land Rovers always felt a little unwieldy with a trailer attached, as though they too were reluctant to leave the station. Bannister cursed as he tried to slam it into first gear but there was the grinding sound of an unhappy gearbox which would not cooperate under such treatment.

"Hey, slow down soldier, a little less brute force," Collins said, putting a warm hand on his and gently easing the gear lever forwards. "As with so many things in life; softly, softly, catchee monkey."

"Yeah I guess that's just me all over honey, just raw, brute force." He gave an animal growl. She rolled her eyes wearily at his relentless efforts at flirting but could not conceal the smirk in spite of herself. To Collins he was a stereotypical Scouser - lots of cheeky banter and potentially a nice guy if only he was not constantly trying it on. Spurred on by the slight encouragement, he growled again and clawed at the air in front of her.

"Okay there tiger, pipe down. You'll make Cujo jealous and believe me, you wouldn't want that."

She raised her hand and Cujo, sat beside Senior Aircraftman Samuels in the rear of the vehicle, instantly licked her fingers. This was Cujo's first time outside the station as well as hers. She was decidedly nervous and hoped her dog had not been affected by her mood. Too many people had already been killed while outside the security of the station, either due to poor preparation or a relaxing of established procedures. She did not want to add to that number. Whilst the measures for operations had been refined since then, it was still a mission fraught with very real dangers. However, she knew how important it was to locate supplies and other possible survivors, and accepted that everyone had to bear the burden of risk with these forays. For all of his bluff and innuendo Bannister was experienced in combat and she trusted him to keep them safe. She also had a reasonable amount of frontline experience, as did Freddie Samuels, and they all understood what was expected of them. Bannister had been off base several times now, Samuels had been off twice and both were at ease but alert.

"Unusual name that, 'Cujo'. Where did you get it from?" Bannister asked, turning to gaze into her eyes.

"It's from a Stephen King novel. It's about a dog that gets rabies, goes mad and kills loads of people."

"Cute and oh, how apt," Bannister snorted. He was glad to get the opportunity to chat to her and relieved that they were not dwelling on the death of Abbott or Emma Pethard. There were enough morbid thoughts these days and sometimes it was just nice to forget about them and discuss more mundane issues.

"Yeah, I guess so," she replied. "If I'd known how life was going to pan out and he was due to be my protector and saviour in this crazy world I'd have called him something else, like Lassie, only Lassie was a girl, obviously."

"Or Rebel, the Alsatian in 'Champion the Wonder Horse' maybe," Bannister mused.

"Ahhh, now you're showing your age. Anyway, that's where the name comes from and he isn't going to go berserk and attack anyone, least of all me, are you my angel?" She turned and stroked Cujo between the ears.

"So who's your favourite TV dog?"

She paused before replying, the realisation brought home to her the poignant fact that she would never again watch television programmes.

"Hmmm, I think I'd have to go with Bouncer. You know, from the children's programme Blue Peter?"

"Yeah, of course I know Bouncer and a good choice, but not as good as Shep, also from Blue Peter."

"Yeah? Why Shep?" she asked.

"Well he was much smarter for starters, being a Border Collie an' all. They're the most intelligent dogs in the world."

"No way. More intelligent than my Cujo?" Cujo was awarded another loving stroke and licked his lips in time with the wag of his tail, unaware that his intelligence was being called into question.

"Apparently so. I read that a Border Collie is about as intelligent as a two-year-old child, something to do with the amount of words they understand, the tasks they can perform, that kinda thing."

"Well Cujo's a lot smarter than that. He's clever enough to realise that it's best for him to do exactly what I tell him without question - or else. You try and teach a two-year-old kid that."

The second Land Rover was driven by Sergeant Harper Hutchison from the MT section, a RAF soldier with nearly as many years of experience as Straddling. He was an uneventful looking man of medium height and average build with the kind of face that one had almost been expecting. He had short brown hair framing personable features and sunken eyes that turned down at the edges slightly, giving him a permanently apologetic appearance. He was an experienced and level-headed soldier but was fairly quiet and happy to blend into the background. Beside him was Flight Lieutenant Walkden on his second mission off-base and in the back was Leading Aircraftman Neale from the catering section, on his first foray. Walkden was the senior officer on the excursion; on his first trip he had been accompanied by Captain Lewis and it had gone smoothly. Although now he was technically in command, in reality he was out of his comfort zone and felt extremely glad for the experience of Hutchison and Bannister in particular.

They drew up to the guardroom where Lance Corporal Millington loitered, his SA80 assault rifle slung casually over his thick shoulder. He stood in front of the vehicles, a reassuringly solid structure, and Collins thought it was just a shame that he was not due to go with them on this excursion.

"Last chance ladies," Millington drawled. "Check your weapons 'n walkies,"

Each vehicle was equipped with a fixed Bowman C4I Tactical Communication System, favoured by British military forces, and it was through these sets that they would keep in contact with base. They all had their own Personal Role Radio or PRR, which was a short distance UHF radio. The range of these was only approximately five hundred metres but often considerably less, depending on the surroundings. They went through the well-rehearsed procedure and gave a thumbs-up.

"Be careful out there, call in every hour and don't forget the new body-search procedures when you return," Millington rumbled with a smile. "Now y'all be good and don't make me have to come and rescue you."

"Stick the kettle on amigo, we'll be back in time for tea and medals," Bannister called out.

Millington flashed him a big grin and moved aside, unlocking the gates. As they passed he looked up at the sky with a frown. It had been a promising start to the day and he only wore a light, khaki shirt but it was turning threatening now and he shivered.

Leaving the security of the station behind gave Collins a flush of nerves and she felt vulnerable. Her palms were sweating and she gripped her SA80 tightly to her side as she tried to calm herself. For all of her worries though there was an enormous sense of morbid curiosity and she scanned the surroundings as much through fascination as fear.

171

The initial stretch was just one long, straight road. It was relatively pleasant and rural and did not look very different from how it must have been for the last few decades, although none of them were able to appreciate it on this occasion. Soon they passed a cemetery, its white tombstones catching the sun like sharp, jagged teeth. The normal solemnity of the graves seemed to be lost, given that the dead now literally littered the streets.

Collins turned to Bannister. "I never really understand one thing about cemeteries."

"What's that?"

"Well, once a grave has been used I presume it won't become empty again so the cemetery just fills up more and more. People have been dying every day since man first walked the earth. How is it that there aren't more graveyards and they're not all filled to capacity? I mean the world should surely be just one big, overflowing burial ground."

The instant she said it she regretted it. It was an idle thought she had had some time before but not particularly appropriate for these days. The unintended meaning of her comment was not wasted on any of them but Bannister was enjoying her company and happily continued the conversation.

"Well I don't know much about that, but there is one thing that always confuses me. In films you often see people attending a funeral but I can't think of one where there is a cremation. Given that approximately ninety percent of people who die actually get cremated instead of buried, don't you find that's a little unrealistic?"

She thought about it for a moment with a faraway look in her eyes. "You know what, you're right. You're just a constant source of fascinating information."

"Ah, I'm not quite as stupid as I look. I tell ya, stick with me honey and I'll teach you things, never a dull moment."

For someone who did his very best at appearing cheesy and shallow, Collins found herself not for the first time considering that Bannister may have hidden depths.

Although the sun was struggling to shine, everything seemed to be tinged with depressing, grey overtones. He was cheerful at first but Collins could tell Bannister's mood had changed as they drove further from the safety of the station. He became brusque and professional as he scanned for potential threats. His manner made Collins tense and on edge. Samuels just sat silently throughout the journey. At a bend in the road she noticed some flowers had been tied to a lamppost. They had long since wilted - a forlorn reminder of someone's personal grief; an emotion that now seemed so insignificant, being, as it was, currently shared by every surviving soul on the planet.

Walkden was fidgeting with the microphone to the Bowman radio and staring out of the car from side to side. His mind was tormented with thoughts of a previous, disastrous foray. He had been close to Parsons in particular and his death had really shaken Walkden. He wondered who would be next to die? He could not escape the gnawing feeling that this trip would go no better and that this day was going to be his last. Sergeant Hutchison glanced over at his commanding officer. He noticed the clammy skin around his jowls that hung loosely over his collar, the sweat marks on the shirt that was stretched a little too tightly by the portly frame unused to physical exercise, and the way his hands nervously scraped his grey fringe off his forehead every few seconds. Strewth! He's got it bad, he thought. We need him to get a grip.

He tried to calm Walkden's nerves with idle conversation. "How did your first excursion go boss?"

"Huh?" Walkden replied after a moment. "Oh yeah,

okay I guess." He paused, before making further chat. "And you, how many times have you been off station?"

"With this trip now, that makes five so far. A couple were uneventful, a couple less so. But hey, all in a day's work, right?"

Walkden just muttered some reply and went back to staring out the window. Hutchison sighed inwardly and made a mental note to be extra cautious. He winked in the rear view mirror at Neale who raised his eyebrows despairingly in reply.

As they neared town Collins became aware of how strange the world now seemed. Only on rare occasions before had she witnessed the streets so deathly quiet, such as during a soccer world cup final, in the morning on New Year's Day or a nationally important event. There was a peculiar, unreal quality to the town, as though they were driving through a large movie set. She found the frequent reminders of normal life truly disturbing. These were impressed upon her memory like snap-shots played at double-speed. She could not help but wonder at the pain and suffering each of these little vignettes must have borne witness to over the last few days and weeks. It made her feel guilty for having been sheltered behind the safety of the base whilst those without literally fought tooth and claw to survive, rather like visiting an intensely poor country as a relatively wealthy tourist. Like all of them it was a time for emotional reverie and she had to force these useless thoughts away. Focus Collins, focus, she told herself.

In the rear vehicle Walkden checked in with Headley Court on the radio. He heard the reassuringly chirpy voice of Senior Aircraftman Ric Masters, a reminder that safety was only a short drive away, although a few miles can sometimes be an awfully long way. Hutchison and Neale both grew silent and morose, straining to see any potential hostiles; or possibly even friendlies.

Many windows were smashed and glass and debris littered the streets and pavements, making careful driving imperative. For this reason all vehicles carried two spare tyres. If a car received a blow-out, the protocol was that the mission was abandoned immediately and they returned to base, leaving one spare to cover the return journey. It was just too risky to be caught out in the open without a fully operational means of transport.

They headed first to a nearby petrol station. Reserves of diesel were running low so in the trailers attached to both Land Rovers they carried several forty-four imperial gallon drums. Although there was no mains supply of electricity there would be the facility at the petrol station to manually pump the diesel from underground reservoirs. It was a laborious process but one that was unfortunately necessary. Whilst they were out they were also going to look for medical supplies and guns. Many rural towns in England have their own gun club and therefore there are a surprising number of firearm shops and suppliers. In the nearby town of Stansted Mountfitchet was a national distributor of shotguns and other weapons, and they were going to see what could be obtained from that store. In order to try to find survivors they would adopt the previous practice, and as they drove Collins called out on the megaphone, accompanied by Bannister this time blasting the horn; however it was thought that the loud noises might attract the infected and so as they neared their destination they would cease and keep noise to a minimum.

The lead Land Rover was approximately one hundred metres in front of the second. The radio hissed momentarily and there was the crackle of Walkden's voice. "Right, we're nearing the petrol station. Only about a mile to go so quiet now."

Bannister looked at Collins with a sly grin. "Seems I have to stop giving you the horn, sorry about that."

She answered with a slap on his arm. Yeah, she thought to herself, you aren't quite so tense after all.

There was a tangled car crash blocking the road so Bannister drove up onto the pavement to skirt around it, resisting the urge to toss out any double-entendres about mounting the pavement together. It appeared as though the cars had collided head on at some pace and then caught fire leaving a metallic sculpture dedicated to destruction. Wreckage had been scattered over a large distance and as Collins glanced at the cars she noticed to her horror the charred remains of someone at the steering wheel of one of them. It was hard to make the figure out clearly as it seemed all that was left were some burnt rags and bones with a little scorched flesh, but it was enough to make her gasp out loud.

Banister put a genuine and reassuring hand on her arm. "Don't look honey - not nice. I'm sorry but there may well be more of that before we're done."

She reproached herself for being weak but would have been comforted to know that both Bannister and Samuels felt exactly the same.

The car accelerated away from the carnage and Senior Aircraftman Samuels looked back. As they turned the corner he spoke up for the first time that journey.

"Hmmm, that's odd."

"What's that?" Bannister frowned.

"I thought I saw the other car stop."

"No way," Bannister was quick to dismiss his comment. "Why would they do that and not tell us. You leave the thinking to me doofus. Just keep a look out for them damn zombies."

At that moment the radio brought Walkden's voice to them for a second time. "Guys, seems we've blown a tyre. It must have been some of that debris by the crash. We're gonna stop a moment and quickly change wheels."

They could hear Walkden and Hutchison debating something with the 'press-to-talk' switch held down and so they waited until they could speak.

Hutchison was looking nervously all around with his hand on his gun. "I don't like this. We've only just cut the megaphone and now we have to stop. This isn't safe."

Walkden did not want to return to base empty-handed as he felt that would reflect badly on him and he answered rather more abruptly then he had intended. "Look, our destination is literally just around the corner. I say the others get started with the diesel and we crack on and change our tyre. It won't take us more than a couple of minutes, and then we can go and join them."

"That's leaving us rather vulnerable isn't it sir?"

"They're only about thirty seconds away if we have any problems. There's hardly any difference between them being here than there. If we get into trouble we can practically shout for help. Besides, if they get started now, they can be half way through by the time we arrive. I just don't like being away from the station any longer than is absolutely necessary."

Hutchison was still not convinced. "Well none of us are exactly happy being off base sir, but we've established protocol that we're supposed to follow. As far as I see it, they come back to us, we change wheels and then we all head back together." He was mindful of Walkden's position of authority but ultimately he was not keen to put himself into more peril than was absolutely necessary, and he was also well aware that Walkden was inexperienced in battle zones.

Walkden's stress level was rising and that was reflected in his voice. "Well, yes, that is correct, they are the procedures we're supposed to follow, but then sometimes you have to think a little outside the box. What I am saying is that we are virtually at our first destination so we hardly need to drive any further *away* from Headley Court. It would be a real shame to go home with nothing, only to have to repeat this exact same journey another time. So, they get started on the fuel, we join them, then we all call it a day and go back. Get some of that tea and medals Bannister mentioned." A thin line of sweat had formed on his brow. He was becoming agitated and talking more and more quickly.

Sergeant Hutchison too was getting frustrated so Neale, from the back seat, nervously leant forwards. "Look guys, we're wasting time. We could have had the tyre changed by now. Whatever we're gonna do can we please just do it?"

At that Hutchison let out a large breath that he did not even know he had been holding, shook his head and looked away resignedly into the distance.

Walkden spoke rapidly into the radio. "You guys go ahead. If we have a problem then be prepared to come and help immediately. We'll change our tyre and then we can all head back together."

Collins looked at Bannister with a frown. Like Hutchison she was unhappy with this plan. "If anything happens to them they'll be sitting ducks."

He paused in contemplation for a moment then shrugged his shoulders and she replied into the radio. "Are you sure sir?"

"Yes!" Walkden retorted sharply.

Bannister sighed and eased the Land Rover back into the middle of the road and on towards their first target. He turned to the other two with a serious expression. "I know you have both seen front line action before so I don't want to teach you to suck eggs, but now is the time to bring your A-game. Concentrate out there and don't let your attention wander. Your life, and more importantly that means my life, depends on it. If you have any doubts then there is no doubt, we all get straight back in the vehicle and discuss it there. Speak up if anything bothers you; believe me you'd rather I bite your head off for being a nonce than they bite you. Understood?"

The vehicle swung in a slow arc around the petrol station's forecourt under cover of the overhead awning. Cujo started to whimper and Collins assumed he was anxious to get out of the hot, stuffy vehicle; she held up her hand and he licked it but she was too preoccupied to think any more about it.

Bannister brought the car to an abrupt stop. "Last check of your weapons. Here's what we're gonna do - Collins, you and Cujo stand guard. I want you to patrol around the vehicle in a small perimeter, looking for anything that moves. Samuels, you're gonna grab the drums off the trailer and put them as close to the diesel reservoir as possible. I'll get the fuel system set up. Then I'll pump, you join Collins, bish, bash, bosh we'll have it done before the other losers even arrive. Questions?"

They shook their heads.

All of them searched outside for signs of the diseased but there was not another living soul in sight. They exited the vehicle together, moving with urgency. Collins had a tight grasp of Cujo's leash as she got out of the Land Rover but he was straining at it and still whining. She yanked the lead and he reluctantly came to heel.

She quickly scanned all around. The petrol station had a large forecourt and a car-wash area at the rear. A discarded shopping trolley lay on its side and there were bricks and debris littered about. Some wooden boards and sticks by one of the pumps looked as though someone had tried to light a bonfire and there were two cars that had their windows smashed. The petrol station itself had a shop attached to it. Next to it was a small car park. Weeds had started to sprout up in the gaps between the paving slabs giving it a scruffy, deserted appearance. There were shops opposite, a supermarket and apartments in the surrounding buildings. All were relatively modern and would have previously been rather smart although again windows had been smashed and one or two showed the effects of fire damage. There was a hardware store and a pharmacy that might have some useful items for later.

Bannister looked over his shoulder to check on his colleagues; Freddie Samuels was still struggling with the first drum and Collins was pacing around them in a tight circle. Cujo tugged at his leash with every other step. Not very well trained for a military dog, he thought. Perhaps it had picked up on all of their nervousness and was reacting to it. Still it did mean that Collins was paying too much attention to controlling it and not enough to her lookout.

He cursed quietly and called out to her. "Are you all right there Collins?"

"Yeah, Cujo seems a little on edge, that's all."

Suddenly there was a loud crash as one of the forty-four gallon drums slipped from Samuels's grasp and tumbled to the hard concrete surface, making an awful racket. They all froze for a moment and stared at poor Samuels who was scrabbling to stop the drum from rolling.

"Samuels you fool, are you trying to bring the entire tribe of crazies down on us?" Bannister snapped. At that moment Cujo started barking, pulling and straining at his leash and snarling as he had done when Emma Pethard had been attacked.

Bannister looked all around. He could see nothing but felt uneasy. "Okay, I think change of plan. I know what Walkden said but sod it. Let's get in the car and head back to them. We can always return together and finish off when they're ready."

Even from where they were, with none of the normal noises associated with life in general, Walkden heard the faint crash of the drum. He stopped what he was doing for a moment and looked in the vague direction his colleagues had taken.

"What was that?" said Neale but Walkden was already on the radio.

"Guys, just thought I heard a bang from your location. Are you okay?" There was no answer.

He looked with a worried expression over at Hutchison who was still undoing the bolts on the wheel. "I think you best get a move on."

Hutchison returned his anxious look. "Yes boss."

"I mean it."

Flight Lieutenant Walkden and his two colleagues were not the only ones to have heard the noise. A dark figure crouching on a nearby windowsill of an upper floor apartment craned his neck out into the sun in order to try to detect where the sound had come from. As he squinted out into the light he could not see anything, but he could sense that action was taking place not too far away. This felt different from the usual activity of the diseased. There was something in the air, a scent of fear or death. Sebastian rose quickly to his feet and jumped to the roof of the building below. Instead of dropping down to the road, this time he remained at height, leaping sure-footedly from one rooftop to the next. He covered several buildings in seconds without pausing for breath, planning his next move before he had even executed the previous one. Finally he looked down upon a scene of developing carnage.

Collins saw them first, a moment after Bannister had revised his plan. They were coming at a low run as though they were winded or trying to keep their heads below an unseen parapet. There were three people, one man and two women, all dirty and wearing ragged clothes. They were splattered in fresh blood and screaming unintelligibly with rage. They came from behind the car-wash, quite a distance, but they covered the ground with speed and were upon the soldiers almost before they had time to react.

"Into the car!" Bannister bellowed, discarding the fuel pump and sprinting for his life with diesel spilling out behind him like blood from an open artery. Samuels was nearest to the vehicle but Bannister still managed to get into his seat and ready his SA80 before his younger colleague. From behind them they heard more screams as another two people ran at them and then another from within the hardware shop.

"Oh my god, there's hundreds of them," cried Samuels as he turned to see where Collins was.

Cujo had gone absolutely crazy, like nothing Collins had ever seen before. She shrieked at him and desperately dragged him back to the vehicle. Bannister leant over from the driver's seat and had the door open for her with one hand, his weapon clutched in the other. Collins forced the dog into the Land Rover. She dived in after him as Bannister squeezed off a round into the body of the nearest diseased - a woman who was wearing a grubby white blouse. She was only a couple of lunging paces away when the bullet knocked her back and she crumpled to the ground.

Collins fumbled with the door handle, then pulled it closed but it did not shut properly. There was a crunch as she tried to slam it a second time and then she felt a hand latch around her ankle. The woman in the white blouse was on the ground at her feet, blood gargling from her mouth as she tried to pull herself up. Collins looked down into her black, unfocussed eyes and yelped as the next of the infected reached her. Bannister again aimed carefully and zeroed a round right between the eyes of the man. But there was yet another right behind.

There was a growl and a flash of dark fur and Cujo leapt straight out of the half open door, into the growing presence. With teeth bared and barking furiously he launched himself at the growing mob, biting and snarling. His attack would have scattered any normal crowd, but unfortunately these were not normal people and they did not know when to be afraid. Their attention was diverted momentarily and Collins lashed out with her boot, right into the face of the woman who determinedly clawed at her leg. There was a snap and crunch of bones and the woman dropped to the ground still shrieking.

Samuels fired three times and now urged from the back seat. "Go!"

Bannister was in the process of doing just that, trying to grind the gear lever forwards when Collins hurled herself out of the vehicle. Her SA80 blasted on fully automatic as she screamed, mindlessly trying to save her beloved guardian.

Bannister cursed but did not delay for a single moment. He too opened his door and leapt after her into the direct grasp of danger.

Cujo's assault and momentum had propelled the horde back a couple of metres from the vehicle. They seemed to be easily distracted. Now the dog held their combined, murderous attention as their rage found a new focus. His ferocious, initial attack had started to wane and they retaliated. They jumped on him and soon pinned him down, with many grasping hands ripping his body apart. His barks and snarls turned to howls of pain and then

183

wails of terror as they attacked him with their hooked claws and gaping, hungry mouths.

Collins was entirely out of her mind with a rage equal to theirs. She screeched as she advanced, emptying her magazine into their bodies, but she sprayed wildly without aiming. Her rounds lacked the effect she needed, either straying wide or burying themselves deep into non-vital organs and fleshy parts of her victims. There were many more of them now, attracted by the commotion and prospect of fresh food. Her attack had fortuitously gained her a little more space as they fell back momentarily. As she stood before them they turned and threw themselves at her anew, just as her collar was grasped from behind. She tried to scream but the effort was choked out of her. Bannister yanked her away from the reach of the nearest. His other hand still held his Browning which he fired once and blew a man's head apart.

With his ears ringing from the gunshot he shouted at her. "Run!"

There was no way they could get back into the Land Rover as the crowd now blocked their path so Bannister pushed Collins towards the petrol station's shop. One crazed woman in a torn, green dress saw Samuels. He was still in the back of the vehicle so she turned her savagery upon him. Scrambling through the driver's door she tried to climb into the back and another was right behind. Samuels leapt from the car in fright and managed to get to the shop first. He kicked its door open but had the presence of mind to turn and fire a volley into the pack as they chased after his colleagues. His shots found the nearest target, striking a woman in the leg and knocking her to the ground. The man behind tripped over her flailing body. That action bought them the second or two they needed to out-pace their attackers and they tore through the open door. Samuels followed but snagged his foot on the threshold and crashed into a display cabinet. He struck his head on a metal shelf and knocked himself senseless in front of the open doorway.

The bottom section of the door was made of steel and there were glass panels in the top half that looked to be reinforced with thin wire mesh. Bannister slammed it shut and hurriedly shoved a display stand forwards against it. The infected rushed at the entrance in fury and the soldiers had only seconds to barricade it. The door rattled and gave an inch as the diseased hammered into it. With Samuels out cold, Bannister and Collins spent anxious moments piling a couple of heavy racks in the hope that it would be enough. Both of them were gasping and trembling. The din from outside was horrific. The mob seemed to have swollen to well over a dozen. They were all screaming and pushing forwards, fighting each other in their eagerness to get at their prey.

When Walkden heard the shots he turned to his colleagues. The usual pink of his skin was pale. Hutchison looked up again as he heaved at the spanner. He had just managed to get the spare wheel on and was trying to tighten the first bolt.

"Nearly done boss," he said apologetically.

Walkden impatiently checked his gun again. Impatient to go to the aid of his colleagues yet terrified of what awaited them all around the next corner. As he looked in their direction he noticed a shambling figure emerge from a building just along the street. He froze as he watched the man stumble in the direction of the petrol station. Neale had seen him too and warned Hutchison in a whisper. Then two others emerged from the same building and started to follow the first. The soldiers did not move. The three dishevelled figures were almost at the corner when one of them looked back and saw them.

He let out an inhuman screech. The other two turned and as one they ran at the soldiers. They seemed to be trying to outpace each other, the sooner to get to their quarry, to tear them apart without compassion and feast upon their fresh, tender flesh.

Hutchison dropped the spanner. He smoothly raised the rifle and flicked the safety catch off whilst assuming a well-practiced kneeling position. He could vaguely see Walkden struggling with something but he was too preoccupied himself to pay much attention. When the people were only perhaps forty metres away he was expecting some command of some sort from Walkden but nothing were forthcoming. He turned to look. Walkden was still standing in front of the Land Rover and frantically fiddling with his SA80.

"Safety!" Hutchison yelled and leapt to his side. With a deft movement he readied the weapon and turned back to the oncoming assault, adrenalin thrilling his body. He tried to steady his breathing and calm his hands, and now spoke up himself. "Let them get a bit closer, then go for head shots. Keep it cool and controlled." He paused and then shouted. "Let 'em have it."

Walkden's rifle was still on automatic and he sprayed out in a gangster style that would have made Al Capone proud, but mostly missed his aim. The woman running at him was spun round and knocked to the floor by the force of a round penetrating her leg but it merely slowed her down. Neale hit his target with two carefully aimed shots. Both hit the upper torso. Although the man sprawled headlong, he slowly and hesitantly got back to his feet and still came limping forwards determinedly. A third bullet in the head as he was about ten metres away finished him off. He sagged forwards. His skull hit the road with a crack.

Sergeant Hutchison had waited the longest, conserving

ammunition. When the third infected, a younger man with a shaved head and a tattoo across his neck, was only a dozen steps away he fired twice. Both shots accurately found their mark. They obliterated the man's face, replacing the tattoo with blood and splattered tissue. Walkden's target was now upon him and he was panicking. He backed up to the vehicle with a frightened, groan. His rounds became wilder and missed their target but a single, cool shot from Hutchison ended the assault.

It was over in a moment. None of them spoke as they searched for more attackers. The blasts from their weapons still reverberated in their ears. They were all shaken but Walkden visibly more so than his colleagues. He was leaning on the bonnet and looked as though he was about to collapse. Hutchison took a deep breath to steady his own nerves and then tried to focus. It was clear that Walkden would now be useless on lookout and so to utilise him to their best advantage Hutchison handed him the spanner. "Here sir, get cracking with this."

Walkden just nodded and took the tool.

"You okay?" Hutchison said to Neale.

"I guess so Sarge."

"Get on the radio. Tell them back at base what's happened and most important of all, keep your eyes peeled. That was a little too close for comfort. We don't want any more surprises."

"Sure thing boss."

Sebastian jumped down onto the roof terrace over-looking the forecourt just as Cujo was giving his life so selflessly. He calmly removed his sunglasses and peered below. He made a quick estimation of numbers and odds, then whistled softly. He knew what he had to do. He was not scared. He merely had a heightened sense of awareness; heightened even for a vampire, as the excitement of the pre-kill flowed through his veins. He had not faced odds like this in an age, since long before on the outskirts of a rural French village in Provence. Humans had discovered his hideout and marched mob-handed to drive him out, armed with basic weapons, farming implements and sticks. He remembered the feel of the blows as he defended himself, at first trying not to hurt anyone whilst only attempting to escape, but then being cornered and forced to fight. That was when the bloodlust had taken over. Others of his sort called it a red mist but that would imply that he had lost sight of his actions and he most certainly had not. For a moment he had become enraged and turned, but only for a moment, into what he despised, but what he had to be in order to survive. He could vividly remember the terror in their eyes and the screams as they attempted to flee, as he slaughtered them all. He had sworn to himself that he would never let that happen again. He knew on this occasion though there would be no terror. The only screams would be of anger, not of fear, and unlike the previous time he could absolutely not afford to allow them to draw blood.

As he was about to step forwards and drop into the maelstrom of hatred below there was the light scent of flowers and another figure landed softly beside him with barely a thump. He turned to stare into the deep blue, unfathomable gaze of Flavia. It was an unusual perfume that she wore, reminiscent of wisteria, but he found it quite endearing, reminding him of times gone by.

Her red lips parted in a provocative smirk. "Hello Sebastian, fancy seeing you here."

He returned her gaze and her smile. "Hello Flavia, where's your boyfriend?"

"I do go out alone sometimes. I'm a big girl now."

"Yes I can see that," and he did nothing to hide the

appreciative glance he cast over her curves, causing her to grin in a self-satisfied way. There was a certain flirtatious tension between them that vanished whenever Farzin was around. As he looked into her eyes he could feel himself involuntarily warming towards her and mentally steeled himself against her spell. He had seen the effect she had on men and did not want to become just another lapdog around her, fool to her charms. He did not particularly trust her, never had, but that probably had more to do with the nature of their first meeting.

"You surely aren't thinking of being the hero all by yourself?"

He looked grimly back at her. "Well come on then, let's do it."

"Just make sure you don't get bitten," she warned as she stepped out over the precipice and launched herself down towards the fracas. He couldn't help but appreciate the irony in her comment, coming from a vampire, before following her over the edge.

Collins watched with horror as the swelling mass pressed against the door which was now bearing an enormous force. The upper hinges would not hold for long so they were desperately trying to manhandle another display rack on top of the initial two. From outside the livid howls were growing in intensity. The glass panels suddenly cracked making them both jump back. The wire mesh still held the glass in place however, but for how much longer?

Bannister grabbed Collins by the arm and spoke quickly. Fear was evident in his eyes although she could see that he was still rational and calm. "That door is not going to last. My SA80 was beside me on the seat and I left it in the wagon when I jumped out after you. All I've got is my pistol. Where's Samuels's rifle?"

Collins looked crestfallen. "He lost it when he took a tumble; it's just outside the shop. Mine's out of ammo. I only have my pistol as well."

"Well, Walkden and the cavalry better get here soon, else we're royally screwed!"

As he spoke the door partly gave way and cracked open. The first of the infected was a haggard looking woman. She wore a black shawl and would not have been out of place playing the part of a witch from Macbeth. She tried to wriggle through the breach but the gap was still not quite wide enough for her. Her head and one arm and shoulder poked into the shop and she stretched out towards the soldiers whilst screaming. Her blood-shot eyes were bulging and the veins on her temples protruding. Collins flung herself against the barricades trying to force the door closed, but Bannister stepped slowly forwards until he was almost within the woman's reach.

Collins watched aghast as Bannister stood a few inches from the woman's fingers. He could feel her hot, rancid breath as she screamed, could see the red lines like crazy paving on her face, the liver spots that had formed across her forehead and the dry, flaking skin on her cheeks and chin. He stared calmly into her incognisant eyes, glaring at him with a total absence of empathy or conception and for the first time in a while he felt pity. This was the closest he had come to one of them; the first time he had ever really contemplated them as anything more than 'zombies'. The woman was probably not as old as she had initially seemed but the ravages of the condition had aged her unnaturally. Hanging around her neck was a small, golden necklace that bore the name 'Giselle'. It struck him as out of place, as much as anything because this small trinket was a reminder of the woman's past, her life while she was still a normal human being that was so at odds with the unrecognisable monster that she had now become. The name also reminded him of his youth, like a blossom, an unusual yet delicate and unforgettable name of possibly the first girl he had ever had a crush on whilst in primary school. The Giselle of his past was now certainly gone too, either dead or one of these 'undead' creatures.

As she tried feverishly to reach him he stepped away from her. He slowly raised his Browning and fired a single shot into her face, ripping her head apart as she jerked back, spraying the inside of the windows with blood and flesh and releasing her from her unholy torment. Her body slumped forwards like a nun praying at the altar. The next was right behind, trying to climb over her and through the slowly widening gap. He was a youth of possibly seventeen or eighteen years old and even as he scrambled forwards, a larger man also tried to get into the shop, causing a jam and preventing either of them from gaining access. For a moment the two of them attacked each other, clawing and biting at each other's faces. This bought the soldiers a moment's reprieve. Bannister turned to Collins with a grim expression that she had never seen him wear before. There was a fatalistic look in his eyes, as though he had already prepared himself for the inevitable.

"Conserve your ammo," he said. "Make every shot count. Go for the head, one round for each lurcher, understood? And if it comes to the end, save your last bullet for yourself. And one for me too. Now try Walkden once more."

"Walkden, where the hell are you?" she cried into her radio as she backed up to the wall in the small shop.

There was nothing but static, no comforting reply from the cavalry about to save the day. Bannister stooped over Samuels's body and removed the man's pistol from its holster, then turned back to the door with both guns aimed at the creatures without. He too backed up against the wall beside Collins. She felt the reassuring press of his arm against hers, feeling incredibly small and vulnerable. Despite his words and despite his show of bravado, clearly he did not want to die any more than she did.

As they looked out at the multitude there was a sudden commotion and for a moment the infected all seemed to be diverted by a flash of movement and a shadow.

"Walkden?" Collins asked, but Bannister did not answer.

Both of them stared in amazement, not quite sure they could believe what they were seeing. It seemed that two figures had entered the fray at the back and were attacking with nothing more than their bare hands. And they appeared to be winning.

Sebastian landed right after Flavia and just beside her, only a step away from the fight. Both of them initially lashed out with well-placed kicks, slamming the two nearest diseased into the group and knocking several to the ground, but only for a moment. Both vampires pressed forwards into the skirmish. With reflexes like striking cobras they attacked. Sebastian took hold of a woman by the collar of her jacket. He picked her up and sent her flying backwards, taking care to avoid her snapping teeth. She crashed hard into a wall with enough force to stun a normal human. The woman gave a piercing shriek and staggered to her feet with one arm hanging loosely from her side and a gash across her head. She did not seem bothered by the injuries but was more concerned with tearing the eyes out of her enemy. The other infected now started to turn their wrath from the shop. They quickly became intent on ripping apart this most recent foe. These initial manoeuvres by the two vampires bought them a little space and had the effect of scattering the assailants so that the attacks did not all come at once, but they had not actually reduced the infected and there was still an alarmingly overwhelming number.

The first to get to Sebastian was a large, black man with short, dark hair and a savage wound on his cheek. He came in low and tried to throw himself around Sebastian's waist like a rugby player. Sebastian dodged to the side and brought an elbow down hard on the man's spine sending him to the floor. He instantly slammed his heel down onto the man's thick neck and felt a crack as it broke like a chicken bone. The man flinched, his legs spasmed and he moved no more. It had taken Sebastian a mere moment to kill the man, effortlessly and indifferently, and he leapt forwards at the next victim.

Flavia's first assailant was an elderly woman with an old-fashioned blue rinse in her grey hair and a dirty, flowery house-coat. She still clutched the cloth handbag that had probably not left her side when out of the house during the past twenty years. She was relatively slow and Flavia dispatched her with ease. The woman had come at her from behind but Flavia sensed her and aimed a well-placed kick backwards at the woman's head with a vicious lunge and a snarl that bared her long, sharp teeth. The single impact cracked the woman's skull to the side, leaving her lying motionless on the ground with a faint trickle of dark liquid oozing from the fissure. The two vampires now found themselves back to back with the infected surrounding them and approaching somewhat more warily. Although the diseased knew no fear they seemed to be able to learn and reason, to an extent.

There was a rush of activity and several attacked at once. They were considerably slower than the vampires but their sheer numbers made fighting them a challenge. Sebastian grabbed the first and threw him to the side. Simultaneously he lashed out with a boot sending another stumbling. A third came at him immediately, a young man probably in his early twenties with long, dank hair and a pointed goatee beard. He tried to grab at Sebastian and seemed to be smiling as he leered at his prey. Sebastian was way too quick and easily manoeuvred out of his reach but then darted back close enough to grasp the man's head between his hands. He rotated it with a sudden movement until there was the unmistakable snap of bones and the man hit the ground. At this stage it was all about trying to make space and slowly erode their adversaries.

Two more lunged forwards and managed to grasp Sebastian's arm. He retreated and stumbled over the large man he had killed first. From within the shop Collins gasped in fear for the stranger without really knowing why. Maybe she already felt some inexplicable connection with him, or perhaps she just saw the two strangers as their salvation.

Sebastian went down on one knee. He felt the throng press forwards. For a moment he could foresee them falling on top of him and making it impossible to escape. Another darted around the side with a strange, blood thirsty gurgle, sensing the opening, but Flavia reacted much faster - faster even than Sebastian. With stunning speed she yanked the man by the neck backwards off his feet and tossed him behind her with an air of utter disdain. Then she leapt at the two who had grasped Sebastian's arm.

Both of them were on top of him, thrashing and snapping as he held their combined weight with one arm, his other hand momentarily steadying himself on the ground. Flavia braced herself and then reached for them, hauling them both off their feet in a massively impressive display of force. She swung around and then released them with a righteous scream, sending them tumbling back into the melee, buying a moment of breathing space.

She turned back to Sebastian, grabbed him by the hand and hauled him to his feet. "Get up you pussy, this is no time to rest."

He could see there was a glint in her eye. Her chest heaved beneath the scant corset and he was sure she was enjoying herself. Then she twirled about to fight with a hiss of pure aggression. He observed her for the briefest of moments. He was undoubtedly stronger than she, but there was an effortless grace to her movements. She had an efficiency that made her absolutely lethal and awe-inspiring yet elegant and beautiful to watch. The way she pirouetted from one victim to another without pause was truly impressive. The slightest flicker of a smile traced across his lips as he too returned to the fray.

From within the shop Collins stood quite still and silent. She was awestruck, finding it hard to believe what she was seeing. To her the two figures looked sort of like normal people, albeit tall and willowy, but their actions were more feline than human. The woman in particular fought with a poise and refinement, as though she was going through the motions of some cold, deadly dance, and the speed with which they both moved was absolutely breath-taking. They seemed to anticipate each other and acted accordingly, complementing and covering each other perfectly like paramours. To Collins the woman's outfit only seemed to enhance the image of the performance, a gothic ballerina playing the part of an enraged killer in some truly macabre, apocalyptic ballet. She was mesmerized by the phenomenal display of agility and ruthlessness as attacker after attacker was felled.

Bannister too was rapt by the strange woman whose

feminine figure and outfit seemed at odds with the master-class in dispatch that she was providing. He watched the creases of her tight leather trousers, the swing in the lace around her corset, the pout in her beautiful, red lips and the lightning glances in his direction, real or imagined, as she leapt like a mongoose playing in a den of vipers. For a moment the troubles of the last few minutes faded. The woman outside was everything.

He was revived from his contemplation by a groan from Samuels. He checked the man's pulse and prised opened his eyes to see if there was any reaction to the light. Samuels moaned again and seemed to be coming to his senses, so Bannister, relieved that he was okay, returned to the scene outside.

"Who are they?" Collins breathed, captivated now by the tall man in black who moved with a little less poise but seemed equally capable and deadly, and held himself with a detached fearlessness. His was less the action of a dancer and more that of a boxer or martial artist, an economy of effort with huge power, using strength instead of subtlety.

"I don't know but I'd sure like to find out," Bannister murmured, absolutely spellbound now.

"You're not thinking about actually going out there are you?"

Collins glanced at him in surprise that he could seem so relaxed at a time like this and then returned her gaze to the man outside who had just pounded the skull of an infected woman into the pavement. He leapt to his feet and glanced in their direction. For a moment she could see his light, hazel eyes searching inside the shop. She instinctively went to crouch down but he turned his attention back to more urgent matters such as killing and survival.

196

The woman at his side seemed to be taking great delight in the mêlée. She would leap high into the air and then come down hard on the back of an attacker, grinding them into the floor. She would then quickly finish them by smashing their heads on the concrete or pulling their necks forcefully back until the bones splintered. This move she typically finished off by violently twisting the head and pulling, which seemed to leave the skull hanging limply. A middle-aged man in a black suit came at her so she grabbed his arm and swung him around before releasing. The momentum that she had generated she then used to propel herself gracefully through the air and landed with a boot in the face of a young man, sending him to the floor. She paused hardly a moment on any one combatant before using the energy and impetus to strike at the next in a truly dazzling display of slaughter.

The fight had barely lasted a minute. In that time Walkden had tightened the second and third wheel bolts and was about to start on the fourth. Sergeant Hutchison grabbed him under the arm and hauled him to his feet. "Right, that'll do, into the car," he yelled urgently. "We're not going far, it'll hold. Let's go."

Neale was already in the driver's seat, revving the engine like a boy-racer at the traffic-lights in Southend-on-Sea. Even before Hutchison's door closed he had popped the clutch and the wheels span. Hutchison had disconnected the trailer from the Land Rover. As they careered along the road he checked his gun and ordered Walkden to do the same. Walkden complied without saying anything. They rounded the final corner practically on two wheels and it was only then that Hutchison first realised that the sounds of gunfire had stopped. He could see the other Land Rover ahead by the petrol station and a load of bodies on the floor around it.

"Good lord, it's bloody carnage!"

Bannister was already pulling at the barricade as the last of the infected was killed.

"Come on, help me," he urged.

Collins hesitantly went to his assistance. As she bent down a shadow swept over her. She looked up and shuddered. Both of the strangers were standing at the broken window peering in with odd expressions on their faces, somewhere between euphoric recognition and the shyness of anxious children on their first day at a new school. She felt the male's eyes fixed on her as she staggered back in shock, her knees nearly going from under her.

What happened next was a little unclear when she later tried to recall it, but one of the strangers pushed hard at the door which effortlessly seemed to shove the remaining display unit out of the way. Bannister sauntered forwards as though he was sleep-walking. Collins backed up nervously against the shop counter as the man entered. She vaguely noticed Bannister step close to the woman. After a moment of saying something to him, she seemed to enwrap him in an embrace.

The tall man advanced with long, purposeful strides. He stopped a yard away as she raised her pistol. He looked down at the gun and then fixed his eyes upon her and smiled. It was the most unexpected expression. After the battle that they had just witnessed with all that bloodshed, and the fact that she was pointing a gun at his head, a calm, friendly smile was the last thing she expected. But there it was, reassuring and intensely disarming.

"Do not be afraid."

His words seemed to come from some deep, inner part of him like rumbling thunder in the distance. It felt as though she had imagined them as much as heard them. He held her stare and his eyes were hazel coloured although they seemed to flash an intimidating dark. When someone has a gun pointed at them their entire attention tends to concentrate solely upon it, a response known as 'weapon focus'. Everything else at that moment pales into insignificance and for a short while the weapon becomes the centre of that person's world. Although it was she that held the Browning, that was exactly how Collins felt. Like tunnel vision, anything outside the man's eyes and voice seemed irrelevant. She stared at him and was captivated. Only then did she notice that she had unconsciously lowered the gun. In surprise she was jerked out of her semi-trance and raised it again but this time a little less decisively.

"You have nothing to fear from me," he said with a smile and this time she held his gaze and lowered the gun deliberately.

"Who are you?" she whispered, entranced.

He opened his mouth to answer but never got the chance to speak.

There was the squeal of brakes from outside as the second Land Rover announced its arrival. The tall, pale woman called from outside.

"Sebastian."

He turned to look, flashed one last, lingering smile at Collins and then leapt through the door.

Hutchison was already out of the vehicle and trained his gun on the two figures. "Stop!" he shouted, but they ignored him and ran to the building beside the petrol station. Hutchison dodged around the petrol pumps and corpses and followed them but by the time he reached the area they were already gone.

Like a rush of blood to the head after standing up too quickly, Collins felt dizzy and steadied herself with a hand on the counter. It was as though the world was returning to her senses in a giddy rush of colours and sounds with the beating of her heart thumping in her head. Only then did she notice Samuels was now awake, propped up against the shelf unit and staring curiously at her.

"Thank God you are okay." She went to him, still unsteady on her feet. "Are you hurt?"

"I'm fine. Sorry for... for not being there to help out. Are you okay?"

She was not sure if there was extra emphasis on 'you', having witnessed her encounter with the strange man.

"I'm fine," she said. Then to change the subject she continued in a flustered voice, "Bannister's outside."

"I know. I saw him."

Hutchison entered the shop. He seemed to have assumed command and checked them all over to make sure no one was injured.

"Has anyone been bitten?" They both shook their heads dumbly. "Okay, all the infected outside are dead. Who the hell were those two people?"

Bannister drifted back into the shop and seemed to Collins as though he was still half asleep.

"I have no idea who they were," she said, "but if they hadn't arrived when they did we wouldn't be standing here right now." She looked at Bannister for support but his eyes were glazed over and he was not his normal talkative self. "Isn't that right Bannister?" she prompted.

"Oh, yes, definitely. They came at a good time," he said. Then as though coming back to reality he rounded angrily on Hutchison. "Where were you when we needed you?"

Hutchison glanced at Walkden who stood keeping guard. "Yeah, sorry, we ran into a little trouble of our own but nothing compared to what you faced here."

They all turned to survey the scene outside, lost in contemplation and amazement. Bodies were scattered all around the forecourt with twisted, broken limbs and dark liquid oozing. It was a dreadful scene and quickly reminded them where they were.

Hutchison nervously walked to the door. "Let's head back to base. We can debrief there."

They got rapidly back into their Land Rovers. Collins inspected the building the strangers had climbed in their swift departure. It was a two storey shop with a sloping, tiled roof. It had windows on upper and lower levels but as far as she could see there was no obviously easy way to scale it, and yet they had gone up it in moments without any apparent difficulty. She could see no sign of them now however as the vehicles pulled away and headed back to Headley Court.

The drive did not take long, Hutchison quickly established radio contact with base and informed them briefly that they had encountered hostiles but nobody had been seriously injured. The voice of Senior Aircraftman Masters replied. He told them he had copied the information and that he would pass it on to Group Captain Denny.

As they drove, Samuels spoke from the back seat in a hushed, shaken voice. He was pale with a trickle of blood on his temple.

"Guys, I'm really sorry, I screwed up back there. I guess I took a tumble. Thanks for saving my arse."

Bannister was morose and even more curt than normal. "Just don't do it again, idiot."

Collins scowled at Bannister then looked back at Samuels. She was trembling, partly through shock and partly through adrenaline, but Bannister's reply annoyed her. "Actually if you hadn't given us covering fire and slowed them all down we may never have made it. You bought us some vital time so you didn't screw up too badly." She smiled reassuringly.

He still looked puzzled, as though something was bothering him. "When I came round all the infected were dead. Who were those other two?"

Collins and Bannister exchanged a glance. "I'm not sure who they were," Collins answered, "but they single-handedly tore that crowd apart. They were unarmed and they went through the lot of them like a bunch of school kids."

Samuels had not lost his frown. "They looked kinda odd, foreign or something and they dressed funny. And then I'm not sure I was quite with it yet, but from where I was lying it looked like she bit you Bannister."

"What would you know?" Bannister rounded on him. "You were concussed, fool."

"Well that's how it looked to me too," Collins said irritably. She stared hard at Bannister, waiting for an answer.

He was silent for a moment, brooding with an angry look on his face. "It all seems a little hazy," he said eventually, without taking his eyes off the road. "I think I'm still a bit traumatised from the whole episode, but no, no she didn't."

Collins then noticed a small prick of blood on his neck, just above the collar. Just a single red mark but a tell-tale sign nevertheless, denouncing his lie. She reached over and rubbed it. "Blood! She did bite you."

Bannister was getting more cross now and pulled his collar up to cover the mark. "I don't know," he said sullenly, "it seems really weird. I don't know why I went to her. I guess I was going to thank her for saving our lives. Then she hugged me. Like I say, I was still in a state of shock but maybe she did, I'm not sure." He became contemplative once more and this time the hush remained.

As they neared the base a sense of reality started to return and Collins's thoughts went to Cujo. Her face creased and she buried her head in her hands, her shoulders shaking with grief. Bannister looked briefly across at her but for once he was distracted and did not bother to use the occasion of her tears to put an arm around her shoulders or ingratiate himself towards her. At the moment he felt cold and emotionless. With his eyes resolutely fixed on the road in front, he drove back to the station, his mind full of his own troubled thoughts.

CHAPTER 10

Flavia was faster than Sebastian, faster than any of them, but she paused on a flat piece of roof, allowing him to catch up. Her eyes were glistening and flashing animatedly as the excitement from the encounter still coursed through her body. She reminded him of a champion thoroughbred that has just won its race, her sides heaving with exhilaration and exertion.

She turned to greet him with a broad grin as he approached. "Kinda reminds you you're alive, huh? And they call us undead - pah!"

"Hmmm," he was contemplative. "You enjoyed that?"

"Of course, what's not to enjoy? Don't tell me you didn't. I could see it in your eyes - when you finally got into the spirit of it."

"No."

"Not even a little bit?"

He was annoyed now but more with himself than her and tried to keep it from his voice. Facing the distinct possibility of death, yet coming out victorious had undoubtedly given him a heightened sense of elation and an appreciation of life that was too often missing, especially in an existence as prolonged as theirs. He did not want to admit to himself that he had enjoyed the experience but there was a certain, undeniable truth in what Flavia said.

"They are humans, or at least they were once," he replied tersely. "I feel sorry for them and wish that had not been necessary."

"That's right, they were human once, but just like us they're not any more. Their humanity is as far behind them as ours is behind us. And it was necessary - very. They would have torn you apart and eaten your flesh given half a chance. They're now nothing more than animals acting on basic urges. They don't feel pain, they don't get frightened, all they do is follow their instincts and that instinct is to kill you and eat you. I suggest you follow their example and become a little more concerned about saving your own skin, rather than not hurting theirs. I may not be there to save you next time. That's twice I've saved your arse. We wouldn't want to lose such a fine body part would we now." The look in her eyes was playful and mischievous but Sebastian could see there was a serious tinge to it. "Just remember that you owe me. Twice."

"Yes, thank you. I'll bear that in mind."

He always felt that she was more relaxed around him when Farzin was not there, but lately it seemed as though she was being a *lot* more flirtatious. The end of the world had brought many things to a head. Was she acting differently towards him, or was it just in his imagination? He was briefly taken back to a time, many years previously, but tried to focus on the present.

"So you actually *enjoyed* killing them?" he asked.

She thought about it for a moment before replying. Her bottom lip jutted out in a slight moue that he always found endearing, even now. "I guess not, the killing wasn't the important thing for me. Like a matador I enjoy the sport of it, but personally I do not actually feel the need to *kill* them. That is merely a consequence. For me I enjoyed the fact that there were so many of them, that one wrong move at any time and they would have been upon me. I'd have been bitten and then who knows what would have happened. Now Farzin, he would have enjoyed the killing itself just for the sake of it, but not me."

Sebastian could agree with the sentiments although he would not have admitted it to her. He wondered whether she was just saying what she thought he wanted to hear, and if that was the case, then why? Did she really want to endear herself to him? Or perhaps that actually was just how she felt? He wondered if he would ever really know and suspected not. Ever since the collapse of mankind, things in the vampire clan had become even more strained. They were all suffering together.

She was watching him closely and could see that her comments had hit a nerve. Again she was perplexed as to why he was such a closed book to her. There was one more thing that bothered her though. "The girl - why did you not take blood? You had just saved her life. You didn't need to end hers but you could have drunk to satiate your thirst, as repayment of her debt. Why did you not?"

He knew this was not something he could easily explain to her or to any of the other clan members. As vampires they saw it as their justifiable right to do what they had to in order to survive. Drinking a human's blood did not necessarily condemn them to death, nor to a life supposedly after death. Perhaps though, being the most recently 'turned' of his clan members his connection to his past human life was the strongest and this tended to discourage him from the blood of humans.

There was something else though; possibly because of the elation after the fight, but for once he *had* been tempted to drink from her. The girl's expression however, the look in her eyes of wonder and awe, had stopped him. And although he had deliberately calmed her fear and put her at ease with some gentle mind-manipulation, it was *he* who had felt disarmed and *he* could not get her image out of his head. The feelings he experienced through once again being close to humans was unsettling.

"I guess the second vehicle arrived too soon," he muttered darkly.

"Nonsense. You had time, if you had wanted to. Don't tell me you felt something for the girl?" She had read him well.

"Of course not," he snapped irritably but she was smiling now.

"Sebastian, all these years you could have had me and now you fall for a human. Just wait till I tell the others," and with that she ran to the roof's edge and leapt out into space, her arms wide open like a cliff-diver at Acapulco. He watched her admiringly for a moment, all grace and purpose and agility, and then followed her half-heartedly, hanging back. He played her words around in his mind somewhat ruefully, knowing that although she was teasing him, this was not the whole truth.

By the time he arrived back at the church the sun was setting and the shadows in the graveyard were growing. He alighted on the first floor window ledge and with hardly a pause vaulted through. Flavia was already talking to Farzin and Alec and all three looked at him when he entered. Unless he was mistaken, a certain tension entered the room along with him.

Farzin spoke first. "I hear you have encountered the humans. And you defended them from the infected. An eventful day it would seem." Then without waiting for a reply he turned back to Flavia. "And what is this on your mouth my dear? Human blood?"

There was a slight red stain just by the corner of her lips and she smiled. "Yes my love, I saved it for you."

"Ahhh, but how sweet of you." He cupped the back of her head in his hands as though he were holding a large chalice and bent forward to lick the blood from her with great satisfaction and an overly theatrical display of delight. Just as he finished and pulled back she glanced at Sebastian to see if he was watching. He turned away from her smug smile.

Darius and Max alighted on the window sill and climbed swiftly inside. Darius surveyed the scene

207

quizzically and turned to Max. "I sense there is something afoot here. Has anybody got anything to tell me?" He looked almost accusingly around the room.

"Yes my lord," Flavia answered with a slight, deferential bow of her head. "Sebastian and I happened to chance upon a party of some three soldiers under attack from a group of the contaminated. We killed the contaminated and defended the soldiers from certain death. I tasted human blood, the first time for a while."

Her mention of blood brought a faint gasp from Darius and Max who reacted like addicts denied a shot of their drug of choice. They stooped forwards slightly and seemed as though they would start to salivate.

Darius mulled this revelation over before speaking. "This is interesting news indeed. And how did you leave the humans?"

"More arrived suddenly. They were all armed and we thought best to depart before any 'misunderstandings' could occur."

"Yes, very wise. And?" This was good news that further encounters with the group of humans had occurred so soon, but it was not enough in itself to get overly excited. They needed to know where the humans were based in order to make proper contact.

"And I feel sure that I will be seeing at least one of them again presently. I believe I left him feeling as though he wanted a little more from me. I will find out where they stay and report back to you as soon as possible my lord." She bowed again but glanced at Sebastian who remained silent.

Darius saw the glance, frowned slightly and turned to Sebastian. "Very well. Do you have anything further to add?"

"No my lord," and he too bowed. "It was exactly as Flavia has said." He wondered why she had not mentioned his omission to drink human blood, whether she had decided better of it, or had chosen to store that information for another time more useful to herself.

"Good, I hope to hear about further encounters before too long. Perhaps the two of you can take me out to show me where you met with the humans. Perhaps we can pick up their trail and find them again."

"Of course my lord," they both answered in unison.

However Farzin was not content to leave the conversation at that. As far as he was concerned this represented a prime opportunity and although he knew only too well how the conversation would progress he could not contain himself.

"So the humans have seen how pathetic their attempts are at staying alive without our intervention. Now would be a good time, would you not agree my lord, to press our advantage. When we find out where they reside we should go to them and take what is ours. Now they have seen us we need to act fast."

Sebastian could see that Darius was angered. The Clan Leader took a step towards Farzin who stood his ground, a defiant glare smouldering in his eyes. How long, Sebastian wondered, until those glowing embers became ablaze with the unquenchable flames of revolt? Ever since Sebastian had joined the clan, Farzin had been difficult; testy and wilful. Long had he assumed that he would ultimately replace Darius as Clan Leader and Darius's preference of Luca was clearly a source of continual annoyance and had caused division. But Sebastian knew, as Darius and the rest of them also knew, that Farzin would not make a good leader. Even before the rift had begun to form he had been too impulsive and aggressive, and doubly so of late. Frequently he would react with unnecessary hostility when a more measured approach was preferable. He was certainly a strong character, had a charismatic air, and had played a part in keeping them all together over the years, but it would not be wise to put him in a position of overall authority. Luca had been in the clan longer than Sebastian and so was the obvious choice. Farzin seemed to bear no malice towards Luca and had even remained cordial towards Darius, until very recently with all the troubles in the human world, when his defiance could no longer be restrained.

Darius replied to Farzin with control and reason, his voice low and calm and persuasive. "I agree with you Farzin, now is indeed a good time to press forward our advantage. The humans have seen that they cannot hope to exist in this new world without our benevolence and protection. Now is the perfect time to go to them with our offer of assistance in return for their 'allegiance'. Now is the time to forge a perfect, symbiotic relationship, with each party aiding the other, not to become parasites and feed off them, giving nothing in return."

"I do not seek only to take. They will be receiving the gift of life, which is something that they will not have for much longer without us."

"And what is this 'gift' of life without freedom? If once we start down this route then forever will they see us as the enemy, and if they once again gain the upper hand then woe betide us for treating them thus."

"I would have it so that they will not gain the upper hand again. We are in a position to create as large a vampire army as we require and enslave the humans to serve us as we see fit. There is no longer a need to hide in fear. We are the dominant race and it is time that we take our rightful position as such."

At this point there was a soft swish from the window and Luca sprang lightly and elegantly through, landing a couple of metres into the room. His dark hair glistened in the dim light and was slicked tightly back against his thin head. His usually pristine white shirt was ruffled and there was a tiny stain of blood on the end of the exposed collar. He wore clothes from an expensive Italian designer. A fitted, graphite, cashmere gilet was over the shirt, tailored charcoal trousers met brown suede ankle boots and a cobalt cravat finished the look. The only item that was not Italian was a slim Swiss watch with silver dial, black face and black strap. He looked as though he belonged on a catwalk or adorning the pages of a fashion magazine as much as in a vampire clan. He glanced around the room questioningly, clearly aware that a heated debate was going on, and felt slightly aggrieved that yet again an important conversation was occurring in his absence. He said nothing though but waited until a more appropriate moment to interject with his own not insignificant news.

Farzin turned now to Sebastian with a look that could have been aggressive or conspiratorial, it was not clear which. Sebastian always tried to avoid getting involved in these quarrels, just as he had in human life. He did realize however that the time was coming to take a side and be willing to back that up. Killing a human, whether diseased or otherwise, was not something that he relished, but like any animal, if his own life was threatened and there was no alternative then he would do what was necessary. However, if things within the clan became hostile and violence erupted, then killing a vampire would be a much harder thing. He did not even really know how it could be physically done and doubted whether he could bring himself to do it emotionally.

The relationship between Sebastian and Farzin had at times been tense, largely due to Sebastian's association with Flavia, but each of them would, he assumed, always have looked out for the other. Current events in human civilization had precipitated a radical and rapid change in

211

Farzin's attitude and it was clear that matters were coming to a head. He did not fear Farzin. He knew that he had a size and strength advantage over him. However, strength is not always the best way to win a battle. Farzin was undoubtedly cunning and savage, and to underestimate him would be folly. Farzin was more vicious and unpredictable, and over these last few days and weeks being in his company had been akin to being sat in the same carriage as an unpleasant drunk on a night train; one just never knows what he is going to do next and it is wise to keep one's distance unless one is actively pursuing trouble.

"You were there Sebastian. You have seen the humans. How did it feel to be so close to such delightful nourishment only to see it disappear once more out of reach? Do you not feel as though having defended those pitiful creatures from certain death you now deserve your reward?" A small amount of spittle was projected as he spat out the word 'pitiful'.

Sebastian wondered again why Flavia had not mentioned his omission to drink of human blood. Perhaps it had been to avoid causing him a confrontation, as clearly Farzin would not understand his attitude. He looked deeply into those baleful eyes full of resentment and held the gaze, not aggressively but without fear or cowering. Over recent weeks he had seen the anger in those darkened pupils grow as the self-control dissipated, much like the infected humans. Not long now, he thought. Not long.

"I agree with you in that the humans today would undoubtedly have perished without our intervention. With our aid their likelihood of survival is indeed greatly increased but exactly what we would be due for our assistance is not a matter that we can conclude by ourselves. In this negotiation there are two parties and we cannot say what they should be willing to give up for our custody. You ask me whether we should take what we deem is our due by force; I would rather be ruler by dint of love or admiration or respect than through coercion and fear."

"So at last your position is clear." He said the words with a hint of a sneer. "I must admit to being a little disappointed in you." He glanced briefly at Flavia as he spoke.

"I am happy to disappoint," Sebastian replied evenly. His final words caused a further flicker of anger to ignite in Farzin's eyes as he glared back.

Flavia watched the interchange more closely than the others as she stood between the two. Tensions and passions of more than one kind, that had long been buried deep, were now bubbling close to the surface and were detrimental to the stability and status quo of the clan. Flavia could sense the feeling of frustration in her partner and she understood it. He believed wholeheartedly that the time for the vampire was now. The moment had come to right the wrongs of the last thousand years, to end the days of oppression and hiding and become the rightful masters at the top of the food chain without the need to barter for that position. Like the tiger stepping out of the forest and in amongst the weary villagers, he believed they should be able to go where they pleased and take what had been denied them for far too long. Flavia agreed with him; to an extent. But there was truth in what Sebastian said also, although she was careful to avoid saying as much.

Even now with emotions high and their guards removed she could still not fully read Sebastian and it frustrated her. Not that she could actually read the minds of others, it was more an extension of 'women's intuition'. As a human she had always been extremely insightful. Her instincts were so acute they had gained her a reputation for being a witch. This was something that did no one any favours back in those days in France, and led to her having to flee Paris and head south before she was turned and became vampyric. Now, like all vampires, she had fine-tuned that skill so that she knew intuitively what people were thinking, and she was without doubt the virtuoso amongst them. The slight dilation in someone's eyes, the tiniest of frowns or pouts, a faraway look, a quickening pulse and small beads of perspiration forming upon the upper lip, an overly stressed vowel, a slight indrawn breath after a certain word whilst rubbing ones hands nervously together; these little signs were all as clear to her as the correct course for the vampires was to Farzin. She read this secret language like a story in black and white. She often guessed what someone was going to say before they spoke and knew how they were likely to react. But that was not now, and never had been, the case with Sebastian. It may have been due to the manner of his turning, she did not know, but it vexed her, and if she were to be honest it fascinated her as well, a fact she realised she would do well never to mention to Farzin. She stepped close to his side and mouthed something in his ear and the tension seemed to leave his shoulders and hence the room. As Flavia led Farzin gently away, nobody, not even she, noticed the smug smirk that fleetingly tainted his lips.

Darius turned briefly to acknowledge Luca but then strode to Sebastian's side and in a conspiratorial manner took his arm by the elbow. "These confrontations are becoming more common and increasingly vehement, I do not like it."

"No my lord, and neither do I."

Darius quickly changed the subject as though it gave him displeasure even to talk about it. "I would have you show me where you last saw the humans."

"Now, my lord?"

"Unless another matter preoccupies you? The sooner we regain their trail the more chance we have of tracking them. I have already wasted too much time in procrastination."

Sebastian bowed slightly. "As you wish, I am ready."

Luca had been waiting patiently to speak to Darius. "My lord, I too have news," he said, but Darius raised a hand to silence him.

"I am sorry Luca, I must go immediately. This is of the utmost importance. Can this wait until my return?" but it was a rhetorical question and he did not pause for a reply.

As Sebastian and Darius leapt through the window, Alec, who had remained standing in the far corner, now stepped forwards into the light. He noticed the sullen look on Luca's face and nodded almost imperceptibly at him with an expression that may possibly have been pity or empathy, before stalking from the room after his companions. Max, who had also lingered, noticed the brief exchange and it filled him with grave misgivings although he was not sure why. He was deeply concerned about the rift that had grown in the clan and wondered about Luca. He followed Darius and Sebastian, leaving Luca alone in the growing gloom with his inner torment; even vampires have their own personal demons to contend with.

Luca heard the other three in another area of the presbytery and wondered whether he should go to join them but decided quickly against it. With all that was going on he did not feel totally welcome or at ease in their company. He now noticed the speck of blood on his collar and wondered why the others had missed it. A fresh blood stain would not normally go unnoticed. It caused him to reflect on his own events of the past few hours. He

215

checked the rest of his attire, smoothing his clothes down and then rubbed in irritation at the blood. He had never quite lost his pride in his appearance, coming, as he did, from Italy.

Luca was born in a village called Modanella in central Italy where superstition and the myth of vampires was an everyday part of life amongst rural villagers. He had made the voyage to England aboard a container ship that was leased by a merchant of expensive coffins to export his wares to wealthy clients in the UK. Whilst it was mere fable that vampires spent their nights asleep inside a coffin, on this voyage however it had suited Luca's purpose. He had stolen on board with relative ease and spent the crossing in a state of trance-like catatonia inside a rather flamboyant casket with purple, felt lining. Ironically it was designed for the use of an elderly bishop from the diocese of Bath and Wells with ostentatious tastes, who would never know that its first occupant was somewhat less than accepted by his church.

Earlier, before the latest confrontation between Farzin and Darius, Luca had been some distance from the presbytery, enjoying the curious feeling of searching for sustenance with no particular caution or hurry. As for all of them, since the collapse of society this freedom to wander was such a complete novelty and he found pleasure in the most inconsequential of things. He had stood for a while in the middle of the street with his arms outstretched, staring towards the heavens, marvelling at the wonder of the sky and the clouds that scurried nervously by.

Luca's senses of smell and hearing were extremely acute even for a vampire, and as he meandered in an unknown area he had encountered a desirable scent, that of uncontaminated humans. It gave him an enormous thrill, like a child waking up on Christmas morning to the promise of untold gifts. The odour was faint and intermittent and seemed to be coming from a hospital that he was passing. A bead of perspiration formed on his brow and upper lip and he hardly noticed the fact that he was panting.

Harlow's imposing Princess Margaret Alexandra district hospital had been built of beige brick in the post-war years. Glass covered the road which gave a crunch to his normally silent footfalls, and for some reason there were hospital beds scattered outside the entrance, mostly overturned and splattered with blood. Lower windows were barricaded although a few of the boards had subsequently been torn off, and there were signs that some parts of the building had been ablaze. Various other medical accoutrements littered the grassy verge leading up to the main entrance, including a stethoscope, a pair of crutches and some bandages strewn like the aftermath of a rowdy football match.

Luca dropped into a crouch. He was no longer blinded by the tunnel vision of excitement. Guardedly he approached the entrance. His senses strained to detect the slightest anomaly. He paused regularly to sniff and listen. As he entered his eyes quickly adjusted to the gloom within. He passed through the entrance hall on the lower floor. There was nothing but broken chairs and tables and smashed glass. Puddles of dried blood still held the noxious odour of contagion. A discarded shoe was smeared with gory remains, a ragged ankle bone protruded from it. He wrinkled his nose in distaste. Over the smell of burnt wood it was hard to detect any other so he proceeded towards the main staircase where he caught the aroma once more.

He silently started to ascend with his back pressed to the wall. On each floor he paused. He tested the air like a serpent, then quickly moved on. He negotiated his way carefully around the detritus, chasing the scent with increased urgency. When he reached the fourth floor he suddenly became aware of a slight change in the atmosphere. It was as though someone was nearby and their shadow had momentarily obscured the light, or of the slightest of drafts stirred up by movement. He could see nothing above him on the staircase but felt that he was no longer alone. He froze, straining to hear what awaited him. He considered whether it was wise to continue, not that he was afraid, but just that the thought of becoming cornered in such a confined space by a horde of the diseased was folly. Then he caught another subtle whiff of humans and the decision was made.

He peered up the stairwell. Nothing moved in the gloom. There was not a sound, just a tomblike stillness so he proceeded more cautiously to the top floor. More broken furniture here littered the stairs. The perfume was strong and he began to feel intoxicated.

Just short of the top step a man was laid on his back. There were dark stains on his shirt which had been pierced several times and blood had pooled around his upper torso. It was not clear whether he had died from these injuries or from smashing his head open as he lurched backwards down the stairs. What *was* certain from the odour and the flies that swarmed as Luca approached was that he had been dead for several days already, that and the fact that he had most certainly been contaminated.

There had been a significant barricade placed at the top of the stairs. Desks and chairs had been piled virtually to the ceiling and bound together blocking access, although clearly the infected had done their best to try to break through. Beyond, some wardrobes had been stacked and secured. The entire array looked firm, well thought out

218

and seemed to have served its purpose.

There were splashes of septic blood all over the furniture. The bodies of three more contaminated men and a woman were arranged in various poses over the nearer desks like a ghoulish still life exhibition. The woman had several blatant, fleshy wounds festering around her shoulders and face, and a sharpened chair leg was still protruding from just under her jaw. The men were similarly marked and it looked as though there had been a horrendous struggle; the infected following nothing more than basic instincts and trying to get to fresh food, the defenders behind the barricades fighting desperately for their lives and to avoid the most horrible of fates.

Luca leapt at the obstructions now, dispensing with caution as he felt his goal nearing. He could not contain himself any further. He tore at the tables and sent them crashing down the stairwell. He smashed his way through the wardrobes without noticing the splinters that speared his fists. He was too excited to notice that despite the ruckus he was now creating, no humans came to attack him.

After a minute of hard work he finally smashed through the last wardrobe and stepped free into the open space beyond, all caution and subtlety had long been abandoned. By this time he was in a frenzy and no longer acting like a rational being. The tantalizing fragrance of his victims was overpowering and reminded him how much he missed the taste of human blood.

There was no sound or sign of anyone from within. There was an open area with beds, medical monitors and all the equipment of a normal operating hospital ward. Everything looked in fairly reasonable order with none of the chaos that was apparent on lower floors. This level had obviously remained devoid of the infected and had

219

served well as a safe-house, or perhaps as a prison. Leading away from the main section was a corridor and several smaller rooms which included offices, counselling rooms, lavatories and a treatment area that was cordoned off with curtains. In all areas there was no damage to furniture or windows. Everything was still very much in order and probably looked similar to how it had looked every day for years. There was evidence of survival in one of the rooms where a fire had been lit and empty food containers littered the floor. The lavatories stank of unflushed human waste and Luca did not loiter.

It was not the state of the place that was of interest to him however, he took all this in with a swift glance and a sense of disregard; he was solely interested in the presence of survivors. As he progressed he grew more and more agitated. In one of the offices he found the corpse of an adult male. The man had been dead for possibly a couple of days. He was lying on a trolley bed with his arms and legs bound securely to the frame. His shirt had been ripped and was stained with blood and his face had a distinct crimson hue to it. There was a large, open wound at his neck where he had been repeatedly stabbed by something sharp. It seemed odd that an ill person would have been kept in this safe haven for no good reason, but he was of no use to Luca who passed by quickly.

The other humans were in one of the further wards and looked as though they were sunbathing, lying side by side on their backs in the light from the far window. There were three of them, two men and a woman. One of the men was dressed in a torn, white shirt and grey suit trousers. The other two wore nurse's uniforms. Neither of the men had shaved in a while and their thick stubble and dishevelled appearance meant they probably did not look very different in death from how they had looked for the last week whilst still alive. Their waxy countenances bore the fixed expressions that they had worn as they died.

Luca rushed to the corpses and checked them over quickly yet thoroughly. There was no sign of infection and he could not smell anything to cause concern. There were no human bite marks on the cadavers although he did quickly discover other teeth marks - those of a vampire!

The three humans had undoubtedly died recently - very recently. A vampire would possibly recognize the bite marks of other clan members and Luca felt reasonably confident that they had not been killed by any of his fellows. He looked around and the only way he could think that the killer had gained access must have been through the window. With the significant revelation of others of his kind nearby he suddenly felt the presence of danger. In times such as these one could not be too careful, and he became vigilant once more. He had searched the adjoining rooms well enough and was quite sure that this vampire was no longer there. Nevertheless he could not be absolutely positive. He froze, sniffing, tasting the air and straining for the slightest sound. It was only then that he heard it - the distant creak of floorboards from somewhere below in the hospital, a rasp of laboured breathing, a heavy footfall on a stair. He looked towards the broken furniture of the barricade and saw nothing, so he quickly turned his attention back to the cadavers. He knew that whatever was making the noise below was most certainly not vampyric but may well arrive at any moment, and he would have to work quickly. Time was precious and escaping fast.

The nearest body was the female. He dragged her closer to the window and propped her legs up on the sill in order to pool the blood towards her head. An aficionado in death, he probed her corpse for a couple of seconds. He pressed her face and watched the colour drain away and then return, a sign that the blood had not yet started congealing and a fairly accurate indication of her time of demise. Her muscles were still very pliable and rigor mortis had not even started to set in. These factors, together with her temperature, indicated that she had probably not been dead more than a few minutes. The initial incision had been on her wrist so he chose her neck. As he leaned close he could detect the smell of many days of unwashed sweat and grime masking a faint hint of cheap perfume. He ignored these odours and found her carotid artery with a single tooth, opening it up with a small incision. On a live person the pressure created by the heart would have sent a spurt of blood which he would have expected to fill his mouth with warm delirium and pleasure. On a fresh corpse he would have still expected a certain amount of residual pressure behind the flow of liquid. As he opened up her artery however there was barely a trickle to greet his avidly hopeful lips which showed how deeply the previous vampire had drunk. He created a larger hole with his tooth and sucked hard, raising her entire body now to pool all the blood towards her neck and was rewarded with a few meagre mouthfuls. Obviously there was a lot more blood in her still but it was just hard to get at it from one puncture point with the time he had available to him.

He had become distracted in his excitement and had forgotten about the noises from below, but now they clamoured for his attention once again. There was the snap of breaking wood from the top of the stairs and a strangled choking. Luca did not move from the woman's neck as the sounds drew close. It was only when the man entered the small ward that he even bothered to look up.

He was in his late thirties. His head had been shaven but now sported possibly three weeks of dark stubble and

222

lesions. His face was scarred beneath the scabs and open sores that had formed, and his eyes were an unhealthy yellow with red lines around the edges. He wore ripped black jeans and black boots but was topless. Menacing tattoos spread across his broad chest and all down his thick, muscular arms, ending only at his stubby hands which were bejewelled with chunky gold rings. He looked as though he had stepped straight from a gangster movie in the role of a henchman and would have been the kind of person one might cross the street to avoid in normal life and normal times. He stopped as he entered the ward and glared at Luca with boundless hatred and fury, emotions which fitted his cruel, blunt features admirably. He threw his head back and screeched as loud as he could, a scream that sounded totally eerie and unnatural coming from a human mouth and seemed to be formed of words but none that Luca could understand. He crouched and charged his significant bulk with arms reaching and grasping, still frothing and shrieking.

Luca released the girl letting her fall with a thud but remained close to the floor. His eyes burned into his assailant, his mouth open wide with long, cruel incisors showing. His hiss turned into a roar of irritation at being disturbed whilst feeding. His yell was entirely more terrible than his assailant. A deep, primordial scream, it was a sound that originated back in time and had prevailed against adversity and fear and hatred. It was a sound that had silenced brave men before and made them lose control of their minds.

He hardly moved as the man neared. Just as his attacker stretched out his arms to grasp, Luca abruptly stood with mighty force. He grabbed the man's neck and crotch, maintaining his momentum. He swung the man around and then released him, hoisting him up and casting him through the window in a single, smooth, effortless movement. The glass and wooden frame shattered easily. The man's shriek lost none of its rage as he sailed through the air with a graceful poise that he most certainly would not have possessed in his life before. His body described a gentle arc and he subtly rotated to face the sky. His scream did not stop until he landed with a snap on the ground, five floors and fifty-five feet below, his spine shattered and broken and the life from him utterly extinguished.

Luca heard more sounds approaching but for now he was only concerned with his feed. He turned to the two men and repeated the procedure on the nearest, drawing a little more sustenance. The front of the rabble now entered the ward and rushed at him. Luca continued to ignore them as he sucked at the remaining blood and turned to the last corpse. They neared him just as he bit. He had time only for the briefest of feeds before they were upon him. There were possibly eight or nine already in the ward and several more that he could see streaming up the stairs behind. He had delayed longer than was prudent and the first of the infected swiped at his neck as he stood up. With a roar he lashed out with his foot. The man was sent hurtling back into the throng which scattered and bowled over the next few. Another lunged at him. He grasped Luca's collar with both hands. Luca whipped round and tried to knock him aside but the man was driven by rage and hunger equal to his own, and his fingers had become entangled in Luca's clothes. He slipped to the side but clung on and struggled back to his feet, biting at Luca's face. Luca leapt in retreat over the three human corpses, dragging the man with him as the others now got back up and surged forwards. With the first hint of concern Luca calmed himself. He took a strong hold on the man's forearms and quickly twisted them outwards, snapping both with a clean break. The wrist bones pierced the skin and the flesh around the injuries immediately started to blacken. He shoved the man backwards into the on-rushing attackers, scattering them once again.

Had Luca been clearer minded he would have used the brief respite to make good his escape as their numbers in such a confined space were overwhelming even for a vampire. However he had just had his first, tantalizing taste of human blood in a long time. It had whetted his appetite and the fact that he was being chased off the kill sent him into an unrestrained rage. He lost control, bellowed at the oncoming infected and hurled himself forwards.

He grabbed the nearest to him firmly by the head, a woman, probably in her late sixties. She wore an old, pink dress with a thick silver chain and crucifix around her neck. Her dark hair still displayed the remnants of a bad colouring job but her grey roots had long ago started showing through and now a lot of her hair had fallen out in clumps revealing a scabby, mottled scalp. Most of her teeth were missing, those that remained were discoloured and her gums were bleeding and dark. He savagely twisting her head through ninety degrees and yanked it to the side. It had become apparent to the vampires that the contaminated would not be stopped merely by the pain of injury. They only seemed to feel anger and hunger and so in order to kill them, or at the very least immobilize them, it required a significant trauma to the head or spinal cord.

He felt something snap in her body and pushed her away as he turned to the next of the infected, an overweight, bald man wearing dirty, brown pyjama bottoms and a stained, white string vest. Luca wasted no time on this attacker. He recoiled quickly and then as the man leapt at him, punched with all his might, a single blow to the head. Large as the man was, he was knocked completely off his feet and sent hurtling into the wall with a satisfying crack of bones.

Luca now found himself all but surrounded. He stood panting and glaring at the mob for a moment. They too seemed to pause, or was it just his imagination? Perhaps they were now becoming aware that he would not make easy prey, and on some level were considering their next move. Or perhaps they were just a little slow at negotiating the fallen bodies. Either way the slight breather gave him time to consider. More had entered the ward cutting off any option of escape down the stairs and he was putting himself in jeopardy by remaining purely to vent his frustration. As they attacked anew he jumped as high as he could in the direction of the window. There was a small man blocking his path but Luca struck him in the chest, clearing the way for escape. He launched himself gracefully through the window and into the cool afternoon air. He paused on the sill to take stock of his position and the nearest of the diseased rushed forwards and swiped at him. Luca easily evaded the clumsy attack but grabbed the man by the wrist and hauled him out of the window, dropping him to his doom below.

The distance to the ground seemed much too far to contemplate jumping so he found a convenient ledge from which he could access a pipe and shinned quickly up and to safety, leaving the angry cries behind.

On the hospital roof he crouched, regaining his composure as he scanned all about. The sounds of the turmoil below were initially of anger at the prize that had escaped them but soon became petty squabbling as they started fighting each other over the three corpses. He shut the noises out and checked around for any sign of the mystery vampire. Ordinarily meeting unfamiliar vampires should not necessarily be a problem, but these were far from ordinary times and he was wary about encountering any in the open by himself. He could see or sense nobody and so felt slightly more at ease. He arranged his clothes and smoothed back his hair.

If Farzin and Sebastian had polarized attitudes about killing the infected then Luca's opinion was positively equatorial. Normally he did not take actual pleasure from it but neither did he shy away from it. He would not deliberately go out to kill for sport but if it was necessary and the easiest option for him then he would do what he had to without hesitation or remorse. On this occasion however, in a confined space with such numbers attacking him, he knew that it would have been foolhardy to remain and fight. He had come as close to peril as he cared. Even staying as briefly as he had in order to exercise his frustration had been foolish, although his anger had been assuaged somewhat. Satisfied that he was now safe, unobserved, and content that he had indulged in at least a modest amount of human blood, he had then returned to the church and to Darius's apparently decreasing esteem.

Darius and Sebastian's search in order to try and pick up the human trail from the petrol station was to prove fruitless. This was disappointing, although as yet they did not appreciate exactly how significant the ramifications would be for them all. If they had known how important this was, they may well have hunted longer and more determinedly.

Luca now stood alone in the presbytery in the gathering gloom. He rubbed at the blood stain on his collar, with the sounds from Farzin and his entourage faint and hushed in muted conversation in another room. There were several reception rooms and bedrooms, enough that they all had their own privacy and space. The furniture and décor were unusual but tasteful. There were several old works of art that could have cost a significant amount, some of which dated back several hundred years. The priest who had lived there had obviously had an eye for historical pieces and it made the clan members feel at home amongst articles some of which were as old as Darius and Max themselves.

Luca stood staring vacantly at a small painting from Iran hidden away behind some tall, wilting plants in a corner of the room. It depicted a great battle between hosts of opposing armies. There was a central figure, presumably a famous hero, whose body shone with a kind of radiance. For the first time in a while Luca did not hear the soft footfall behind him and he was startled by the faint voice, virtually a whisper, at his shoulder.

"One of the most famous artists of the Khajar period in the sixteenth century, Mohammad Kamal-ul-Molk." Farzin's voice had taken on a strange edge to it; perhaps it was talking of his home-land that made him exaggerate slightly his usually faint Persian accent. "He painted many scenes of war from Persian folklore. This one portrays Fath Ali Shah Qajar, our most celebrated ruler, in a great battle in order to demonstrate his fighting prowess. Here he is depicted with his arch-enemy Zakhak, a celestial being of evil origins." He pointed now to a cowering figure in the shadows, who sat upon an exhausted horse that wore faded, black armour. From his shoulders grew two serpents, both attacking enemy soldiers.

"Sometimes Zakhak is shown as being guarded by these vipers that grow out of his body, but occasionally in rare, more ancient works of art, his defenders are two stooping, hooded creatures with claws and long teeth who drink the blood of their enemies."

Luca turned in surprise and Farzin smiled. "Yes, even back then in Persia they had knowledge of us. When I lived there no one would talk of us in the open but there were folk tales of people who became infected with a terrible disease and were cursed for eternity. It is just in more recent times that they have become blind to the truth. Modern living has led them to forget such old tales; luckily for us I would say."

He turned back abruptly to the painting. "In truth Fath Ali Shah Qajar never went into battle himself. Instead he sat dictating the fate of his minions from the comfort of his royal court whilst those serving him fought and died in his honour. He would suffer no betrayal or cowardice amongst his troops. Anyone who did not excel themselves on the battlefield or who showed the enemy the slightest degree of mercy was thrown into a pit of snakes on returning home. If anybody died before taking the blood of an enemy then their family was thrown into the pit, a fairly successful method for encouraging his troops. However he rewarded his victorious armies well and was both revered and feared by his own in equal measure. He had a strict code, a protocol, which he followed, in life as in death. It's that protocol that elevates us all from animals. He was a truly great leader for a truly great time."

Even in the gloom Farzin's eyes were positively luminous, shining and glinting with an excited zeal that Luca had never seen before. He said nothing further and after a pause backed slowly away with a bow, leaving Luca alone once more, wondering which quality Farzin most admired – that which inspired fear, or reverence. He also wondered exactly what that brief exchange had all been about. Had he really been merely discussing art from his homeland? Was he tentatively trying to extend the olive branch of peace towards Luca? Or more ominously, was he trying to imply that like the great leader in the painting, he too would suffer no cowardice or betrayal? It left an uneasy feeling with Luca as the shadows lengthened and gathered all around him.

CHAPTER 11

Lewis was waiting by the guardroom when the two Land Rovers arrived. A worried-looking Millington flung the gates open. This time there was no big, welcoming flash of teeth and full-bellied laugh, but instead a look of consternation and concern. Behind him Denny and Singleton stood looking pale and grim. Sergeant Straddling paced up and down scowling and tutting under his breath in an uncharacteristic demonstration of nervous energy, not his normal dispassionate state.

The gates were closed resolutely behind the vehicles and the six soldiers were ushered into the guardroom.

"I am delighted that you all made it back here alive." Denny spoke gruffly with no procrastination. "Well done and thank goodness. Has anyone been bitten?" He scanned the group who all stood in front of him with sullen expressions. He looked to Flight Lieutenant Walkden for an answer but it was Sergeant Hutchison who spoke up.

"The three of us missed the majority of the action but none of us were bitten in my Land Rover sir."

Denny nodded. "Good. And what about you others?"

He looked directly at Bannister who caught the look in Collins's eyes. He shifted uneasily but said nothing.

"Well, was anyone bitten?" he demanded.

Collins glared at Bannister and he cleared his throat. "Seems I may have… been bitten sir, although not by any of the infected," he added quickly. All six of the soldiers looked awkward and none of them said anything further.

"What? Bitten by whom then?" Denny was perplexed.

"I dunno sir," Bannister said, but he lacked his usual bravado and slumped back into silence.

Denny exploded, now getting irate. "What on earth are you talking about? What do you mean - you don't know who bit you? That's ridiculous!"

"Look, tell us what happened?" Lewis asked more calmly, trying to encourage some information out of him. He was beginning to appreciate that Denny was perhaps not the best person to be asking the questions in such tense situations as this.

"The other Landy blew a tyre just up the road from the petrol station," Bannister muttered, "but as it was so close we thought it would be safe to go ahead and start to get the fuel."

Denny raised his hands in exasperation and started to draw breath to speak but Lewis gave him a withering glare and he shut his mouth.

"Before they got to us," Bannister continued sullenly, "we were attacked by some diseased and had to take shelter in the petrol station shop. There were loads of them, trying to break in to get at us. They would have killed us too but suddenly two people came from out of nowhere. They just jumped down into the middle of them and started attacking. They completely took them apart, killed every last one of them. I've never seen anything quite like it. They just totally ripped through those zombies.

"I think at that stage I must have been in sort of a state of shock, but afterwards the two came to the shop and one of them sort of…" he paused and rubbed at his throat, embarrassed to say it, or perhaps just unsure of exactly what happened as it all sounded too far-fetched. "She sort of bit me." He pointed to the small prick of blood on his neck.

Nobody said anything at first but Singleton started to examine the tiny wound and Denny was stunned, trying to take in the information.

"Were they infected, these two strangers?" Lewis asked.

232

"No, I don't think so sir."

"How can you be sure?"

"Well they weren't acting like the rest of the diseased. They were controlled and rational. They did seem kinda unusual but they were attacking and killing the rest of them, so no, I really don't think they were lurchers."

"Well who were they then?"

"I dunno sir."

"So let me get this straight," Denny said, finding his voice again, "a group of the Great Impure were killed by just two strangers, then one of them bit you on the neck but you don't know whom they were or anything about them?"

Bannister shrugged again, having run out of words and explanation. He glanced down at his feet and Charlotte Collins found she could not bring herself to look up at Denny either.

"I don't understand, I just don't understand." Denny raised his hands. "If they weren't contaminated why the hell did one of them bite you?" He turned now to Hutchison. "Did you see these two individuals?"

"Err, yes sir," Hutchison mumbled. "I got a brief glimpse of them."

"Well, did they look diseased to you?"

"It's hard to say sir, I didn't see much of them. They fled as soon as we got there but they didn't seem to be infected, no sir."

Lewis could see the interrogation was not really getting anywhere. He stepped forwards, partly in front of Denny, and half-turned to look at him. Denny caught the expression and let his shoulders droop.

"Well, at least none of you are dead, that in itself is a blessing," Lewis sighed. "After the twenty-four hours we've had, I hope you're right and that's not a contaminated bite. I'm still not sure what you're talking

233

about but let's sort this out inside. I'm sorry but you'll have to be quarantined Bannister, obviously. Look, let's get you all checked over, then we can debrief you in the mess."

Denny seemed unhappy with this solution, but he reluctantly agreed to continue inside the main building. Lewis thought that it would allow his commanding officer time to calm down and they might actually get somewhere with their questions. He turned now to Collins, remembering something. "Where's Cujo?"

Immediately her face crinkled and the tears recommenced as her shoulders shook with grief.

The sky was grey and had clouded over, as bleak and depressed as the mood on base. At times over the last couple of weeks there had been glimpses of normality at Headley Court, sporadic episodes of black humour as one might find on a hospital A&E ward. Occasionally each person had spells where they briefly forgot their own woes and for a time went about with a temporary suspension of reality. Everyone knew that their survival thus far was extremely fortuitous and this helped to keep them focused on the present, rather than on the past and lost loved ones. As for the future, that remained out of bounds to all. After recent events however, the atmosphere throughout the base turned disconsolate. A spontaneous period of mourning sprang up and the malaise of collective depression sank like a veil over them all.

Singleton, Dr Handley and the rest of the medical team thoroughly checked all those who had been off base before clearing them as 'unbitten'. When it came to Bannister they were still completely bewildered as to what had happened. The only bite mark on him was a single puncture would on his neck. It was a small incision

234

with no significant sign of bruising around it and no other obvious teeth marks. It did not resemble an attack from one of the infected and none of them could conceive of a reasonable explanation, despite what Bannister told them.

Finally all six soldiers were assembled in the conference room where Denny had held his meeting only hours before. Whilst the mood then had not exactly been light-hearted, it was decidedly grimmer now and tempers were getting frayed. Everyone else from the meeting earlier in the day was already assembled, sitting in gloomy silence.

"Okay does somebody want to tell me again what happened out there today?" Denny started. "I thought we agreed earlier, no more cock-ups? How the hell did it all go so badly wrong? What happened to implementing new, safer procedures?" He was nearly shouting already, and had gone red in the face. He thumped the table as he spoke.

Lewis glanced at him and groaned inwardly. He half-stood and gave an imploring look towards his commanding officer. He was under enough pressure of his own without constantly having to placate both his commanding officer and his senior sergeant. It also irritated him that Denny could sit in judgement when he would not leave the base himself. "I guess that's all very well to sit here in the comfort of this function room and decide that we are going to do everything more safely, but ultimately out there things do not always go according to plan, sir. Out there sometimes we have to make instant decisions in situations that one couldn't possibly have expected. Perhaps it might be worth finding out exactly what happened before we make any judgements and cast any aspersions?"

Denny was one of the longest serving military personnel on the base. He had spent a lot of time running training or logistical establishments in the UK, but compared to some of the others around that table his experience in the battle zone was extremely lacking. This only added to the stress that he was under. He not only had to keep everybody safe and motivated but also felt totally out of his depth. He was trying really hard to adapt his knowledge to a new way of operating, as a front line base under siege by a strange, uncompromising enemy.

He took a deep breath, stared at Lewis a moment and then sank into his chair. "Yes, Thomas, you are quite right."

"So?" Lewis looked around the table at the six soldiers. "What did happen?" His question was a general one but slanted more at Flight Lieutenant Walkden as the senior officer on the scavenging party, another whose experience for this type of scenario was woefully inadequate.

Walkden was staring glumly at the table but looked up at Lewis and then at everybody else. He recounted the day's events in a concise fashion but sparing no important details. When he mentioned the decision that he had made for the leading Land Rover to proceed alone he paused expectantly, waiting for criticism. A few eyebrows were raised and Lewis cast another warning glance at Denny who had to stop himself from berating Walkden, but nobody made a comment and Lewis prompted him to continue. Walkden spoke in glowing terms of the actions of his two soldiers, in particular praising Hutchison for keeping them all focused and maintaining clear control of the situation. To his credit he did not try to exonerate himself or explain away how he had frozen when faced with the attackers. He merely said that his experience in the field was wanting, and that had showed through. He spoke with the humiliated voice of someone spent and defeated.

He finished by describing the final moments as they approached the petrol station. Until then he had been composed and clear but now he coughed, became unsure of himself, and rubbed his chin as he spoke. "When we finally arrived we thought these three must surely be dead. There were corpses everywhere but as we were pulling up we noticed two strange people running away. From what I could tell one came out of the shop where Collins and Samuels were, and the other seemed to have been standing with Bannister just outside, as though saying something in his ear or something like that. We got out of our Landy as fast as we could but they were gone already."

"Where did they go?" Lewis asked.

"I didn't really see but it looked as though they must have climbed the wall of the building beside the petrol station, but then…" he stuttered and ran out of explanation.

"But then what?"

"Well, it's just a bit unlikely, that's all. The building was quite high and we would have seen them climb it. It would have taken them a while but we were there a moment or two later and they were gone already."

Hutchison and Neale were both nodding furiously at this stage too, in clear agreement with Walkden.

Singleton interrupted now, more interested in the people themselves. "When you say 'strange', what exactly do you mean?"

Walkden was genuinely embarrassed and clearly quite perplexed. "I didn't get a close-up view of them, but from where I was they both seemed quite tall and lanky. They sort of moved in an odd manner, effortlessly, as though they were floating an inch or two above the ground. I don't really know how to describe it other than that." Again he could not think of anything further to add and fell silent.

They were getting no closer to understanding what had occurred. Lewis felt his hackles rise as this was starting to become extremely creepy. He exchanged a worried glance with Singleton. The six soldiers from the scavenging trip were all obviously shaken and disturbed, and he had not seen Walkden, or Bannister for that matter, so stuck for words before.

"That's it? That's all you can say?" Denny was getting frustrated again. "Tall and lanky? And floating? What kind of description is that?"

Walkden shrugged apologetically and remained silent.

Denny now turned to the other three soldiers with a frown. "So does one of you want to talk us through your experience, from when you left the other vehicle behind?" He could still not keep the tone of disapproval from his voice. As Bannister started to relay his version of events, Collins held her head in her hands and started to sob.

"We arrived at the petrol station. Everything seemed to be okay so we started preparing to get the fuel. Collins and Cujo were on guard and Samuels was unloading the drums. I was preparing the pump when Samuels let a drum slip out of his hands." He scowled accusingly at the man who looked crestfallen. "It made an almighty racket, then Cujo started going loco and the diseased appeared nearby and attacked us. We got back into the Landy at first but there was some confusion. Cujo managed to get out and attacked the crazies that had already gathered around us. I tell you, they came out of nowhere and they were fast; really fast.

"Then it all happened so quickly. Collins went after Cujo and got into a spot of bother so I dragged her into the petrol station. Samuels followed but managed to knock himself out in the process."

Lewis noticed another contemptuous glare at the young

soldier. For some reason Bannister seemed overly irritable and was giving the man a hard time which was quite unnecessary in the circumstances. They had all been through enough already. Lewis made a mental note to keep a keen eye on Bannister.

"We managed to barricade the door," Bannister continued, "but the lurchers had gathered outside and there were loads of them. I mean, I don't know exactly how many but maybe fifteen, maybe more. They started to break into the shop and we really thought we were goners. We shot a couple but if they had got in that would have been it - game over. We just didn't have enough ammunition."

"And then?" Lewis tried to keep him focussed on the facts and move the story along.

"Then these two people just plunged right into the middle of the crowd. I guess they must have been on the forecourt's awning above, watching it all happen. They just swooped right down into the middle of it all and started ripping them up."

"With what?" Lewis asked. "Guns? Knives?"

"No sir - with their bare hands. They just punched, kicked, whatever. They smashed the infected's heads into the ground; they snapped their necks, whatever it took. And they were fast too, they moved like no one I have ever seen before. Just like Flight Lieutenant Walkden said, they moved like ninjas or something. I've never seen anything like it sir, it was pure poetry in motion."

In the confines of that room Lewis could detect a real rift starting to form between those who had witnessed the incredible events and those who were struggling to comprehend and believe what they were being told. Tempers were rising.

"Hang on there a moment," Straddling was incredulous and it was his turn to interrupt. "Are you saying these two people just appeared right in the middle of a load of festering mutants and killed the lot of them, ten, twenty, however many, with nothing more than their bare hands? No guns, no knives, no initial stun grenade, just their hands?" He stared hard at Bannister without trying to hide his disbelief.

Bannister glared back at him with some measure of hostility, leant forwards in his chair and spoke more slowly and deliberately now. "Yes Sergeant. That's exactly what I'm saying. They tore them apart with nothing more than their bare hands."

Collins's eyes were blotchy and her face was red but she spoke now sounding coherent and calm despite everything. "That was exactly it. They really did move with a kind of grace that you normally only see in a dance or a ballet. There really *was* a poetry to their motion. And yes," she turned to Straddling, "they killed the lot of them with nothing more than their bare hands. It was phenomenal."

Nobody spoke and Bannister scowled defiantly at Straddling and anyone else who would meet his gaze.

Lewis's feeling of unease had multiplied. He had the strange feeling of someone who has been told by a respected friend that he has seen a ghost or that aliens have been sighted and he has to try to believe it. He could not help but notice the almost dream-like way that both Bannister and Collins spoke when referring to these two strangers. He discreetly surveyed the others around the table, feeling very isolated at that moment. Dr Handley was leaning over and whispering something to Singleton who looked ashen and shaken herself. Denny's face was bright red and he was vigourously rubbing his hair, while Straddling just sat grimly shaking his head, with his arms folded angrily on his chest.

"You're all crazy or lying, or both," Straddling

grumbled moodily to himself.

The mood in the room was stifling and once again Lewis tried to calm things down. "Okay, let's leave that and move on. So after these two people had somehow killed the lot of them, then what?"

"I… I'm not sure exactly." Bannister now lost his angry demeanour and became more sullen and sheepish. "Like I said earlier I think I must have been in a state of shock or something. The two people just smashed aside our barricade and I guess the woman kind of bit my neck."

"Bit your neck? Like a vampire?" It was Handley's turn to sound scornful. He gave a muffled snort of disbelief and Straddling stood up suddenly pushing his chair back, and started to pace around the room, mumbling to himself.

"I don't know, I guess so. I didn't really notice her biting me so maybe I just cut myself, I dunno."

For the first time Senior Aircraftman Samuels spoke up. He had been sat meekly in one corner, trying to avoid attention, but now cleared his throat. "I may have been unconscious for much of the fight but I came round at the end. I can tell you what happened…" His voice was shaky and uncertain but all eyes fixed decisively on him and Straddling stopped pacing as he continued. "I was lying near the entrance to the shop where I knocked myself out I guess, so I could see it all. These two characters did just push the barricade aside. I mean it had been keeping the entire lot of infected at bay but they just shoved it out of the way as though it was nothing. The man came into the shop and was talking to Collins. He was speaking really quietly and I couldn't make out what he was saying, but I was distracted by Bannister anyway. He walked out to the woman as though she had summoned him, and she seemed to say something to him.

Then she kind of slowly put her arm around the back of his neck, pulled him into her as though she was going to embrace him or something and she bit him. It must have lasted a few seconds. She seemed to be kissing or sucking at his neck where she had bit him, I couldn't really see. Then the other Landy arrived and they scarpered."

This time the hush lasted more than a few seconds. Singleton flashed a glance at Lewis that could have been suspicion or could possibly have been fear, and he felt a chill pass over himself. He shuddered.

"So let me just get this all straight," he said, breaking the silence, "these two ninja-like characters jumped into the middle of the infected, killed the lot of them with no weapons, drank your blood like a vampire and then scaled a wall without ropes?"

Bannister, Samuels and Collins all nodded, all of them looking uncomfortable.

"This is about as weird as the mystery of Sinna and Rohith's disappearing bodies. Great - so not content with zombies, we now have vampires too. All we need is Frankenstein for a full house." Lewis scoffed and gave a laugh although he did not feel remotely amused.

"Well actually Frankenstein was just a normal man," Singleton said acerbically. "He was the doctor. It was the monster that he created that you're probably referring to - Frankenstein's Monster." She would normally have relished the opportunity to correct Lewis but this time it sounded hollow and childish.

"Touché," he replied and smiled at her in spite of himself, appreciating that he would have made exactly the same type of comment himself. Time to build some bridges, he thought. A release of tension rippled around the room as Lewis also stood up and rubbed the back of his neck. "This is all too weird."

Singleton was still more concerned with their

appearance. "Can any of you tell us what these two strangers looked like?"

Collins looked puzzled, as though trying to recall a pleasant but elusive dream. "It does all feel a little hazy, as Bannister says. I can remember what they were wearing but not really their features, except the eyes. He had these amazingly piercing, hazel-coloured eyes. Really quite extraordinary."

Freddie Samuels again filled in the gaps. "I got a clear look, at least of the male. He was tall, probably 6'5" or 6'6," or something like that. He looked sort of Eastern European, with pronounced cheekbones and distinctively shaped eyes, if you know what I mean?" Singleton was nodding enthusiastically, encouraging him to go on. "He looked really kind of sinister and eerie as he was so tall and unusual, but friendly and calming at the same time, if that makes sense? And yes, his eyes were really piercing, a really clear hazel colour, they kind of drilled right through you." Samuels blushed and became quiet and brooding.

Denny still felt totally out of his depth which was now manifesting itself as anger. "I just don't believe this. I can't believe that you all think they killed a load of infected without weapons. They must have had some that you didn't see. And then one of them bit you? No, I'm sorry, I don't buy it." He carried on mumbling to himself under his breath.

"Well did they say what they wanted, whom they were, anything at all?" Lewis asked.

"He said to me that I have nothing to fear from him and that I shouldn't be afraid," Collins said somewhat wistfully. "Then the second Landy arrived and they ran away"

"Look, we call the contaminated 'zombies'," Straddling said as he returned to his seat, "but we all know that there is logical explanation for their illness, an explanation that is based on medical fact. There was a cause and there is probably a cure. In reality there is nothing supernatural or fantastical about them, and I am sure the same can be said for the two people whom you saw today. I mean let's face it - we're all under a hell of a lot of stress. Collins had just lost her dog, Samuels had just knocked himself unconscious and it's very possible that you were all experiencing a stress-induced hallucination or something." He tailed off, seemingly satisfied with his explanation and defiantly waited for comment.

"Well yes, there are indeed stress-induced hallucinations," Handley said thoughtfully, "but not hallucinations that are shared by three or even six people, totally independently. That's just not possible."

"So you think it's more likely that they were saved by vampires?" Straddling sneered.

"At the moment I don't know what I think," Handley answered, "but a shared, group hallucination, induced by stress or anything else for that matter, is totally out of the question. Right now though I'd like to try and deal with the 'zombie' situation before we have to face anything else."

Singleton latched on to the argument and interrupted. "But as Sergeant Straddling has just said, the illness that these people are suffering from did indeed have a cause and so surely it *must* have a remedy too." She left the sentiment hanging. Everyone knew how strongly she believed in finding a cure.

Denny had been quietly trying to compose himself and now he spoke again with more control. "Yes, I know what you are getting at Anna. You still want us to capture one of the diseased for medical studies, but after the day we've just had I think we'll leave it for the time being.

We need to try to stay alive a little longer before we go and expose ourselves and everybody on the base to even greater threat.

"Look, let's call it a day. Whoever these people were, it's without doubt a blessing that they arrived when they did and saved you all. However I don't think we're any closer to actually understanding what happened and I don't think we have quite got to the bottom of this yet. I just can't quite believe what you have told us, but we should take a break. We *will* come back to this though, I assure you." He looked sternly at the six soldiers and then turned to Lewis. "We still need to get more provisions which does unfortunately mean we have to go off base again, but I think we can sort that out later, after dinner tonight or tomorrow."

Lewis nodded. He was well aware that when Denny said '*we* have to go off base again', he was not actually volunteering himself. After his first unnerving experience of leaving the safety of Headley Court he had remained firmly behind locked gates. Lewis said nothing however. In truth he would rather his commanding officer *did* stay on the station, as he would be too much of a liability to take with them. In reality Lewis had come closer than any of them to the truth when he mentioned the vanishing corpses, but alas nobody had stopped to think about it further.

They all filed quietly out of the conference room. Singleton put an arm around Collins's shoulders and spoke to her comfortingly as they walked away. Lewis hovered at the exit, waiting for everyone to leave. Denny still sat in his chair, rocking back and staring out of the window while he tugged at his lower lip, lost in his thoughts. Lewis watched him for a few seconds before speaking.

"You okay boss?"

Denny did not hear so Lewis repeated himself. "Boss, are you okay?"

Denny heard this time and looked up with a frown that turned into a forced smile. "Hi, yes, fine. Why?"

"Nothing, just…" he searched for the right word, feeling a little uncomfortable, "…just you seem a little strung out, that's all. Is everything okay?"

"Yes of course it is." Denny was visibly irritated.

"Boss, I don't mean to pry. We're all going through the works right now. We've got to look out for each other, that's all."

Denny relaxed and smiled again, a little more genuinely this time. "Yes, you're right. I guess I am pretty tired. It's been particularly hard of late. Let's face it, every day is hard right now."

"Yes, I know. We're all suffering. You don't have to carry the burden for us all by yourself though - we're in this together. If you want to offload at any time, you can talk to me. Or, I'm sure, to Singleton," he added reluctantly.

"Thanks."

Lewis turned to go and Denny called out to him. "I mean it Thomas, I appreciate it. Thanks."

As Straddling had left the room he cast a furtive glance over his shoulder and then collared Hutchison, drawing him aside and pausing briefly. The two had served together a long time and were close friends.

"I don't like it," he said when they were out of earshot of the others.

"Huh?" Hutchison turned to face him.

"It's all very sloppy. Procedures are not being followed off base and there's always a good reason for that." He did not give Hutchison time to reply before continuing. "It comes from the top. If a football team is failing you sack the manager, it's always top down. Mark my words, this is a sinking ship and personally, I am not going down with it."

"What are you saying?"

"I'm saying the time may be coming when we have to make a stand…"

Collins went back to her room and sat on the bed, immersed in her own grief. After all that had happened she could not bear to be alone in her cell, so she aimlessly wandered out with no real plan or purpose. The corridors of the mess were quiet and sombre, and she soon found herself outside the rooms where Wood, Reggie Pethard, and now Bannister were being held. Corporal Bell from the catering section sat outside looking bored with his sleeves rolled up. A book lay on the floor under his chair and he was slouching back against the wall flicking his cheek to mimic the sound of a dripping tap. When he saw Collins approach he brightened up and flashed her a brief smile that was quickly extinguished when he noticed her demeanour.

"Really sorry to hear about Cujo," he mumbled and started to get up out of the chair.

"Thank you," she tried to smile in return but it was not forthcoming. News travels fast, she thought, especially bad news. "How are the patients?"

"Good as gold. Pethard's been asleep a lot of the time and The Ice… err, Woody's bored and hungry, just like me."

"Can I go in?" She gestured towards Sergeant Wood's room. His immediate reaction was to protest that nobody was allowed in. However, the look on her face and the fact that she seemed to be about to burst into tears quickly persuaded him otherwise. Better to let someone else have to deal with a blubbing girl, he thought.

"Of course." He quickly fumbled for the keys and

opened the door for her.

Wood lay on his back on the bed. His shoes were off and his hands were folded behind his head as he stared at the ceiling. As the door opened he leapt up expectantly. He smiled at her but there was sympathy in his eyes. Clearly the update of the day's events had reached him too. "Hi. I really am so very sorry to hear about Cujo."

"Yeah, well at least none of us were killed, it could easily have been so much worse," she said, trying to put a brave face on it but the tears were already starting up again.

He was standing on the other side of the room and took half a step towards her. The distance between them seemed an awfully long way and in his reserved manner he did not know how to cross the divide, but somehow he got there and they ended up in front of each other. Gently and timidly he put his hands on her and pulled her in to him in a comforting hug as her shoulders shook, the first proper physical contact they had ever had together. She felt the warmth of his chest and the strength of his arms as he stroked her hair, and she relaxed a little as the tears flowed. There was nothing to say, nothing that would make any of the pain and fear and frustration of the past couple of weeks go away, just the knowledge that they were all in this together, there for each other for better or for worse until death do they part, as it almost certainly would. Gradually her shaking subsided. Gradually she looked up at him into his steady, brown eyes and gradually the comforting hug became a different kind of embrace.

Bannister was in the room on the other side of Wood. He heard Collins's voice in the corridor and heard Wood's door being unlocked. Ordinarily this would have filled him with jealousy as he had developed a soft spot for her, as had several of the soldiers on the base.

However on this evening his dark, brooding thoughts were fixed on another. He could not shake the image of that strange woman approaching him, the captivating stare of her beautiful, timeless eyes, the flowery scent of her perfume and the touch of her cool breath on his neck. It really did all feel quite dreamlike but to be honest most of the last couple of weeks had felt surreal. It was as though he had been drunk and could not quite recall with clarity the episode, but at the moment he could think of nothing else. His mind was rumbling away with what felt like the thoughts of someone else, as though another was constantly chatting away in the background, but he could not quite hear what they were saying and it made him both anxious and relaxed. It disturbed him yet he found himself slowly but relentlessly relinquishing control to this unseen other. It was a precipitous slope that he did not even realise he was starting to descend.

As Singleton and Handley approached Denny's closed door they exchanged a concerned look. In the last two weeks his door had always been open except when he was having a meeting with someone, and as they knew that Lewis was not with him now it seemed strange that his door should be shut. They knocked and waited but heard nothing. Singleton knocked again, louder and after a pause Denny answered.

"Yes?"

She opened the door wide enough for both of them to peer in. "Sir, we're going to check on the patients. Just wondered if you wanted to come and see them for yourself?"

"No. That's fine."

"How much longer do you want to keep them confined? If they seem normal are you happy for them to be released?"

He was staring absent-mindedly out of the window as she spoke and so did not answer immediately. Finally she prompted him again.

"Sir?"

"What? Oh yes, whatever you think. What *do* you think?"

"Well as they weren't actually bitten, if they still seem fine then we had thought it would be okay to allow them to leave confinement."

"Yes of course, that sounds absolutely reasonable."

Singleton and Handley stood waiting for him to say something more but he had returned to his contemplation of the evening's darkness outside.

They closed the door and again exchanged glances as they walked soundlessly on the carpeted corridor towards the patients' rooms upstairs.

"He seems a bit odd," Dr Handley mouthed.

Singleton nodded feeling worried. On the way they stopped at Lewis's room. The door was open and it appeared as though he had just arrived there himself. He glanced up as they approached, raising his eyebrows quizzically. Despite everything that had happened, and even though the two of them did not always see eye to eye, Singleton marvelled at how normal and relaxed he appeared. She could recognise the indicators of stress and grieving on most of the base personnel, herself included, but he still seemed to be handling everything remarkably well. She wondered if it was all a front, but even if it was, it was good for the morale of others.

Lewis noticed the look of concern on her face and put down the tray he had been holding.

"Have you got a mo?" she asked him.

"For you? Certainly doc." He flashed a genuine smile at her. It was the first warm gesture she had received all day and she felt disproportionately grateful to him for this small consideration.

"We've just been to see Denny to ask him if he wanted to come and check on Pethard and Wood with us. He seems really rather distracted, he could hardly concentrate on a two minute conversation. I think maybe the stress is getting to him. I know we're all up tight at the moment and everyone is grieving for somebody, but I just thought it was worth mentioning, that's all."

Lewis's face dropped as she spoke. The playfulness vanished and he now looked at her with a truly serious expression. "Yes, I had thought exactly the same. Actually I was going to come and talk to you. I think he is certainly feeling the pressure of trying to carry us all and he's starting to behave somewhat unpredictably. I'll look in on him in a sec, and let's all keep an eye on him; and on each other."

Lewis watched the two doctors continue on towards the patients' rooms. It was the first conversation he had had with Singleton for a while that had not carried an irritable edge. He was starting to realise that with Denny acting more erratically, he and Singleton would rely on each other more and more. Lewis made his way first to speak to Straddling and Hutchison, who he found chatting furtively in a dark corner of the ante-room which had previously been used for coffee after dinner, and then on to see Denny. The door was closed again so he knocked loudly twice and waited. As before there was no answer so he just opened the door quickly. Denny was sat in his chair staring out of the window into the dusk as he had been when Singleton had left him alone. To Lewis's alarm he was holding his Browning casually in his hand, as though it was a pen or a mobile phone. He did not look round when the door opened. It was only when Lewis cleared his throat that he acknowledged him. He turned and to Lewis's shock there were tears in his eyes.

"Sir, are you okay?"

Denny smiled weakly when he saw the expression on his colleague's face, looked briefly at the gun and lowered it to the table.

"Sorry, I didn't mean to alarm you. It just makes me feel comforted, the feeling of cold, hard metal. Something tangible and real, you know? When we're surrounded by all this craziness." Then he changed the topic radically. "Thomas, do you believe in God?"

Lewis was taken aback. "Well, yes, I was born and raised a Catholic, and yes, I guess I still do believe."

"Despite all this?" Denny waved a hand at the window indicating the world outside.

Lewis scratched his head and thought for a moment before answering. "Yes, I do. People tend to either blame God for natural disasters and large losses of life or say that these events prove that there is no god. The typical argument would be, 'how can there be a god if he allows this to happen?' I don't agree with either argument, I see it differently. For example, should God intervene every time there is a catastrophic loss of life? If so then at what stage should he stop intervening? I mean, if there is an earthquake and a thousand people die, does that mean there cannot possibly be a god that allows that to happen? If a plane crashes and a hundred people die, does *that* mean there can't be a god? What if a car crashes and four people die? And so on. At what stage do you just say, 'do you know what, that is the way of the world; that is just how life happens'?

"I don't expect *him* to intervene if there's a tsunami that kills thousands, and I don't expect him to intervene if little Jonny falls over and bashes his head. So all this happening at the moment, I don't know, it's terrible and horrific and any other word one cares to use, but is it God's fault? Or does it mean that there cannot possibly be

252

a god who would allow this to happen? Personally I don't think it means that at all. Unfortunately it's just the way of the world."

Denny's eyes were shining and he was leaning forward and listening intently now. He shrugged and turned back to the window and waved at the dark sky. "Maybe so Thomas, maybe so. But do you know what? I don't think you are right. I don't believe in any god any more. If he ever existed then I think he has abandoned us. Out there, out there are a hundred billion galaxies, each with hundreds of billions of stars and immeasurable billions of planets. The universe is so inconceivably immense. Here, you and I, those of us surviving on this base and any survivors all over the world even, we are so infinitesimally small and insignificant. The universe doesn't care what happens to us today and it won't remember what happens to any of us in years to come. It really won't affect anything beyond the confines of our miniscule planet. Tomorrow, next year, next century, when we are all dead the universe will go on just as it has for billions of years and no one or nothing will care. What does it matter what happens to us?"

"It matters to me. And it matters to everybody on this base."

"Really?" There was a note of scorn now in Denny's voice.

"Yes. Absolutely. There's no point in thinking that our lives don't matter. They do; they matter to us, right now. And maybe in a hundred years it won't matter anymore, but all we can do is what is right for us, for everyone on this base, right now, today, tomorrow, until we are all dead."

"So what would be your survival aims then?"

Lewis answered without hesitation. He had put a lot of thought into this already. In fact it seemed to him as though most of his waking hours of late had been spent furthering this aim. "Short-term, day-to-day survival, we make Headley Court as secure as possible. We ensure procedures off base are as tight as we can, and we try to keep everyone feeling positive.

"In the medium term we amass sufficient supplies to maintain us for a while and develop basic farming practices within the base. We find other survivors, as there must be some out there, and perhaps find other locations that we could move to at short notice if need be.

"In the longer term we try to outlast the infected, as sooner or later they must surely die of starvation or through killing each other or something. Or perhaps better still, we try to find an antidote and save as many people as possible. We set up a new society and rebuild. Slowly."

He waited for a response and Denny seemed not to have heard him as he did not answer for a while. Finally he just said "Highly admirable. I wish you good luck with all that."

Both the brevity of his answer and the look of finality in his eyes were disturbing.

"Sir, are you sure you're okay?"

Denny saw Lewis glance nervously at the Browning and pushed it gently across the desk away from himself. "Yes, Thomas. I'm fine." He smiled again. "Really, don't fret about me, I'm just a little tired, that's all. Look, what will be, will be. We'll muddle through as best we can, as that's all there is left for us to do. And really don't worry." He glanced down at the weapon. "I'm not going to do anything stupid. I'm saving that for those buggers out there."

Lewis left feeling more troubled than before. He had intended to ask if Denny wanted to help them plan their next scavenging mission but now thought it best to leave

him in peace for a while. Hopefully a little less
responsibility and stress might be good for him.
Hopefully his irregular behaviour was just a momentary
blip and he would return to normal soon. Hopefully - but
somehow Lewis did not really believe that.

Singleton and Handley opened the door to Sergeant
Wood's room to see him sat on the bed with Corporal
Collins beside him. There was an awkward silence and
then Collins stood up, red in the face presumably from
crying and smoothed her blouse down.

"I'll see you later," she murmured to Wood, then
turned and nodded politely to the doctors, brushed past
them and left.

Singleton turned back to Wood. He seemed calm and
examined them with a measured expression. Singleton
could not help but feel that *they* were the ones under
scrutiny, not Wood. "How are you feeling?" she asked.

"Ma'am," he stood now, always very respectful,
bordering on cold or aloof, even though he was her
subordinate, in theory at least. Standing this close to him
she was reminded of how quietly commanding his
presence was, without his even doing anything at all. "I
feel absolutely fine. I appreciate that these procedures are
for the benefit of us all on the station, I don't have the
slightest problem with that. But really, I am *not* infected.
Hungry and bored? Yes. But infected? No. How long do
you need to keep me here?"

Singleton looked at Handley who nodded almost
imperceptibly.

"I think you are fine to go now," she said.

"Thank you, ma'am, I appreciate that." He nodded and
moved past them with a certain confident ease of
movement, leaving them in silence.

As they opened the door to Pethard's room he did not

get up off the bed where he lay, nor did he look to acknowledge them. The tranquilisers he had been given had done their job but the sound of the door opening did cause him to stir a little. Gradually he came to and looked in their direction. Singleton approached and sat on the bed next to him, taking his hand in hers, feeling his forehead and assessing his demeanour.

"How are you feeling Reggie?"

He tried to answer but found his mouth too dry again so took a slurp of water from the glass beside him. "Okay thanks. I think I have been out cold all this time, but I feel a bit better for it." There was great sorrow in his eyes but no hint of insanity.

"Do you feel strange, any headaches, fever, anything at all?"

"No ma'am. I don't think I'm diseased. Just tired. And sad."

Singleton took his pulse and temperature, both of which seemed normal. The two doctors looked at each other with less certainty than with Wood, but finally Handley just shrugged and said "I guess so."

Singleton turned to Pethard. "Look, it seems as though you are fine. I think you are okay to go to your room or maybe go get some food from the kitchen if you are hungry?"

"Do you mind if I stay here for tonight?" Pethard asked in a husky voice. "I don't think I can face going back to our room. Not just yet."

Singleton blushed. She had almost forgotten for a moment the reason he was in confinement. "Of course, that's no problem at all. I am sure we can get you another room in the mess if you like?"

"No that's okay thanks. I'll be up to going back to it tomorrow; it's just tonight I can't really face it."

As they left him and closed the door he lay back down

256

on the bed and was asleep again almost immediately.

Singleton and Handley wandered slowly away. "We still don't really know much about this condition, do we?" she said quietly.

"No not really." Dr Handley stopped and turned to face her with a look of doubt. "Why? What's on your mind?"

"Only that we have just allowed both men out of quarantine, but in reality we have no idea how long it might potentially take for different people to be affected."

"You mean individual susceptibility?"

"Exactly. As we've already discussed, it may take one person less than twenty-four hours to show any symptoms, yet another might take significantly longer."

"That's true. So what can we do about it? It's not really practical to keep them in quarantine indefinitely."

"No. I guess not. All we can do is to keep a close eye on them both, check on them regularly and look for the first sign of any unusual behaviour."

"And then what?" Handley asked.

Singleton had no solution to the question and left it unanswered, as so many questions were of late.

Wood was just wandering into the dining hall when he found Sergeant Vallage pottering around and managed to tease some food out of him. Lately it seemed possible to find Vallage ensconced in the kitchen at just about any time of night or day, and although he was always somewhat gruff to those who arrived out of meal times, he never failed to come up with something simple to eat. He had never been so accommodating in normal life before but realised that morale was at an all-time low and quietly did his part to try and help people get through this nightmare. He complained incessantly whilst he prepared Wood's meal but it was more for show than genuinely intended, and his grumblings were often accompanied with a glint or wink.

After eating, Wood paced along the corridor in the direction of Collins's bedroom and passed the ante-room. There were raised voices coming from within and as the rest of the building now seemed devoid of life he glanced in their direction. For a moment he observed the animated discussion discreetly, quickly taking stock before entering and interrupting the dynamic.

"Mind if I join you?" he asked pleasantly, pretending he had not noticed the heat being generated.

Lewis was talking with Straddling and Hutchison. Maps and charts were illuminated by the candles and, as often seemed to be the case of late, Straddling was being uncooperative and tetchy. He looked up and scowled as Wood came towards them.

Wood raised his hands, defensively. "Don't worry, I'm not sick. I heard voices, that's all."

"Please," Lewis gestured to a vacant chair with a flicker of relief passing across his features. "We're just discussing the next outing for tomorrow. Given that the one today failed, we've got to go out again."

Wood settled into an armchair slightly set back from the table. "Mind if I ask what you have planned?"

Over the last couple of weeks Lewis had become aware of everyone's military history and Sergeant Liam Wood was one of the most experienced there. His Special Forces background and front-line exposure leant the others to view him with a certain amount of awe, although no one had really delved too deeply into his past and he had kept himself largely to himself. Lewis had not had much of a chance to speak with him in depth so far, although he was aware that he had arrived at Headley Court in pretty bad shape and had sustained some sort of back injury. Further than that, Wood did not seem to be the type to volunteer personal information, and there was something about him that made Lewis uncomfortable prying. He had not yet made up his mind about him but was grateful for any advice from anyone with relevant skills. The three men shuffled around and made a space for him to join them. Lewis quickly outlined the intended route for the next day's outing and what they were hoping to find. Wood sat quietly throughout, gently pulling at his lower lip.

Sergeant Wood was not an overly big man, perhaps a shade over six feet tall, but he had an athlete's poise, looked fit and toned, and perhaps for that reason he seemed more physically intimidating than his size would otherwise suggest. The sleeves of his khaki, army shirt were rolled up revealing taught forearms like those of a cat's lean limbs. He carried no extra flesh and through years of active life was honed ready for swift, decisive action. He had self-possessed, brown eyes that held one's gaze unnervingly. Lewis could not help but wonder what atrocities he had seen in his life in the military, or perhaps more poignantly what atrocities he had himself committed.

When Lewis finished Wood just grunted and nodded. "Seems fair enough, you've clearly thought through exactly what supplies you need and where to get them from. That's good. No point in wasting time out there. How many people are you taking out with you?"

"Well so far we have just discussed taking the same as today - two Landies with three people in each. Each Land Rover will have a trailer. Everybody will have a Browning and an SA80."

Wood now leant forwards, the candlelight picking out his dark, steady eyes. "Excuse me for asking, but exactly why are you not taking one of the Bedfords?"

"Ahh, good question," Lewis said with a mild look of triumph which made Straddling scowl even more.

"Initially the Station Commander thought that the Land Rovers were more manoeuvrable which could be handy out there. Also he thinks that the lorries need to be ready at all times in case the security of the station is breached and we have to make a quick getaway from Headley Court. Denny wants us to leave them at the MT section, fuelled and fully operational for immediate use."

"If you don't mind my saying that seems a little short-sighted," Wood said. "The Station Commander isn't the one going off base so he is hardly in a position to make such a call."

Straddling raised his eyebrows and sniffed but Wood ignored him and continued.

"By not using them you necessitate going out on many more missions pointlessly. Personally I wouldn't thank you for that. And yes, I can see that manoeuvrability would be a big bonus out there, but with the trailers attached to the Landies are they really much more manoeuvrable? Might I make a suggestion?" He did not wait for permission but continued regardless. "Would it not be better to take the Land Rovers without trailers, in support of a Bedford? That way you increase their manoeuvrability and also the amount of supplies you can bring back, hence reducing the number of times men are exposed to danger. Take as many people as you can reasonably fit in the vehicles to give you the maximum defence. Go out there, get as much of absolutely everything that you can in one hit, then come back, lock the gates and dig in."

Lewis smiled and rubbed his chin. "Well, yes, I do kind of agree with you and I was just saying something along those lines actually. We have lost too many men and I think it may be time to reconsider our procedures. Okay, we'll plan on taking one of the lorries." He cast a challenging glance over at Straddling and Hutchison who both nodded.

"And can I suggest four men in each Landy, at least two up front in the Bedford and a few more, say three or four, in the back?" Wood continued. "It will help with loading supplies, it will be much easier to move any vehicles blocking our path and it will mean more pairs of eyes and guns for when you really need them."

"A total of thirteen or fourteen men?" Lewis replied. "That doesn't leave many to guard the base and it means putting more people at risk."

Wood nodded, his eyes not leaving those of Lewis, ignoring the other two sergeants who sat quietly without interrupting. "I think the base will be just fine as it is. It's those on the outside that I would be more concerned about. The risk will be less for all and at least there is a greater prospect of everyone coming back alive that way. We're all in this together. Why should just a few people face an unreasonably high probability of death when the gates are opened. I'd suggest you share that risk and increase the likelihood of success for everybody."

Lewis contemplated for a few seconds and then nodded. "Okay." The advantages were obvious and he kicked himself for not having implemented these measures before. Despite Wood's blunt attitude Lewis found himself warming to the man.

Wood had not finished yet though. "And I'd like to come on this trip. My back's fine now, I won't be a hindrance."

"Are you sure?"

"Yep. Definitely. I might be rather useful to you out there." His gaze was again unflinching and unyielding. "I've acquired various 'skills' in my time in the forces that might just come in handy."

CHAPTER 12

As he waited by the main gates for all the troops to assemble, Lewis stared out at the road stretching away before him. There was a row of large trees lining the street on either side. The branches had fairly recently been chopped right back leaving nothing more than stumps in order to prevent them from becoming too large and overgrowing the road. There had been absolutely no leaves remaining, no small branches or twigs, just the main branches looking like twisted skeletons. Nevertheless new shoots were already springing forth with buds and leaves. He found it incredible that despite such a severe cleaving the trees still thrived, still bore the evidence of new growth, such incredible tenacity to cling to life. He was caught in personal reflection, steeling himself for the day, wondering what to expect and what trials would test their own determination to survive when a voice intruded on his thoughts.

"Can I ask you something sir?" Private Darby from the MT section stood at his elbow.

"Hmmm," Lewis barely acknowledged him, still looking at the outside world beyond the security of the gates.

"Just that some of the lads have been talking about Armageddon, sir. This being the 'End of Days' or something like that. Do you believe that sir? Do you think this is God's will?"

"No," he answered distractedly in reply, but the silence from Private Darby jolted him into realising that something more was required from him and he turned to face him. "No Darby, I do not think this is divine retribution or 'God's will', or anything like that. This is a man-made problem, this is nothing more than science gone mad and the solution is going to have to be man-made as well."

"So you don't think we're being punished here on earth, that god is wiping us all out just to start afresh? You don't think that it doesn't matter what we do, we're all going to die anyway?"

Lewis practically snorted in derision but controlled himself. "No Darby. I do not. There is nothing Apocalyptic about this, it's just an extremely unfortunate series of events. Every day when we go out there we face peril but ultimately our fate is down to us, how careful and professional we are, how we act as a cohesive force and whether we make any mistakes. Any one of us *might* die but my aim is to try and bring us all home safely. Even you Darby, as long as you don't continue asking such daft questions. Okay?"

"Ah fab, thank you sir." Private Darby looked relieved, giving the impression that he thought he had just been awarded a personal guarantee of safety. He wandered away, kicking at a piece of gravel with his hands thrust into his trouser pockets and whistling quietly to himself, as though the conversation had been casual, about the weather or the Saturday football or something. Lewis watched him go and smiled to himself; the boy was a marvel, he really seemed unperturbed by events, which was potentially a good attitude to adopt but only if he did not take it too far. Or perhaps he was just not really appreciating the gravity of the situation, which was a more worrying state of mind. As he watched Darby, his attention was piqued by Straddling, who was nearby, hunched in conversation with Hutchison and Newman, an army corporal from the medical section. There was something about the way they spoke in muted tones with occasional furtive glances cast in his direction that worried him, and he wished he could hear what was being discussed.

263

"But that's treason," Corporal Newman said, aghast. "What you're suggesting is mutiny."

"No it's not," Straddling retorted angrily. "The structure of the military no longer exists. There's nothing but us left now, so by rights, military rule no longer holds any sway over us. Before, we were part of one big institution. We had to toe the line otherwise it would all descend into chaos and otherwise we'd be punished. Now though that's all gone. We're already living in the midst of chaos. All that remains for us is to survive."

"So what's your point?" Hutchison asked somewhat warily.

"Just, that we no longer *have to* follow orders. Our main aim now is to stay alive. So if someone gives us an order that we think compromises that prerogative, we don't *have to* obey. It's as simple as that."

Corporal Newman was now nodding in agreement but Hutchison still looked doubtful. "I don't know. I don't feel good about that."

"Look, I'm not saying we actively disobey. That would only lead to anarchy and endanger us all. All I'm saying is that if we're told to do something that places us in mortal danger then we no longer *have* to do it. Ultimately it's every man for himself, survival of the fittest, and all that. It's a dog-eat-dog world right now and I don't intend to let any of these damn festering mutts nibble on my behind."

Lewis sat in the front of the first Land Rover beside Darby who was an adept driver and had seemed relatively unruffled by his two missions off base so far. Lewis wanted to spread the experience and training amongst the three vehicles as much as possible. Behind him and with all eyes trained unwaveringly on the surrounding roads and countryside were Corporal May Williams from the medical section and Wood.

Lewis watched the base receding into the distance then turned to Darby. "Keep it nice and easy, we're in no rush. Anything you don't like, please speak up, and better to keep the car moving, albeit slowly, than come to a complete stop."

"Yessir. No problemo." Darby's concentration never left the road as he stared ahead with his hands gripping the steering wheel tightly.

Lewis tried to hide his smirk. Much of the time he acted the fool but that may have just been a reflection of his youth. Put him behind the wheel of a car and his attitude changed; he clearly loved driving and took it seriously. Sometimes.

Lewis now turned to the soldiers behind him. "You two okay?"

It was the first trip off-base for both of them. Corporal Williams sat looking terrified and hardly noticed Lewis's question until he nudged her.

"Oh, err, yes, I'm okay sir, really." She did not sound convincing though.

"Look just relax. There are loads of us out today so we should all be quite safe if we engage any hostiles. Keep your wits about you and keep that weapon pointing somewhere else." He gently put his hand on her Browning which was aimed upwards and lowered it away from them all. There were not enough SA80s on base to be given to everyone, so they had been shared out appropriately and May Williams only had a Browning.

Wood had not been thought to be medically fit enough to venture out on earlier missions so this was his first excursion. He now sat quietly attentive, soaking it all in. He had a pistol at his side and held one of the rifles.

"I'm fine," was his blunt reply. He seemed to be a man of few words.

Lewis smiled despite himself and felt strangely bolstered by the other's company. Wood was not the most outwardly charismatic of individuals but seemed to exude confidence and ability, and that was exactly what Lewis needed right now; someone who was competent, able to handle the pressure and did not cause unnecessary complications – unlike others in the party. He wondered again why Denny had not come out to see them off; in his opinion that was a significant error of judgement and perhaps indicated his commanding officer's relentless decline under stress.

When Lewis had mentioned to Denny about the change in plans and their intention to take the lorry and more troops out on patrol, Denny had acted as though he had been in favour of it all along. "Well absolutely, of course you should. That seems to be the obvious thing to do," he had replied in a vaguely patronising tone which had made Lewis bridle somewhat, as it had most definitely been the initial orders of the Station Commander *not* to take the Bedfords. Lewis had refrained from pointing this fact out but instead accepted the decision in good grace, breathing a sigh of relief that the request had been granted without further argument. He had made a mental note to himself to take important decisions alone without consulting his commanding officer in future. It was easier that way. The military chain of command seemed to be breaking down. He would now have to assume a lot more responsibility and consider himself to be in overall command. He was aware that was not the 'military way' but in these uncertain times they had to adopt new practices.

Increasingly he was trying to avoid confrontation with Denny and not to put further pressure on him as his actions seemed to be getting more and more erratic. Even at the late hour when Lewis had turned in for the night he noticed that there was still the dim glow of candle light

266

coming from under the closed door to Denny's office. He had half expected Denny to surprise them all and come with them on this mission. He had fully expected Denny to come to the gates at the very least for a final briefing and morale-boosting words of wisdom, but there was no sign of him, just as there had been no sign of him at breakfast.

As Lewis had left the dining hall that morning he had bumped into Singleton and Handley.

"Please check up on Denny and keep an eye on him," Lewis asked them. "I think he's starting to lose it."

Handley nodded on behalf of both doctors. "I'll go and find him right now and make sure he's okay." He turned sharply on his heel and strode away.

Singleton paused in indecision and appeared to Lewis to be decidedly awkward about something. He was about to walk away himself but delayed a moment.

She finally seemed to make up her mind. "Look, we've lost too many good people already," she said quickly. "Please don't take any chances out there. We don't want to lose you too."

Lewis smiled inwardly but for once demonstrated some composure and restrained the big grin that threatened to break loose. "Of course. I'll be as careful as I can and make sure I bring them all back safely."

As he started to walk away he paused and turned to her. "And thanks, you know, for caring and all that."

"Sure," she smiled briefly. "Well, the base needs you, that's all."

The second Land Rover was driven by Corporal Kevin Berthon who had been an army patient at the station for just over three months. Like so many of the patients going through Headley Court in recent years he had been injured in Iraq. He had sustained a back injury from an explosive blast and had been unable to walk for several weeks. He had also received some minor flesh injuries, had needed small skin-grafts and had lost one finger off his left hand. Before the state of emergency had been declared he was showing good progress and had been walking, albeit with the aid of a walking stick, and since then he had improved somewhat. It was far from ideal to take injured people out on patrol but the numbers of able-bodied troops had fallen in recent days, and if they were to take such a large contingent out then they had to improvise somewhat. His back would probably ache after a day in the driver's seat but he would not be expected to get out of the vehicle and that would release another more mobile soldier to perform other duties on the patrol. In addition, Corporal Berthon was an experienced soldier and would be unlikely to be disturbed, any more than anyone else, by the horrors beyond the gates of Headley Court. Sat in the front with Berthon was Straddling and in the rear were Corporal Newman and Lance Corporal Millington. Newman had not been out on any patrols either, although he too had combat experience.

The Bedford was driven by Walkden as it was thought this would be an easier role for him than actively engaging in fighting. He was supported by Hutchison and in the rear of the truck was Sergeant Vallage with Leading Aircraftmen Neale and Patrick Scovell, all from the catering section of the base, and Charlotte Collins.

As before, whilst they drove they used the loud speaker announcing their presence to any possible survivors, although it had been agreed that they would cease this well before arriving at their destination. The only signs of life, at least at first, were some birds that pecked at rubbish scattered all over the pavements and a few stray dogs that seemed to have formed a pack. The dogs had already lost their groomed, household air, and had taken on the appearance of a more feral troop of mangy strays. One or two of them limped, had obvious sores and injuries, and they all looked very hungry.

It was an overcast day and as they left the base it started to drizzle with the wind spraying the sides of the vehicles. Just outside Bishop's Stortford they saw the first infected, two old ladies standing approximately fifty metres away down a side road. They each wore similar jumper and skirt outfits although both were dirty and one had torn the skirt right across her bottom, revealing a large amount of flesh. Had the troops been closer they would have been able to see the open scabs that ran all across her upper legs. The two ladies seemed to be fighting over something. They were pulling at an unidentified object and screaming at each other incomprehensibly.

The small convoy did not stop and the women either did not hear them or paid them no attention. As they drove on, the tussle turned more aggressive with one of the women attacking the other and striking at her head, before a third appeared on the scene. Wood had kept his rifle trained on them throughout, but as the distance between the convoy and the women increased he relaxed and lowered the weapon. Williams had whimpered and hid her eyes at first but took a deep breath and forced herself to look.

"They seem to group together," she murmured. "Why?"

Wood just shrugged, but he wore a puzzled frown as well.

"It seems to me," Lewis mused from the front, "that the condition or infection or whatever it is that they have got, is not so dissimilar to the dementia it was supposed to cure. I mean we call them zombies, septics, or lurchers, but in actual fact they are just humans who have forgotten how to behave and are acting on basic instincts."

"I'll remind you of that sir next time you're up close and personal to one of them," Wood replied, leaving a thoughtful hush in the car, but despite what he said, Lewis's words had got him thinking.

Their first destination was the weapon shop in Stansted Mountfitchet that they had intended to go to on the previous outing. In order to get there they had to drive around the periphery of Bishop's Stortford and then along a country road, the B1383. Every once in a while their passage was prevented by abandoned vehicles. Each time the Bedford was able to shunt it out of the way without too much of a problem. It left them all stationary and feeling exposed, but did not cause any further problems.

At the far side of town as they were approaching the intersection with the B1383 their route was again blocked. A double-decker bus had toppled onto its side partially obstructing their passage and an ambulance had crashed into it, barricading the rest of the street. Behind the ambulance there were several other cars that had smashed into each other making an impassable mess. It was a fairly large road junction but there was no way around the jam.

Lewis was on the radio immediately to the other two vehicles. "Stay put guys, not quite sure what the best option is yet but don't do anything hasty. Keep your eyes peeled for any septics and remain in your vehicles. Any bright ideas, I'm all ears." Then he turned to the others in his car. "Well?"

"I'd say that ambulance is too heavy for the Bedford," Private Darby said. "Even if it did manage to ram it out of the way it may well damage the lorry."

"Agreed. We can always try to find another route, but this is the start of the B1383. We may have to drive quite a way to find an alternative and even then there are no guarantees that other roads won't be blocked as well."

"This is a reasonably open area," Wood said from the back. "There doesn't seem to be anywhere for the infected to jump out from and surprise us, so we'd likely get a fair bit of notice if any approach. That should give us enough time to get back into vehicles or shoot them. Why not get out and check it out more thoroughly?"

Lewis nodded. "Yes, that's my feeling too."

May Williams was looking very unsure about the plan so Lewis tried to put her at rest. "Corporal Williams, I need someone to stay by the Landy with Darby here, to keep a good lookout and warn him of anyone approaching. Are you up to it?"

She nodded enthusiastically, clearly delighted at the prospect of remaining near to the relative security of the vehicle.

Lewis then got on the radio again. "Right I think we're going to take a closer look at this mess." He issued a few brisk orders, looked carefully around the area once more, rechecked his weapon and then turned to Wood. Wood had done the same and returned the tense expression.

Standing away from the base and outside the Land Rover for the first time since Headley Court had been sealed left Wood feeling very vulnerable. It reminded him of walking the streets of Kabul, Baghdad or countless other hostile cities when you knew that an enemy sniper was in your area, possibly even drawing a bead on you at that very moment, and you still had to continue on patrol, hoping and praying that today would not be your day to die. He did not stop to contemplate it for any length of time though; he had a job to do and quite frankly, que sera, sera. They had discussed situations like this the night before and he knew where he was most valuable. His back had recovered a lot since his injury but he was still not at full strength. However he had certain talents that could be of use to them all. He did not go to help investigate the crash site. Instead he climbed as quickly as he could onto the flat metal roof of the Bedford and took up a guard position. He would be the early warning for the others which would hopefully mean that they could continue with their duties in vague safety.

Lewis was joined by Straddling, Millington, Hutchison, Vallage, Neale and Scovell, all, to some extent or other, looking uneasy. Newman, Williams and Collins remained by their respective vehicles patrolling within a few paces and covering all angles of approach.

Lewis took his troops cautiously around the wreckage of the bus, which they were clearly not going to be able to move, and towards the ambulance. There was a possibility that they may be able to shift the other vehicles, or at least that was what he desperately hoped. Otherwise they were running out of options. As they approached the bus there was a terrible stench that made them all gag. Inside were a few bodies in various states of decomposition; some were still intact but rotting, others had clearly been largely devoured. The funk was overpowering and none of them looked too closely at the carnage.

The front of the ambulance had embedded into the off-side corner of the bus, denting the ambulance's bonnet. Its front tyres were flat which would make pushing it much harder. It looked as though it was a total write-off but was the only choice they had. In the driver's seat a body was slumped over the wheel. Again the stench was nauseating and made them all instinctively back away. Someone had to get closer though and it seemed unfair to order another person to do it, so Lewis stepped forwards whilst talking to his troops.

"Don't be distracted by this mess. Keep your eyes and ears open for aggressors. Just 'cos we've got some lookouts we can't rely on them to keep us alive. Stay focused and take up defensive positions."

With the chassis bent the door had jammed and it required help from Millington to force it open. In doing so there was a loud screech of metal scraping on metal that made them stop what they were doing and look around nervously.

From on top of the truck Wood peered anxiously at the group and scanned around for any signs that the noises were drawing attention. His vantage point meant he could see a fair distance along all the adjoining roads leading to the junction. He did not want to raise the alarm unnecessarily but he had already spotted one infected person staggering past at the next road junction to their left. The man had not noticed them and seemed to have tottered away now, so rather than halt the proceedings he had said nothing. Instead he kept an eye on that general area and tried to work out if there was any other road by which the man might yet approach them. He glanced around to see if anyone else had noticed. Collins saw him looking in her direction and smiled nervously at him. Clearly not, he thought.

Meanwhile Lewis had dragged the driver's decaying corpse from the ambulance amidst a barrage of feasting flies, and climbed into the seat. It absolutely reeked of decomposing flesh and made him feel dirty and defiled just sitting there so he tried not to breathe in through his nose. He ensured that his soldiers were suitably fanned out in a defensive formation then placed the ambulance out of gear and attempted to start the engine. The first time he tried it there was just a clicking sound and nothing further. Then when he tried again the engine seemed to turn over but it obviously was not going to start. He attempted it a couple more times and then stopped.

He turned to Hutchison. "Can you do anything for it?"

Hutchison rubbed his chin thoughtfully with a frown. "Hmmm, if I had my tools, the theme tune to 'The A-Team' and a day or two, I could possibly salvage something from this wreck, but unfortunately I didn't know I was going to be repairing write-offs. I can try and get the starter-motor turning over a bit more, which we could use to crank it forwards little by little and out of the way, but that's probably about it boss."

"Okay, that'll have to be enough then. See what you can do. The rest of you, I want you to clear that car from behind."

He pointed to a silver Daewoo Lanos that had smashed into the back of the ambulance. It had caught fire and there was very little left of its innards. In both front seats there was nothing more than the charred remains of two bodies, which was good from the perspective of reduced odour and flies. It too had flat tyres and the front axle had been pushed under the body of the car making it impossible to just knock it out of gear and roll it. As the five soldiers gathered around it and began to try to move it by a mixture of bouncing and lifting, Hutchison wrenched the bonnet of the ambulance open with another grinding screech of metal. Lewis walked a few paces beyond it and stood guard, raising his rifle as he scanned about for movement. The noises from the ambulance and now from manhandling the car were making him nervous. If the diseased were indeed attracted by sound then they were enticing unwanted attention to themselves but what choice did they have?

Another few noisy moments passed and he was becoming impatient. He turned to the soldiers anxiously. "Keep it down boys." The soldiers exchanged exasperated glances and continued to move the car whilst trying, somehow, to be a little quieter.

As Lewis turned back he noticed that Wood was no longer standing on top of the Bedford but had adopted a marksman's kneeling position. He was aiming his rifle towards the adjacent road junction. Lewis followed his line of vision and saw what he was watching so keenly; a lone man with a ragged blue coat hanging from his shoulders and a vicious wound running right across his face was about forty metres away. At that moment the man turned and saw the activity, let out a screech and started running towards them with surprising speed, considering the fact that only a moment before he had been limping.

"Infected!" Lewis barked, feeling a rush of adrenaline and the soldiers immediately stopped what they were doing and stared at him blankly.

Millington was the first to react; he shoved Neale, starting him off towards the military convoy and shouted. "Run!"

The safety of the Land Rovers was only about fifteen metres from them and they covered the distance quickly despite the vehicular obstacles. Hutchison had been in the ambulance at the time and it took him a moment longer to clamber out and over the side of the bus where the two vehicles had collided. Lewis waited agonising moments for him but still insisted on bringing up the rear.

As the man roared and rushed ever closer Wood trained his sights and followed the man's path, waiting for him to approach. He slowed his breathing and relaxed his shoulders, timing his shot with his breaths. He became aware, out of the corner of his eye, of other movements further up the road, but ignored them and focussed on the one target. Williams, Collins and Newman all behaved admirably; as briefed they anxiously stood their ground with their backs to their respective vehicles. They waited for their companions to get in, watching out for any approaching infected, until they too took refuge, but that wait for their colleagues, although only a few scrambled seconds, dragged on and on for all three of them.

Hutchison and Lewis had only just arrived at the Bedford when the first shot rang out, a single bullet, precise and effective. The man's head shattered and his body pitched backwards onto the road with a thud. Everyone apart from Wood shuddered at the sound. Wood was already aiming at the next attacker.

At the same road junction there had appeared five more diseased. It was unclear what had attracted them, but what was fairly sure however was that they too were now coming towards the group at pace. The three drivers had kept the engines ticking over throughout and so were ready to go if need be. All the soldiers apart from Wood had got back into their respective vehicles and weapons were readied and aimed. Darby and Walkden were both waiting for the command from Lewis to start driving but the command never came. Firstly Lewis wanted to check how many infected there were. If they were able to repel them all then perhaps they could continue and clear the path. Secondly he was aware that Wood was still on top of the Bedford and any sudden movements or acceleration could send him falling to his death. It was just too risky at the moment and so they would have to remain where they were.

Because there were more targets this time, Wood decided he could not permit himself the luxury of allowing them to get as near as the first infected had. He fired at the closest when they were still roughly thirty-five metres distant. The bullet's impact twirled the man around and knocked him to the ground but as it only clipped his shoulder it did not kill him outright and in a few seconds he was back on his feet after the others. Wood's next shot came when they were twenty-five metres away. This time it found its mark perfectly; elderly man in torn white shirt - head-shot. Wood again slowed his breathing and timed his shots with the brief pause between exhalation and inhalation. Breathe out, pause, bang, breathe in. Breathe out, pause, bang, breathe in. It was rhythmic, controlled and well-practiced. Fifteen metres, middle-aged man in check jumper, shot through the throat, his blood splattering the woman behind. At this stage the sound of more guns rang out. The initial Land Rover was closest to the oncoming attack and both Lewis and Williams fired. It was the first time that May Williams had ever fired a gun in anger and she closed her eyes as she squeezed the trigger. It was impossible to say whose round found its mark but the woman collapsed to the ground twitching and no longer alive.

In the second Land Rover the soldiers within now aimed their guns as well. At ten metres, a fifty-something woman in black, velvet trousers wearing one shoe and a large, grey bra but no shirt was shot through the head, her scalp erupting like a divot of grass being hacked away by a bad golfer. Then the discipline evaporated and a random volley rang out from all three vehicles as the last of the attackers was sprayed with ammunition. A young girl in her late teens who would have had a full head of blond hair in a former life, died just short of the vehicles. For a long moment no one spoke. Their ears were all ringing and pulses racing. Then Lewis leaned out of the window and looked up at Wood.

"Any more?"

Wood was already on his feet scouring not only up to the road junction but all around them. After a few seconds he looked down and shook his head. "I'd say that's it for now. Good job everybody. That went pretty well."

"Pretty well?" Williams was virtually hysterical. "I just shot a woman at point blank range and you think that went pretty well?"

Lewis turned around and put a gentle hand on her knee. "Corporal. Corporal! Relax. You did the right thing, you know you did. That woman was not the person she once was and you really have just helped to put her at peace. Lord only knows what it must be like to have this disease but you can bet your bottom dollar that she is happier now than she has been for weeks."

Williams still sobbed and nodded with a heart-broken expression on her face.

"Besides," Lewis added, "you missed her. I shot her." Williams stifled a laugh which, between the sobs turned into a mix of a squeal and a snort causing the three of them in that vehicle to collapse in a release of nervous laughter, drawing strange glances from the rest of the soldiers.

Finally Lewis composed himself and got out of the Land Rover. He looked carefully around and then addressed all the soldiers. "Okay that *did* go pretty well. Well done to you all, I don't think we could have done anything better. With a few elementary precautions we can make this as safe as can be. And thanks to you Sergeant Wood. Nice shooting."

Wood nodded from on top of the lorry, still scanning all around them for further diseased.

Lewis continued. "We still need to get through this barricade so, as you were. Check your weapons, keep the lookouts alert and get this ambulance out of the way."

Tentatively at first they disembarked from the safety of their vehicles and took up their previous positions, each anxiously fingering the triggers on their weapons. The Daewoo was swiftly moved clear and Hutchison declared with a grim face that he could do no more for the ambulance. He himself got into the driver's seat and prepared to turn the engine over as all available hands gathered around. He kicked it into gear, nodded solemnly through the cracked windscreen and the troops all began to push it as he cranked the starter motor. At first it was silent and the ambulance remained fixed resolutely in position. Then after a second of agonizing resistance it turned over once and then twice. Because the vehicle was in gear, each revolution of the starter motor forced it forwards a foot or two and with the troops shoving, they slowly started to make headway. They were creating an awful lot of noise though and Wood impatiently shuffled around on top of the truck.

"Hurry up, dammit," he spat. The gap had widened to a metre, then two, enough to squeeze the Land Rovers through but still insufficient for the Bedford. It was taking too long and making too much of a racket, and he could not contain his feelings of foreboding.

The next infected came from a different area and almost caught Wood by surprise. He had been focussing more on the adjacent road junction from where the others had emerged. Had it not been for the screech that the woman let out he may not have seen her until too late. She ran from the far side of the pile-up directly at the soldiers who were pushing the ambulance. She must have been at least thirty metres from where Wood kept guard. Immediately he assumed a marksman's kneeling position and sighted. The troops pushing the ambulance hardly had time to react themselves before the shot rang out and the woman fell. Lewis looked around at Wood with a raised eyebrow and Wood just shrugged.

Lewis turned back to the troops with urgency in his voice. "Okay, faster. Come on, get this done."

Wood turned to Newman, Williams and Collins. "Go help, I'll cover you all. Now. Move." The three ran, somewhat hesitantly on the part of Williams, to the ambulance and aided the pushing.

Two and a half metres now and each slight movement of the two-ton vehicle came at the cost of a lot of noise and effort. Lewis stepped back a moment from pushing to examine the gap. "Nearly there, final effort, come on."

Three metres and Wood was screaming. "Everybody back in the vehicles. Back in the vehicles, now!"

Several more diseased were running at them, from both previous locations. They were coming fast. There were about a dozen of them, screeching their inane babble as they ran. Wood started firing from his position aloft. He made no attempt to get into a vehicle himself. He hit the first at forty metres. Then another, but they were coming too fast for him.

"Run," Lewis shouted at his troops. The infected tearing at them from the far side of the pile-up were nearer to him than to Wood, so Lewis took up a firing position. He started to shoot at them while his troops ran for cover. Straddling joined him. Both leaned over the bonnet of the ambulance for support and defence as the rest of the soldiers fled. The sound of more shots came to them from the direction of the Land Rovers and Lewis glanced over his shoulder.

Grabbing Straddling by the arm he propelled him in the direction of the vehicles. "Go!"

Straddling started off for the Land Rovers and Lewis fired twice more, dropping another man, a black youth probably in his late teens, before following his sergeant. Collins, Neale, Vallage and Scovell had all climbed into the back of the Bedford and were firing from there.

From his vantage point Wood was shouting out orders. "Conserve your ammo, control your fire. Go for the headshot."

Hutchison made it back to the Bedford just in time. He dived in beside Walkden and slammed the door shut, just as one of the diseased crashed into it. Hutchison scrabbled for his pistol and then fired down into the boy's face, turning it to mush. Wood was kneeling and firing quickly now. He was hardly pausing to aim. He no longer slowed his breathing. There was just a continual volley, picking off the nearest of the diseased each time. But he was not able to shoot them all. Straddling did not have time to get to his Land Rover and instead hurled himself at the rear of the Bedford. Neale and Scovell had raised the metal tailgate to waist height. From their elevated position this gave them sufficient protection against any attackers at road level but still allowed them to fire out. Straddling leapt at it and vaulted over in a moment, gasping for breath through fear and exertion. This left just Lewis and Wood outside as the infected reached the Land Rovers. Wood was safe on top of the Bedford. Lewis was not. A man jumped at the Land Rover and landed on the bonnet. He quickly scrambled towards the windscreen baring his teeth, causing Darby to yelp in fright. He had kept the engine running all the while and now nimbly popped his foot off the clutch and the car shuddered forwards, sending the man sliding off. Darby momentarily dabbed the brake, then accelerated again and the man went under its wheels with a jolt and screech as his bones shattered.

The next attacker got to the Land Rover just before Lewis, cutting him off from safety. His anger was initially aimed at the vehicle but diverted to the soldier, and he lunged at Lewis with venom. Lewis had been careering towards the vehicle and only just had time to slow up as the man turned on him. He instinctively kicked out, catching him on the thigh with enough force to knock him to the ground. Right behind him the remains of the mob from the far side of the pile-up were now only a few steps away. Lewis had no time to hesitate as they all converged upon him. They screamed in delight as they finally caught their prey. Hands outstretched in triumph and fingers snagged his clothes. He flung himself frantically at the Bedford, but in his panic he had jumped from slightly too far away. He hit the tailgate half way up, but as he still clutched his rifle in his left hand he was not able to cling on. He fell back into the grasp of the enraged, screaming multitude. Wood fired his last two rounds into the throng and killed another but it was not enough and there were still too many. The nearest of the diseased snatched with loathing in his eyes and grabbed hold of Lewis's shirt. Another swiped at his face, drawing blood across his cheek. Lewis tried to jump once more but unfortunately the hands now gripping onto him prevented him getting sufficient height and again he fell back into peril. Wood helplessly watched it all unfolding in front of his eyes as he tried in vain to release his pistol in time to save his commanding officer from a hideous death. The diseased now surged forwards, all but surrounding him, even as he struck out at them, trying to clear a space. He swung his rifle around, knocking one to the ground, and fired a short burst into their writhing mass. Williams shrieked as she watched them fighting each other to rip the poor man limb from limb. Just then two things happened simultaneously; there was a loud bang as Collins fired into the face of the nearest attacker, splattering the ground with blood and releasing Lewis from his clutch, and two grasping hands reached over the tailgate from within. With tremendous force Lewis was yanked up and away from the clutches of the furious infected.

Lewis landed in a heap on top of Millington who had single-handedly hauled him to safety, undoubtedly saving his life. Some of the diseased remained screaming and reaching up at the soldiers in the Bedford. Several others now turned on the next easiest target, the Land Rover. Five or six of them raced furiously towards it. One leapt onto the bonnet and the others tried to smash the windows and access the tasty morsels within. Corporal Berthon instinctively reacted to the man right in front of him and reversed with a screech of tyres.

Wood was still on the roof of the truck but away from the reaching hands of the attackers. He now grabbed hold of a loose cord and banged the side of the cab. "Drive."

Walkden did not need to be told twice. The lorry leapt forwards at the gap and slammed into the nearside of the ambulance with a crash. For a moment everyone inside was thrown forwards and it seemed as though the Bedford would not get through, but the ambulance lurched an extra foot and they were free, spat out like a champagne cork with the Land Rovers and several infected chasing after.

Walkden checked his mirror to ensure that they had got clear of the danger and was about to stop to allow Wood to get off the roof but he need not have worried. At that moment Wood slipped down from his perch and through the lorry's open window, landing on the seat beside Hutchison. His face was covered in perspiration and he had somehow managed to cut his chin which bled freely, but his eyes were shining and wide open as though he had just come off a roller-coaster. For a moment the three men exchanged glances and then Wood whooped and yelled and banged the dashboard several times, shouting in elation. It was the biggest display of emotion either Walkden or Hutchison had seen from him and they shared in the moment.

Lewis got unsteadily to his feet in the rear of the truck. He was still trembling with fear and adrenaline but composed himself quickly. "Thank you for that," he said to Millington. "I think you just saved my life."

"Ah no man, it was nothing," Millington started to protest, but Lewis cut him short and placed a shaking hand on his shoulder.

"No. You saved my life. Seriously, thank you."

As the sounds of gun-shots rang out in the still air of Bishop's Stortford, with very few competing noises they could be heard from a long distance away, especially to the keen ears of a vampire. When she heard the first shots Flavia was just making her way out of the presbytery alone. She stopped still for a moment, discerning the direction of firing, then set off at a dazzling pace, leaping from roof to roof without paying any heed to subtlety or caution, disturbing occasional roof tiles and bricks, sending them clattering to the road below.

Unbeknownst to the soldiers, had they lingered only a few minutes more at the scene of the attack she would have caught up with them. She arrived at the wreckage as the remaining diseased still roamed about the site. She silently cursed, sniffing the air, listening and scanning all around and ignoring them with complete disregard. The diseased quickly realised that a new quarry was in their midst and turned their unending torrent of rage against her. This proved to be a bad decision as Flavia was not in the mood to be harassed. Out in the open with vehicles to impede their access, giving her plenty of platforms from which to spring into attack and create her ballet of death, she was a truly lethal weapon of destruction and it did not take her long to dispose of them all.

CHAPTER 13

The roads were not entirely free of burnt-out vehicles, but the soldiers did not face any more significant obstacles and arrived at their initial destination without having to stop again. They did see several other diseased wandering aimlessly. Lewis's close encounter made him contemplate his earlier words about the similarity between the infected and people with dementia. It reminded him of his own mother who had died from Pick's disease several years before. It reminded him of Wood's words of warning.

Stansted Mountfitchet was a small green-belt town. It had well-groomed gardens and a mix of modern, detached properties on the outskirts with older, more traditional cottages in the centre that had pretty wooden beams and thatched roofs. It was a pleasant yet sleepy town and the carnage that they found in its quiet streets seemed all the more shocking because of it. The village green in the middle had several wrecked cars abandoned on it. Some of the houses had caught fire and burned freely. The taint of smoke still lingered and the overall effect was one of a village in the Middle Ages that had just suffered a pillaging from marauders.

The soldiers drove slowly, taking it all in and looking for the weapons store. In a location that looked as peaceful as this Lewis found he could envisage quite clearly the horrors that must have occurred, as though he could still hear and see the chaos. Neighbours, who had lived side by side uneventfully for years or even decades, turning on each other and savaging each other in the night. It made him feel nauseous so he tried not to think about it. Instead he focussed on the soldiers around him, under *his* command now and largely reliant on him to keep them alive for one day at a time. He had recovered after the trauma of his near-death experience; the scratch down his cheek was not very deep and had stopped bleeding. Mentally he tried to prepare himself to take charge once more and present a strong figure to his troops.

On the far side of the town they found the small industrial trading estate, hidden away behind a copse. The estate was little more than a cul-de-sac. The units were mainly involved with plumbing and carpentry supplies, and the weapons store looked quite out of place. It was a single storey building with white brick walls and heavy, metal shutters. To the right side of the building there was a reception area that led to the shop but the door to that also had a metal grill in the glass and a large padlock. What neither Lewis nor any of his troops noticed was that the padlock was on the inside.

The vehicles stopped twenty metres away. There was no movement or sound from anywhere so Lewis warily got out of the truck and went over to both Land Rovers. He quickly appraised the state of remaining ammunition and redistributed it to all the troops appropriately. It was important that everyone had at least a few rounds, but with some notable exceptions that was just about all that anyone would have. He cursed under his breath and silently prayed that they had no more unfriendly encounters. They just could not deal with it right now.

"As before, defensive positions. Turn the three vehicles around in case we need to make a quick exit. Williams, Newman and Collins, I want you guarding your respective vehicles again. Neale and Scovell, I want you two to do the same, keep your eyes open. Straddling, Hutchison, Vallage and Millington, you are coming with me inside to tool up. Wood, do you mind taking up your position again?"

Wood was the only person that Lewis asked, rather than just ordering. He nodded and silently turned to climb back onto the roof of the truck as Lewis grabbed the bolt cutters from his Land Rover and strode towards the shop door. It was only then that he noticed that the bolt was on the inside which seemed a little odd, but he was preoccupied and ignored it.

Lewis beckoned Millington over to him. "Come on then, put that enormous brawn of yours to use." He handed the bolt cutters to the big man. "Get to work."

Millington smiled his broad smile. "Step back little people," he rumbled, his deep voice commanding respect despite his lowly rank.

He shattered the glass with a swing from the bolt cutters, the noise making them all edgy. Millington looked around and then started hacking at the metal grill, severing each link in a painfully slow process that made Lewis impatient. They were all scanning the surrounding buildings. All but Millington faced away from the weapons store so nobody noticed the inner door in the shop crack open an inch. Even Millington, who was feverishly working away, did not see the muzzle of the shotgun protrude from within. Briefly it withdrew as though there had been a change of plan but then the blast made them all jump. May Williams gasped, dropping her pistol, and Lewis and his troops all dived for cover on the ground, shielding their heads.

Straddling was the first to crawl over to Millington to check him for wounds. His eyes were wide open, the whites staring out as Straddling grabbed his shoulder.

"You okay?" he mouthed.

There was no reaction at first. Then Millington blinked and to Straddling's amazement he smiled.

"Yeah, sure. It didn't hit me, just scared the bejeezus outta me that's all. Strewth man!"

Straddling let out a deep breath.

"What the hell was that?" Lewis said, already back on

his feet and standing to the side of the shop entrance. He was shielded from the interior and the anonymous shooter, his rifle up and ready.

No one had a chance to answer though before a coarse voice spoke from inside. "Try that again and I'll shoot to kill next time. I don't care who you are, just bugger off."

The voice was rough and heavily accented from Devon or Cornwall perhaps, sounding like a farmer scaring people off his land, almost in a satirical parody. However it had a disturbingly unhinged quality to it, as though the man had just woken up from a drunken slumber and had not yet fully come to his senses. Everyone froze where they were. This was the first contact they had made with anyone in a couple of weeks and it unnerved them all.

Lewis answered him, trying to keep his voice level. "We come in peace." It seemed like a lame thing to say but was the first thing he could think of. He shrugged at Straddling and continued. "Who are you?"

"Who I am is not important."

"Are you sick?" There was no reply, just the soft but distinct click of metal on metal.

"Is there anybody else in there with you?"

Silence.

Straddling started to stand up now, peering in through the glass of the door and there was another boom as the man fired again. The ceiling of the reception area just above the door exploded in choking, white dust as the shot blasted a hole into it, deafening them all again and sending Straddling back onto his belly with his hands over his head, cursing.

As the dust cleared Lewis crawled over to Straddling and tried to reason with the man. "We mean you no harm, we aren't contaminated. We're military, from RAF Headley Court medical base. All we want is some ammunition. We're running seriously low and we really need your help."

"If you try to come in again I'll kill you."

"Why don't you come with us? We can help you. We have medical supplies, doctors, secure grounds and plenty of space for other people. Just please, help us and come with us."

"I'm staying right here. It's not safe out there and nobody's coming in here either. As far as I know you're probably all sick. Go back to your base 'cos the next time I really will shoot to kill. I mean it." The voice rose in pitch and sounded hysterical now.

Lewis was getting more and more despondent and Straddling placed a hand on his shoulder. "Come on boss, let's go and talk about this out of his firing range."

It was a desperate situation. They had come a reasonable distance and faced death only to be foiled right at the end when their goal was practically within reach. The man within was clearly not interested in either helping them, nor in being helped himself, and as far as Lewis could make out he sounded decidedly unbalanced.

Lewis could not think of an alternative and he reluctantly turned now to his troops. "Well, we can break in, which let's face it will probably result in a fire-fight and mean we have to kill him and anyone else who is in there. Or we can leave him in peace with all his ammo and return to base empty-handed. Thoughts?"

Straddling answered without hesitation. His view of the world was a lot more straightforward than that of most of the others. "It's quite simple; we desperately need the ammunition. He's got plenty of it. If he isn't willing to let us have some then effectively he is sentencing every one of us to death, and I for one am not about to let that happen. I say we go in and if he tries to get in our way then we shoot him."

Lewis looked around at the soldiers all huddled about

289

him with pitiful expressions; anxious, downcast and waiting for a solution that he just did not have right now. Vallage, Newman and Scovell were nodding their agreement and Neale looked uncomfortable and would not meet his eye. Clearly they, at least, were in favour of Straddling's plan. He felt the pressure of leadership and wished for an obvious answer to their dilemma.

He looked up at Wood who was crouched on top of the truck. "Well? Any ideas?"

Wood looked grimly down at his boss with a hard stare and Lewis wondered if he might actually agree with Straddling.

"There is truth in what Sergeant Straddling has said," he started, confirming Lewis's fears. "We do really need that ammo. We aren't going to survive for much longer without it. I just wonder if there might be another option. Instead of killing him, why don't we shoot to disable him? Take him down, then quickly get in there. If he is still alive then take him back to the base and get the docs to patch him up."

Hutchison looked uncertain though. "I don't like the sound of that. Shooting to disable him? How would we be sure that he won't still be able to fire? And how would we be sure there aren't loads more people in there?"

"We won't," Wood replied curtly, "but that's the chance we take for maintaining a small element of compassion."

Straddling was tense and the delay was making him angry. "That's all very well but your sense of *compassion* may well get some of us killed. I say he has brought this upon himself with his own selfishness. It's dog eat dog, either him or us. We should just get in there and get the job done. That's what we came for so let's do it." He cast a wary glance at Hutchison as though to say, 'I told you so.'

They were all silent, all eyes resting with great weight on Lewis. Clearly there was not going to be a solution that appeased everybody so he would have to make a decision and bear the responsibility himself. He just hoped that whatever he decided would not lead to mutiny. He had to balance these thoughts against what he believed to be the right course of action.

May Williams, who still stood by her vehicle, was becoming increasingly agitated by the discussion. She could contain herself no longer and rounded angrily on Straddling. "You can't be serious. What you're talking about is murder."

"A casualty of war I'm afraid my dear, and by refusing us ammo he has effectively become the enemy," Straddling repeated with a grim expression.

"Well it's not right," she choked the words out. "He has as much right to life as we do and whatever you say it *is* still murder."

Lewis looked at each of them with an earnest expression. "Yes, you *are* right; we *do* need the ammo - badly. And yes he is indeed endangering us all by refusing. But I can't sanction going in there and killing him. He's trying to survive, like we are, and just because there are more of us does not make it okay to murder him. Whilst in war there are indeed casualties, there is also a code of honour; morality, human rights and all of that. None of that has gone away just because of the collapse of civilisation. We can't just go in there and kill him. It's when things are at their very worst that we have to maintain our sense of humanity. That's as important now as ever. Otherwise what have we got left?"

His plea was impassioned and left him feeling out on a limb. In normal times his soldiers would follow him and obey his commands because of his rank, if nothing else. He was very well aware that the framework of the military, the discipline and the potential for punishment kept the majority of soldiers in line most of the time, but that was no longer the case. With the collapse of civilisation there was no longer a military structure and there was no realistic, viable potential for punishing anyone who disobeyed him. The reason they all followed him and would continue to do so, or not, would increasingly be because his decisions were sound and by sticking together as a cohesive unit they would survive better than by insubordination and individual action. But he knew only too well that the moment his decisions put their lives in jeopardy, what was to stop them from overthrowing his rule and doing what they wanted? There were unquestionably different ways of looking at this particular dilemma and he had made his choice. The others now also had the same choice to make, a decision that could potentially tear them all apart. He looked around at his colleagues imploring them to do as he asked. Straddling had been the most enthusiastic exponent of fighting their way into the weapons store. He was the senior sergeant and what he said carried great weight with the troops. He was undeniably the linchpin in Lewis's plea.

As they stood arguing, Collins had taken herself away from the others slightly and stood near the store entrance. She thought she heard scuffling sounds from inside. Gingerly and timidly at first she pleaded with the unseen man in the store.

"Please mister." There was no answer but she continued anyway. "Please, we really need your assistance. We don't mean to harm you. We're scared just like you are. You don't have to come with us; you don't even have to open the door. All we ask is that you let us have any ammunition and weapons that you can spare. All we're trying to do is to survive for one more day but we can't do that without your help. Please..." Her voice faltered and she started to sob and turned away from the door.

Still silence.

The soldiers stopped their conversation for a few seconds, staring at the store hopefully and none more so than Lewis, but there was no answer from within.

"I'd say he has just made the decision a lot easier," Straddling said gruffly. He quickly raised his pistol and flicked the safety catch off. "He's jeopardising us all and I am not going to allow it. You speak for yourself sir but not for me. I'm going in." He glanced at Hutchison as he stepped defiantly towards the shop. "Anybody else backing me up?"

Hutchison's hand went to his pistol but flickered there hesitantly. Straddling glared at him and he slowly drew it, as did Corporal Newman who fell into step behind him.

Lewis could feel the eyes of the group heavily upon him. Like lead, his hand raised his own pistol and aimed it at his senior sergeant's back.

"Not one step further sergeant." His voice did not sound like his own but came from a distant place. "I am in charge here and I have made my decision. We are *not* going in and that's final."

There was silence. Everyone froze in the little vignette that was playing out. Hutchison and Newman both wavered, looking uncertain. They glanced at their senior sergeant for a cue. Straddling looked back over his shoulder in amazement at his commanding officer. With the colour draining from his face he took a deep breath.

"To be honest, *sir*," he said slowly with a sneer on the last word, "I am in charge of my own destiny. We desperately need more ammunition, otherwise we are all going to die. So actually, I *am* going to go in there."

"There is an alternative," Lewis reasoned, his gun still

pointing directly at Straddling's back. "There's another gun shop nearby - we can get weapons and ammo from there."

Hutchison and Newman looked at each other and slowly stepped backwards, away from Straddling.

"Stradz," Hutchison pleaded, "let it go."

Straddling ignored him. "If you're gonna pull it then you'd better be prepared to use it," he said to Lewis, "'cos I'm still going in there. You're just gonna have to shoot me in the back if you want to stop me."

"Straddling!" Lewis barked.

He never got the chance to finish his sentence, nor carry out his threat. There was the sound of metal scraping and a muffled voice called out from within. "Wait."

The voice was quiet and Collins was uncertain that she had heard correctly. The soldiers all looked at her, standing near the weapons store. Nothing more was said and they shifted impatiently where they stood. Nobody moved. Lewis and Straddling looked like two figures from a frieze. Then there was a bang and a grunt. The metal shutter rattled and was raised a couple of feet off the ground by unseen hands and the stench of human waste wafted out from the darkened interior. A large, wooden box was shoved out and then the shutter clattered back to the floor and there were several more banging and scraping noises as padlocks and chains were reapplied. Then silence once more.

Collins knelt by the box and slowly raised its lid, squinting inside before delving in and rummaging around. Apart from Wood, all the other soldiers now peered keenly at her and Straddling quickly moved to her side. Wood had distanced himself deliberately from the proceedings in order to keep watch and not get distracted.

Straddling looked up. "It's the correct ammo for both

SA80s and Brownings. Quite a lot of it too. I think we're sorted."

"Anything else?" Lewis asked.

"Nope, but that should just about do us I'd say; for a while at least."

"Okay everybody back in the vehicles," Lewis quietly released the breath he did not know he had been holding. "And thank you," he said to the silent building but there was no reply. Collins also called out her thanks and she could imagine the man within deliberating whether to reply or not. Straddling cast a dark glare at the building and then scowled at Lewis's back as he climbed into the Land Rover. His hand fingered the pistol as he closed the door.

As they drove away Private Darby, whose eyes were still glued to the road ahead, spoke with a frown. "Wow. That was intense, phewee."

"Just drive Darby," Lewis muttered.

"But how did he know what ammo we needed? We never told him."

"Hmmm, I guess he must have been watching us quite closely," Lewis mused. The thought of whoever was inside the building scrutinizing them all the time they spoke, probably with a gun trained on them throughout, chilled him. Would they have opened fire the moment Straddling and accomplices returned to the entrance? Exactly how close had they come to being shot by that unbalanced man and how many would have been killed?

Wood leaned forwards from the back seat. "Admirable move back there boss. A man with principles, I admire that." He clamped a hand on Lewis's shoulder.

"Thanks." It had been an extremely tense moment for Lewis and Wood's support was comforting.

"That could have played out very differently."

"Hmmm." Lewis still had the distinct feeling that his

position of command was now tenuous at best and he may not withstand another confrontation. He was extremely grateful that they had not come away empty handed; even more that the situation had not deteriorated further. "Could have done with a few shotguns though, that would have been really handy."

"Well as you said earlier, there's another gun shop nearby so we could always try there. Where exactly is it?" Wood asked.

Lewis looked round at him with a sheepish expression. "To be honest I haven't got a clue where any other gun shop is. I was just trying to diffuse the situation."

"Sheesh man!" Wood said with a grin, and sat back in his seat.

The next item on the shopping list was fuel. They had passed a small petrol station on the edge of Stansted Mountfitchet and that was where they now headed. Pulling up outside Lewis ordered them into defensive positions as before. There was no sign of life anywhere as they started to unload the forty-four gallon drums from the back of the Bedford, being careful not to drop any and attract unwanted attention as Senior Aircraftman Freddie Samuels had on the previous scavenging mission. Sergeant Vallage had not been off base on previous missions and was decidedly nervous although he would not admit it. He chatted animatedly as he passed the drums out of the lorry. It was the most talkative that either Neale or Scovell had ever seen their ordinarily dour sergeant. If they had not known him better they would have said he was actually in good spirits as he cracked jokes and bantered with the two of them. He repeatedly told them they were doing well and praised them for keeping their cool during the earlier fire-fight, so much so that it almost became embarrassing.

"Think the boss has had a personality transplant. Either that or he's totally lost it," Leading Aircraftman Neale confided in his friend when Vallage had climbed into the rear of the lorry, out of ear-shot.

"Nah, he's just crapping himself." Leading Aircraftman Patrick Scovell was a large Geordie with a mass of unruly black hair, a galaxy of freckles and a distinct turn of phrase. He had been in the RAF for a little over six months, having joined straight from school, and was only just nineteen years old, but the events since the state of emergency did not seem to have ruffled him unduly. Since joining the military he really had come to accept his fellow soldiers on the base almost as his family and had adjusted to the structure and regulations of military life admirably, as if it was what he had always needed. As he carried the barrels he seemed at ease, as though it was merely an ordinary day's work in a completely normal situation. Neale watched him surreptitiously for a moment and marvelled at how unaffected he appeared. He couldn't help but wonder though if it was all a front, if it was just easier for him to block everything out and act totally naturally.

The petrol station had a small supermarket attached to it. As they prepared to collect fuel, Lewis sent Millington, Newman and Straddling, who still appeared to be smarting, to have a look inside for any supplies that they could salvage. The building was a low structure with a corrugated roof, blistering white paint that looked as though it had not been maintained in many years and peeling adverts in the windows. The posters were largely outdated and showed glossy images of impossibly tasty snacks, chocolate bars and permanently fizzy drinks. Surrounded by the terror and death of recent weeks they could not have seemed more out of place and meaningless. The shop would have looked tired and uncared for even when it was still serving customers regularly but now with all that had happened in recent weeks it looked alien and made Millington feel peculiar. He could imagine the chime as customers walked through the door to pay for fuel, the banal conversation of the cashier and the chink of coins being deposited in the open maw of the cash-till. As they stepped up to the front door he noticed a crack in the window at the bottom corner. A slither of glass had fallen out onto the ground and splintered, indicating the start of the building's demise, as though if he came back every week another part of it would be lying abandoned and broken until there would be nothing left except the eternally shining candy bars and a few dusty remains blowing in the wind.

Bang!

The door flew open as Millington heaved against it. The rusty lock splintered, sending the frosted glass door crashing back against the inner wall, making Corporal Newman jump. Everyone stopped what they were doing for a second and glanced first at the three soldiers entering the shop and then at the surrounding area. There was no movement so slowly they returned to the activity of gathering fuel and patrolling.

Straddling looked at Millington and Newman. "Let's at least try to keep it quiet, hey? Guns and torches ready, we don't want to get caught with our trews down." He checked his Browning's safety catch again, even though he knew it was set to 'off' and gave his torch a shake which then burst into life. Millington smiled and did likewise. Newman nodded more seriously and hoped that he did not look as afraid and on edge as he felt, then held his pistol in front of him as he had seen done in films.

They slowly entered the small shop, their feet crunching on broken glass that seemed to lie everywhere without any actual indication of where it had come from.

Their torches probed the gloomy interior, picking out the detritus from weeks of neglect. It reminded Millington of an old church or an ancient, undisturbed tomb. They were all listening and looking so intently that it took a moment to register the stench of decay. The shop had three narrow aisles. Shelves were piled high with products and there was rubbish, cardboard and tins strewn all over the floor. The soldiers gradually and carefully moved into the shop and peered between the aisles, one at a time, pointing their guns ahead of them in case anyone tried to rush at them. However the shop was empty.

Straddling tapped Millington on the shoulder and pointed towards the cash till. They moved as silently as the broken glass would permit towards the desk and peered over. Nothing. Straddling lowered his weapon and a loud a sigh of relief escaped from Newman.

"I think we're safe, it's clear," Straddling said but there was a muffled clatter from nearby that made the three of them freeze. Millington pointed behind the cash till at a black, wooden door. It was partially hidden behind some boxes that looked like they had been piled there for years and in the gloom they had all failed to notice it. Weapons raised they advanced towards it. There were no more sounds now and Newman started to doubt whether the noise had actually come from within the store at all - wishful thinking perhaps.

The three soldiers took up position at the door, with Newman at the back and Millington and Straddling poised to open it. Millington tried the handle but it was locked so he lowered his weapon and took another step back. Straddling looked around at Newman and nodded. Newman's eyes were wide and he was sweating. He could hear his heart pounding and he felt as though he might faint. He tried to smile as Millington had done earlier and returned the nod although he felt far from convincing. Then Millington launched himself at the wooden door and the frame splintered.

He sprawled forwards into the darkened room and tried to regain his balance, quickly raising his weapon and aiming into the room defensively. Straddling's torch worked back and forth immediately. After the initial bang there was momentary silence as they searched the interior and their eyes adjusted. Then in the far corner behind some crates there was an abrupt flurry of activity and a pinched, unintelligible scream. A body suddenly flickered in the shadows from one corner of the store room to another and Straddling tried to pick the movement out with his torch. Newman saw a silhouette loom in the dark that was exaggerated by the eerie shadow it cast. He took an involuntary step back in shock with a gasp. His finger squeezed down on the trigger at the same moment.

"*No!*" A dark figure stepped in front of Newman as Millington threw himself in the way of the weapon. Straddling knocked the gun up and the shot fired deafeningly into the ceiling.

"No you fool, it's not one of the infested," Straddling snapped at the shaking soldier and Newman sagged back and almost collapsed.

Millington had immediately grasped the situation. He swiftly sheathed his weapon and with surprising tenderness for such a large man stepped forwards and lowered himself onto his haunches. Behind some boxes, in the light of Straddling's torch he saw the pale and dirty face of a very frightened little boy. "Hey little fella, it's okay, we're here to help." Millington spoke softly as he edged nearer, holding his hands out in a placating gesture.

The boy stared wild-eyed at him, screamed and bolted for the other side of the room, sheltering behind the boxes. Millington changed direction and patiently approached him once more, making soothing overtures all the time. "Don't be afraid. We're not going to hurt you, you have nothing to fear, it's all gonna be okay now."

The boy again tried to escape but Millington was close enough to grab his arm, gently but firmly, and pulled him close. The boy wailed again and lashed out, catching Millington in the chest with his shoeless foot and in the face with his bunched fingers. Millington ignored both and held the boy steady in his arms, continuing to make calming noises. The boy's protests continued but gradually, as Millington held him fast, they turned from screams of fear into the whining sounds of desperate anguish and tears started to flow down his grubby cheeks. Eventually he quietened down as Millington rocked him. His face buried in Millington's large shoulder and his body went still and lifeless as he passed out.

After the gun shot there had been an alarmed shout from Lewis. "You guys okay in there? What's going on?"

As Millington dealt with the boy, Straddling sheathed his weapon and turned around to brief him on the latest turn of events. Millington now stood up and walked out of the store room into the light, clutching his most precious loot. "God only knows what this little guy has been through."

Lewis, Wood and Hutchison were standing in the shop's entrance with weapons drawn and frightened looks on their faces. All Hutchison could say, over and over again was "Good Lord!"

The biggest smile broke across Wood's face and Lewis immediately turned around and summoned Williams. "Please come over here. I think that Millington may need the calming assistance of a woman."

The boy was absolutely filthy, emaciated and stank, as he had clearly soiled himself. Millington sat him down in the back of the Land Rover but ensured that the door on the far side was locked in case he regained consciousness in a panic and tried to escape. May Williams found some water and a cloth in the supermarket and dabbed his face gently, enlarging the paths that his tears had already cleared through the grime. Gradually the boy came round and at first, as his eyes flickered, he was docile and still. Then swiftly as he became fully aware his legs shot out rigidly in front of him, he screeched and moaned and pushed himself violently away from his rescuers towards the far side of the vehicle. Williams slowly got into the Land Rover beside him and sidled across the seat until she was up close to him, taking the kicks to the stomach without complaint. Little by little she managed to calm him down until she was able to put her arm around him. He eventually seemed to accept this and buried his head in her chest and started to weep once more.

The forty-four gallon drums were all filled and everything of value had been taken from the store. Lewis set up a defensive cordon around the vehicles whilst Williams and Millington calmed the boy down. There was a real buzz amongst the hardened, cynical soldiers, a momentary reprieve from all the futility and anguish. The fact that there was a survivor seemed to fill them all with optimism, if only for a moment. In the depths of their darkest despair, amongst all the traumas and trials, finding a survivor, any survivor but particularly one so fragile and vulnerable, was a real beacon of hope for them all. Neale, Scovell and Vallage shared a cigarette, Wood chatted with Collins as though out on a date in the country and Walkden cracked a joke with Hutchison. Lewis was surprised to find that he was keen to get back to the base in order to show their finding to Squadron Leader Singleton of all people. For the briefest of moments all was well with their small world. Even Straddling was caught with a broad grin, a rarity in such times.

Finally Lewis walked over to the Land Rover, not wanting to alarm their new charge. "Look I hate to rush you but I'm getting nervous. Are you guys ready to go?"

"Sure thing boss," Millington beamed, his smile bigger than ever. "We'll be ready in just a mo."

Lewis noticed that the big man had tears in his eyes. Williams had slowly ascertained that the boy's name was Josh. He was eight years old and had been hiding in the store for several days since his father had brought him there, although he was unsure as to exactly how long it had been. The reason his father had abandoned him was not clear but Millington suspected he had become ill and wanted to make sure his son was as safe as possible whilst he still had time. Possibly he had hoped that his boy would be found by some looters who were not sick and taken into their custody, which was in effect what had happened.

Throughout their gentle interrogation Josh continually asked in a small voice where his father was and when he would be joining them, which made Williams break down.

"I'm not sure poppet," she said as her stomach wrenched. "He may be gone a while, I really don't know. But you are safe with us in the meantime. So why don't you come with us and maybe we can find your father later?"

The boy nodded with a mixture of heart-breaking sadness and obvious relief at having been found at last. He clung to Williams's arm and hid his head behind her shoulder. Millington loomed over her other shoulder still beaming and chatting to Josh as though they were old friends.

Lewis came over to them again. "Okay, ready?"

Williams looked at Millington and he nodded. "Yes sir."

303

Last on the agenda was a stop at a large supermarket on the outskirts of Bishop's Stortford. Private Darby, driving the front car, was filled with the weird sensation that it felt vaguely like a normal day out. As they arrived the scene was quiet, there was no obvious menace and it reminded him of driving with his mates in happier times. Cars really were his passion. He and his friends delighted in tearing around empty car-parks in their pimped-up motors using the lampposts as obstacles. They had spent countless hours parked up together and admiring the engines or body-work of each other's rides with music pumping out into the night sky. He felt himself slipping into morose reminiscing but a closer inspection as he drove through the car park entrance revealed a different picture and brought him back to the present. A few vehicles were scattered around and it was obvious that they were not all parked neatly. Some had clearly crashed or had just been left randomly in the middle of the car park. Shopping trolleys had been strewn all over the area and the Land Rover had to shunt some out of the way as they approached the glass entrance doors to the store.

Darby perked up as they approached and turned to Lewis beside him. "Reminds me of my youth this does sir."

"What? An abandoned supermarket?"

"Nah, going to the shops before anyone else was up and doing a few doughnuts in the car park. You don't mind if I do a few now do you sir?"

"Doughnuts?" Lewis asked.

"You know, hand brake turns, wheel spins, that kinda thing."

"I don't think so Darby. Not just now."

From the back seat Wood rolled his eyes in exasperation and shook his head.

Several of the store's windows had been smashed. A shopping trolley had been thrown through one and a car driven through another.

As before the three vehicles were positioned ready for a quick exit if needed. Williams stayed with Josh in the car and this time Collins, Scovell and Millington guarded the three vehicles with Straddling on top of the Bedford. Lewis wanted Newman to accompany them into the store in order to gather medical supplies. Wood, Neale, Hutchison and Vallage also went in so that there would be enough troops to split into two sections. They each collected a shopping trolley as they entered. It felt totally surreal to be in a party of soldiers in uniforms, all brandishing weapons but pushing trolleys.

Neale cursed as they went into the shop. "Why do I always get the micking trolley with a dodgy wheel and a mind of its own?"

"Shhh," Vallage cuffed him round the back of the head and scowled. "Quiet."

With torches slicing through the dark interior they walked silently amongst the aisles. They tried in vain to avoid stepping on the debris that festooned the floor. They were now not only looking out for diseased, but also for potentially armed and unpredictable survivors. Lewis took Wood and Neale down one aisle, the other three took the next. Lewis first wanted to sweep the shop to check it was clear before becoming embroiled in their task of gathering supplies.

"Keep your eyes open and take no chances," he whispered. "I don't want a repeat of whatever the hell happened to Sinna and Rohith."

There were over a dozen aisles. The first contained an assortment of cheap electrical goods and the store's own brand of clothes. There was little disturbance in this area and it could have felt normal but for the stale air and sickly-sweet, lingering odour of rotting food coming from somewhere within. Lewis spoke in a hushed voice to the two men by his side.

"Wood, you go first. Neale keep your eyes peeled, don't let your concentration lapse and keep your finger off your trigger" he said as he pointed to Neale's hand which already hovered nervously over the trigger. "I don't want you firing in error."

Lewis brought up the rear and continuously looked back over his shoulder. Wood moved at a steady, measured pace, sweeping his torch from side to side and up and down in graceful, lazy movements as though he was writing his name with a sparkler at a fairground. The first aisle was clear. They regrouped with the other three and Lewis exchanged a glance with Hutchison who nodded tensely. Lewis pointed to the next row and they proceeded wordlessly.

As they continued, aisle by aisle, they could all hear an odd sound, sort of a wet slapping noise that got louder as they moved through the shop. It stopped occasionally and was interspersed with a faint rustling. The subsequent aisle contained fruit and vegetables and it was here that the odour of decomposing matter was strongest. There were some items that had spilled on the floor and been trodden on, and Neale nearly slipped on the mess, earning him a stern glance from Lewis.

Deeper into the store they were further from natural light and it became reasonably dark, making progress slower and more nerve-wracking. The frozen goods section showed particular signs of disturbance. Blood and raw meat were spread all over the floor. It looked as though animals had been there and eaten through the plastic wrapping. Neale trod very carefully on the slippery surface, keen not to embarrass himself again. The reek here was strong and Lewis wondered how anything could eat the rotting meat when it made him want to retch.

They had worked their way through most of the store when the lapping sound returned and there was a commotion from somewhere indeterminate. Hutchison and his two soldiers froze, not sure where the disturbance had come from. Hutchison looked at Vallage who shrugged so he quickly led them to the end of their lane where Lewis was already waiting. He decided that it was safer not to separate while they searched the remainder of the store.

They started down the penultimate aisle of biscuits and cereals. In the gloom there were shadows moving towards the far end. Wood, who was still leading the way, held up his hand and they came to an uneasy halt. He waved them all back and they turned and retraced their steps. When they had rounded a corner they stopped.

Lewis leaned close. "What was it?"

"I'm not sure how many, but there were a few diseased down there. Maybe two or three, maybe more, I could only see vague shadows. They were all huddled together, eating something I think."

"Did they see us?"

"Nope. We could take them out but then I'm not sure if there are others nearby that might be attracted to the noise. Alternatively we could just quietly gather whatever we need from other areas, and maybe get out of here without any trouble."

"Sounds like you prefer the latter option," Lewis said.

Wood nodded. "If they're all happily eating then hopefully they won't hear us. Even if they do maybe they won't be interested."

"Okay. Let's make it quick then." Lewis said. It seemed to be intuitively wrong to be continuing, knowing that some infected were only a few metres away, but he too thought at the moment it was probably the better option. "Hutchison - take Vallage and Neale. Get as many tinned and dried goods as you can. Maybe some pasta, rice and cereal, that kind of stuff. We'll get medical supplies and toiletries and whatever else we can find of use. Five minutes max, then we're out of here. And stay focussed, don't let anything sneak up on you. Only one of you gets the items whilst the other two are on guard."

Hutchison nodded and the three men silently slipped into the dark while Lewis led the other two quickly through the store to the section with medical items. He was still not happy with the plan and hoped he would not shortly be ruing his decision.

As Neale started loading the trolleys Vallage and Hutchison took up defensive positions on either side of him, impatiently standing with weapons and torches facing out like the bodyguards of a reclusive star. Many of the shelves had already been ransacked and goods were spread over the floor. Neale appeared to be having a bad day as a tin slipped from his grasp and clattered as it rolled and rolled. The noise disturbed the silence and they all froze, fearing the worst, but after several seconds there had been no outraged cries from the diseased, only a few aisles away. Vallage tutted furiously at Neale, who avoided his eye contact and continued loading goods with his head down.

When Newman had filled two of the trolleys with toiletries, first aid items, vitamins and other things of use, Wood pointed at the adjoining row. Lewis glanced over and realised that they had forgotten to get any drinking water so he quickly stopped Newman and redirected his efforts. He looked back and Wood seemed to have disappeared. With a puzzled expression he probed the gloom with his torch but there was no sign of him. He had not mentioned splitting up so it seemed quite irregular and bad practice to abandon them for whatever reason without warning.

He hissed into the darkness. "Wood?" But there was no reply.

Is this what happened to Sergeant Sinna and Private Rohith? He could not help but wonder anxiously, but he did not want to leave Newman. After a minute a shadow sneaked around the edge of the shelving and Wood slipped up to them. His arms were laden with bottles of brandy which he added to the trolley.

Lewis was puzzled and slightly annoyed, but there was something about Wood's demeanour that made Lewis hold his tongue, as though he had been doing the most obvious thing and clearly they should have known where he would be. He was becoming more familiar with how Wood operated. He could imagine that the man was used to acting alone and on his own initiative. He doubted that Wood ever did anything when in the combat theatre without careful thought. Instead of admonishing the man he looked quizzically at the brandy.

"Cocktails," Wood replied with a twinkle in his eye.

Later, thought Lewis. This is not the time to ask. Get everybody to safety now and ask later.

Lewis gave a sharp 'psst' and Newman stopped what he was doing. Lewis drew a flat hand across his throat in a guillotine motion, and pointed to the exit. He checked his watch; four minutes although it felt like forty. Long enough and time to go. They had been fortunate so far; best not to try their luck too much.

With the three men pushing a heavily laden trolley each they slowly worked through the rubbish on the floor and made their way back to the light. Every squeak of one of the trolley wheels made Lewis cringe and listen for sounds of onrushing infected. With every step he had to fight the urge to run. The feeling of relief washed over him with some enormity as they approached the exit. Hutchison had obviously had enough as well as they arrived at the same moment.

"Time to go," Lewis mouthed and ushered them all out. He tapped Wood and Hutchison on the shoulders, pointed to his eyes and then the exit. Hutchison nodded and silently the two men stepped back into the store, watching out for any of the diseased whilst the rest of them loaded up the lorry.

Wood shone his torch into the depths of the supermarket and could make out vague shapes dancing in the shadows. He watched them carefully, silently cursing the slow progress being made loading the supplies onto the lorry.

It was easiest to just put the trolleys directly into the back of the Bedford. Millington hauled them up virtually by himself, with only superficial help. It only took a minute and they were done. Lewis made sure they were all in their vehicles before jumping into his. For a moment he did not speak and found it hard to focus or elucidate a command to his driver. Everything seemed to have gone too smoothly. There was a nagging feeling that they had forgotten something or left someone behind. He had become so used to mishaps, death and bad fortune that for the little shopping spree to have gone entirely according to plan just felt wrong. With all the responsibility for everyone's lives in the field solely burdening his shoulders he could empathise with Denny and the pressures that he had been under for the previous couple of weeks. It was a reminder to him, both to check up on Denny on his return to Headley Court, and to keep an eye on himself and his own levels of stress.

"Boss?" Darby looked at him with a concerned expression on his face, waiting for instructions.

"Yes, sorry. Let's get out of here."

Darby immediately gunned the engine and threw his occupants all off balance as he raced the vehicle away with a screech, leaving rubber tracks on the road and chuckling to himself as he drove.

The convoy did not encounter any more hostiles although they did see a number of diseased scavenging in bins, chasing dogs or just wandering aimlessly in the road. Lewis was thoughtful and spoke out loud as much to himself as to the others in his vehicle. "I wonder if the disease has passed to animals yet."

Wood turned and watched the dog that had been lying in the middle of the road and just scampered out of the way of the Land Rover in time. "I guess for that to happen, if it's even possible for the illness to be contracted by animals, one of them would have to be bitten but not actually killed by one of the infected."

"And that could easily have happened. I wonder if there would be a difference in how they act and whether we would be able to tell a sick animal from a normal one. Perhaps we should start to treat them with caution as well."

In the second Land Rover Josh was sandwiched between Millington and Williams. He spent the journey torn between looking out of the vehicle and hiding his head behind either of them, both of whom kept chatting to him throughout.

As they passed the road junction with the wreck of vehicles, several large, black ravens took to the air. They had been feasting on the corpses of the dead that the convoy had left behind. Lewis shuddered and turned round to talk to Wood again.

"I think we can add birds to the list of potential carriers, as well as dogs. Maybe they don't need to actually be bitten; maybe it's enough for them to just eat contaminated flesh themselves."

"Well God help us all if that's true." Wood looked out at the crash site with morbid curiosity, examining the bus and ambulance and remembering where the Bedford and two Land Rovers had been parked. He contemplated how they could have made everything safer for themselves whilst away from the protection of the vehicles. Could they have positioned the Land Rovers differently perhaps or set up a more effective defensive cordon? Had he looked more closely he might have noticed a figure sat in the shadows on the roof of a nearby building, dressed in black leather trousers and a lacy, black top. She was quite still and very patient, waiting and watching for her quarry to return. She saw them when they were still distant but made not the slightest movement. In fact had Wood seen her he could have been forgiven for thinking she was nothing more than a rooftop statue. She watched the vehicles pass, enjoying the sounds of the chatter from within and the scent of human flesh, watching them disappear as she stood and climbed carefully down from the roof. She was certain that nobody in the vehicles had seen her and she was quite correct, but had *she* been more observant herself she might have noticed another even more stealthy pair of eyes watching her as well.

CHAPTER 14

As the convoy approached the gates Lewis could see a few people awaiting their arrival. Flying Officer Oliver Frost, a young trainee helicopter pilot who had been undergoing aeromedical training on the base was on guard. He was hurriedly unlocking the gates as they neared. His rifle was slung clumsily over his back and as he stooped to open the padlock it kept slipping down and striking his hands, knocking the padlock from his grasp and delaying the process. Just behind him and standing outside the guard room were Singleton, Dr Handley and Private Hanson, a tall, skinny, army medic who had been serving on the base for only three months. Senior Aircraftman Masters's beautiful wife Vida also stood huddled with them, her long, dark hair bouncing and looking immaculate as she jumped from foot to foot impatiently. There was no sign of Denny.

The three vehicles drove through the gates. The occupants disembarked and Lewis went first to Singleton and Handley.

"Successful mission I hear?" she smiled, looking relieved, then noticed the wound to his cheek. "Are you okay?" There was genuine concern in her voice.

"Ah, it's nothing, just a flesh wound," he grinned. "And yes, we did have a pretty successful day out, all in all." He motioned for Williams and Millington to bring their charge over and Singleton got down on her haunches.

"Hello there, I'm Dr Singleton. How are you?"

Josh did not answer but hid his face in Millington's coat and Millington answered for him. "His name's Josh, ma'am."

"Well hello Josh and welcome to Headley Court. I'm sure you'll be very happy here and we'll take great care

313

of you." She could not contain the grin that broke free and spread across her face.

Straddling stalked past with an expression of thunder and Singleton looked quizzically at Lewis.

"What's put the bug up his ass?"

Lewis sighed and rubbed his face wearily. "Ahhh, tell you about it later." He looked quickly around at the assembled group. "Where's Denny?"

She shrugged with a frown and was about to answer when they saw him walking along the driveway towards them from the main building, looking as though he had just woken up. His hair was dishevelled, his uniform un-ironed and he looked as though he had slept in it overnight.

He walked up to the group, saluted stiffly and addressed them all in a loud voice. "Well done to you all, it's great news that you have all made it back safely, I'm absolutely delighted. I understand that you have brought back lots of good supplies for the base and even one new member?"

He looked at Josh, strode towards him and thrust out a hand. Josh hid again behind Millington and Denny coughed in embarrassment. "Oh well, cat got your tongue, eh?"

"He's just a bit shy sir, a bit shell-shocked is all," Millington answered for him again.

"Well maybe later then. Anyway, well done everybody." He stood for a moment looking round at them all as though he was searching for someone in particular, then turned on his heel and strode away.

Lewis stared after his retreating commanding officer then turned back to Singleton. "How's he been today?"

She sighed. "I think he's okay, he just seems really stressed. I guess the responsibility is wearing him down. Every time someone gets killed he takes it very personally and that makes it hard for him whenever anybody leaves the base I think."

"I know how he feels," Lewis replied and truly meant it.

There were too many people around them to discuss the matter further and there was too much to be done so the subject was postponed. The two doctors checked everyone over thoroughly for bite marks before the vehicles were driven up to the main buildings and unloaded.

"I'll come and see you later," Lewis called out to Singleton as he walked back towards the Land Rover.

"Yes, I'd better check that scratch on your face," she replied with a smile. He felt that the normal sense of antagonism between them was slowly dispersing. Perhaps she also realised that with Denny losing the plot, the two of them would be the most senior officers on base and would be increasingly reliant on each other. Maybe she had started to construct a bridge on her own bank of the river.

Before departing Lewis called Millington and Williams over to him for a moment. They spoke quietly out of hearing of anybody else. Williams nodded enthusiastically. Millington gave one of his characteristically big smiles and softly scooped the boy up into his thick arms before carrying him towards the medical section. Lewis watched them go with a grin and a warm sensation in his stomach, replacing the ever-present gnawing anxiety. He marvelled at the gentleness that Millington displayed, such tenderness that only the completely self-assured seem to possess. The man very clearly had a good and genuine heart, which was probably why every single person on base was so fond of him.

By the time Singleton returned to check Josh more thoroughly he hardly resembled the boy they had rescued from the petrol station. The grime had all but gone and he was starting to talk a little. When he spoke, regardless of who had addressed him, he directed his replies to Williams or Millington. They had the distinct feeling that tears were never very far below the surface and tried to keep conversation and questions as light as possible. There was plenty of time later to dig a little deeper and find out what had happened to his parents and whether he knew of other possible survivors. Medically he seemed fine; he had not been bitten and there were no obviously broken limbs, cuts or wounds. He was just pitifully in need of a good feed, some proper sleep without nightmares and a little loving care.

Lewis stuck his head around the door and smiled at the three of them. "You ready?"

Corporal Williams nodded and led Josh by the hand out of the medical centre.

They found Corporal Reggie Pethard sat in a deep, green velvet armchair in the ante-room beside the dining room. He was dressed neatly in uniform, his hair was combed and he was clean and shaven but he stared into space, not moving, hardly breathing and not really looking as though he was actually awake at all, apart from the fact that his eyes were open. Lewis signalled to Williams to wait outside. He coughed as he approached but Pethard did not appear to hear. It was only when Lewis sat down in front of him that he was forced out of his daydream and to focus on life.

"Oh sorry sir, I didn't see you there." He went to stand up but Lewis put a gentle hand on his shoulder and encouraged him back into his seat. His eyes were red and he barely looked at Lewis at all.

"How are you doing?" Lewis asked in as calm a voice as he could muster.

"Oh okay sir, you know, it's still really hard but I'm

getting there."

"Pethard, it's only been a day. Of course it's hard and it's going to continue to be hard for you, we all know that."

"Yes sir, but we've all been through similar things, there's nothing special about my situation. I've got to just face up to it and get back to work. We all need each other, now more than ever." There was a lot of truth in what he said but few people on the base, if any, had had to witness the death of a loved one at such close quarters and in such a brutal manner. There was a profound sadness in him and Lewis could not help but admire him for his stoic attitude. Although his heart was breaking he still realised his place on the base was as vital as everyone else's and that others depended on him After all, he may still one day be needed to save someone's life. This only made Lewis even surer that he was doing the right thing.

"Well if you feel up to it I have a special request I'd like to make of you. But I'll quite understand if you feel that this task is not for you at the moment."

Pethard tried to summon up a look of enthusiasm but it remained well short of convincing. "Yes sir, of course. What is it?"

"We found someone today off base. A survivor. Someone who needs to be looked after and I wondered whether you might be able to help with that?"

He beckoned Williams in and both Lewis and Pethard rose instinctively to their feet.

"What?" Pethard was dumbfounded and speechless. Lewis had seen men unable to communicate effectively when surprised, spluttering and getting their words mixed up, but to be so completely at a loss was rare. Pethard looked at the small boy in front of him who stood meekly staring at the floor and then back at Lewis, his eyes wide open and his mouth flapping. No words came out, just a strangled, moaning sigh.

Lewis could feel his eyes becoming prickly and strived to control his emotions. "We found him today," he said, trying to keep his voice level. "He was hiding in a petrol station just outside Stansted Mountfitchet. He's all alone and needs someone to look after him. I just wondered whether you might be up for the task? Perhaps you and Williams can both look after him between yourselves, you know, make sure he gets somewhere comfortable to sleep, make sure he gets fed with everyone else and just be there for him in general.

"I mean obviously we'll all help to take care of him as needed, but maybe just to have you and Williams in particular to look out for him, it would be a great help. You think you can manage that?"

At last Pethard found his tongue. His eyes were shining and tears had started to flow but he turned his back and quickly wiped them away. "It's a miracle!" That was all he managed to say at first and Lewis found himself now unable to stop the tears and dabbed surreptitiously at the corners of his eyes as the explosion of emotion from Pethard caught them all up. "It's a miracle."

Without knowing why, all three adults found themselves laughing hysterically. Pethard turned to Lewis and, forgetting rank and place, actually clapped him on the back and pumped his hand vigourously, and for another brief moment their microcosm in the shadows of the ante-room was only just big enough for the four of them and too small and solid for any outside horrors to break in.

Josh stood in the middle of the adults, staring up at them in confusion, not knowing whom they were, where he was or where his father was, but on some level realising that for now at least, he was safe and amongst people who would take care of him. Even he, young as he was, felt the slightest inkling that not all was bad with the world just then and tears came freely to all four of them in that little cosmos in the ante-room.

Lewis left Williams and Pethard with the boy and walked slowly away with a broad smile on his face, to the station medical office. He found Singleton and Handley sat facing each other on chairs, chatting in low voices. Privates Hanson and Howes were pottering around in the background, teasing each other and winding each other up with little quips and digs. Private Howes had been serving in the medical section for just over a year and although Private Hanson was new on base the two had bonded quickly. It was a real love-hate sort of relationship. Howes was much shorter and dumpier and yet seemed to be the more elegant, graceful and quick-witted of the pair. Hanson was always the one to play the fool to Howes's wise-cracks and the two were a humorous double-act, bouncing off each other.

"Knock knock." Lewis stuck his head through the door and flashed a large, genuine smile, a rarity at these times.

"Come in, we were just talking about you actually," Singleton replied warmly.

"Oh yes?" He resisted the urge for smutty banter.

"Just wondered how you had got on with young Josh and Corporal Pethard? By the size of your grin I'd have to guess things went pretty well?"

"Oh I think they'll do just fine. I think that's exactly what each of them needs right now." His smile grew and became infectious.

"Sounds like you had a successful day out?"

"Well, we got just about everything we went out for. We fought off a few septics, no one was too badly injured and best of all we found a survivor, so yes, I'd say that it was an immensely successful day; for once."

They all beamed at each other. It was amazing how one

happy event could so radically change the atmosphere on base and replace the bleak feelings of the previous couple of days, albeit temporarily.

"Now let me have a quick look at that scratch on your face."

Lewis watched her closely as she came near to him. A look of concentration was on her face as she dabbed at the wound with some antiseptic cloth, making him wince.

"Oh you big baby, it doesn't hurt does it?" she laughed.

"It could have been a whole lot worse, believe me," he smiled, still feeling extremely grateful to be alive.

"Have you been to see Denny yet?" Singleton asked, her eyes narrowing.

"Nope, that was next on the agenda. Has he been out and about much today?"

"No, we've hardly seen him."

"Personally I can totally understand the pressures he's under and how he must be feeling," Lewis said. "That's pretty much how I feel every time I take troops out with me off base."

"Well please don't let it get to you too much. If you start to feel stressed then do come and talk to me about it. Or I mean talk to any of us," she added quickly

Lewis had never seen Singleton acting so concerned about him and he was genuinely touched. He had not previously realised how helpful it was to have a little support from her.

"How are you sleeping?" Dr Handley chipped in.

"Oh you know, like everybody else I'm sure. Nightmares, waking up in the middle of the night in tears, not knowing where I am and then suddenly everything comes flooding back. Just the usual, until I get so tired that every once in a while I sleep for about twelve hours straight and wake up completely spaced out but vaguely refreshed."

Handley nodded. "Yep, sounds familiar. Well, we have some drugs for that, if you need them."

"Thanks. I may take you up on that. Have you had this same chat with Denny?"

"Well we intended to today but he's not been in his office and we couldn't find him. We'll try again later. It's important that we all look out for each other."

"Hmmm." Lewis was pensive. "Look I was thinking. Finding a survivor today, and one so vulnerable, has given me pause for thought and reaffirmed what I had already been thinking. It really is not enough to seal ourselves off from the outside world. If this young boy can manage to stay alive then there will undoubtedly be many more survivors out there. We have got to try and find them."

Singleton leaned forward, her eyes gleaming with excitement. "I am so glad you said that. I couldn't agree more. And what about my suggestion to capture one of the infected and study it?"

Lewis looked doubtful. "I just don't know. I have to say that I think, at the moment, I would tend to agree with Denny still. I can see your angle and there may well be benefits but it really would be so bloody dicey and I certainly wouldn't like to try it." Her expression blackened and he found surprisingly that he did not want to disappoint her so he tried to soften his remark. "We can continue to think about it though and see if we can't come up with some sort of plan in case the opportunity presents itself. But it did make me wonder; what about trying to come up with an antidote?"

Handley and Singleton exchanged a look that sent goose bumps up Lewis's arms. Hanson glanced at Howes, for once with a genuinely earnest expression. The two of them slunk off to a rear room to avoid the serious discussion that they knew was about to ensue.

"Funny you should say that," Handley said. "We've been discussing that very subject today actually."

"Yeah? As a matter of fact I've been contemplating it today myself," Lewis replied. It seemed that he was not the only one thinking of matters beyond their own existence. "So what did you guys conclude?"

"Well, we thought that for everyone on the base I guess the most important goal must be just plain and simple survival, day to day stuff. Getting through each day without dying, basically. But after that, then what? That's all good but that kind of closes our eyes to the outside world, letting everybody else perish whilst we few survive? That doesn't feel right to me.

"As you say, now that we have found a survivor, and such a vulnerable one at that, it really must mean that there are indeed many more of them. There may be people hiding alone or in groups. They may be in remote locations away from other sick people or just in particularly secure places, who knows. But what is probable is that they won't survive indefinitely without help; our help.

"We both think that our aim now, our moral duty even, should be to try to help others. If it's not safe at the moment to capture one of the infected to study then perhaps we should be making more effort at finding survivors. But also we should be thinking about trying to create a cure or immunization. We *are* a medical establishment after all."

Singleton was leaning forward again looking hard at Lewis whilst her colleague spoke. Lewis regarded them both with veiled eyes but he could not hide his interest in what they were suggesting, nor the sudden sense of excitement at having a worthy cause to focus on. For once their lives would have real meaning, something that had been lacking for the past few days and weeks.

"Okay, that sounds reasonable," he said cautiously, "and I think I would agree with you, especially after finding Josh today. Why do I get the impression that you have already worked out a strategy?"

Handley and Singleton broke into big grins and Private Howes, who had been listening through the half-closed door, gave a soft chuckle.

"Well of course," Singleton said, "we've had precious little else to do today with most people off base, and we needed something to stop us going stir-crazy."

"Okay let's hear it then." His goose flesh had returned with a vengeance and he could feel himself wanting to buy into the plan before he had even heard it. The desire for more than just their own basic survival was overwhelming. The need to have a goal to give them all some hope for the future was all-consuming.

"Well as you may know, the research for the drug Mnemoloss was conducted largely at GVF Laboratories. They are on the outskirts of Cambridge. That's only about twenty miles away, straight up the motorway. Jump on the M11 and less than half an hour later, bingo, easy as that."

Lewis smiled ruefully, remembering the troubles they had gone through in order just to get to a nearby village. "Well, almost. And you think the cure might be there?"

"No, probably not," said Handley. "They would never have predicted side-effects like these and when they realised that things were going so badly wrong I doubt they would have had time to do all that much about it. But an awful lot of the research may still be there; the data, test results, just about everything anyone would need to start to look into a cure or an inoculation. It's without a shadow of doubt the best place to begin, ground zero."

Now Lewis was leaning forward as well, nodding enthusiastically. "If you had mentioned this to me yesterday, I would probably have said something like, 'that sounds like a great idea but is too much of a risk,' because it would be a risk; and an enormous one at that.

"Now though, having found one survivor my outlook has pretty much changed. I agree with you; hiding inside the protection of the station is not the answer. We have got to do something more, something to help humanity recover. So I guess I'd have to say, absolutely. When do we go?"

The three beamed at each other for a few seconds, as happy as if they had actually completed their new mission already.

Doubts returned to cloud Lewis's mind though. "Do you really think it'll be possible to make a cure? Are you guys qualified in these areas?"

Singleton's grin faded as well and she frowned. "Well it's a long shot at best. There are many potential hurdles and any one of them could totally thwart us. We may get there and find the place has been trashed by diseased or it may even have burnt down like so many other buildings have done. If it *is* all still there we may not find what we're looking for anyway. And if after all that, we do find the data from the research done on Mnemoloss and can actually access the information, we may not be able to do anything with it. Both of us have studied a wide range of medicine and we do have some experience with neurological disorders but the guys who designed this drug were specialists, experts in their field and brilliant at that. For us to be able to make head or tail of their research is possibly the longest long-shot of them all. But it really is the best option we have and I personally would risk my life for it."

She looked absolutely determined as she held his glance. He was humbled by her unwavering selflessness. How could he possibly refuse to at least consider it when both doctors were so clearly willing to offer their lives in sacrifice for the remote chance of helping others? He simply nodded. "I'll go and talk to Denny but rest assured you have my utmost support in this and I *will* make sure it happens. God speed us, we'll need all the luck and help we can get."

Denny was not in his office when Lewis entered, having knocked and waited at the closed door. He had a quick look around while he was there, although he was not totally sure what he was looking for. What exactly are the signs that someone is having a mental breakdown? Maybe some empty bottles of spirits, a carelessly abandoned weapon or macabre and disheartened scribbling? He found nothing and did not like lingering and snooping amongst someone else's personal effects, so he left quickly.

From his vantage point by the tree outside, Denny had seen Lewis enter his office and watched as he poked around. It was dark now and he knew that he would not have been seen from within. Denny mumbled under his breath something about inappropriate behaviour of a subordinate but found it hard to muster any great feelings of righteous indignation. He had been outside for nearly three hours, patrolling the grounds of the station in case there was a breach of security at the main gate.

"There's no way I'm going to allow any of these damned creatures onto my base," he muttered. He no longer felt sure that he could trust the soldiers on guard to be rigorous enough. There had been too many incidences of lapsed concentration or poor judgement, and too many people had paid for these failings with their lives. It was high time that he took matters into his own hands and ensured the safety of everyone. As he stamped his feet he idly flicked the safety catch of the Browning off and then on again before continuing his solitary patrol.

Lewis checked for Denny in the dining area but again to no avail. Pethard and Williams were there though, chatting away to their new charge enthusiastically. The room was the busiest Lewis had seen it for some time and there was quite some buzz. Having such an unexpected yet welcome responsibility to look after had indeed been just about the best thing that could have happened to Pethard. He looked to Lewis to be relatively content and relaxed. Or perhaps he was just temporarily distracted, but either way is was beneficial.

Earlier when Pethard and Williams had first entered with Josh, everybody in the hall had gone quiet before erupting into excited chatter. The effect that Josh had upon the station was amazing and really quite uplifting. Pethard felt proud to have been given the task of looking after the boy and had thrown himself into the role enthusiastically. He had found a table in one corner and seated Josh and May Williams while he went to get food for them. Even Sergeant Vallage was in good spirits, and on seeing the trio, he came out from the rear of the kitchen to welcome Josh to his dining hall. He had made a small cake for the boy with some dried eggs that had been found in the supermarket, and he presented it to Josh with great flourish and a beaming smile. Neale and Scovell were both being kept busy in the kitchens by the large number of people, but that did not stop Scovell from constantly teasing Neale for having dropped the tin of peas in the supermarket. Whenever Neale went to clear anybody's plate Scovell seemed to be looming behind him.

"Careful with that, you might drop it. Look, you clean the table, I'll carry that."

All Neale could do was to try and laugh it off but the joke wore thin fairly quickly.

Having been checked over, Bannister had been released from his confinement and sat in the centre of the hall on a table with Millington, Corporal Gillen and Freddie Samuels, who had a bandage on his head where he had knocked himself unconscious. The medical centre had kept a close eye on him but he felt relatively normal and his only side-effects were a mild headache and slight, intermittent nausea. Bannister sat quietly as the others chatted away but he was not hungry. He played with his food, pushing it round his plate and occasionally looked up and faked a smile in response to something that Millington said. Otherwise he did not really contribute much. His thoughts were still dark and brooding and the prospect of eating did not appeal. He sat at the table for what seemed like a reasonable length of time before excusing himself and leaving. Normally Millington would have noticed his friend's ill humour but for the fact that everyone was so overwhelmed at the new arrival. As Millington had been the one who had found Josh he had assumed a level of responsibility for him in some way too, and was very keen to ensure that the boy was okay. Samuels was naturally more introverted than Millington and as he felt somewhat delicate due to his injury he had been quite reserved over dinner. It was he who noticed that Bannister had not really engaged and had hardly touched his food, both of which were atypical for Bannister who was usually boisterous and had a large appetite.

When Bannister left, Samuels leaned forwards with an earnest look in his eyes. "Did you notice anything about him?"

Millington had been chatting to Straddling on the next table but turned back to Samuels when he saw the serious expression. "Hmmm, can't say that I did. Why?"

"I dunno, he just didn't seem himself. I mean, I know

we are all pretty strung out most of the time, but he hadn't really seemed to have been affected as much as most people until now. Tonight he hardly spoke, and look, he's barely touched his grub. You know Bannister, normally he likes his groceries."

"Yeah maybe you're right," Millington said. "Maybe he's still bothered by the little fire-fight you all got into yesterday."

"That could well be it. He hasn't been himself since then. I went to visit him a couple of times during the day today and he's hardly had a good word to say, at least not to me anyway, although that could be 'cos I screwed up."

"No you didn't," Millington rumbled with a chuckle as he clapped a large hand on his friend's shoulder. "From what I heard, if you hadn't given them covering fire who knows what would've happened. Anyone could have taken a tumble. Look, if it makes you feel better I'll go and have a word with him, all right?"

Wood and Collins were leaving at the same time, having had dinner together on a table by themselves. Wood touched Collins on the arm lightly as they got to the door. "Hang on a second would you?"

She watched as he ducked into the kitchen quickly, and came out with a bottle partly concealed under his arm.

At that moment Lewis glanced in. "Oh, I meant to ask you earlier," he said to Wood, "what was with the spirits from the supermarket?"

Wood smiled. "Like I said - cocktails."

Lewis looked puzzled. "What?"

"Of the Molotov variety. Thought they may come in handy sometime."

"Ahhh," Lewis grinned. Of course. He reproached himself for not having guessed already.

Wood led Collins gently by the elbow. Now it was her turn to be confused. "Cocktails? Really?"

328

"Well no, not exactly. Molotov cocktails are basically fire bombs, named after the Soviet foreign minister during the Second World War. If you stick a wick of some sort in the top of a bottle of flammable liquid, light it and throw it you have a fire bomb that's really easy to manufacture. I just thought that a few of those might be useful sometime."

"So is that what that's for?" she said, pointing at the bottle under his arm. "Are we going to go and make some now?"

"No. This is for our personal consumption. After all, all work and no play is very boring."

He smiled, a half smile that lightened only one side of his face. Collins thought it was as though he could not be bothered with the effort on both sides, too economical with his emotions. Or perhaps the expression was forced and not genuine enough, as though he was detached and merely reacting as he thought she expected of him. However it somehow suited his laconic attitude and she was getting used to it. Maybe she just needed to get to know him a bit better, if only he would let her in. He had also managed to acquire a couple of decent brandy glasses. On seeing them Collins laughed.

"What's so funny?" he asked.

"Crikey, Sergeant Vallage really must like you if he gave you the mess's finest brandy glasses. That's not like him at all to be so generous."

They lay on the bed facing each other and chatting as they swirled the fiery liquid in the tulip glasses, allowing it to gently warm. It was not the best of brandies but Collins was not normally particularly keen on the liquor anyway, so even the finest would have been mostly unappreciated by her. Her father used to drink it sometimes. She would sit on his lap with the scent of his aftershave mixing with the fumes from his glass. As he slowly sipped it he would tickle her neck with his stubbly chin, the prickles just like the tears that prickled her eyes now. She blinked them away quickly, not wanting to ruin the moment. Most of them on base were at times given to morose reflections these days. No one questioned it, nobody felt the need to ask, it was just accepted as part of life now, the remorse and regret and painful memories. She did not know if Wood had noticed her tears and did not look to him for comfort. The mildly choking scent of the liquor and the whole time-consuming experience seemed to her, back then, like an exotic, adult ritual, but try as she might she had never been able to acquire the taste for it. Nevertheless on this occasion it seemed perfect; the gradual slowing down of time as they worked the glasses, the liquid sloshing up towards the rim as they chatted and then the burning hit as the fluid coursed down the back of her throat, slightly painful and not entirely pleasant and a gentle reminder that they were alive. Perfect.

As the first sip of brandy made its way down they heard a distant noise from somewhere along the corridor as Millington knocked forcefully at Bannister's room and then pushed the door open. Bannister was standing with his back to the door and swung round guiltily as Millington entered.

"Are you all right mate?" Millington was genuinely concerned.

"Yeah, sure, of course. Why wouldn't I be?" The sharp tone to Bannister's voice went unnoticed.

"You hardly ate anything tonight." Millington walked fully into the room and plonked himself down into a chair.

"Didn't I? Oh, I guess I'm just tired."

"That never normally stops you."

"Ah well, maybe a little preoccupied after everything

that's been going on, you know? All the killing, the death, especially the patrol yesterday."

"Yeah, I guess." Then Millington noticed Bannister's military boots were by the door. Also, Bannister was wearing his field jacket. "Are you going somewhere bro?"

"No, I was cold, that's all, so I put it on."

"And the boots?" Millington was getting suspicious now. Samuels was right, Bannister *was* acting strangely.

"Err, I was just going to polish them." Bannister blushed slightly as the lie stumbled inarticulately from his mouth.

"You what? You? Polish your boots? You gotta be kidding me." Millington threw his head back in a loud laugh. "You are the scruffiest person on base, we all know that. You haven't polished them since the state of emergency was declared."

"Well that's exactly the point. I thought it's about time I made some effort. Raise my game a bit."

"Are you still trying to impress Charlotte Collins?"

"Yeah," Bannister forced a laugh. "Something like that."

"You know you're rubbish at polishing. Look, give it here amigo." He grabbed the nearest boot and found some black polish and a swab of cotton wool under the sink. "Give it to the master and let me show you how it's done." He spat on the boot and started working the polish into the leather in small circles, peering closely at his work.

Bannister stared down at him for a few seconds, glaring malevolently. They had been best mates for several years but now he could not help but curse his insatiably cheerful friend. Right now Bannister just felt like taking the other boot and clouting him with it. After a few moments Millington looked up from his toil.

"Well the other one isn't going to get polished by itself, is it? Here." He chucked the polish and the cotton wool at him. Bannister had no choice but to sit in the chair beside him and start on the boot, still mentally attacking the other with shadowy thoughts. The frown that creased his brow went unnoticed, and had Millington seen it he would have put it down to something other than his own intrusive help. The two sat in silence with Millington occasionally looking up and comparing their efforts and laughing good naturedly. Bannister watched the time tick by and cursed inwardly.

Lewis had virtually given up on finding Denny but tried his office once more. The door was slightly open as he approached, although he was certain that he had closed it when he had left. He knocked and quickly entered. Denny stood in the middle of the room and whipped around as he entered, the pistol in his hand pointed straight at him. Lewis jumped back in fright but Denny smiled and lowered the weapon.

"Sorry old boy. I didn't mean to scare you. Just making the weapon safe."

"Doesn't seem very safe to me," Lewis said under his breath. "I've been looking for you all over sir. Seems nobody's seen you all evening."

"Really? Well I've been here."

"I came myself to see you, you weren't here then."

"Oh right, I must have just slipped out, toilet or dining hall maybe. Anyway, I'm here now."

"Are you okay sir? You seem a little," he searched for the correct word, "*distracted*, of late."

"Yes sure, thanks, never better."

Lewis had to admit that he did indeed look well at the moment. The heavy, preoccupied shadow that had been hanging over him seemed to have lifted and in fact his cheeks were red and his eyes were shining fervently, like a crazed disciple in some strange religious cult.

"How's the boy settling in?" The force of his interest took Lewis aback.

"Very well sir. I've given him to Pethard and Williams to look after. It seems to have done Pethard the world of good, just what he needed to take his mind off things."

"Yes, very good move that, well done. Any sign of any more of those vampire creatures out there?"

"No sir, no sign at all," Lewis answered with a frown. This was the first time anyone had mentioned the occurrence at the petrol station since the debrief and it made him feel extremely uneasy. It brought it back to him that it was still very much an unresolved issue and one that he needed to address, when finally he had some spare time and energy. Denny nodded as though this had been a perfectly normal question to have asked.

Lewis continued. "I've been talking with Singleton and Handley. They suggested going to Cambridge, to the GVF research labs where much of the work on the Dembuster was done, to see if we can find anything that could help us make a cure. I think it's a great idea, we'd like to go. Soon."

"Hmmm, yes, yes," Denny was nodding enthusiastically, perhaps a little too enthusiastically and Lewis started to think that he had not really taken in what he had said. He decided to push it a little in order to check.

"We're hoping we may find a cure, save all of mankind, that kinda thing."

"Yes, yes, an excellent idea, I totally agree," Denny bumbled.

Lewis was surprised at the ease with which he acquiesced but decided that Denny was probably not really devoting much attention to the conversation, as though he was just paying lip service to it in order to get

rid of him as fast as possible. He had not asked any
questions about the proposed plan, not pointed out any of
the obvious, inherent problems with it, nothing. He had
just immediately and whole-heartedly embraced the idea
as though it had been his own.

"Would you like to come with us when we go?" Lewis
asked, pushing further still.

The question brought Denny up sharp, as if he had
been slapped. "No. No I don't think so. My place is here
on the station. You go and bring some more survivors
back and maybe a cure. I'll stay here and guard the base."

The conversation faltered and Lewis was at a loss for
anything further to say. After an awkward pause he said,
"Well I'll be off then. Are you sure there's nothing I can
do for you?"

"No, that's quite all right, very kind of you though."

As Lewis turned to leave he noticed a plate with some
half eaten food on the edge of the desk. He could not
remember having seen it there before and wondered when
Denny had fetched it. Obviously the boss had taken to
eating in his office alone now, surely not a good sign.

As he got to the door Denny spoke again, seemingly as
an afterthought. "Thomas, I know I have not exactly been
myself lately and I am aware that you are concerned. You
don't need to worry though, I'm fine, really. Just a little
preoccupied and tense, like everybody I guess. Really, I
am fine though."

Lewis turned back to him and smiled although he had
to try and force the warmth into the expression. "I'm
happy to hear that. I *was* worried but I'm glad you are
okay."

When the polishing was finished Millington stood up and
stretched his back. He showed the boot to his friend with
an elated smile. "Check it out. Am I the best or what?"

"Yeah man, you're the dog's danglies." The sarcastic edge went unnoticed.

Bannister watched as he strolled casually from the room. He listened attentively as Millington made his way along the corridor and wondered whether he was going to go to bed now and leave him in peace for the night. He started to prepare himself again to go out, but a moment later the door swung open once more. Millington stood in the doorway waving aloft a bottle of cheap whiskey like a victorious footballer holding the winners' trophy.

"What on earth is that?"

Millington mistook the irritation for amazement and his grin stretched a little further.

"Scottish mouthwash. It's one of a few I've got. Been saving it for a special occasion but I figure tonight is as good a night as any, whilst we're both still alive and kicking, and able to appreciate it. We don't know how much longer that will be the case." He was still under the misapprehension that his friend was stressed and in need of company and distraction. He did not have a clue about Bannister's true intentions that night, nor that his company, whilst not at all what his friend wanted, was exactly what he needed at that moment, and was doing him a favour that neither of them could possibly imagine.

"Ah man, look I'm really tired," Bannister started to protest but Millington had already unscrewed the bottle and tossed the cap disdainfully over his shoulder. It landed by the sink.

"We won't be needing that again," he said as he raised the bottle in a salute, then poured two generous measures into a couple of coffee mugs. He thrust one at Bannister, raised his own in a toast and then quaffed the lot in a single gulp. He glanced at Bannister expectantly over the rim of his cup. Bannister returned the look but his thoughts were entirely different from those of his large friend, his best friend and comrade in arms. They had been inseparable for several years since going through initial army training together and had seen each other through many scrapes, both in peace time and war. Together they had been shot at, arrested and even shared women. Bannister knew that his pal would do anything for him and yet as he stared back at him on this night his thoughts were full of loathing. At that moment he despised his friend for his constant, even temper, his good nature and the fact that he never seemed to get angry. He despised him for his eagerness to help others and his sometimes overly protective attitude towards Bannister. But most of all he despised him at that moment because as long as Millington stayed in the room with him he would be unable to go out into the night, escape the base and find *her* again. The smile remained in place on Millington's face and Bannister had no choice but to reluctantly return the toast and finish his drink.

The bitter burn of bad Scotch made him gasp and gag a little, and Millington laughed and clapped him forcefully on the back.

"That's the spirit. And another."

As Millington's second measure disappeared Bannister sank back into his chair in resignation and glared balefully at his friend. All the while the second hand of the clock on the wall ponderously counted away the night which expired considerably more slowly than his patience. Whilst Bannister's thoughts were never far from Flavia, hers, in turn, revolved largely around him.

The vampire's lengthy existence inherently meant they had a greater propensity for patience. As the night slipped slowly by and Bannister became more angrily resigned to staying on base, Flavia shifted her position overlooking the petrol station forecourt and stared out into the night

336

below, looking like an alluring, gothic Sphinx. She was confident that the wait would be worth it but keen for it to end. She found it a real pleasure to be able to enjoy the quiet, uninterrupted panorama and stare at the stars without having to disguise herself from human view, but also without the peace being disturbed by the unnecessary cacophony that humankind constantly inflicted. The air already tasted fresher without the continual belching of fumes from industry, and she had surprised herself by finding that she appreciated the timid re-emergence of wildlife into urban areas, for various reasons.

Below her a scraggy, solitary dog padded softly by, its tail hanging limply between its legs with an unnatural kink in it that hinted at some recent battle for food or dominion. As it passed underneath Flavia stepped from the ledge and plummeted to the ground, landing with a thud right beside the animal which jumped and whimpered in fear. A moment later and it was dead. Flavia looked warily around her, more through the habit of long years than because of a current need for caution, before snapping the dog's head back, biting its vein and drawing a thin line of fresh, warm liquid into her mouth. She grimaced at the musty taste and held her breath to slightly lessen the unpleasant flavour whilst feeling the surge of life-blood gush through her body.

She wrapped her arms about her shoulders and shuddered involuntarily. It seems someone's walking over my grave, she thought with irony, as her limbs welcomed the explosion of warmth. The tentative tendrils of dawn snaked along the horizon as she casually tossed the canine corpse aside and made her way wearily back towards the vampires' lair. For a minute nothing else stirred but the hint of light in the east. Then imperceptibly, almost too slowly to acknowledge, a shadow detached itself from a rooftop overlooking the scene and moved delicately but deliberately after the diminishing vampiress.

Flavia hauled herself through the window to the upper floor where Darius and Max were standing, talking in low voices. As she entered they turned and bowed to her with an elegant and respectful flourish. Darius tilted his head questioningly.

"No," she sighed, for once not having to feign disappointment. "Still no sign of the human but I am confident that it will not be long now." She returned the bow and glided past them.

Darius turned away from Max and stared out of the window, thumping his hand down on the frame as he silently cursed. Had he made a grave error and left it all too late? "My friend," he spoke over his shoulder, "I believe that events are overtaking me. This may well be a storm that I will not weather."

"We have seen troubles come and go before, and we have overcome them all, my liege."

"Yes that is true; you have stood by me through many previous battles. You have been a long and faithfull ally and I thank you for that from the bottom of my heart. However I believe this may now be slipping beyond my reach."

Max put a supportive hand on his shoulder but could not in all honesty say much to dissuade his leader and friend from his negative presentiments. Deep inside himself he found that he was of the same opinion.

As the sky became lighter Darius's mood grew ever darker and his portentous forebodings ever stronger.

CHAPTER 15

The next day heralded a bright blue sky. There were only a few wisps of cloud starting to form like the first vultures to gather over a dying animal on the savannah. The temperature was crisp with a light dew enveloping the ground and a gentle breeze mocking the trees. To a casual observer it could have been any peaceful autumn morning. For Josh it was the first time he had slept properly in way too long and he did not stir until nearly midday. Pethard checked on him several times, concerned that he was still breathing. Initially, when finally he opened his eyes, he smiled, confused and dazed. Pethard was slouched in a chair by the window where he had spent the latter half of the night, dozing on and off with disturbed dreams. He leapt up when he heard Josh wake. Very quickly the boy's smile creased and deflated and was replaced by tears. Pethard sat on the edge of the bed trying to comfort him and occasionally turning away to hide his own tears until Williams joined them and she too broke down.

Bannister woke up with a headache that did not feel completely due to the alcohol. He was cold and shivery, and his limbs ached as though he were going down with the flu. He deliberately avoided Millington; in fact he tried to avoid everyone and took his breakfast back to the solitude of his room to eat alone. Most other people on station however were in good spirits. The arrival of Josh had momentarily lifted the dark veil from the base and there was the slightest hint of optimism circulating amongst them.

Through the gentle and compassionate efforts of Williams and Pethard they slowly put Josh at ease and even as the day wore on he became less tense and started to open up to them a little. Clearly the presence of other humans was a panacea for his terrors; he craved company and hated to be left alone. They teased out of him a little information regarding the events leading up to his being found. Although he did not know for how long he had been in the petrol station, it had indeed been his father who had deposited him there with a promise that he would return within a day or so. He did not know the whereabouts of his mother; as far as he knew she had disappeared some indeterminate number of days before and he had not seen her since. The reason his father had left him was still unclear. Pethard did not want to probe too deeply but Josh mentioned injuries that his father seemed to have sustained on his arms which pointed towards the possibility that he had fought with some infected and did indeed realise that he had little time left to safeguard his son. This was all pure speculation but did tie in with what was already suspected. The fact that he had survived all alone for as long as he had was nigh on a miracle and it seemed as though he was as important for the station as they were for him.

Lewis requested a meeting with the two doctors as well as Hutchison, Straddling and Wood. Although Wood had only been a patient at the base and not a serving member of personnel, his experience was invaluable and nobody outwardly questioned his presence at the meeting. He was fast making himself an invaluable member of the fragile community. Lewis also invited Flight Lieutenant Walkden, although only through courtesy to his rank rather than because he expected any great input from him, and Denny, although he did not expect the group captain to attend. He was therefore surprised when Denny walked into the conference room after breakfast with bloodshot eyes, wearing a somewhat creased uniform.

When Straddling entered the two men initially ignored

each other and the tension in the room was frigid but Lewis tried to get over it and pretend that nothing had happened. He knew that everybody in that room and on the base was suffering in their own personal hell and so perhaps it was best to put events down to the pressures they were under, rather than make an issue of things. He intended to talk to Straddling at some stage but the opportunity had not yet presented itself. He just hoped he had time to smooth things over before the issue resurfaced. That could prove disastrous for everyone.

He spoke about the plan to go to the GVF laboratory and search for survivors and any information on the Mnemoloss drug that may help them develop an antidote. His sketchy outline raised eyebrows and prompted whistles of surprise from the sergeants, but Walkden said nothing and Denny seemed barely to be listening.

Singleton then spoke in about exactly what they hoped to find. She concluded by detailing what was of utmost importance to them. "I would guess that in any laboratory like this there will be areas where they have conducted animal tests. There is bound to be a large amount of empirical data in this area which may well be very important. Results of tests from various steps of drug development, what the different stages showed and what the side effects were, how different animals reacted and so on. This info will probably be on computer but it may also be backed up with paper copies.

"There may be an area with powerful computers where they have produced all the computer models. An awful lot of drug development these days is done this way and again this will be very useful if we are able to take the data away with us and access it. Lastly there will probably be offices of the different analysts, technicians and scientists, and goodness knows what we'll find there but it will quite possibly be of enormous value. It's

341

extremely hard to say what we need to bring back with us until we are actually in the laboratories but as long as you are all aware of the kind of things to keep an eye out for then that is all we can ask."

Straddling interrupted her now rather abruptly. "You said 'we'?"

"I'm sorry Sergeant, what?"

"You said 'we' ma'am. Until *we* are actually there. You mean to say you think you're coming with us?" His bluntness was now bordering on rude.

"Yes, of course. Both Dr Handley and myself will be coming along."

"With all due respect, ma'am, this is no picnic. We're probably going to encounter some festering diseased and some of us, maybe all of us, might get killed." He turned now to Lewis. "Is it really a good idea to be carrying deadwood with us when we're out there? No offence ma'am."

The room went silent. For the second time in as many days Lewis felt that the authority of his command no longer carried sufficient weight to dictate the actions required to his men. He now had to come up with solid reasoning and convince them of the merit of his ideas. If not then what was to stop them from just saying 'no'? Besides, Straddling did have a point; the doctors were not trained in battle and this was likely to be a perilous trip. They needed the best, most experienced team possible and the doctors would complicate matters and potentially make the mission more hazardous.

Lewis paused for thought and chose his words carefully. "Firstly the whole aim of this mission is to try and find a cure for these diseased. The longer we leave it the more potential survivors will have been contaminated and the more people will have died and be beyond our reach. This is the single most important thing that we, as

342

survivors, can do right now, so much so that both the doctors and myself are willing to die for it.

"If we go to the labs without the doctors then yes, we may strike it lucky and find something that they can use but we'd be clutching at straws. I most certainly don't know what data we'll be looking for. Do you Sergeant? At least with the doctors there we can make a proper, thorough search and increase the likelihood of finding something important. I know what you're saying and there's some truth in it. Having inexperienced people with us may increase the risk a bit but on balance we need them with us."

He stopped, leaving his words hanging pendulously in mid-air, looking at the others around the table.

Straddling still looked dubious at best, bordering on belligerent and nobody would meet his glare. He shook his head and growled in reply. "It's hard enough out there as it is. We've lost soldiers already, good men, experienced men who knew what they were doing. If we go out there with people who've had no battle exposure then we're just increasing the possibility that something will go wrong and we'll lose even more troops." He shook his head and banged the table as he spoke and his cheeks were flushed with colour.

Lewis deliberately took his time before answering, trying to phrase his words as non-combatively as possible. He had expected this line of argument and there was no denying the truth of it. It really did come down to a question of whether or not taking the doctors was too much of a hindrance, or was the added benefit worth taking the chance for? It was a question that each soldier had to answer for themselves. It was from an unexpected corner that assistance came.

Walkden spoke softly and hesitantly whilst looking down at the table, as though he did not believe his opinion really counted for much, which was in part the truth. "Look I know that I don't have any real, combat experience but I think I agree with you Tom. I agree that this is without doubt the most important thing that any of us can do right now. The fact that it carries with it a great risk, well, so what? Even living at the moment is tough. If we are going to do this then we may as well do it right. I can't imagine we're going to want to go back to the labs again in order to find the information we need.

"If what you say is true and we go there without the doctors then it sounds as though there's no point in going at all. We won't know what we're looking for and we're just jeopardising our lives for nothing. So why don't we go there just once, do it right first time and get everything we need. If it makes it more dangerous taking the two doctors along then surely that is still better than having to go back to the labs more than the once."

Lewis could have kissed the man and immediately felt guilty for his negative perception of Walkden's usefulness. He nodded furiously and looked searchingly around the table again.

This time it was Wood who sealed the debate with a little light-hearted humour. "Well said sir. What the hell, I've got nothing better to do with my time right now. I'm sick and tired of this place and all your ugly mugs. Count me in."

Straddling coughed and cleared his throat. "Well I can't have a couple of English ponces going and me too scared to join you. Sod it, when are we off?" There was a shift in the tension around the table and the decision was made.

Walkden promised that he could have a third Land Rover prepared in time and the team for the mission was selected. They were to depart the next morning. They dispersed, all buzzing with anticipation and nerves.

As Lewis got up to leave, Walkden, who was not one of the soldiers chosen to go, confronted him. "I meant what I said Tom; even living is precarious at the moment. I know I screwed up last time but I'd really like to go on this mission. This is something that I truly believe in. I can help. Please, let me come along."

Lewis clapped him on the shoulder, impressed with the man's bravery and wishing that certain other members of his team were as compliant and willing to be of assistance. "You already have helped me my friend. More than you know, but this one is not for you. No disrespect but we need the most battle-experienced soldiers out there. You can best aid us by making sure those vehicles run like dreams. We don't want any problems with them when we're off station."

Walkden beamed. "Well *that* I can do for you, yes indeed."

Lewis was about to follow him out of the conference room when he noticed, like the time before, that Denny had not moved and was still sat at the table, staring out of the window.

"Sir?" He paused and addressed his commanding officer.

Denny did not look round but mumbled faintly, as though to himself. "They'll never take this base you know. Never."

Lewis frowned, puzzled but was too distracted and did not have time to stop and question the matter further, and by the time he would remember the comment it would already be too late.

The day was spent in a blur with much activity and preparation. Just before dinner Lewis summoned everyone on base, other than the guard at the front gate, into the dining area for a briefing. Denny was noticeably absent. There was a hush as Lewis outlined the plan for the following day and the moment he stopped speaking there was a murmur of anxious chatter. Vallage had outdone himself and somehow created a huge pan of steaming chilli, although nobody dared to ask him what he had used for the meat. For once he was in a good mood and actually emerged from the kitchen himself in order to serve the diners.

When Wood went up to him for food Vallage grasped him by the arm. "Good luck tomorrow sonny. I know you'll keep them safe."

He slapped an extra-large dollop of chilli on Wood's plate.

"Hmmm, someone's flavour of the day," Collins teased him as they walked back to their table, "although if that means you have to eat more of that slop then I'm quite glad it's you and not me."

Collins and Wood spent another evening together, but as she was not going on the mission the following day, she had been assigned guard duty for later that night. In order to let him sleep she slipped out of his room at around midnight with a kiss. Although she was quiet and discreet her exit did not go entirely unnoticed.

The atmosphere had been virtually like a party with just about everyone in the dining hall together for once. Lewis and Singleton had gone in search of Denny at various times during the night but his office always looked as though he had just vacated it. On each occasion they found his window open and the curtains flapping but no sign of the man himself.

Singleton was clearly on edge. Lewis stopped her in the corridor as they walked towards Denny's office for the last time. The light from his candle cast eerie, dancing shadows on the wall like a cadaverous puppet show.

He placed a hand on her arm. "Are you okay?"

She smiled, looking a little embarrassed. "Yeah I guess so. I think that the reality is starting to hit home. It's one thing to be brave and volunteer for this mission when it's just a remote possibility but now that we are actually going to go I guess I'm a little frightened."

He grinned reassuringly. "It's okay to be frightened."

"Really?"

"Yeah sure. I'm scared every time I leave the base. In fact if I'm honest with you I'm completely scared witless. It's natural; you'd have to be a fool not to be. And anyway, it's a good thing."

"How's that?"

"It keeps you sharp and focussed and that keeps you safe. If you weren't at least a little bit scared then you'd probably be careless and that would get people killed. So I suggest you don't try and fight it too much, recognise that your fear may just keep you alive and be thankful for it."

She released a large sigh and let her shoulders drop. "Okay, that makes me feel a bit better. Thanks."

"And if it makes you feel better still, I'm gonna put you in my Land Rover so I'll look after you. Just stay close, don't do anything silly, and for heaven's sake, don't accidentally shoot me in the back."

She laughed. "Well, all right, I'll try not to, but only because you ask so nicely."

They were standing close to each other, huddled in the small flickering halo of light. Lewis was suddenly aware that this was about as close as their bodies had ever been to each other for any length of time. He could feel her breath on his cheek, smell the faint hint of dried sweat that lingered around them all these days, the cloying scent of stale perfume and the smell of the gum that she chewed to clean the remains of chilli from her teeth. He could even see how dilated her pupils were in the dim light. It was the first time he could recall ever noticing the colour of her eyes. For a moment they held each other's gaze and he thought that she might just be having a similar realisation. In fact for the past couple of days he thought they had probably got along better than ever before.

"Huh!" He smiled, stepped back slightly and broke the moment.

"What?"

"I never knew before what colour your eyes were."

She too smiled, although her smile was a little sheepish and embarrassed. "Yep, plain old brown, all my life, although I used to want blue eyes. In fact when I was at med school I used to wear coloured contact lenses. That's pretty sad, I know."

"Really?"

"Yeah, I thought that piercing blue eyes would be much more desirable. I guess you always want what you haven't got."

"Well I think yours look really quite nice as they are."

"Is that a compliment, Captain Lewis?" She pronounced his title somewhat deliberately, feeling very self-conscious.

Now it was his turn to look embarrassed. "Well, I guess it is, Squadron Leader Singleton." Both of them realised, although neither said it, that it was actually the first compliment he had ever paid her.

Once again Denny's office was empty when they arrived and again the window was ajar, although again Lewis closed it.

Later that night Lewis lay on his bed wearing only his boxer shorts. The curtains were open and the light from a pale moon illuminated him. It was a cool night but he had a high metabolism and usually found that he felt warm while those around him shivered. Tonight, especially with so much going round and round in his head, he was sweating slightly and could not sleep. He was going over the plan for the next day, mentally checking that they had prepared as best as they could, had chosen the right people for the sortie, which vehicles to have them all in and so on. He thought he heard a soft knocking at his door and sat up. There was no sound. Thinking he must have imagined it he sank back down but again, a hesitant, uncertain knocking, as though whoever it was did not want to actually wake him up if he was asleep, but was also fairly insistent and was not going away unanswered. He got up and opened the door. Singleton stood there wearing only a thin, pale vest and skimpy knickers. The gossamer top followed the silhouette of her otherwise naked figure closely, subtle details being picked out by the moonlight. She was a slim lady, she had very obviously kept herself in good shape and it was the first time he had ever thought about her body in such a way. She looked apologetic and embarrassed as she hugged herself, for once a shy teenager rather than the brash, authoritative medical officer that she normally portrayed.

"Sorry to disturb you, I can't sleep. Guess I'm a bit more scared than I thought."

Lewis was surprised to see her and did not immediately respond which she took as a rebuff and started to recoil, stammering.

"Look this is a really bad idea, I shouldn't have come. I'm just going to go back to my room and try to sleep. Forget I was here."

"Hey." He said nothing else but it was enough to stop her backing away. In times such as these, each new day brought the very real possibility that any one of them might face their doom. The mission to the GVF laboratories the next day had brought that fact sharply into focus. Whilst it was something that was clearly vitally important, nevertheless they all appreciated that it

349

may very well bring with it more deaths. The thought of it was praying on the minds and souls of everyone on base. Every last chance to embrace the fact that they were still alive was to be celebrated. Every opportunity for levity, every moment of compassion - or of passion - was one not to be wasted. He opened the door a fraction more and moved aside to allow her in before closing the door gently behind her.

After the jovial atmosphere that had momentarily prevailed, the base was now quiet. Not everybody had been in a party spirit however; Bannister had been in a foul mood all day. His headache had not shifted and he had tried his best to avoid company, although Millington had infuriatingly been keeping a close eye on him. Bannister had also been involved with preparations for the forthcoming mission. Now that he had been released from quarantine he was one of the more experienced soldiers and was an obvious choice to go, along with his frustrating friend.

Tonight however Millington had retired to bed, as had most people, and at around midnight Bannister found it easy to slip out of his room unnoticed. His brain pulsed with strange thoughts that did not entirely feel his own. His torch was not turned on and so when he practically bumped into Collins as she vacated Wood's room, she fortunately did not see him. He froze to the wall and held his breath as she turned away and shone her torch down the opposite length of the corridor, in too much of a contented daze to consider the fact that she was not alone. He watched her pert buttocks bob away into the darkness with the soft, swish-swish sound of starched military trousers. Although theoretically he was not yet doing anything wrong he still felt like a criminal and his heart was racing.

He stared at the door to the room she had just vacated. Wood! He always seemed so smug and self-assured, so patronising and judgemental. At that moment Bannister truly loathed him. He paused outside the door as the alien thoughts throbbing in his skull filled with anger and violence, and he actually half-considered going into the room and sinking a knife deep into the man's throat. He would be able to do it whilst his unsuspecting victim slept, no problem. See how smug he would be then, huh? But his interests were elsewhere tonight and at that moment he could not have cared less about Corporal Collins and her firm little rump.

Like a panther he stalked through the corridors of the mess, freezing at every creak of floorboard or sigh of settling beam. In a fuzzy, dream-like state he found himself outside and gasping down the cold air as his breath formed vapour in front of him. The night came to him in brief glimpses of clarity, interspersed with a confused jumble of images. He was astride the perimeter wall at the back of the mess as far away from the main guardroom as possible with a ladder propped up just below him. A moment later and he was outside the station and walking along the grassy verge, his Browning held listlessly in front of him, guiding his way. On some level of consciousness he knew that what he was doing was incredibly unsafe and he really should be afraid for his life, but he just could not muster the enthusiasm for fear, so consumed was he by his own private mission and so scrambled was his reasoning.

He carefully avoided the guardroom and the next glimpse of clarity had him out on the open road heading towards town. A moment later and he was further from the base near some houses with parked and abandoned vehicles. On the lawn of the closest was a Ford Fiesta. Amongst other crimes Bannister had committed during his misspent youth, he had stolen various cars, and this skill was to come in handy now. Fords were renowned for being the easiest to hotwire and this one presented him with little problem. Before he knew it he was proceeding sedately along the road as though he were out for a drive in the country. His actions were slow and ponderous and he could barely remember smashing the window and forcing the ignition. In truth he did not even manage to get the car out of first gear, although he was completely unaware of that fact.

Sat once again on her perch overlooking the petrol station Flavia saw the lights of the car before she could hear the sound of the engine. "At last. What took you so long?" She smiled a thin, self-satisfied smile revealing long, sharp incisors at the corners of her red lips and stood to flex her elegant limbs.

Simultaneously above a nearby house another shadow detached itself from the rooftop and keeping low to the building, slid carefully away into the night, out of sight and hearing even of Flavia's acute senses.

When she had bitten into Bannister's neck before, Flavia had taken blood from him but she left a little something nestling deep in his soul. Once under her enchantment it was like a drug that Bannister found very hard to fight against, just as she herself could barely resist the allure of human blood. Flavia had known that sooner or later he would return to her at the place she had told him to come to, just as Sebastian had also guessed. So now Sebastian noted where he first glimpsed the lights of the car and made his way to that spot to wait. At some stage later that night he realised Bannister would return to the military base. Sebastian did not have the use of a vehicle himself at this time. He knew it was unlikely that he would be able to keep pace with this car. However, he reasoned that if he went now to wait just beyond the spot

where he first saw its lights, when it later came past him
on its return journey to Headley Court that would give
him an advantage and he may just be able to track it all
the way back.

As the car approached the petrol station Bannister's
head was pounding. He felt his body start to gently throb.
He got out of the car. The unnerving way his breath
curled around him in the headlights just added to the
surreal shroud that the night had donned. There was a
slight fragrance of flowers. Immediately he sensed, rather
than felt, the presence of another person standing behind
him. In a sudden panic he span around.

"Fear not my little one, 'tis I."

And there she was, a vision, or perhaps an apparition.
She loomed closer and closer in the still night and then
his brief moment of awareness became a blur. At some
stage on some level he heard her talking to him,
whispering in his ear with her mouth rubbing against him,
brushing him tantalizingly with murmurings of seduction
and half promises and he answered; he mentioned the
base and the people within and the mission to the
laboratories and felt her lips caress and pull at his neck as
they had done before, and then her lips pressed against his
and her strong, cold arms wrapped firmly about his back,
preventing him from struggling, although to struggle was
the last thing on his half-crazed mind, and he felt his body
relax and the pounding in his head retreated and he
pressed himself against her and the shaking in his limbs
subsided, and then, eventually, even the dreamlike blur
dimmed and faded.

Some long time later but all too soon he realised he
was back in the car and already driving home towards the
base although he had no recollection of their parting. He
found himself approaching Headley Court and then he
was outside the car and trudging through the

undergrowth, and a moment later he was at the foot of the ladder. It was propped against the wall allowing him to climb back into the base although he could not actually recall having hoisted it over, so long ago now, and then he was back in his room and nobody had seen him and he was tired, oh so tired, and then finally, at long, long last, he slept, blissfully unaware of the damage he had already done.

The alarm sounded like a claxon violently ending her slumber for the night. Collins groaned and sat up, rubbing her eyes. It felt as though she had only been asleep for a few minutes and she cursed whilst fumbling for her torch. The walkie-talkie on the bedside table crackled into life.

"Collins, Collins, you awake?"

"Yes, I'm awake Corporal Gillen," she replied somewhat grumpily.

"Your turn. You've got fifteen minutes to get here."

"Right, I'll be there."

She lay back down on the bed and closed her eyes for a moment, coming round slowly. The radio crackled and blared out again.

"What was that?"

"Yes, I heard. Fifteen minutes, copy, roger, wilco, whatever. I'll be there." She swung her legs off the bed and shivered. It was cold.

She had had strange dreams where she had been in an unfamiliar house and was searching unsuccessfully for something. A dark figure with piercing eyes had been present and nearby although he remained largely unseen. No matter how hard she tried to turn and see where he was, he stayed one step ahead, in the shadows and constantly out of her field of vision. She could not remember if the individual had been intimidating or protecting her but it had left her feeling anxious. There

354

were other horrible manifestations with bits of rotting flesh hanging off their faces and hands, all chasing her. She was aware that if ever they touched her she was doomed to suffer the same plight. At one stage she was with another soldier but he disappeared and she was totally alone. She just accepted that it was useless to search for him. He was gone and would never return. Somewhere in the dream Cujo had been with her. He had been dragged into another room that she could not enter and his screams haunted her from behind closed doors. She had woken with her heart racing and was not upset to leave the dream behind.

Gillen was delighted when she poked her head through the guardroom door. "Ah, there, you are. Thought you'd gone back to sleep for a mo." He was way too cheerful for someone who had been awake all night. "There's nothing to report here, it's just a quiet and chilly night. I'm off. Have fun, see you tomorrow."

"Bye," she said but he was already gone. He could not get out of the guardroom fast enough. She closed the door behind him and sat down, rubbing her hands together and blowing into them before reaching for a thermos flask of coffee that he had left behind. She stared out into the night and could feel her eye-lids becoming heavy as she struggled to throw off the tiredness. Her dream bothered her as it reminded her of the unanswered questions that had been all but forgotten on base, questions about the missing bodies of Sinna and Rohith and about the strange couple that had saved them at the petrol station. Since no one could provide any answers to either conundrum and there was already enough to preoccupy everyone, both issues had died a death on the station and had hardly been mentioned since.

The door creaked slowly open making her jump. A chilling surge of air flooded through the guardroom causing an involuntary shiver. She wearily got to her feet to close it. The coffee mug slipped from her fingers as she recoiled. The gasp was lodged in her throat and did not make it out. The scream was even further down her oesophagus. Standing right in front of her with beguiling, hazel-coloured eyes was the man she had last seen two days before at the petrol station. She instinctively backed up several steps as he took one long, deliberate stride towards her, holding out his hands in a placatory gesture.

"Do not be afraid, you have nothing to fear from me." The same words he had spoken to her before in the shop. She felt the fear subsiding as a warm feeling washed over her.

"Sebastian." It was what she had heard his friend, the female, call him. She said it not as a question but more just a blunt statement of fact or a prediction that has come to fruition at last. He smiled but did not query how she knew.

"How did you find me?" she asked breathlessly.

"I have been searching for you for a long time." She did not know whether he was talking figuratively or literally and did not notice or care that he had ignored her question. Once more she was totally consumed by the irresistible pull of his hazel eyes, the light sparkling from within and the aura of powerful calm that radiated out. She suddenly realised that this time she had not removed her pistol from its holster and glanced down at it instinctively.

He saw the look and smiled. "You won't need that with me. Save your bullets for others."

She felt herself being drawn into his eyes, her focus narrowed and the peripherals of her vision began to grey out as she started to sink down those endless, honey-coloured wells to the black depths below. She put a hand out to steady herself and her knees wobbled beneath her.

Before she knew it he had closed the gap between them, his arms were behind her head and cradling her under her legs as he effortlessly scooped her up in mid-swoon and set her gently down on the edge of the table. It was as though she weighed no more than a small child and he still supported her until she regained her balance. Although they were so close now, for some bizarre reason she was distracted by the total lack of odour from him which was odd if only because of its absence. His touch was cool; comforting yet unyielding, like gripping hold of a statue honed from immovable stone. He had pronounced cheek bones, perfectly coiffured hair and those piercing eyes again. She felt as though she must drag her gaze away but found it so very hard. The entire effect was of one enthused with health and vitality and full of life, which seemed ironic given that he was a vampire.

"Who are you?" she was finally able to stammer.

"As you said already; I am Sebastian."

It was hard to formulate or elucidate any thoughts and so she continued with an uncharacteristic stutter. "You saved us. From the infected. Thank you."

"You are so very welcome. It was my," he searched for the right word, "my pleasure."

She blurted out the next words before she even had time to think about them and she was not sure where the thought came from. It seemed completely evident, indisputable but something that her mind had been denying, eluding and hiding from in the quiet of the night. At Headley Court people had avoided the subject, not allowing themselves to believe the account of the attack at the petrol station yet not having any other potential explanation. It had been easier to avoid the subject but now it seemed to Collins that there was no other possible explanation.

"You are a vampire."

He inclined his head slightly and again did not directly answer her, other than through implication. "I was human once, just like you."

There were so many questions. Unlike a moment before when she had found it hard to think straight, now it was difficult deciding what to ask first. She tripped over her words as they tumbled out of her mouth, one sentence forming before the previous one had even been finished.

After a slow, slightly awkward start they spoke at length about his past, his life while he was a human and how he was 'turned' into a vampire. He had been born in Bordeaux although she could not exactly work out the year and he seemed either reluctant to say or did not fully know himself. His life had been reasonably unremarkable until he had moved to Marseille and started working at the docks as a rigger on French merchant sailing vessels, and frequenting certain bars of lesser repute in Marseille's slum areas. He described life in detail, in what she assumed must be roughly around the middle or towards the end of the nineteenth century and it was totally enthralling to hear him speak of it.

Just before he had become turned, he had been involved with a woman and had got into a fight over the affair. His attacker pulled a knife on him but Sebastian had managed to disarm him and used it upon his aggressor. The man had not died but had been able to identify him and Sebastian was blamed and vilified. The woman turned out to be well-connected and married to a ship-owner. Although Sebastian's advances had been encouraged and appreciated by her at the time, as soon as the liaison became common knowledge she changed her story and claimed that his attention had been a nuisance and that he had been molesting her. One night shortly after the fight, he was hunted and chased through the streets of Marseille and cornered by a gang of dock-hands who were in the employ of the lady's husband. They would surely have killed him but for the intervention of a certain stranger.

In one of the ale-houses that he frequented there was a small group who always seemed to occupy a remote, gloomy area of the bar. They kept themselves to themselves and wore dark cloaks and hoods much of the time, as many did in those days, so that he had rarely seen their faces. He occasionally had the weirdest feeling, as though they were watching him although he had never actually made eye contact with them. As he was cornered by the dock-hands Sebastian feared for his life but one of the strange, hooded people from the bar jumped down in front of him from some roof above, startling the gang and creating a brief distraction. As usual, the stranger was wrapped in a dark cloak as though feeling the cold, even though the night was stifling with hardly a breath of air. At first the hooded character bantered with the gang but the men were crazed through cheap alcohol and bloodlust. As the assailants turned back to their vengeful task and tried to get at Sebastian the stranger lashed out and in a few moments one of the attackers lay dying, blood dripping from a wound that had been opened with unseen blades. This obviously enraged the gang but seemed to have an even more startling effect on the stranger who entered some kind of killing frenzy, moving amongst them with poetic speed and grace as though the attackers were all motionless whilst the hooded figure slashed and whirled. Within mere seconds the rest of the men had been slaughtered.

Now Sebastian was convinced that his death was surely imminent. The hooded figure approached as Sebastian stood cowering. The fear and exhaustion seemed to overcome him and he lost consciousness and that was the last that he would be fully aware for some time. His memories of the subsequent events were hazy. He was unconscious for a while, how long exactly he did not know although it might have been merely hours or perhaps days. During the brief moments when he was awake it was to a blur of people and activity. There were patches of lucidity interspersed with strange visions and nightmares. He could not distinguish reality from illusion, was he dreaming of being awake or having a waking dream? It was hard to know which memories were real and which his brain had invented. At times he found himself in a strange room in an unfamiliar house but was not sure whether he was imprisoned or being cared for. He could remember shivering so hard it hurt his limbs, and feeling feverish and aching all over his body, right down to the very core of his being. He was nauseous and there was a burning deep in his belly. Then the next thing he could remember was waking up with a ravenous, insatiable thirst and being introduced to the vampire clan as its newest member.

Sebastian had not spoken of such things in a long time and the flush of memories were all still vivid and carried with them strong emotions. He found the conversation with this human strangely liberating and totally different from any he had with his comrade vampires. He spoke about some of the nicer times of his long life and it reminded him how much he missed being human. Now that society had collapsed he understood how much he had yearned to be part of it again all these long years. Darius had directed them all to go out and find the humans in order that they might forge a relationship with them, and he was just doing what he had been told to do, but it was an easy order to follow as his heart craved this interaction more than he had realised.

Collins sat in silence, spell-bound by his account,

transfixed by the images of life in those days gone by. There was something about the way he talked and stared at her, so intense and earnest, that brought his words to life. Throughout his tale she could imagine the cool, salty wind blowing off the sea. She could smell the docks, hear the clank of chains on the masts and envisage life as it was then.

It was talk of the vampires however, that particularly engrossed her. "My God, I just can't imagine what it must have been like; waking up to discover that all of a sudden your existence was never going to be the same again, from that day on you would be a vampire."

"Yes, it took some getting used to," he nodded soberly.

"So what are the rest of your clan like then? I mean, that woman from the petrol station, is she like, your girlfriend?" She felt silly saying it, like a jealous sixteen-year-old schoolgirl and the word 'girlfriend' seemed woefully inadequate. For some reason though she did feel an inexplicable twinge of jealousy although she had no idea why and tried to banish the emotion.

"Flavia? No." His answer was swift and sharp, almost an admonishment. "She has another mate, another from my clan."

"Oh, I guess I just assumed..." Collins did not know what she was saying. She was nervous and the words were just babbling out before she could think about it. She immediately regretted sounding even more juvenile than before.

He paused and looked uncertain, then shook his head, looking down at the floor.

"No. She has been with her mate for quite some time, since before I knew her."

"So do you have a... a 'mate'?" Again she felt that confusing surge of irrational jealousy and tried to stop herself from blushing. She hardly knew this man, this vampire before her, and as beguiling as he was, she had absolutely no business feeling any such emotions. She did not know why she felt as she did and she could feel herself acting completely out of character. Perhaps it was the improbability of the situation or his effect upon her. Perhaps.

"No. I do not."

He returned her look evenly and unblinking, his hazel eyes boring deep into her. It was hard to tear herself away from his stare and her attention never strayed far from his gaze. As they spoke she became aware of small details of his features. His lips were thinner than she remembered but with a perfectly neat little dip in the middle of the top one, and when he smiled he tended to do so with a closed mouth. She had yet to see his teeth and found it simultaneously intriguing and terrifying to contemplate what they might be like, the supposedly killer incisors of legend. His nose was thin, vaguely Roman she would have said, but somehow majestic or arrogant and he flared his nostrils occasionally when he spoke as though testing the air. He had a full head of luxurious, thick hair and she could imagine him having been immensely proud of it when he was still human. However, for some reason she could not envisage a vampire preening himself in front of a mirror, if they used mirrors at all, or did they avoid them as in fable and folklore? But it was to the eyes that her attention returned mostly; she completely forgot about the time while they conversed in their private little room, ignoring the outside and everyone else.

"How many of you are there in your clan?" she asked.

"Seven. I was the last to join."

"That sounds a lot. I guess I'd always imagined vampires of mythology to be solitary creatures really."

"Yes, in truth it is quite a lot – probably too many. It leads to…" It was his turn to be lost for words, "…to tensions."

"So are the others much older than you?"

"Yes. I am the newest member; some of the others have been vampires much, much longer than I. Darius, our Clan Leader, has been a vampire for many human generations, I do not know exactly how many. I do not think he knows himself. After a while it ceases to matter."

"Was Darius alive in the time of Dracula then? And was he a real person, a real vampire, or was he purely fictitious?"

He smiled. "I wondered when you would ask me that. I know that in your society there are many different stories and rumours as to whether Count Dracula was a real person or perhaps as many believe, based on Vlad The Impaler.

"Vlad was a bloodthirsty ruler in the fourteen hundreds who lived in Wallachia in Romania. There are many who think that Vlad was an actual vampire himself. The truth is that the Count Dracula from the book by Bram Stoker was not a real person but merely a character created by the author. It is correct however that he was indeed loosely based on Vlad, also known as Vlad III of Wallachia or Vlad Dracula. However Vlad was not a vampire and although he did impale his victims, the reports of his brutality are, as is so often the case, grossly exaggerated and have grown with the passage of time. The tales of his gory reprisals towards his enemies were embellished in order to create an aura of fear around him.

"His father, Vlad II, was a Romanian hero who fought the invading Ottoman Turks. Because of his bravery and services against the Turkish army he was admitted to the Order of the Dragon which was founded by Sigismund, King of Luxembourg, Hungary and various other countries, as well as, most ironically, being at one time the Holy Roman Emperor. Sigismund founded the secret

Order of the Dragon which was created to uphold Christianity and defend the empire against the infidel Ottoman Turks. After being admitted to the Order, Vlad II took the name Vlad Dracul, dracul being Romanian for 'the dragon', or alternatively, and again quite paradoxically, 'the devil'.

"His son Vlad III took the name Vlad Dracula; dracula merely means 'son of dracul'. He continued where his father had left off, by slaughtering thousands of Turks. His favourite method of killing them was by impaling them on a sharp spike earning him his name, Vlad the Impaler. Vampires were quite commonly known about through folklore in that part of the world in those days. However most people would not openly admit to believing in them and certainly wouldn't talk about them in public. It was said that Vlad the Impaler drank the blood of his enemies as it dripped down the spikes because he believed it gave him unnatural strength and long life. In truth he was not a vampire and did not drink blood although he embraced and harboured these stories as much as he harboured actual vampires behind the walls of his castle.

"He was the patron to a very small number of extremely powerful vampires, exactly how many I do not know. He provided for them a safe haven where they could rest unnoticed and unmolested, a practice that has continued throughout history and even, occasionally, to this day. When they went forth at night in order to feed throughout the superstitious villages of the surrounding lands they were occasionally sighted by people who only rarely lived to tell the tale. Perhaps it was they who drank the blood dripping down the spikes of impaled victims, I do not know for certain. The stories were that Count Vlad Dracula himself wandered the lands preying on the simple people, taking their blood and leaving most for dead. This gave to Vlad a truly fearful reputation that he encouraged and it dissuaded many potential enemies from attacking him. So Vlad was indeed Count Dracula in real life, but he was not the vampire Dracula from the book.

"When Vlad III finally died the vampires spread such fear amongst the servants who worked in the castle that some fled the castle babbling insanely. Any that remained became lost to relatives and friends on the outside and continued to serve their new masters. It was believed that Vlad the Impaler lived on after death and although his armies no longer served his cause, the castle was never attacked again. Slowly with the passing of many years fewer people went anywhere near the area, believing it to be cursed. The lands and paths leading up to the castle became overgrown and virtually impenetrable. The castle had been well placed anyway in a location that made access rather difficult and hence kept the castle safe from marauding armies. It was forgotten about by all except those who lived in its shadow and remembered the terrifying tales from days of yore. The stories turned into myth and legend from the darker days and were rarely repeated, fading with time. But the vampires liked this anonymity that it gave them and they were still very much alive within the walls of their home. Or at least that is how the stories go that I have been told."

Collins was silent throughout, speechless and absolutely riveted by this window into the distant past that linked together fable and fact, transforming the fantasy of Count Dracula into a very real and terrifying reality. Had it not been for the last couple of weeks she would have found it all too hard to believe. Now though having seen society come crumbling down and normal people turn into crazed, bloodthirsty creatures not dissimilar to zombies, she was more open to the seemingly fantastical. Besides, Vlad the Impaler was a real figure with historical truth behind him. And she was sat at that very moment talking to a real vampire.

Her head span, she felt almost like she was watching herself from outside of her body, as though she may pass out at any moment. She gripped the table edge and closed her eyes for a second. It took her several seconds to regain her composure.

"That sounds like a whole lot of killing going on. They sure were ruthless. So if Darius is really old has he also killed a lot of people then?"

Sebastian winced and she instantly regretted saying it. She dug her nails into her hand until it hurt as a penance.

"We do not always drink human blood. It is quite suitable and nourishing for us to feed from animals and that is often easier for us to come by. Even when we do drink the blood of humans it does not have to lead to their death, unless we specifically want it to. In your society can you not donate blood and function quite well with a temporary shortage? And so it is the same if one of us were to feed from a human."

"Why don't you all just drink animal blood all the time then?"

"The blood of a human is far more nutritious and animal blood does tend to have a peculiar taste to it which puts many off the concept. It is a personal choice, just as some humans will eat animals and others prefer not to, no?"

Sebastian was frowning and looked wistful. Again she regretted asking these questions and making that beatific face look so dejected, but she found it all absolutely fascinating.

"So Flavia drank my colleague Bannister's blood the other day?"

He nodded.

"Does that mean he will become a vampire?" For the

first time she suddenly considered the dreadful, potential implications of this meeting.

He shook his head with another dazzling smile, banishing the melancholic expression. "No, drinking your blood is not enough to turn you into a vampire. For that to occur you must become blood-brother to a vampire. Some of a vampire's blood must mingle with yours."

"How?"

"It is easily done; when biting a human's neck it would be very simple to bite one's own tongue for example, draw forth a little of one's own blood and then just allow it to mix in the human's vein."

Just like a virus; the vampire blood mixing with a human's, turning them into a vampire as well. Just like the infected who now roamed the streets turning humans into zombies. She did not say it but she thought it and he saw it in her eyes.

"Yes, we are not so dissimilar from those who were once normal and are now sick thanks to GVF Laboratories. Like them, we were human once as well, and like us they now bear little resemblance to those whom they originally were. But is that not the same with many human conditions? Mental disorders, for example the dementia that the Mnemoloss was created to cure, take away the essence of the person, leaving only the body; a husk and a reminder but no longer the same person as once was."

"I guess so. I hadn't thought of it like that before." She was quiet a moment. "So you know about the infected and GVF Labs then?"

"Of course," he smiled. "We may be a lot older than you, coming, as we do, from the past, but we live in the present, with televisions and radios and cars and guns. We have to adjust to changes, just as you do."

"Oh." She felt naïve and continued speaking to hide

her embarrassment. "So if you are used to our technology does that mean you mix readily with… with human society then? You interact just as normal people do?"

He shook his head solemnly. "We have always kept to the fringes of your society. I do not think our species were ready to accept each other before. I am not sure they are ready now either."

Something he had mentioned just occurred to her. "You said 'it *would be* simple' for you to bite your own tongue and mix it with the blood of a human. Does that mean you have never done that yourself? You have never 'turned' someone before?"

"No. I have not. As I said, seven is quite a lot for one clan and the justification was never there, before."

She was not sure exactly what he was implying. Did he mean purely that he had never had justification? Or did he mean that *before* he had not had justification, whereas now he did? And if so, was he implying that because of the collapse of civilisation he now had justification, or perhaps because he had now found someone that he would like to 'turn'? She was confusing herself and decided not to push that train of thought, but the flood gates of curiosity had been prised open and she was not sure what to ask next. There were just too many questions.

"Were you tempted to… to drink my blood? … You know, when you saved us by the petrol station?"

"Yes, there is always temptation but on this occasion I chose not to. It is not that I never drink human blood. Just that I choose my times more *selectively*, shall we say, than do my clan members."

She nodded thoughtfully and fired the next question at him without pause. "Vampires are supposed to be able to hypnotise people into doing whatever they want, sort of like putting them under a spell. Is that what happened to

Bannister? Is that why he let Flavia drink his blood?"

He paused now, considering. "Yes."

"Why didn't you do that to me?" She knew the question was poignant and if he had been a human she felt that he would be blushing now. It was her turn to hold his gaze.

Again there was the dazzling smile. "You are very direct, aren't you." It was not a question, just a statement.

She returned the smile. "Well..?"

"Well if someone is going to do something for me then I would prefer them to do it because they actually want to, because of what they genuinely feel in their heart for me, not because I have put them under my 'spell', not because they are beholden to me, my slave, and they have no choice." He was silent for a moment. "I guess I'm just an old romantic, huh?"

His demeanour was that of someone from another period, another civilisation, and yet every once in a while she caught herself being surprised by how modern he could sound, and each time it made her smile.

Is that what you want from me? She wanted to ask the question but dared not.

"I searched for you for a long time. I would not want to force you to do something that was not your desire." He spoke as though having read her mind. Had the question been that obvious? Or had he indeed been privy to her thoughts?

Just then she looked out of the window and noticed that the darkness was already withering. Dawn had arrived. She checked her watch and gasped. "Oh my god! The time - I'm late. I should have radioed for a replacement ten minutes ago but if he's already set an alarm he could be here any moment." They had been chatting so long and she had been so rapt by him that she had not realised how fast the hours had slipped by. He stood, looming over her, tall and imposing as he gazed down at her.

"It has been a pleasure, but for one thing."

"Oh?" She was momentarily taken aback, disappointed. "What?"

"You have not told me your name."

She laughed, relieved. "Charlotte. And it was a pleasure for me too. Where will you go now?"

"To the only place I can go. I must go back to my clan. There is nowhere else for me."

"Will I see you again?" She was aware that she sounded desperate and tried to keep it from her voice. She did not know why she suddenly felt a wrench in her heart and she was confused.

"Ah yes, most definitely, I am sure of that." He was still standing close to her and leaned forwards slightly. She froze as he moved nearer. Her breath caught in her throat, unsure of what to do if he kissed her. Instead he deftly moved a curl of her hair out of her eyes with a long, slender finger then turned and in a single step was at the door. He looked back for the briefest of moments, and then he was gone into the remnants of the night leaving her alone with the turmoil of emotions, the memory of his intensely burning eyes and the ever-circling doubts about the future of them all.

As Collins spoke into the radio to summon her replacement, Sebastian merged effortlessly with the darkness. He paused before scaling the perimeter wall and had one final, long gaze back at the guardroom. He watched the woman move around the small building, the heat from her body and her scent still lingered vividly in his memory. The proximity to her and the feelings of being in human company once again were all fairly overpowering and it was reluctantly that he dragged himself away when the soldier shortly came to relieve her. The time with her had passed quickly, but he had no idea how fast things were about to change, for him and for the humans.

When Flavia had returned to their lair she had sat on an open window sill waiting for dawn and the return of Farzin. Her body buzzed and pulsed with energy from her successful night and she felt more alive than she had for an age. She did not have to wait long before the dark figures of Farzin and Alec materialised. Their countenance suggested they had been energetic and their eyes shone with the thrill of death.

"My love." As Farzin approached and reached to embrace her he paused. "Ah, what is this? Do I detect the scent of a human? Perhaps the same one as before?"

She nodded with a sly smile and described the incident, leaving out only one or two minor details.

Farzin was pleased and could hardly contain his excitement. "That is most wonderful. Let us not speak of this to Darius just yet. The time is not quite right." He turned now to include Alec in the conversation, putting one arm around the shoulders of each, conspiratorially. "And so the noose draws tighter, finally. We must concoct our plans for we have much work to do. We must make our move with all haste; there is no time to lose. Now my friends, it is our time. The daybreak of a new era beckons us forth."

As dawn approached, creating doubts and shadows, Farzin started to plot and scheme. Bannister had unwittingly conveyed more than he realised back into the presumed sanctity of RAF Headley Court. He had ignited the fire that would be beyond any of their powers to extinguish. The soldiers and medics started to awaken with trepidation for their imminent mission to the GVF laboratories, and quite rightly so, as they had absolutely

371

no idea what lay in store for them. But beyond that, beyond the ghastly yet tangible realm of science gone mad, there awaited something far more terrible and incomprehensible, far more in keeping with their previous misguided notions of what amounted to the supernatural. If they thought that the past three weeks had been filled with fears and tragedies, then in reality those horrors were only just about to begin.

END OF BOOK ONE

Coming soon...

"Once Bitten, Twice Live"

Book two from 'The Blood of the Infected' series.

When death is the best option, survival is no longer
enough...

With a growing realization that their continued existence
bestows upon them a debt to humanity, the survivors look
to create a cure for the insanity that has brought
civilization to its knees. But that only encourages
disagreement and infighting, and comes at a heavy price,
bringing various shocks and surprises.

Tensions amongst the vampires are escalating,
jeopardizing the very existence of the clan itself. A battle
for supremacy seems inevitable and their future is in the
balance. How far will Farzin go to achieve his aims -
domination of the vampires and humans alike? And how
terrible will his vengeance be against any who stand in
his path? Their interaction with the humans threatens to
increase and not necessarily for the benefit of either
group.

Meanwhile the wrathful infected grow ever hungrier...

When every day is a struggle to stay alive, survival of
the fittest is never guaranteed.

CHAPTER 1

As his mother's teeth fixed firmly upon his arm it was not the pain that he had felt initially but the shock; total, numbing shock and disbelief. For the briefest of moments he had not reacted. He just stared at her as she sank her jagged teeth into him. Those teeth had been responsible for nibbling loose ends of thread while darning his jumpers when he was a child. Those teeth had, all his life, been flashed at him in a loving and ready smile. Those teeth were now tearing his flesh, sinking into his forearm and bringing with them his doom…

Please check the website   **www.oncebittentwice.com** for updates and info on books two and three.

Book three from 'The Blood of the Infected' series

"Twice Bitten, Twice Die"

When there's no one left to hear you scream…

Thank you for taking time to read "Once Bitten, Twice Die". If you enjoyed it, please consider telling your friends and posting a short review on Amazon. Word-of-mouth referrals are an author's best friend and much appreciated. Many thanks. Also, feel free to contact the author through his website with comments or with feedback: www.oncebittentwice.com
Or through Instagram: OnceBittenTwiceDie
Facebook: https://www.facebook.com/ajsobtd
Goodreads, Smashwords or Twitter: @ajsobtd1
The author cannot guarantee to answer every email, but will make every effort to try to do so… Thank you.

The Author's Biography

"Once Bitten, Twice Die" is the debut novel from Antony J. Stanton. The book is the first of 'The Blood of the Infected' series, in the 'post-apocalyptic action thriller' genre. Stanton was born in London in 1970. Even as a child he always dreamed of becoming a published author, and he started to write a book. But, having watched the film 'Top Gun,' he was swayed into a becoming a military pilot. After no more than a glancing blow of a career in the British Royal Air Force he decided that his long term future lay elsewhere and he became a commercial pilot and remains thus to this day. Hence much of this trilogy was written all around the world, generally at unsociable times when jet-lag meant that normal people were asleep.

During a holiday with three friends, a bet was made amongst them. Each had a task to fulfil within the year - Stanton's was to write a book. A little late, but five years on and his challenge has been completed. Three times.

His period spent in the RAF helped him write the military survival aspects of this book, and a kidnapping incident in Kazakhstan and shooting in Ghana, amongst other 'adventures', provided him with a dark well of experience to draw from. Life is, after all, one big adventure. A combination of the aforementioned, along with his love of the darker sides of literature, and the results are this novel and the next two in the trilogy.

And all it took was the impetus of a friendly challenge to spur him on to his creative dream... He still lives in South London and is very much looking forward to watching his friend fulfilling *his* part of the challenge: demonstrating his (not-so) newly acquired break-dancing skills, surely a sight to behold.

Acknowledgements

Many thanks to Dark Angel, Lilith Draconia & Lumia Dark of The Crypt, and Tim from the Cheltenham Horror Club, for their encouragement. Also to Ric Mayoh of www.PlaneTalking.com for excellent web design and marketing expertise, and to all those who helped with cover design – you know who you are… Many thanks.